W9-BYK-364
3 9094 03077 8284

FOUR WIVES

FOUR WIVES

WENDY WALKER

ST. MARTIN'S PRESS

NEW YORK

This is a work of fiction. All of the characters, organizations, and events portrayed in this novel are either products of the author's imagination or are used fictitiously.

www.stmartins.com

Book design by Ellen Cipriano

LIBRARY OF CONGRESS CATALOGING-IN-PUBLICATION DATA

Walker, Wendy, 1967–

Four wives / Wendy Walker.—1st ed.

p. cm.

ISBN-13: 978-0-312-36771-8

ISBN-10: 0-312-36771-6

1. Female friendship—Fiction. 2. Suburbs—Fiction. 3. Wealth—Social aspects—Fiction. 4. Married women—Fiction. 5. Self-realization—Fiction. I. Title.

PS3623.A35959 F68 2008

813'.6—dc22

2007032494

First Edition: February 2008

10 9 8 7 6 5 4 3 2 1

For Andrew, Ben, and Christopher

ACKNOWLEDGMENTS

I would not have succeeded in this endeavor without the help and support of the steadfast people in my life and others I have met along the way. It is therefore with humble gratitude that I thank:

Jim (who is in no way depicted in this novel) for being a fabulous father *and* a scratch golfer; my father for boundless ambition; my mother (who can squeeze twenty-five hours out of each day) for dogged determination; my family near and far for their love (and also for the great material); my suburban mommy friends for being my readers and cheering section; the circle of lifelong comrades who help me keep my head on straight; agents Matt Bialer, Emilie Jacobson, and Dave Barbor for taking a chance on me; editors Jennifer Weis and Hilary Rubin Teeman at St. Martin's for their expert input and overall enthusiasm; authors Jane Green and Jill Kargman for their generosity (which still overwhelms me); writing professor and author Brooke Stevens—without his encouragement and instruction everything I've ever written would be at the bottom of my sock drawer; and, finally, my children for being the cake under all this frosting.

FOUR WIVES

ONE

JANIE

HER HEART WAS POUNDING as she sat in the car. Before her was the house, a giant white colonial with black shutters, a quaint portico, and the three-car garage set off to the side where she now found herself, wondering. *What have I done?*

She took a breath to stave off the panic that was beginning to seep inside her. She needed to be careful. She reached for the garage remote, then thought better of it. The chain runner would cut through the still night air like a buzz saw. She killed the headlights, then the ignition. Her hand slipped inside the door latch, pulling it slowly until it clicked. She pushed open the door and swung her feet outside the car. She removed her shoes, her favorite strapped heels, and hung them on her fingers. She draped her purse around her shoulder, then, as softly as she'd opened it, closed the door with her hip. The soft silk of her skirt was deliciously sensuous as it brushed against her bare leg, testing her will to stay focused. To forget.

The sound of the neighbors' sprinkler coming to life startled her as she began to make her way around the back of the house. Her feet stepped like a cat's paws on the asphalt, and for a moment she was frozen in place, listening to the initial burst of water followed by a rhythmic pulsating—the *pinging* of water drops as they hit a small section of a flagstone terrace on their way around. Placing the sounds, she pictured the neighbors' yard, the two acres of flat green grass, the free-form pool, the stone wall that divided their property from her own. Then her yard and back door, up the stairs to the children in their rooms, the husband in her bed. The reasons she was creeping about under the midnight sky.

Taking another breath, she carried on, around the outside of the garage to the patio—through the maze of wrought-iron furniture, kick balls, plastic toys, and gas grill, and finally to the sliding glass door that opened into the kitchen. It was unlocked, and she pushed it slowly, then looked inside, making out the shapes of things in the dark room—the oval table that was still piled with remnants from the dinner, a bottle of ketchup, *The New York Times,* a plastic sippy cup. It was the heart of their lives, this kitchen. She could see the babies, four of them in eight years, sitting in the high chair that now resided in the basement with the rest of the childhood monuments. She could see them running around the island as she chased behind them, their shrieks of laughter filling the room as they avoided capture. She could feel in her bones the toll from the daily struggles—getting them to eat, umpiring fights, and saving them from spilling over as they climbed upon their chairs like unruly savages at dinnertime. This was the place where they played, talked, cried, and fought with each other. And though she felt drawn to it like a time traveler returning home from a long journey, she remained frozen at its threshold, not yet able to enter.

It was not a terrible life. Janie Kirk was a suburban housewife, the steadfast bottom of an inverse pyramid upon which the demands of her family balanced. It was a life founded at its core in her love for the children who lay sleeping inside. From there it grew heavy with the weight of their needs, and those of her husband, which she had carried on her shoulders for so many years. School, soccer, ballet, swimming. Doctors, dentists, speech therapists. Food on the table every day. Laundry, yard work, pets. Birthday parties. Dieting. Sex. It was an odd existence when she stopped to consider it, but so completely common that she rarely did, and it occurred to her that it would be close to perfect if she hadn't contracted the unfortunate disease of discontentment.

She was standing now between two worlds, her eyes taking in her life, her mind reliving the feel of his hands on her body not an hour before—his face replete with desire as he approached her. In that desire, she had seen the teenager in the back of his father's Cadillac, the young man whose heart she'd so foolishly broken in high school, then the college lover who'd broken hers. He had been, in that moment, every first kiss, every curious glance from across a room. All the things she'd left behind so many years ago.

She recalled the firm hand gripping the back of her head and pulling her to him, the other hand reaching for her back. The hold was strong, powerful, and she'd given into it without the slightest hesitation, without a second thought. Then came the kiss, and with it a warm burning under her skin. She'd opened her eyes and pressed her mouth harder against his, no longer someone's wife, someone's mother. Just a woman. And he was nothing to her but a man she desired. He had tried to speak, *You're so beautiful* . . . But she'd pressed her mouth harder against his and waited for the sound of his voice to disappear from her mind, along with everything else she knew about him. The shape of his face, the color of his eyes, his house and family. All of it had vanished. There had been no place for talk, no need for reassurances or stating one's intentions. The confines of their social structure that kept the wheels turning in this privileged existence had been suspended, and for the first time in her life she had not cared what her lover thought—if he was comparing her to past lovers, assessing her performance, her body—whether he would call her, see her again, marry her and buy a house, have children and live happily ever after until they were both dead in the ground.

She closed her eyes now, wanting to remember for one moment more the feel of his weight over her, her legs wrapped around him, pulling him closer—her mouth on his, nearly consuming him in a frantic embrace. And yet her life was waiting, pulling her back in.

She opened her eyes and took a breath. How could she have imagined that this would be possible, that she could walk through that door and up the stairs, kiss her children, then crawl beside her sleeping husband? She had wanted this night for a long time, and the thought of this night had somehow managed to coexist with her inside those walls. Now that she had given life to her thoughts, now that she had given in to what was, at best, a purely selfish act of weakness and depravity, she felt alive. Her body, her senses, her mind. Everything was awake again. It was a feeling of intoxication, and though she was nearly sick from it, she knew she would have to have more. There would be war between what awaited her and this narcotic flowing through her blood, and there would be no chance of reconciling the opposing needs that would now demand attention within this house.

What have I done? she thought again, knowing she had cast them all on a different course—an uncertain course. With a quiet resolve, she stepped inside.

TWO

LOVE

THROUGH THE OPEN BEDROOM door, Love heard the baby crying. She fumbled for her glasses on the night table and checked the time. For the shortest of moments she hoped for four o'clock, though the fog inside her head was thicker than a 4 A.M. wake-up. It felt more like three, definitely not five. At five o'clock she could actually hold a thought together. She would not hope for five, only to be disappointed. But *two*? The red numbers did not lie: 2:15 glared at her from the small black box. It was no better than the night before, and an hour worse than the one before that. It was regression, and in the face of sleep deprivation that was now chronic, she could feel the frustration taking over her entire being. This child was *never* going to sleep through the night.

She untangled herself from the appendages of her sleeping husband, pushing off the limbs that felt like dead weights around her. She pulled the covers back and walked around the bed. The room was a small converted study, and even their double mattress frame had trouble staying out of the way when she made these walks in the darkness. She turned sideways at the foot of the bed, her back pressed to the wall. As she shuffled through the confined space, she wondered how the man had slept through it. First, it had been three-year-old Jessica. At midnight, she'd wet through her pull-up. The bed, the child—all of it needed to be changed. Now, the baby was having a turn.

The crying stopped for a moment. Baby Will was listening for her footsteps. Not hearing them, he turned it up a notch. Love continued her shuffle to the door, studying the figure under the covers, the rise and fall of the large lump in the bed. He really was dead asleep. *Confounding*, she thought. It was simply the nature of his world, she supposed, a world apart from hers—work, eat, sleep. It was a world where someone *else* woke up in the middle of the night, where someone *else* remembered when to feed them, what to pack for school, to watch them in the tub so they didn't drown. These things were decidedly on her, and lately she felt wholly incapable of tending to them.

In the hallway, the dim glow from the nightlight cast shadows on the wall, images she knew well after six years of answering the calls of her children. The huge black stripes from the stair rail cast to her left, and the outline of her own round, pudgy shape always keeping one step ahead of her as she walked to the nursery. Time might as well be standing still. Will was seven months old now. The grace period was over for the baby weight, but there it remained. Twenty pounds of flesh that hadn't budged. It was unforgivable. Not just because it was a testament to her weakness for bakery items. Or evidence of their relative poverty in a town where every self-respecting housewife had a nanny and personal trainer. She was the doctor's wife—people understood that she didn't have access to the things that help afforded, what with managed care and all. Not that being a doctor didn't carry the respect it always had. Doctors, lawyers—the years of training required to earn a professional degree still impressed people. There just wasn't any money in it, at least not the kind needed to keep up in this town. Hunting Ridge was driven by careers in Manhattan's financial institutions. Tens of millions in accumulated wealth was commonplace, so much so that its relative enormity was no longer recognized. Just over a million dollars had bought Love and Dr. Harrison a house and a ticket into the superb school system. But it hadn't been enough to buy a room for each child, or sufficient floor space to accommodate even a queen-sized bed. Crammed into their tiny house with two kids bunked in the old master bedroom and one in a modest nursery, looking after three children and eating bagels and donuts and leftover mac-and-cheese because she was too tired to inspire even a trace of will power—it was no wonder the doctor's wife couldn't get the fat off her ass.

Still, for Love it ran deeper. She wasn't just an overweight housewife living in the "poor" part of town. If she were just that, it might be bearable. If she had not fallen so far from what she had once been, there would not be this bone-deep humiliation. Rather, there might be acceptance, contentment that all was as it should be. *Yes,* she might be thinking, *this is how I always thought I would turn out.* But that was not the case. She was miles from where the old Love Welsh had been, and the distance grew with every day she remained on this trajectory of marriage and motherhood. Miles from the career she had imagined for herself as a child. Miles from the excitement and fulfillment she had expected would fill her day-to-day life. It was more than two decades gone, the possibility of that existence, but it still lingered inside her. Tormenting her at moments like these.

Of course, she had still grown up, and into quite an attractive woman. She was tall like her father, with the long, wavy auburn hair of her mother. Her hips had curves that were accentuated by long legs, and her face had beautiful structure. All of this was still with her now—the basic scaffolding that made the person. But to Love, who saw none of these virtues in herself, it was simple. She had been a golden girl. Now she was a pudgy shadow on the wall.

She opened the door to the nursery, then quickly got out of its way so she could close it again and contain the noise. She looked into the crib. Baby Will was flailing—arms and legs reaching for the sky as if they could somehow grasp an invisible rope to facilitate an escape. His cries were loud and now interspersed with gasps of breath. *Gasp . . . cry . . . gasp . . . cry.* It was desperate. And it got Love every time.

She reached down and lifted him out of the crib, eliciting a vice grip of little arms around her. He nuzzled his face deep into her neck, and she whispered in his ear and kissed his cheek. *Mommy's here.*

With a slimy wetness now reaching from her face to her shoulder, Love sat down in the rocker and held him tight until his sobs turned to deep sighs. *What took you so long?* they seemed to say, and the guilt found its place inside her. She knew what she was supposed to do now. Put him back in the crib. Leave the room. Let him cry for ten minutes. *Repeat torture of child until child cries himself to sleep*. And though it wasn't in her to do it, she knew from the pounding in her head that it was either Baby Will or her. And it made her thoughts drift toward things existential, questions about the Divine Creator, mastermind of the universe, who had placed a mother's needs against those of her child. But these were thoughts for another time. At the moment, she had a choice to make. Someone was going to have to suffer.

After a short while, the infant loosened his arms from his mother's neck, then reached with his whole body for her chest. His hands patted her breasts and he started the sobbing again. She thought about the rules. *Whatever you do, don't feed him*. She pulled him close to her and rubbed his back. "Shhhhhh," she whispered. He was barely out of the womb. Ripped from his safe haven where he hadn't wanted for a damned thing. Now everything he wanted she was supposed to withhold. *Don't rock him. Don't nurse him at night. Don't give in*. Why had raising children become about denying them the very things they craved?

To hell with it. She lifted her shirt and put Baby Will on her breast. His body melted like a chocolate bar in the sun, molding around her until every part of him was touching her. One arm wrapped around her back and the other reached out for her face, resting on her cheek. Through the fog in her head and the bewildered resentment at the mysterious force that created humanity, Love couldn't hold back a smile as she watched her baby's eyes roll back in his head before closing. He was nothing short of blissful, doing what he did best—sucking on his mother, filling his tummy. He was satisfied. And she was a complete failure.

Settling into the state of defeat—a familiar place now—Love kissed Baby Will's hand, then rested it on her chest. She closed her eyes and tried to sleep, but the adrenaline had begun to flow and now had her heart racing. Rocking back and forth with the baby in her arms, she could feel the love here, the truest kind, the kind that forces its way inside the most stubborn soul and takes root. And it filled up every space inside of her, except the one that could not be penetrated.

It always came in these moments of peace, when the house was quiet and she was alone in the conscious world. At night, that was when it came—the disoriented, *where the hell am I?* feeling that somehow managed to coexist within her, right next to the fierce devotion she held for her children. The baby in her arms, the two curled up next door—Jessica with her stuffed pig and Henry with his Lego directions under the pillow. It felt inhuman to not be content. But there it was just the same. The haunting force of her other life.

On most nights she didn't fight it, letting her mind go as it so liked to do—wandering beyond the façade of certainty she maintained in the daylight. Back in time it would carry her, changing things that could not be changed. Sitting in the darkness, her wits not fully alert, she could think of how her career ended without feeling the monstrous shame that generally kept her away from the subject. She could picture her life laid out as a storyboard. One after another, years were erased and rewritten with stories of unprecedented achievement and the humble admiration of her famous father, *the Great Alexander Rice*. It was a fantasy thought cocktail—a weaving together of truth and untruth—that on most nights settled her nerves.

But not tonight. The regrets of the past, along with the fragments of hope that she might someday reclaim her destiny, could no longer be indulged. Instead, tonight, her body was trapped in a kind of shock. She thought about the letter tucked away in a kitchen drawer, buried within a pile of papers no one ever bothered to sort out. She could see her father's handwriting on the page, and through some kind of visceral subconscious connection, she could smell his cologne from nearly twenty-two years ago—the last time she'd seen him. Was he really going to do this to her? Would he expose her after all these years? Her secret, the one she kept hidden beneath this life, had become over the years a muddy river of memories and emotion that now flooded her body. She pictured her friends, what their faces would look like when they learned the truth about her. She imagined the agony it would inflict upon her husband, having thought all this time that he had seen her darkest corners and swept them clean. And she wondered how long it would take to reach her children.

With her sweet baby now fast asleep in her arms and her heart pounding within the walls of her chest, she could feel the fear inside her, searching for a place to take hold. From the moment she'd opened that letter, it had been growing like a fungus, corrupting her body, her mind. And she could not help but wonder if it was her own desire, her midnight fantasies of being more than what she had become, that had brought this about. She was her father's child, no matter how much time was now between them. That his letter had arrived just as her desires had begun to resurface seemed more than coincidental. Yet it could not be more than that. For all his vast talents, Alexander Rice was not psychic. His letter was about nothing but himself, his world and his desires. Still, it was within this letter, and all that it held, that Love was beginning to sense her own undoing.

THREE

GAYLE

GAYLE HAYWOOD BECK HEARD the soft click of the brass door latch. Light from the hall sifted into the bedroom as the door swung open, then disappeared again. Across the floorboards, she heard him walk slowly past the bed, through the sitting area into his dressing room. Another door closed, then the light from the dressing room appeared from under the door.

Lying still, Gayle strained her eyes to read the clock. It was well past two. Surely he would be tired. Through the closed door, she could hear him remove his clothing—the clicking of the belt latch, the shoes dropping to the floor, one and then the next. His starched shirt was unbuttoned, pulled from his body and tossed on top of his shoes, where it would be left for the maid to sort out in the morning. Then it was quiet. Lying in bed, waiting, Gayle could hear her heart pounding in her ears. Still, she closed her eyes and began to breathe deeply, feigning the breath of sleep.

He went next to the bathroom. First to brush his teeth, then into the shower. But only for a moment. The room fell dark again. She heard the floorboards give way to steps as he approached their bed, then the pull of the covers as he crawled in on the other side. She could smell him now, the crisp lavender soap on his skin, his wet hair, mint toothpaste. She heard him sigh and roll over, settling into the bed to sleep, and it sparked a wave of relief that was nearly euphoric.

How quickly these moments came and went now, how easily her emotions were pushed and pulled by even the smallest event. First, there'd been the anticipation. *Is he coming home tonight?* It was so much easier when she knew from the start, when he gave her some kind of schedule. She could gauge her mood, her tolerance for her husband that night, and make the decision which pill to take, and how many.

She thought about the pills now, sorted carefully in small brown prescription bottles in the bottom drawer of her vanity. Dr. Theodore Lerner—known affectionately as Dr. Ted to Gayle and the rest of the Haywood clan—had written out the instructions with great care and precision. Two blue Zoloft with breakfast. One white Xanax at lunchtime to prevent the afternoon anxiety. Then, if needed, Ambien just before bedtime. The regimen had started as just that—a strict menu of mood-altering drugs. Of course, over the years, Gayle had taken to some experimentation to see how much relief she could actually squeeze out of these resources, and she had become quite skilled as her own personal pharmacist. She took the Zoloft, a popular antidepressant, as written. Its effects were subtle and constant, making it useless for any immediate purposes. The Xanax was another story. There were some afternoons when two or three made their way out of the bottle, and others when she skipped it altogether. In the early evenings she could multiply their effectiveness with a glass of wine or a nice martini. She was careful not to overdo—rehab would not be good for someone as visible as Gayle Haywood Beck. She knew what she needed, when she needed it. Two Xanax and a drink usually made it possible to be Troy's wife, and this was why it was so crucial to know her husband's schedule.

Tonight had been left open. Troy had been invited to a late afternoon golf outing at the club, followed by a cigar dinner. Those always went late, and Gayle counted on this. But for some infuriating reason, he wouldn't give her an answer as to whether or not he would attend.

"Does it really matter?" he'd asked after her third call to the office.

She'd made the excuse that she needed to let their cook know about dinner. "If you go out, I may have Paul make me a sandwich."

He'd held out until nearly four o'clock, calling on his cell as he made his way back from the city. He was going to play after all, and stay for the dinner. It seemed like months ago, the blissful relief that had come at four o'clock. She'd skipped the Xanax and enjoyed just one glass of wine after her son went to sleep. Now it was the middle of the night, the drugs were out of reach, and Troy was home in their bed.

The scent of his favorite soap—his signature in Gayle's mind—filled her nostrils as she inhaled, provoking a memory that struck like a fist to her gut. It was a memory of another time, the first time she'd smelled that smell, a time when she'd found it enticing, even comforting. That this same scent now made her recoil with fear was the very dilemma that formed the base of her illness.

The sessions with Dr. Ted had helped her understand this—the acute frailty of her demeanor—the underlying condition that her mother had always reminded her of. This was life. Marriage was tough. Ups and downs. Good and bad. Troy had his *issues*. What man wouldn't be affected by a wealthy wife? The evidence was all around her, at the book groups and luncheons, the charity functions and bake sales—what woman was consistently happy in her marriage? They told her to take the pills and forgive herself for needing them to live a normal life. She had the first part down.

Troy Beck rolled over again, then cleared his throat. Across the mattress, his wife lay perfectly still, fighting to hold back the tears that might give her away. She calmed herself, breathing slowly, though her body was rigid, her every muscle tense as she prayed for him to fall asleep.

FOUR

MARIE

IN THE HOUSE NEXT door to Love Welsh, Bill Harrison, and their unruly clan, Marie Passeti stared at her husband. In the darkness of their bedroom, she could make out little more than a silhouette of his face, but it was enough. The evidence was adequately apparent. *For the plaintiff,* she thought, her head now propped up in the palm of her hand as she leaned over him for a closer look. *Receding hairline, chubby cheeks, beer on the breath.* Evidence of the downslide, the effects of their suburban existence. Work, beer, TV, golf, not necessarily in that order. Anthony Passeti hadn't been to a gym in three years. Beneath the covers, she watched the rise and fall of the round ball now known as her husband's stomach. *Exhibit four.* It was confounding, really. Men were fit in this town. After all, this wasn't some middle-of-nowhere American suburb. It was Hunting Ridge, for Christ's sake. There were certain standards to maintain, beauty being near the top of the list. Just beneath wealth, but slightly above college ranking, breeding, and social connections.

OK. It was time for the defense to make its argument. *Exhibit one—still smart, very smart.* Marie watched his eyes flutter beneath their lids. *Where have you gone?* It had been a very long time since she'd seen exhibit one. They'd been here just under seven years, and in that time Anthony had gone from CNN to the Golf Channel, from *The Economist* to *Golf Digest.* From pondering the universe to air swings. Was it a disease? If it was a disease, maybe the twenty pounds were a good sign, a deviation from the norm that perhaps indicated some resistance to the illness that seemed to permeate the inhabitants of this quaint little village. Maybe it was Anthony Passeti's quiet *F-U* to the suburbs. But if he wanted to send a message of defiance, could he not have chosen one more beneficial to her? Like giving up his golf game and staying home with the kids on the weekends? Or emptying the dishwasher once in a while? No self-respecting Hunting Ridge man emptied the dishwasher. That would be a good one. Maybe he'd chosen the beer gut to drive her farther to the other side of their bed.

Go to sleep! These midnight wakings were doing her in. She'd pass out from exhaustion just after ten. But then the panic would strike, making her pop up, open-eyed, staring at the figure lying beside her, desperate to understand what was going so wrong. Still, as much as she resented the disruption, it was in these moments, and only in these moments, that she could get some of it back—the feeling that she actually knew this man.

It was the goddamn suburbs. That was it. Life had been sailing along just fine in the city. A fierce litigator, Marie had been on the fast track in a New York law firm before having her first daughter, Suzanne. She'd had every intention of going back after her maternity leave, but the pull of her child had been too strong, and that had been that. The first mistake. For all her intelligence and two Harvard degrees, Marie had been easily seduced by suburban lore. She'd quit her job, moved the family to Hunting Ridge where the air was clean and there was grass outside their door—grass that was now littered with black spots that some fungal epidemic had claimed. Olivia came next, and after her birth Marie resigned herself to joining the ranks of her peers. For two years—time that seemed to stand still—she had endured the endless talk of toys and teething and pediatricians. She went to the playgroups, met at the park, sang "Old MacDonald" sixty million times at mommy-and-me music class. It was mind-numbing, anxiety-producing.

Crazy-making. And, in hindsight, it was inevitable that she would begin "dabbling" again in the law. By the middle of her third year as a stay-at-home mommy, she had signed a lease for office space in town.

On some days, it actually made her crazy life in Hunting Ridge tolerable. Up at six, get the girls ready for school—breakfast, lunchboxes, homework, notes for field trips and play dates. Shower and dress, organize the papers she'd brought home and worked on late into the night. Then clean up after her husband who, after staying out late at the club, would sleepwalk through the morning, leaving out the cereal boxes and milk, throwing his dirty shirts on the floor near, but God forbid inside, the laundry room. Then to the office, sorting through her work, making out the assignments for her small staff—the two associates whose part-time schedules looked like a small jigsaw puzzle. There wasn't much that got pitched her way that she couldn't hit out of the park. Marie Passeti was the very embodiment of efficiency.

That it had begun to belittle her husband, to shine an even brighter light on his domestic failings of late, was a consequence that could not be helped. Anthony Passeti was perfectly capable of dressing his children and putting away his cereal boxes. He'd done it for years, supporting her career, sharing the responsibilities at home. Then, one small task at a time, he had removed himself from the invisible chore chart Marie kept in her head. And one task at a time, Marie had picked up the slack. It wasn't the only change that had taken place right under her nose. Not long ago, her husband had been fully present in their lives, doting on the girls every weekend, finding creative ways to please his wife—the occasional breakfast in bed, spontaneous dinner plans in the city. And when their second child had put a damper on their sex life, the reserved corporate attorney had surprised her with a series of Internet orders—small packages that arrived in the mail, discreetly wrapped in plain brown paper. *Hardware for the hard up,* he'd joked. And although most of it wound up in the bottom of Marie's underwear drawer, it had returned a sense of mischief to their lives, a flavor that had since been diluted by Hunting Ridge vanilla.

Years had passed since she'd received a plain brown package. Now, all that came in the mail were bills and golf magazines. And while it amused her on some level that her husband had become so fond of sticks and balls, it wasn't exactly her idea of foreplay. Still, despite his downslide, Anthony Passeti was a brilliant man, and on the days she didn't hate him, Marie could still see traces of the man she loved so deeply.

She slid closer beside him and curled up next to the rising gut. She was an infrequent visitor to his side of the bed, and she remembered now how much warmer it was than her side where her slight body barely made an indentation. Carefully, she pulled her pillow next to his and dropped her head upon it, closing her eyes. It was important that he not wake. She was angry at him again, a far too ordinary state of affairs in their house, and snuggling would definitely be a sign of contrition. She heard him snore twice, then shift to the left. *Good.* He was out, which meant she would still have deniability in the morning. *Sorry, must have rolled over in the night.* She let out a deep breath and felt sleep return as she lay beside her long-lost husband.

FIVE

DREAMS

DREAMS TORMENTED JANIE THROUGHOUT the night. *Waking to find two men in her bed, struggling for an explanation. Running after a stack of papers that had been blown from her hands. The feel of his rough beard on her inner thigh.*

She slept in short segments, dreaming then waking, dreaming again. Each dream brought a new dose of panic or relief, tossing her back and forth like a rag doll. The sun peeking through the bedroom curtains should have been welcome, but she knew from the sickness in her stomach that the anxiety would only intensify as she moved through her day.

Daniel was still asleep next to her when she heard a noise from down the hall. The youngest of the four Kirk children was beginning to stir. Not ready to face what she might be feeling, or not feeling, she jumped from the bed without looking at her husband. In the bathroom, she checked for evidence. Clothes were in the hamper, a place with which Daniel would not concern himself. The contents of her purse were put away—compact, lipstick, comb, breath mints—the purse was back on the rack in her closet.

She retraced her steps as she quickly brushed her teeth and pulled back her hair. The novel from the book-club meeting she'd ducked out of was on the kitchen counter. The remote for the garage door was in the basket by the kitchen door where such things were kept. Forgetting it there would be her reason for not pulling in the car. What else? There was nothing else, except the contents of her mind, which she knew from experience would not be detected by anyone living in this house.

She looked in the mirror, checking her neck, her breastbone. There was no trace of his lips there. Dressed in clingy cotton pj's, no makeup on her face, hair uncombed, she would easily pass as the *mommy* and the *honey* they expected each morning—the embodiment of suburban perfection. Long hair, perfectly highlighted in shades of blond. Sculpted legs, firm ass, flattened stomach, new construction breasts—perky size Cs. And a face that was both provocative and subtle. Despite her forty-two years and four pregnancies, she looked damned close to herself twenty years ago. In fact, if she didn't occasionally dress them up and parade them through town, there would be no visible evidence of the four children that she'd borne. And that was how Daniel liked things—just as they had always been.

It was ironic, really, that the things she'd done to herself to please her husband had opened the door to her infidelity. She was reality on hold—no saggy tits from years of breastfeeding, no loose, floppy skin that had been stretched to oblivion again and again. What man wouldn't want the very things he'd once had but could never have again? It was all possible now with the surgical erasing of time. Janie had no illusions as to why she'd found herself the object of pursuit.

She thought about it now, how all of this had transpired in a few short weeks. First, the typical Hunting Ridge cocktail party. Elaborate catered nibbles passed around by waiters, all dressed in white. Tendered bars set up in every room. Rented policemen parking the cars and ignoring the smell of alcohol on the guests when they returned to drive home. She'd gone to the small bar in the back of the kitchen to find a decent bottle of wine. These were friends, and she felt at home in spite of the formality surrounding her. The good stuff would be in the wine fridge, which had been her destination. But the short walk in search of a drink would only be the beginning.

"Check the bottom rack."

The man's voice was familiar, and she'd thought nothing of it as she turned from the fridge with a smile. She'd known him for years.

"I had my eye on a Kistler Chardonnay," she'd said.

"Let's break out the red."

Stepping around her, he'd allowed his body to come closer to hers than it should have. And as they knelt next to one another to examine the bottles on the last three racks, she'd felt the jolt of a subtle, and surprising, seduction. The second step on her path to betrayal.

"Here we go," he'd said, pulling a pinot noir from its slot. They moved back to the kitchen. He opened the bottle, poured two glasses, then handed one to her. His hand brushed against hers, and she smiled in a way that, upon reflection, was reflexively sultry. After years of nothing but benign interaction with members of the opposite sex—a suburban mandate—it had taken very little to sense the flirtation, and her body had responded as though it had been secretly training for this very moment. This was surely not the first time they had been alone in a room, but this time had been entirely different.

Whatever it was they had begun had paused there as they returned to the party, and most of her was grateful when she'd found herself safely tucked away in her bed later that night, next to Daniel, having done nothing, really, but smiled. She could see now how that smile had been the third step. Still, in spite of where that smile had led her, she would never let go of the life she had built, the security for herself and the children. What was this? Lust? The innate curiosity of sexual beings? Passion, desire? Those were nothing but the seeds of fleeting encounters, and complete anathema to the sustaining of a committed partnership. And she wanted that above all else—the companion to look after her when she was sick, when time finally claimed her body. She wanted the father who would walk her daughters down the aisle. But he had found her irresistible—and in the end, that was all it had taken. The final step.

"Mommy," Janie's three-year-old was there now, standing at her hip with a ragged blanket trailing by her side.

She reached down and picked her up.

"Good morning, sunshine."

Her daughter pressed her face next to Janie's, and they watched themselves watch each other in the mirror.

Janie sighed at her angel-faced girl, then turned her head to plant a kiss on the soft, chubby cheek.

"Come on. Let's go downstairs and start breakfast."

Within the hour, it became clear to Janie that she'd been wrong. The anxiety was quieting, perhaps from the rhythm of the morning routine—packing lunches, pouring bowls of corn flakes, measuring coffee. Or perhaps from the ease of hiding.

Daniel breezed in, smelling of shaving cream and menthol deodorant. Standing with her back to him, her apparent focus on the four lunchboxes laid out on the counter, Janie made a conscious effort not to greet him directly as he approached her. This was their way, the casual avoidance of married life, and she was careful not to deviate from it as she worked through the tasks.

"Morning," he said. His face was still warm from the shower when he gave her a peck on the mouth and patted her behind. Then he reached for his travel mug from the cupboard next to the sink.

"Are you catching the train, or do you want breakfast?"

"Train. I've got a meeting downtown."

Janie took the mug from his hands, filled it with coffee, then added some milk from the fridge. Only as she handed it back did she allow her eyes to meet his.

"There you go," she said with a smile.

He smiled back, then looked away quickly, as he always did.

"How was the book group?"

Janie returned to the packing of lunches. "Fine. The usual."

"Was the Rice woman there?"

"Love? No. She's in the *other* group. The benefit committee for the clinic. And she goes by her mother's name. *Welsh*."

"*Ahh*," Daniel said, now shuffling through the morning paper on the other side of the kitchen, the wheels turning.

"We're meeting today."

"How is Gayle? We should see them more." Daniel was talking, though it had that distant resonance, more like he was verbalizing his thoughts than actually addressing his wife. That was Daniel, always plotting, scheming. It was in his nature—why he was so successful on Wall Street. He knew how to work people, relationships, even friendships—and lately, his marriage. It had cost them ten thousand dollars to buy Janie a seat on the clinic board four years ago. It had been an investment, a way to get close to the Becks and the other local power couples. Of course, Gayle had been the primary draw, being a Haywood, of the New York Haywoods, the family that had made its fortune two generations before by founding its investment firm. That made them old money, the best kind, the kind that looked down on the other kinds. In fact, Gayle Haywood Beck was so far beyond the wealth of anyone in this town that she'd been disqualified from the competition. And Daniel had wanted to rub elbows with her the moment they'd bought into Hunting Ridge.

In spite of her disdain for her husband's fixation, Janie had—as always—complied, serving dutifully on the board and befriending Gayle. Not that it had been an unpleasant task. Gayle was warm, genuine, and among the few on the board who actually cared about helping the young girls the clinic served. Now, seven years later, they were firmly embedded in each other's worlds within the Hunting Ridge mainstream—husbands who worked on Wall Street and wives who stayed home to care for the children and manage the help. They crossed paths at school functions, the nail salon, restaurants, and high-end boutiques. They were on the same social calendars, and belonged to the same club. And all of this made Daniel feel like a player.

"Can you set up a dinner?"

"Not at the meeting. It's too rude. I'll have to call her. Maybe in a few days."

"I don't know. You could invite the Rice woman as well. I know they live in town, but it might be fun to know a celebrity."

Daniel was still skimming the paper as he spoke, giving his wife an opportunity to roll her eyes. What was this, rush week at the frat house? Aside from bragging rights, which Daniel exercised frequently, knowing someone in the Haywood family hadn't changed their lives in the slightest.

"She goes by Welsh. And Marie Passeti will be there as well."

"Ahhh. Then you'd better call Gayle in a few days."

Exactly, Janie thought to herself. God forbid they should waste their time on the Passetis—townies who weren't celebrities.

Daniel checked his watch, then turned and walked to the oval table where his children sat, watching TV and spooning up cereal. "See you guys later. Be good." His oldest son held up his hand for a high five. "See ya, champ."

Janie waited until he was at the door leading to the garage.

"Hold on!" she said. Daniel stopped, then watched as his wife scurried to the basket on the floor beside him. She reached into the basket for the remote, then pushed the button. Daniel nodded as he heard the garage door pulling open.

"You have to keep it *in* the car, Janie."

"I know, I know." It wasn't the first time she'd had to leave her Mercedes in the driveway, and Daniel always came close to clipping it when she did.

"Just be careful backing up."

He smiled again. "I won't be too late."

"See you tonight."

And that was it. Daniel, along with his coffee, his briefcase, and his social-climbing plans, was gone for the day. Janie didn't wait for his car to pull out before closing the door. She didn't wave good-bye, completing the façade of normalcy. She looked at her kids, lost in their little worlds. Oblivious.

"Five more minutes, then it's upstairs to get dressed."

No one listened, and this made Janie smile. Her world hadn't collapsed around her. Her children weren't ruined, her husband wasn't heartbroken. She still had the keys to the house, the car. And whatever was churning inside her had, for the moment, been contained.

SIX

PAUL FROM THE KITCHEN

TROY WAS GONE BEFORE Gayle woke, catching the five-fifty train that would get him to the office before the market opened. She rolled onto her back and pulled the covers up to her chin. It was still now, calm. A diffused light from the morning sun entered the room through delicate sheer curtains, the clock ticked back and forth on her night table. And though she could still smell his cologne in the air, her husband was gone. She closed her eyes and stretched her arms wide across the entire bed. She had made it through the night, and now it was her room, her house, for the rest of the day.

She climbed out of the bed, then methodically smoothed the covers, tucking in the sheet and, finally, draping the spread on top. With the bed made, she walked to the balcony doors and slid them open, letting in the fresh spring air. Looking down onto her property, a magnificent eight acres of rolling hills and delicate gardens, she pushed from her mind the details that needed to be tended. A patch of bark on one of the oaks that was black with the fungus that had been spreading across the town, the chewed evergreens that were evidence of a hole in the deer fencing. There would always be something, and there would be time for a list later in the day when the groundskeeper arrived. For now, she needed the feel of cool air on her legs as it swept under her nightgown, the faint warmth of the sun on her face. It was in these small moments of peace that she had come to live.

Under her bedroom floor, she could hear the sound of dishes as Paul prepared the breakfast. There would be fresh ground coffee whose odor would fill the kitchen and linger for hours, eggs, fruit, and cereal for Oliver, her six-year-old son. The table would be set with her grandmother's china, delicate antique silver, and soft linen napkins. Oliver would sit quietly wishing he could watch TV, but he would sit just the same because he was coming to understand his world, and the importance of his upbringing. They would discuss their plans, what he might do with the day off from school, one of those staff-development vacations that never seemed to result in a more developed staff. She thought about the chapter of *Harry Potter* they were reading together, and how she would do her best to step outside of her inhibitions to perform the voices properly—the way that made him laugh.

Six-year-old feet bounded down the back stairs to the kitchen. Oliver was up and hoping to make it down before his mom so he could sneak in a few minutes of cartoons. Gayle smiled to herself as she walked to her dressing room, taking her time, thinking that a few minutes couldn't hurt. She pulled the nightgown over her head, then carefully dressed herself in the blouse and silk slacks she'd laid out the night before. Like her friend Love, Gayle was a tall woman, though she lacked the soft, feminine curves that drew people in. Instead, she had a stalwart presence, a businesslike aura that she subconsciously fostered with conservative clothing and a short, blond "do," a signature mark of professional women from the prior decade. She kept with the old school of fashion. Chanel suits, Gucci shoes and handbags, Tiffany pearls. It made people take her seriously, and allowed her to maintain a safe distance from the endless array of vultures who wanted a piece of the Haywood pie.

Gayle gave her hair a quick comb-through and applied some cream foundation. She chose her shoes, soft Italian leather slides, then descended the back stairs.

"Good morning, Mrs. Beck." As expected, Paul was in the kitchen arranging the breakfast trays.

"Good morning, Paul. How are you?"

"Very well, thank you. Coffee?" Paul asked, pausing in his task of folding the napkins to address her properly, face to face.

"Thank you." Gayle sat on a bar stool at the kitchen island as she watched him pour the coffee into a china cup, the same way he did every morning. Always dressed neatly in black slacks and a white button-down shirt—a self-imposed uniform—he was a presence in the house from sunup to sundown, unobtrusively tending to their every need. His official role was to serve as the cook, though his competence and easy manner had led to an expansion of his duties over the years. With gentle eyes, closely cropped gray hair, and a smile that was genuine, the fifty-two-year-old servant had imbued the Beck household with a peaceful sense of order, and been Gayle's daily tonic for nearly three years.

Returning the smile, Gayle accepted the cup as he placed it in front of her from the other side of the island. She closed her eyes and inhaled the familiar aroma. The room was warm with the morning sun, and Gayle let the sensation drift within her. This room, the fine coffee, the sunshine, and, of course, Paul were like a warm blanket around her, and she was instantly serene. It was this very feeling she had sought from her husband when she'd purchased the Hunting Ridge estate, though it was now glaringly obvious that a simple change of address could do little to reverse the bad turn her marriage had taken. She had complied with her mother's demands to quit work, get pregnant, and oversee the renovation on the 1890s farmhouse. She had complied with her husband's demands to make the house outlandishly expensive. And for years she had waited, and hoped. But the moments kept coming, hidden beneath the immunity of marital relations.

"When will the ladies be here?" Paul asked, interrupting the thoughts that were now visible on his employer's face.

"About an hour."

"I've made some muffins for the children. Chocolate chip."

"Mmmm. They'll be thrilled."

Paul nodded. "And you'll be needing the dining room to discuss the benefit plans?"

"Unfortunately."

"I'll put down some linen." He placed a folded napkin on one of the trays, then stood in front of her.

"Do you have packets as well?"

The "packets" were Gayle's version of place cards, white folders with copies of the minutia for the benefit she was hosting—bids from florists and caterers, linen samples, seating charts, and lists of guests for the invitations. On each folder she'd written a name, one for each of them. Love, Marie, Janie, and herself. It was a small group by design. Janie was a fellow board member of the Cliffton Women's Clinic, and a friend, who shared her vision for the clinic. The other two were volunteers she'd called to duty. The group's familiarity was intended to keep the intrusion into her life at a minimum. And its members had been hand-picked to consist of trusted friends, women whose loyalty was to her. Women who would have her back with the rest of the board.

Paul had stopped folding things, but was still standing across the marble counter—the formal demarcation of their relationship. "Shall I set them out now?" he asked, referring to the packets.

"Please," Gayle said, smiling to herself. She walked to her desk and retrieved the four white folders she had prepared the night before.

"The usual places?" Paul asked.

Gayle nodded. "It seems to be working."

As he took the packets from her hands, they exchanged a warm, knowing look. Paul was deeply perceptive, and there was little about the world that got past him—including the social politics of her friendships. He would seat Marie at the head of the table, closest to the door. She liked to be in charge, and her limited patience for all things suburban (in particular, Janie Kirk) required she be in close proximity to the nearest exit. Gayle would sit across from her at the other end of the table, giving Marie a friendly face in her direct line of vision, and a reminder that her sacrifice was for a dear friend. Love would be to Gayle's right. She was easy—Gayle's oldest Hunting Ridge friend, Marie's best friend and neighbor. She could be placed anywhere, but next to Marie would certainly help matters. Janie would take the seat to the left of Gayle—next to her closest friend in the group, across from Love who had the self-restraint to not gaze at her external perfection, and, hopefully, far enough away from Marie's radar to prevent an overt display of ire.

That Paul knew all of this, that it passed easily yet unspoken between them, was profoundly comforting, and Gayle felt lightness sweep across her face.

Of course, Paul noticed this as well and seized the moment. "I'll take care of it. You enjoy breakfast with Oliver. I'll call him in."

Having her son beside her was all that was missing.

Gayle smiled and nodded. "Thank you."

SEVEN

THE MEETING

"HOW MANY BIDS *ARE* there?"

Marie was annoyed the moment she picked up her packet. Despite Gayle's careful placement, the little tolerance Marie had for Hunting Ridge was expended the moment she saw its very embodiment—Janie Kirk—in the room.

The folders were thick with a sea of papers submitted by every business that wanted a piece of the suburban fundraising action. It was ridiculous to Marie, this winning combination for party vendors, a vast supply of highly educated women with far too much time and disposable income on their hands. With their children at school and their homes tended by staff, the women of Hunting Ridge had taken to three forms of entertainment. Body perfecting, redecorating, and fundraising. Any one of these alone, or in combination with vacation planning, shopping, and obsessive self-assessment, could easily fill the hours between eight and three, five days a week. That they could simply write checks to the charities that caught their attention, or hire planners to run the events, was neither acknowledged nor considered. And this was more than enough to push Marie to the end of her rope.

"Look at this!"

Gayle caught Marie's eye and smiled broadly. "At least we're not doing another statistical analysis of Easter Bunny impersonators."

"*Please,*" Marie sighed, remembering the last committee she'd served on with Love and Gayle. It had been her first—a futile effort to meet people when she'd first landed in this town—and she'd sworn it would be the last.

Marie recounted the discussion. "Well, with the discount on the second bunny we could yield a significant advantage over prior egg hunts. . . . Little Bobby won't have to wait as long in the line."

"Oh, no, but if the lines are longer, little Bobby's mommy might buy more crafts to keep little Bobby happy . . . ," Love chimed in.

"I'm so glad I took out all those loans to go to Harvard. It's come in so handy, and I only have eighty more years before it'll all be paid off."

"Marie," Gayle said, pausing until her friend looked up from the table.

"What?"

"Have I thanked you for doing this?"

Marie sighed. "Only several hundred times. Sorry." And she was, instantly. Gayle's motives were generous and pure, though it was something she tended to forget in the face of the Haywood wealth. Cliffton was the next town over, but in another financial universe. It was a small city, and as such had urban troubles—impoverished women and children being near the top of the list. The clinic provided free medical services, childcare, and after-school enrichment programs. Gayle had joined the board the first year after moving out, and though Marie believed in the cause as well, she believed in Gayle more. Gayle was, after all, a Democrat, a *liberal* Democrat. Educated at Brown. A women's studies major. She believed in sex education, accessible birth control, and political contributions to local officials willing to push for insurance coverage and Plan B contraceptives. Marie was on board with all of this.

What Marie couldn't understand was that, despite the large Haywood contributions, the clinic's finance committee habitually opted to use the yearly benefit money for prenatal care and upgrades to the facility. It was a centrist approach, easily swallowed by the vast Republican majority of their donor base, but it also left a huge gap in the services these women needed.

Now, finally, there was a chance to change all that. The gala had been in desperate need of a new home after the planned venue fell through. And although it would exact an enormous toll on her need for privacy and containment, Gayle had offered her home in exchange for a seat on the committee and a say in how the money was spent.

"How's the vote leaning, anyway?" Love asked.

Gayle shrugged. "I'm working on it."

"She's a brilliant lobbyist," Janie Kirk chimed in. "In all our years together on the board, I've never seen this woman so cleverly infiltrate the enemy ranks." She looked at Gayle and gave her a wink. Gayle smiled back, though they both knew this wasn't exactly the case. Gayle was smart, and she could be clever. But it wasn't in her to engage in warfare, even of the social kind.

Marie knew this as well, and she shot a look of disapproval at Love. Wasn't that the reason they were all here? Within the scope of half an hour, Marie could negotiate every demand Gayle had. These women needed her house, not to mention the ongoing support of the Haywoods. Marie could get it done in her sleep. That she couldn't cure Gayle of her inability to exercise her own power was close to maddening.

Love shook her head in that *not now* way of hers, and Marie threw her hands in the air, but said nothing.

Pulling some papers from her folder, Janie changed the subject. "Anyway, can we at least choose the flowers? I have to go in about three minutes."

"What's in three minutes?" Marie said, her tone laced with judgment.

It did not go unnoticed, and Janie had come to expect nothing else. Marie had a chip on her shoulder from being a working mother. Her very identity was wrapped up in resenting the SAHMs (stay-at-home mothers), especially those like Janie who could afford help.

"I have a session with my trainer," Janie said, rubbing it in just a little.

Marie did not look up. "You should just go then. Nothing gets done in three minutes."

"That's not exactly true," Janie retorted, then paused for the slightest moment. "His name was Allen. Senior year. Two minutes, tops."

Love and Gayle laughed, and Marie gave an obligatory smile.

Having had the last word, Janie gathered her things. "Sorry to leave you with the work."

"It's fine. Go to your session." Gayle waved her off with a smile, and Janie blew back a kiss. Then she was gone, and her exit brought a sudden deflation of energy throughout the room.

"What?" Marie asked, taking note of the silence.

Love looked at Gayle, who shrugged. What could they possibly say about the giant chasm that divided these two women? Marie had a growing disdain of suburbia and Janie Kirk had made a career out of becoming the woman every other suburban woman wanted to be, and that every man wished he had. It was an irreconcilable situation.

"She's too happy," Marie said, finally. "Maybe she's having an affair."

"Marie!" Love said, putting down a florist bid.

"Well . . ."

Gayle shook her head. "I've known her for many years. She's just a happy person."

"OK, OK," Marie relented. "Christ, I can be a real bitch. She just fills me with thoughts from the devil. What's *wrong* with me?" Marie dropped her head to the table with customary drama.

Love and Gayle both smiled. There was something comforting in knowing another person as well as they knew Marie.

"Maybe we can perform an exorcism," Love teased, rubbing her neck.

Gayle let go of her smile, her face growing concerned as she looked at her friend.

"What's wrong with your neck, Lovey? That's the third time you've had to rub it." Her voice had a soft, maternal tone, and it made Love want to curl up in her lap.

"The baby was up again. I fell asleep in the rocker. I'll be fine," Love said, now self-conscious as she removed her hands from her neck. In truth, the pain had been with her for nearly a month—coming and going, attacking and retreating seemingly at random. That it had coincided with the arrival of her father's letter was not lost on her, though it presented a significant dilemma for someone who did not believe in fate or any other kind of metaphysical occurrence.

"You don't look fine," Marie interjected, getting up from her chair. She walked around the table and stood behind Love, then placed her hands on Love's shoulders.

"Really, I'm OK." The feel of the soft hands on her skin reached deep inside her. It had been a long time since she'd let someone try to heal her, to help her even. Standing on her own, taking on as many burdens as she could unearth, had been a necessary distraction to live this life and hold back the currents of the past. But these burdens had become increasingly heavy and they created a powerful longing to be saved—one that she knew she would never give in to. She closed her eyes to hold back the tears.

"Just relax a little." With gentle, caressing movements, Marie started to work on Love's neck. "Now—what's up with the night wakings?"

Love took a long breath as she felt the pain subside. And for the remainder of the hour, they distracted themselves with talk of their lives. Love described in detail Baby Will's sleeping patterns. Marie, who had been through it herself, offered her own stories. Through concurrent interruptions from one or another of their children—Baby Will insisting on a seat in his mother's lap, and a call from the electrician about the landscape lighting—Gayle worried out loud about the gala that would turn her home inside out, and they all plotted the revenge they would seek if the finance committee voted to spend the money on chenille throw pillows for the clinic's lobby when all of this was said and done.

It was a good distraction, a pretty dance around the hot zones that were smoldering in each of them. Love said nothing more about the pain that came and went, or the letter from her father that was threatening to expose her past. Gayle left out any mention of her invisible illness and the pills needed to manage it. And Marie managed to stifle the growing discontentment with her life that was verging on intolerable. With the technical difficulty of a fine tango, they spoke of their children's troubles and tiffs with their husbands without revealing the fears and secrets that held the threat of change. Motherhood could wear you down, but not make you crave something more. Husbands could be difficult, impossible even, but you could never stop loving them. These were the invisible lines that could not be crossed, the lines that held their world together, suspending reality long enough to get them through the day—until the distractions were gone, leaving nothing between them and the bare bones of their lives.

EIGHT

RANDY THE INTERN

At 121 Main Street, above the town eatery known simply as Joe's, were the law offices of Marie Passeti. A far cry from the posh New York address where she had begun her career—the plush wall-to-wall carpeting, spacious enclaves, and mahogany reception desk—her current work space was comprised of two moderate rooms lined with linoleum flooring. The front held an oval conference table and shelves of law books. It was freshly painted and, overall, presentable despite the persistent smell of bacon that wafted through the vents from the tenant below. The back held the office where Marie and her two associates came and went as their cases demanded.

At the door, she dropped her briefcase and searched for the heavy ring of keys that was weighing down her jacket. Finding it, she turned them to locate the right one, then put the key in the door for the daily jiggling-turning-jiggling move that finally got the damned thing to open. Inside, she tossed her briefcase on the largest of the three desks and switched on the row of overhead fluorescent lights. It was damp and musty inside, not at all conducive to a productive meeting. Her client, Carson Farrell—defendant in the odd case of *Farrell v. Farrell*—would need to feel comfortable, at ease. There wasn't much time before their meeting—maybe just enough to turn on the heat, dry the place out, then blast the a/c to cool it down to seventy-two degrees. Dry and seventy-two. It could be done.

After making the necessary adjustments, Marie returned to her desk and opened the coffee, which today had a distinctive, burnt odor to it. It was always a crapshoot with the coffee at Joe's, where they left the pots on until they were empty. Ostensibly a greasy-spoon diner, the eating establishment had been infected by the insidious culture of Hunting Ridge, which seemed to leave nothing within its domain untouched. No longer worthy of its diner billing, Joe's lattés were perfect, rich and foamy, served in luscious oversized mugs. Scones and mini lowfat muffins were shipped in from the city at the crack of dawn. Always fresh. And staying true to Hunting Ridge form, the regular, working-class coffee, and those evil bagels driven into disfavor by the low-carb craze, were downright lousy. Marie had been unusually hopeful to catch a fresh pot, but by the smell of the stuff in her cup, there was no question she'd caught the dregs yet again. And it made her miss New York as much as every other thing in this town. Still, it didn't matter. Musty old office, shitty coffee, the smell of bacon and buzzing fluorescent bulbs that were probably causing a brain tumor—it was all hers, under her command along with the rest of her life.

The case of *Farrell v. Farrell* was another matter. There was no affair involved, which in itself placed it in the minority, as did the fact that it was Mrs. Farrell who wanted out. Carson Farrell worked in the city trading derivatives—solid income, enough for a house in the back country, though there was a significant amount of leverage on their assets. They had a 401(k), stock options, and other financial muck that would have to be sorted out. Like most of the cases, the fight over the kids would bring everything into play. Time with his children would cost him, it always did. But this case involved something Marie hadn't seen in all her years of practice, and how it would play out—in court and in her own mind—was not yet clear. Shortly before the split, the unthinkable had happened. A child had died, and it had been on her client's watch.

That was all she knew at the moment, her client having mastered the art of holding facts close to the vest. But they were beyond that now. His wife was pushing for sole custody, offering Carson limited supervised visitation with their surviving three children. His deposition had been scheduled for next week. Time was out. Today she had to get to the bottom of what had happened to the fourth child, the baby named Simone. The kid gloves were coming off, and Marie was not at all sure how she would view this case, or her client, when the truth was revealed.

It was a dilemma for sure, a real headache. And, her daughters aside, taking it on at the throat was exactly what drove Marie Passeti.

There was a quick rapping on the glass window of the office door.

"It's open," Marie called from her desk as she walked through to the conference room, closing the adjoining door behind her. She heard the familiar squeak of the hinges, then the rattling of glass as the door closed again. When she turned around, a man was there.

"You're not Carson Farrell," she said.

The young man smiled nervously. Barely into his twenties, he was perfectly coifed—cleanly shaven, tucked in, and buttoned up. The suit was interview navy, conservative and entirely devoid of personality, though his face told a different story. His cheekbones were still rounded—he was obviously young. But his eyes seemed far too old to be placed there. Glancing around the room to get his bearings, he came full circle to focus on the briefcase hanging by his side. Black leather and far too small to be useful to a lawyer, Marie could tell by the ease with which he held it that it was nearly empty.

"I'm Randy Matthews. The intern from Yale," he said with the intonation of a question.

A look of surprise came across Marie's face. There was no doubt she had hired Randy Matthews. She'd just gone over the resumé that morning. NYU undergrad, Yale Law School, first year. The cover letter had expressed an interest in family law, particularly custody situations. She'd asked one of her associates to vet Randy in a phone interview, and a glowing report had followed.

Still, in all of that, she'd been expecting Randy Matthews to be a woman. Not that she wouldn't hire a man. There simply weren't many male attorneys who wanted to work for a woman practicing family law. And now one was standing in front of her.

With characteristic ease, Marie recovered. "I've been waiting for a client—thought you were him. Never mind," she said, ushering him around the conference table to the inner sanctum. "You're here a little early, aren't you?"

The young man spoke to her back as they walked. "I wasn't sure how long it would take me to get here. I drove from New Haven. I hope it's all right."

"It's fine."

Marie showed him to her associate's desk in the back room, and the drawer they had cleared for him.

"We've set you up here. Nancy is one of my two associates. She only works three days a week. And she doesn't come in much. I use her to run motions at the court, and she works from home a lot. Are you OK sharing the desk?"

"It's fine." With the awkwardness of a novice, he sat down, then popped back up to unbutton his jacket. Marie smiled and took a seat at her own desk, leaning back in the chair precisely as far as it would go, then crossing her legs. There was no question a male intern had never entered her mind, and she found herself surprisingly unnerved. But as she watched him settle in, it occurred to her that this would have been true even if she hadn't made the wrong assumption about his gender. There was something about him—a sense of inner comfort that was unusual in a person his age. The suit was new. He was in a strange town, a hole-in-the-wall office with a woman superior. Still, he seemed to accept his awkwardness, his inexperience.

Smiling with authority, she tried to put them both at ease. "You can take off your coat. We're pretty informal around here."

As he removed his jacket and hung it on the back of his chair, Marie turned to a stack of books she'd collected from the conference room shelves.

"I've pulled together some of the pivotal custody cases in our jurisdiction."

"Great," Randy said, taking a legal pad from his briefcase. "Is there something in particular I should pay attention to? I mean, a specific case I'll be working on?"

Marie nodded. "We've got a lot of cases in the works. All fathers, different degrees of custody and visitation requests. We don't have any demands for sole custody at present, just clients who want more time with their kids than their wives want to give. But you'll see a list of factors the courts use to make these decisions, and all of those will be relevant to our cases."

She paused then, and let out a long breath. "Then we have the Farrell case."

Randy picked up the first book. "The Farrell case?"

"The client I'm expecting. They had a baby who died, and now the mother wants to keep him from the other kids."

"Oh," Randy said, trying to have the appropriate response but getting it all wrong.

"It's OK to be surprised. This is highly unusual. I've never seen it before, and I can't find any local precedents. You'll be doing research later on, after the discovery. Assuming our client shows up."

"OK."

He sat upright at the desk, both feet planted on the floor. It was hard not to watch him. His dark wavy hair, polished shoes, the gold college ring that was still glistening. His eyes were an average shade of blue, but clear and honest. Not something one saw every day.

"Can I ask you a question?"

Randy turned to look at her. "Sure."

"Why do you want to be a divorce lawyer?"

Randy shrugged, returning his gaze to the closed book on his desk. "I guess the same reasons anyone does. I just feel drawn to it."

Marie smiled to herself. *If he only knew*. Divorce lawyers, though necessary, were usually (and unfairly) seen as occupying the bottom of the ladder as far as lawyers went. Well, maybe not the bottom. Personal injury specialists were tough to beat for that privilege. Still, having come from Harvard and a haughty first job in corporate litigation, Marie had hardly been *drawn* to overseeing the unraveling of families. What she had been was smart. She'd honed in on a highly lucrative niche. Now, after six years, she was not only the best female attorney specializing in paternal custody claims—she was the only one in the county.

It was an odd fit for a strong-minded feminist who had, generally, more contempt for her clients than sympathy. The suburban divorce stories were usually the same—happy marriages crumbling under the weight of kids, financial stress, and a social structure that cast men and women into opposing universes. The husband usually caved in first, seeking solace in other women, falling "in love." Ironically, he would somehow think that the flaw in the first go-around was with his choice of wife, and jump wholeheartedly into a second marriage, a second family. Still, the ones she took on as clients wanted to be a part of their children's lives, and this was, to Marie, worthy of her efforts.

As she had quickly discovered, divorce law could be rigid, presumptive, and arbitrary. And it wielded a great deal of discretion to the local judges—more than some were worthy of. Too often, they used their discretion to pay tribute to the well-defined roles of working dads and stay-at-home moms. Stereotypes provided easy cover to avoid the tough calls. Mom got the kids, but dad usually got financial concessions to afford his new family. None of this was good for the children. It was Marie's job to effect a different result, and doing that job required bitter contention of legal norms, which sometimes verged on belligerence. This bothered Marie not in the least. Over the years, she had come to believe that she was looking out for the real victims of the system—the children.

She'd gone over it again and again, rationalizing her work to herself, her friends, the mothers across the table who looked at her with the worst kind of disdain. That it gave her the income she needed to keep the firm afloat, to contribute to the family, and still be home when her girls got off the bus—that she had made a name for herself—all of it weighed in. On most days, she could live with it.

What, she wondered, could it possibly hold for the young man sitting beside her?

Then he spoke. "There's something about the stories of the people, what's happened to them."

Marie raised an eyebrow. "People stories?"

"Is that OK?" Randy asked, suddenly self-conscious.

"Sure. Fine. But I have to ask—will you be needing time off in the afternoons to catch your soap?"

Randy smiled and let out a slight laugh. "If you don't mind. And a subscription to *The National Enquirer* would be great."

Marie made a few mental notes. *Funny. Quick. Sarcastic.* "Well, in any event, I'm lucky to have you. Your resumé is very impressive and I could use the help."

"Thanks."

Marie got up from her desk and headed for the conference room, her sole purpose to remove herself from the office.

"I'll let you get started."

Randy opened the first book, pencil in hand, determination in his eyes. Marie closed the door between the office and the conference room, then took a seat out of view from the glass partition. She had prepared herself for the approaching months—the Farrell case heating up, golf season trying her patience, the girls home from school, and that ridiculous benefit. She knew what to do with all of that, largely because she had those things figured. Hunting Ridge, the men and women in it, the local judges and lawyers—every social dynamic at play in her insular world. Knowing what was wrong with the things around her kept her sane. She had constructed categories, stereotypes for cookie-cutout suburban dwellers, and Randy Matthews was not fitting into any one of them. Now there was no question she would have to dig until she sorted him out. That she was looking forward to the task more than she should did not escape her, nor did it stop her from returning to the office.

NINE

THE MOMMY

THE MORNING DRAGGED ITSELF along until it was noon and the train was in full motion. Henry Harrison was glued to Nick Jr. on the TV, while his little sister stood on a stool watching the cheese melt between slices of bread.

"Guess what, Mommy," she demanded.

With Baby Will on her left hip and a spatula in her right hand, Love stood at the stove next to her daughter. "What, sweets?"

"When I'm as old as you, I can make the sandwiches all by myself." Jessica wanted to do everything her mother did, and the thought of it was frightening. Between Henry, Baby Will, and the general chaos of her life, somehow there would have to be time to make sure Jessica did not end up like her mother.

"Yes. You will be able to make the sandwiches and do a lot of grown-up things."

Love scooped up the grilled cheese, helped Jessica off the stool with her free arm, then delivered the food to the table. Henry got a plate, though he wouldn't eat. He had nothing but TV for lunch. Jessica pulled the cheese out with her fingers, then used her shirt as a napkin.

"Mommy?"

"Yes, sweets?"

"Can I do that thing to Baby Will?"

Love smiled as she scooted her chair closer to Jessica and moved Will to her other knee. Jessica leaned her head over her baby brother, letting his hair just brush her cheek. She watched everything her mother did, especially with the new baby, and feeling the soft, feathery hair on her face had seemed irresistible. Now, it was a ritual of sorts between the siblings. It was such a small thing, and on many occasions would be followed by a slap on his head or some other transgression. But for Love it was a sign that Jessica was recovering from the loss of her status as the baby of the house—evidence that somehow, in spite of all Love's failings, something was going the way it was meant to.

The sound of her husband on the stairs pulled her back from the moment. He was on rotation for rounds, which meant he'd enjoyed a morning off but would now be at the hospital through the night. He emerged from the front hall dressed and ready for the day. Bill Harrison was a big man, tall and broad in the shoulders, with a full head of sandy hair that was just showing signs of silver. His face was kind and handsome, his manner steady. As he stood before her now, in his neat clothes, cleanly shaved, Love could recognize everything she'd been attracted to on the night he helped save her life. But, like so many things lately, she just couldn't feel it anymore.

"Good afternoon, everyone," he said, and Love felt her neck tighten.

With Henry in TV land and the baby oblivious to anyone but his mother, Jessica was the only one to respond. "Hi, Daddy."

Bill made his way around the table, kissing his family on their heads.

"Any coffee?" he asked Love, looking at the empty pot as he planted his lips on her forehead.

Love shook her head. "Sorry."

"Don't worry. I'll stop at Starbucks." Love read disappointment between the lines. It was so much easier when she could be mad at him. And lately, anything would do. A look, a sigh, even an act of overt kindness that was just a bit too contrived. Love would grab hold, convince herself that he was harboring silent criticisms of her. *Is it too much to ask that coffee be made?* As he worked his way through the cluttered kitchen, searching for something to eat, she infused his every action with hidden meaning. *Is it too much to expect that the house be picked up, organized a little?*

Watching him dig through the fridge for the bread, jars of mayonnaise and jam clanking together as he moved them around, searching, Love felt the pain in her neck sharpen and run down her back. Soon she found herself standing beside him, baby on hip, reaching behind the orange juice on the top shelf for the bread. Without a word, she pushed past her husband and set the loaf on the counter next to the peanut butter he'd pulled from the cabinet. Then she returned to the table where Jessica was waiting for a book to be read.

"Are you all right?" Bill asked his wife. And she stuck to the script. *Husband asks what's wrong . . . wife answers, "I'm fine."* It wasn't fair. She couldn't expect him to know. Bill Harrison was the best of husbands. Home by six, helpful with the dinner-bath-bed routine. Always there for the school assemblies, the soccer games and weekend ballet classes. He went for take-out when she was too tired to cook, rubbed her feet when she was tense. And he did his best to understand why the wife who once adored him now rolled over at night, curled up in a corner on her side of the bed.

Are you all right? They were just a few words, everyday, nothing kind of words. Still, she needed him to see her—to look past the mother, housekeeper, grocery shopper, cook, laundress, accountant, janitor—past his housewife to the woman he used to live and breathe. Maybe then he would know the answer she was not giving him.

There was a time when he could see nothing but her. Love Welsh, renowned child genius of the late 1970s. Not the first one to capture the interest of the public, but her lineage had given the story unusually long legs. Her father was Alexander Rice, a famous modern-day philosopher whose works were still on the reading lists at the world's greatest universities. She had earned her high school diploma at the age of twelve through a course of expensive private tutoring. She spent her childhood in an adult world, surrounded by New York intellectuals and immersed in their cynical view of the public at large. Over time, she came to accept her father's low opinion of her own peers, seeking the approval of the grown-ups who had taken her in. Rice brought her to lectures and to parties at Studio 54, where she rubbed elbows with Andy Warhol, Woody Allen, and the like. He pressed her agent for media coverage, and eventually wrote a book about his experience educating a brilliant child. And then, in the fall of her thirteenth year, she began a college curriculum under the instruction of Pierre Versande, a former professor of philosophy from the Sorbonne. It was that year that her life was so shockingly interrupted.

Her mother had quickly moved her to L.A., and that was where Bill found her years later—the fallen prodigy in need of another road, a road where she could start over, reinvent herself. The humble doctor from Connecticut completing his residency with an ER rotation. She had come in close to death, the immediate result of an overdose and the culmination of years of self-destruction. He had given her an escape. Only somewhere on the road that had transformed her from derelict intellectual to housewife, she had begun to vanish and Bill didn't seem to notice. He looked at her with expectations and dismay at her restlessness. It was, Love knew in her head, understandable. He had saved her from herself once. It was done, over. Problem solved. But in her heart, she needed him to magically see that there was something more to the story—the things she had never told him and that she couldn't bear to tell him now for fear that it would blow their lives apart. The black hole in her past was charging back into her life and Bill was wanting the coffee made. Never had she felt so alone.

"Mommy!" Jessica's screaming brought Love's attention back to the table. "I spilled!"

Jessica's cup was on its side, floating in a pool of juice that was quickly spreading out across the table. The first stream fell on Henry's side, dripping onto his leg.

"Mom!" Henry was yelling now. Love stood up to avoid getting hit by the sticky mess. She watched the juice run off the table in four directions, her two oldest both crying as though the juice were hot lava turning them into ash. From his bird's-eye seat on Love's hip, Baby Will looked calmly from his siblings to his mother, then back again. *What should we do here?* Even he seemed to know that standing and watching was not helping matters. Still, Love could not move. The pain was in charge now, holding her hostage.

"Here . . ." Bill was beside her with a dish towel. He dropped it on the table by Henry where the spill was moving fastest. Then he looked at his wife. "I'm sorry, honey . . . I'm already late." *And I have to go to Starbucks because you didn't make the coffee.*

Love did not take her eyes off the hot lava. "I've got it," she said, waiting for the pain to pass and hoping Bill wouldn't ask why she was so slow to respond. She took a breath to swallow it down. The crest had come and gone. She could feel it receding.

In a moment she would issue the decree to stave off the catastrophe. Wet clothes would be removed and placed on the table. She would get another towel, clean the table first, then the floor. They would use soap and water and scrub brushes. It would kill the hour before Henry's soccer practice, teach them to be useful. She knew how to do this. Still, each day since receiving her father's letter, being the mommy was taking more and more out of her.

She considered the tasks that still lay ahead. Drive to activities, home for dinner. Eat, play, cry, clean up. All of it would require her attention. *Mommy!* The call would be made again and again. She would pull from her memory the things she'd read on handling sibling disputes and Will's separation anxiety. She would try to remember not to let Jessica, the easy middle child, fall through the cracks. She would do things wrong, lose her patience at some point—maybe from Henry talking and talking about Legos or Will grabbing her hair one too many times—either way, it would happen. Then there would be baths, pj's, teeth brushing, stories. Their resistance would solidify like drying cement until, finally, they would relent and fall asleep.

That's when she would feel it the most—the pain that was growing as strong as her attempts to ignore it. After the kids and Bill and the churning inside her gut from that damned letter, she had nothing left to hold the weight of the worry that something might be wrong with her body.

With Bill walking toward the door and the juice still flowing off the table to the floor, she took one more breath and went on with the day.

TEN

FAKING IT

"You coming, honey?"

At the foot of the front stairs, Janie Kirk groaned softly beneath her breath. Her hand was on the rail, her body leaning toward the incline as it would have had she actually begun the ascent to the second floor. But her feet were not moving.

"Be right there." She lifted her right leg and planted her foot on the first step.

Was it always this hard? she wondered. Having just closed a deal two days prior, Daniel had been coming home early, going in late. Standard practice for the partners at Weinberg Investments. Deals came in, work picked up. Deals closed, work wound down. And when the work wound down, and Daniel actually came home for the family dinner—when he greeted his long-lost children at the door, doling out high fives and promises of carpet wrestling matches after their homework was done—rewards would be expected. She knew in the morning when he planted that kiss that it was coming, and she had resigned herself that the weekly performance had been scheduled in his mind for later that evening. Still, now that it was here, she felt like a horse being pulled from the plush green fields to the confines of the stable, and her left foot was cemented to the floor.

What the hell is wrong with you?

Daniel Kirk was an attractive man. The same features that had lured her into his fraternity room their senior year were still prominent, though, perhaps, weathered by the passing of time. And despite the twenty years, he was, essentially, the same man she'd fallen in love with. He was easy to understand. Deals, money, sports, sex. She'd married him right out of college, and her faithful adherence to their implied contract had brought her everything. And having everything was worth the sacrifice. That was what she told herself, even as the truth began to emerge—slowly at first, then falling upon her like an imploding highrise, crumbling to the ground and taking her with it. She had analyzed it to death, reading self-help books, listening to Dr. Phil. But in the end, she saw it for what it was. Bad luck.

Standing on the brink of intimacy with her husband, there was no doubt that the truth had arrived. Janie Kirk, the woman with everything, no longer loved her husband. She had loved Daniel Kirk in college. Loved him on their wedding day, and through their childless years in New York. She'd loved him after their first was born, and maybe after the second. She couldn't remember exactly when it happened, or how, only that it did. Somewhere along the line, she stopped loving him.

The children had been a wonderful distraction. The high of each birth, the relentless work of caring for them through the infant years—all of it had kept at bay the longing that had finally broken through. But now the youngest was three. The sleepless nights were gone, the constant demands for attention waning. An afternoon nap was no longer the object of her fantasies. She'd done everything she could think of to shut it down, the disquiet within her that felt as primal as drawing breath.

That she couldn't be the sexual being she once was had seemed an obvious dilemma, and in the many years she had lived in this world, nothing had surfaced to prove her wrong. Husbands and wives lived in houses together, raised children together, did the same bedroom dance over and over—all the while pretending to be satisfied. She was not the only woman with bad luck. She had thought she could live with it by adhering to the carefully constructed roles, each a unique piece of the puzzle that made up the family unit. But, in the end, she had underestimated her own need.

"Janie . . . I'm waiting . . ." His voice was playful.

Fuck it. She unglued the left foot and propelled herself up the stairs. One, then another, then another. She tried to console herself. *Thirty minutes. On the outside.*

Their house was a modern colonial, with five bedrooms sprawled along a wide second-floor hallway. The master suite was the last on the right, a private enclave comprised of five separate chambers—bedroom, bath, sitting room, and two walk-in closets. Making her way there, she passed the children's rooms, listening for sounds. His voice had been loud as he called for her from under the covers. Perhaps he'd woken one of them? No such luck. She passed the last door without incident.

"Where've you been?"

Propped up on his side of their bed, arms laced behind his head—and naked beneath a sheet that was looking like a little pop-up tent at the moment—was her husband. His side-table drawer was open slightly, the drawer where he kept his magazines, and Janie wondered which one he'd used to get himself going.

"I had a few things to straighten up," she lied. "I'll be right there."

She walked across the soft carpet to the bathroom. Moving quickly now before the resignation subsided, she brushed her teeth, flossed, gargled. Then she dimmed the light and pulled the door close to shut, but not completely shut. Daniel was a "visual" man, whatever the hell that meant, and in any case, the bottom line was that he liked to see her naked. Still clothed, Janie walked past their bed, and the husband who was growing impatient, to her closet. She pulled off her cotton workout jersey, unhooked the support bra and let it fall from her shoulders. She slid off her stretch pants, then the cotton thong, the last article of clothing. And the last excuse. She turned off the light.

His eyes were upon her as she made the walk from her closet to the bed. It was inescapable.

"You look good. The exercise is really paying off."

Made-to-order Janie managed a smile as she stood on the carpet next to the bed. Slowly, she pulled back the covers and moved her body beneath them.

Turning to face him, she smiled again, then closed her eyes and waited for the first move. Within seconds, his hands were on her breasts, squeezing, pulling, rubbing her nipples between his fingers.

"*Mmmmm.*" He let out a moan. She couldn't feel it, really, not the way she used to. The surgery had left the skin desensitized, especially around the nipples where the incisions had been made. But it was more than that. Somewhere along the way, the touches had stopped being about her, about pleasing her. Somehow, they were his tits now, perfectly reconstructed. Perfect perky Daniel funbags. And all of his moves, from the gentlest touch to his most spasmodic thrusting, felt like a kind of taking.

Daniel rolled over on his back and Janie was instantly annoyed. Her mind had been set to a different page of the Daniel Kirk playbook. As she climbed over him, she felt his hands on her hips, gently urging her downward. *Goddamn it!* The escalating annoyance made her feel like screaming. Still, she began the descent. First the token pecks on his chest, then one on his belly. She flipped her hair over one shoulder, getting it out of the way, then opened her mouth and took him in.

Did he really think she was enjoying any of this? Did he not know that his wife had been slowly disappearing for years, living only in the moments she was not with him? *Wake up, Daniel Kirk! Your wife has left the bedroom!*

"That's good," he whispered. She wiped her mouth with the back of her hand, then slid up and over him again. On nights like this one, when he was in the game for more than the first quarter, he liked her on top because, again, it was the best vantage point for seeing her breasts, and fondling them if he was so inspired. Tonight, he was into the motion of things, holding her hips, directing the action. And with little of her body now engaged, Janie slipped quickly into a state of detachment.

On most occasions, this was the point in time when her mind would fill with trivial things. The morning schedule, errands, grocery lists. Tonight, oddly, she was in a reflective mood, and the thoughts were curious, and then entirely obvious. She had spent more than a little time wondering what had happened to her in this bedroom, how she went from lusty passion to indifference—and tonight utter recoil—at her husband's touch. In her short but productive pre-Daniel, post-virgin sexual career, she had gone to bed with virtual strangers. And liked it. She had made love to crushes, after the crush had died, but before finding the nerve to break it off. Not the greatest of moments, but still not like this. It was that one time—the time she had not consented, or consented after realizing it was going to happen either way—that had found its way back into her thoughts after so many years. It was a college thing, and as she suspected, a common enough experience for girls who liked to party the way she did. And she had thought little of it, except the occasional pondering over the curious fact that it had not seemed to have caused any lingering trauma in her psyche. Still, it was the distinct feeling of that boy on top of her, the weight of his body bearing down against her folded arms—the futility of her attempts to push against his chest—that was now on her mind.

Straddled over her husband, watching his face contorted with pleasure as he closed his eyes for the home run, she knew there was no one holding her down. No one but herself. And the fact that tonight was requiring unprecedented will could be easily traced to that impulsive encounter, that damned lover who'd awakened the woman who had become a stranger in this house. Janie Kirk had been resuscitated, and now, curiously, the same act she'd performed thousands of times was close to unbearable. *Taking, taking, taking*. That's what this was, and she was done being on the losing side of the transaction.

When it was over, she rolled off Daniel and smiled.

"I think I'll catch the end of the game," he said, pecking her on the mouth as he climbed out of the bed. "Love ya."

"Love you, too," she said back to him, with an insidious sarcasm. When he was gone, she removed herself to the bathroom and took a shower.

ELEVEN

PINK NAILS AND CEREAL BOXES

"Do you like my nails, Mom?"

Marie studied the little pink fingertips that were being held so close to her eyes that she had trouble focusing. "They're great, Suzanne."

It was just after eight and the girls were in their beds, ready to be tucked in. Suzanne lay down and pulled the spread up to her chin, leaving only her hands exposed. She turned them around to face her and inspected the manicure one last time.

"Do you think the color is right?"

Sitting on the edge of the bed, Marie was doing her best to take the beauty nonsense seriously. To her vexation, this had become a mandatory job requirement in mothering her third-grader.

"There's no right or wrong with nail color, Suz. It's just what you like."

Her daughter seemed to ponder this, though her discomfort was still palpable.

"Katy Kirk picked dark purple. It's really cool. I think pink is for babies."

"Then why did you pick pink?"

"Because I liked it at the time. But sometimes I like the wrong things."

Marie sighed, then gently pressed the back of her hand to her daughter's cheek. "Everyone does that once in a while." *Believe me.* "But with nail polish, there is no wrong," Marie said, at the same time realizing that she had already tried that tack to no avail. Then, giving in to the evil forces of society that objectified women and were seeping into her home like one of those bird flus that had everyone so apoplectic, Marie said what needed to be said to get her child to sleep.

"I think the pink is pretty, and it will go with most of your clothes. Dark purple would have clashed. You'll see, Katy Kirk will have a new color by the end of the week."

Suzanne's eyes narrowed as she thought about this, and Marie felt a pang of regret as she read the girl's mind. *Yes! Katy will have to wear purple all week.*

"OK?" Marie asked.

Suzanne smiled as she snuggled into her sheets. Marie gave her a kiss, then turned out the light, closed the door, and left the room. She went next to tackle Olivia across the hall. Having fought with her sister over what show to watch before bed—and lost—it was more than likely that she would be lying awake, plotting her revenge. But by some stroke of luck that tonight felt like nothing short of divine intervention, she had drifted off. Marie pulled up her quilt, gave out the last kiss of the evening, then headed downstairs.

Dressed in sweat pants and a T-shirt that clung to his growing belly, Anthony was standing in the kitchen, staring at the two cereal boxes he'd left on the counter that morning.

"What are you doing?" Marie asked as she walked through the room, picking up toys, homework, and anything else that remained misplaced.

Looking at his wife now, his expression one of contained annoyance, Anthony asked the witness his first question. "Are these out for a reason?"

"Am I on trial, counselor?" Marie was now standing in place by the sink, meeting her husband's eyes.

"Come on, Marie. Are you trying to make a point here?"

"Yes."

"And that would be?"

"That I am not your maid."

He knew that was coming. Still, it was necessary to have it on the record. "So let me get this straight. After thirteen years of marriage, thirteen years of give and take, you think putting away my cereal boxes one morning—a morning, I might add, when I was running late for the train—somehow relegates you to the position of maid?"

Marie swallowed hard, then dug deep to get out her patient mommy voice. "It wasn't one morning, Anthony. It's nearly every morning. And it's not just cereal boxes."

His face was now contorted with an honest bewilderment. She'd never mentioned cereal boxes until tonight, and for the life of him, he could not remember whether he'd left them out before or not. Lacking a solid defense, he decided to play offense.

"And the time I turned off your car lights? Or ran out for milk at ten P.M. because you forgot to put it on the grocery list? I've done a lot of little things for you."

"Those things are different."

"How so?"

"They just are. Doing nice things for someone once in a while is different than having to clean up after them on a regular basis. Cleaning up after someone makes you a maid," Marie said, her mommy voice taking on a sharper edge.

Anthony sighed and crossed his arms. Marie did the same, though she was already feeling vindicated. While his absentmindedness toward all things domestic drove her to her limits, it was now coming in very handy.

"Fine." Anthony turned from his wife, opened the cabinet, and slid the boxes back on the shelf. He then closed the cabinet gingerly and turned once more to face Marie. "I'm sorry I made you feel like a maid. It was not my intention when I *accidentally* left out the cereal."

It was a lame apology—totally lacking in remorse and failing to account for the numerous other times he'd left things for her to clean up. Still, she'd been expecting more of a fight and was feeling quite satisfied.

"Would I be pushing it to ask what's going on with the grass?" The grass, the most coveted asset of suburbanites, was a responsibility that was specifically assigned to Anthony. Grass and car maintenance. The manly things.

"What's going on with the grass?" Anthony looked instinctively out the kitchen window, though the night sky offered no opportunity to assess the state of the yard.

"There are black spots everywhere. Some kind of fungus."

"Fungus?"

"Yes. That's what everyone's saying."

"Oh."

"So . . . what should we do?"

Anthony shrugged, then quickly pulled back the *I don't have a fucking clue* expression he was considering. "I'll ask at the hardware store."

"Great!" Marie said, smiling at him.

As they did every night when the kids went to bed, Marie and Anthony retreated to the family room with their briefcases. They sat side by side on a corduroy-upholstered couch, their work laid out on the coffee table in front of them. On most nights, the TV was turned on, but only as a token reminder of days long past when they actually had the time to watch something.

"Mind if I turn to the golf?"

Yes, Marie thought. But having won the battle in the kitchen, a fact that was beginning to make her wonder (there was a time when Anthony Passeti would have fought to the death just for the fun of it), she decided to let him salvage the remains of his manhood. "Whatever. I have some documents on the Farrell case to go through."

Anthony grabbed the remote and hit the *Fav* button that stored his most beloved channels. Tiger was playing a tournament in Arizona, and he instantly felt the pull, even with an unruly memo on his lap that needed his attention. Not to mention the wife next to him, whose silence, he knew, was grounded in the expectation of conversation. What would he give, he wondered, to turn up the volume, crack open a beer, and watch every glorious shot?

"How's that going?" he asked his wife instead.

Marie let out a groan. "Dead baby. Need I say more? Farrell never showed up today. I left a message to reschedule."

"That's strange."

Marie nodded in agreement.

Anthony moved to the last item on his mental checklist of things a good husband would ask his wife. "And the new intern?"

"Randy Matthews. Started today. Seems good."

"Think she'll be helpful?"

With the speed of light, Marie processed her options, then devised an answer that would not require the use of a personal pronoun.

"Yes. I think so." It was not a lie. Nor was it an omission that constituted a lie. It was a failure to correct an assumption, one which she could easily deny having heard. It was one letter, hardly anything at all, though it now seemed to be sitting between them on the couch.

"I'm tired. You go ahead and watch the tournament," Marie said as she packed up her work. "I think I'm gonna go to bed."

There was a time when this would have had Anthony worried. Either worried or jumping up to follow her to the bedroom.

"OK. Get some sleep."

Marie leaned over and kissed her husband. "Thanks for understanding about the cereal boxes."

Then she left him on the couch with his golf.

TWELVE

THE WORLD THAT DOESN'T SEE

IN THE NORTH END of the Beck home, Gayle leaned over her son to say good night, and he hugged her tightly.

"Thanks for playing with me," she said, kissing him on the forehead.

They had spent the afternoon in the playroom—a modest name for the massive enclave in the back of the house that was home to Oliver's things. With vaulted ceilings, professional game tables, and built-in shelves storing an enormous arsenal of toys, the room was a child's paradise.

"What was your favorite part of the day?" Gayle asked, still holding her son.

He didn't hesitate. "Beating you at Uno!"

Gayle pulled back and looked at his face. "Beating me at Uno?"

"Uh-huh." Oliver nodded with a wide grin. It had taken four tries for the cards to fall in his favor. But winning was everything to a six-year-old boy, and he'd been a patient loser—somehow certain that his luck would change.

"I liked the hotdogs in front of the TV," Gayle said. It had been a day of irreverence all around. Sending Celia, their overpaid nanny, out to run errands, skipping bath, reading stories well past bedtime. It was long overdue, she thought, as she tucked him into bed. How this could be true felt very wrong to her tonight. She had servants to handle every task, every piece of life's tedious minutia. Shopping, cooking, cleaning, errands, yard work. Her role had been reduced to supervision, even when it came to caring for her only child. Could it be possible that she devoted more time to analyzing Celia's performance playing with Oliver than to playing with him herself? Was she not inherently better suited to raising her son than a nineteen-year-old? School wasn't out until three. What did she do all day?

"I love you, Mommy." Oliver said the words first, and they provoked a swell of emotion within his cautious mother. She'd forgotten how easy it was to please a child with nothing but time. She watched him roll over on his side, waiting for the covers to be tucked in around him, tight under the mattress like a large cocoon. Gayle took a deep breath as she finished the task, then went to dim the light. She made one last trip to her child's bed to stroke his hair, the only part of him not trapped now, beneath the covers.

As she leaned over to see his face, his eyes began to close, his face relaxed with the peace of sleep, and Gayle believed without question that she would sell her soul to stay in this moment—this perfect moment when her blood was still, her insides not churning like an incessant whirlpool.

But, like most of the good in her life, it proved fleeting, and fickle, quickly folding beneath the panic that awaited her outside the room. Even as she shut the door, her heart full to the point of eruption, she felt herself drawn to the prescriptions, her mind making calculations for her escape. It was after eight. Troy could be home any time now.

"Mrs. Beck?" A voice came from downstairs. Paul was tidying the kitchen when he heard her steps overhead, and he'd walked to the foot of the stairs in hope of catching her.

Gayle stopped, pulling herself back from the pursuit. The pills would have to wait.

She walked to the foot of the landing. "Good evening," she said with unusual formality, nervous that he might somehow know where she'd been heading.

She was expecting a quick update on some household matter, a polite good night, and then an exit. But Paul surprised her, stopping himself before his words came out, then climbing the stairs to meet her face-to-face on the landing.

"You seem tired, Mrs. Beck," he said, looking at her with concern. He had stood beside her hundreds of times. But it was never at these times when they spoke of personal things. Those conversations were left to the mornings when there was a task before him and a counter between them. Somehow, having coffee to pour and napkins to fold made it possible to stretch the rules of their relationship. She would talk of her day and he would ask appropriate questions, at the right time, looking at her with politeness, and from a distance—the width of the marble-topped island.

Gayle brushed him off. "I'm fine," she said, meeting his eyes for barely a second, hoping he couldn't really see her the way he seemed to.

It was Paul who looked away now, hanging his head slightly as he smiled, a hint of embarrassment on his face. It was something Gayle had not seen in the three years he'd been in their employ.

"This is out of place, I know, but I've been meaning for some time to ask if I can help with the fundraiser. I was a hotel event planner another lifetime ago, and I could take some of the weight off."

Gayle let out a nervous laugh, relieved that the worry over her had been deferred.

"No, I couldn't ask you to do that."

"You're not asking. I'm offering. Really, I might have to take offense if you turn me down."

Gayle smiled as she looked at him, waiting this time for his face to turn. "I wouldn't want to keep you from your life. You already do so much."

"I don't mind."

"Why?" The question came out before she could pull it back.

Paul seemed surprised. It wasn't like her to press him on his life outside these walls. Still, his answer came with ease. "I don't see my life in terms of work and not work. If I can be helpful to someone, that is a gift. Isn't it?"

His words provoked a moment of clarity. How many things she had overlooked, small details this man had tended to, keeping everything exactly as she needed to not go insane. And never once had he looked at her the way Celia always did. Never had he judged her. Instead, he had stood beneath her, catching the pieces she couldn't hold, and putting them back in place—simply because he could.

"I'm sorry."

"Don't be sorry. Just give me a task."

Gayle nodded. "All right," she said, mostly to herself. Then, looking at Paul, she said it again, this time with conviction. "All right. But you'll have to let me do something for you. I'll owe you a favor."

"I'll take a glass of wine."

"Not exactly a favor, but OK!" she said.

Paul turned to descend the stairs, then looked back—expecting Gayle to be just behind him. Her hesitation was brief, part of her still hearing the pills calling from down the hall. In the end, it was the fear of having to explain herself that kept her from retreating.

"After you." Paul stepped aside and let her pass. They walked silently, awkwardly, to the butler's pantry and opened a bottle of Bordeaux. Gayle poured the glasses, then handed one to Paul.

"To the benefit," Gayle said, lifting her glass.

"To the women who need the clinic."

"Yes—and the hope that our efforts don't get wasted on throw pillows."

They finished the toast with a taste of the wine, then walked to the dining room where the flower bids had been carefully sorted and laid out on the table. On the breakfront were brochures and order forms for china, silver, glassware, serving plates, and the like. And spread out on the floor, because there was nowhere left for it to go, was the master floor plan for the backyard setup.

"So much muddle," he said, taking it all in. "And all for one party."

That was exactly what it was to Gayle. A huge muddle taking over her house, threatening the order she fought so hard to preserve—the order that made the rest of life possible. She could see on his face a slight smile, a mix of disapproval and amusement. Necessity had made her perceptive that way, able to see things through the eyes of another from just one look, and she saw through Paul that way now, at what all of this really was. Trivial. One party that would come and go. Guests who would approve or not. Life would go on, and this entire episode, this drama she had woven out of meaningless threads, would have no consequence at the end of the day. Why could she not see this on her own? When had her judgment, her reasoning, become so corrupted?

She had not always been so compliant. There was a time when her life had been a quiet mutiny, a series of subtle variations to her mother's plans. An Ivy League college, yes, but Brown—the most liberal among them. Living in New York, yes, but in the Village, working as a cosmetics marketing executive—a job she had procured on her own merit. She'd gone to the club, learned to play tennis and golf, but done so without enthusiasm. And, finally, succumbing to the pressure to marry, she had chosen Troy Beck as her groom.

"What's the biggest hurdle?" Paul asked, interrupting the sadness that was settling in.

Gayle picked up the floor plan and handed it to him.

"I'm trying to keep it out of the house as much as possible."

Paul nodded, then took the sketches.

"Come on. Let's go outside and try to see it."

Gayle poured more wine, then brought the bottle to the wrought-iron bench at the edge of the patio. Looking out at the property, they talked about dining tables, buffets, and the flow of traffic as guests moved about. It was far less complicated than Gayle had imagined, and the decisions were made within an hour. Still, the conversation carried on, flowing from their shared dislike of the Hunting Ridge social minutiae, to the places they had traveled. Paul spoke again of his time as a drifter, working for families around the world, holding few possessions. He had never intended to spend his life this way, but here he was at fifty-two with no reason to change. Gayle, in turn, told more stories from her childhood, the outrageous incidents of the wealthy that cannot be perceived but from within.

"I forget sometimes that you come from that world," Paul said, and like the chill of the night air on her skin, the waywardness of her actions was suddenly upon her. She had spoken to Paul about her life before, in brief snippets from across the counter. But this was different. This was social conversation, give and take, over a bottle of wine. Somewhere between the playroom and this bench, they had broken the rules.

"Can I bring you a jacket?" Paul asked, but Gayle refused. Running alongside the chill from the air, and the discomfort at roaming so far beyond the confines she had constructed for herself, there was a deep longing to stray even further—and a kind of exhilaration she hadn't felt for years. With every story, every glimpse into this man's thoughts, she felt the joy of unhindered human connection, which had been lost inside her. Only with her son had she held on to it, yet it was different with a child—a one-sided flow of understanding and reflection. Looking at this man now, she felt the desire to reach inside him for more.

"What world are you talking about?" she asked, engaging his eyes.

Paul thought for a moment, searching for a succinct description. "The world that doesn't see."

Gayle looked at the darkening sky, her face lit up with an unnerving sense of comfort. *The world that doesn't see.* She thought about her mother's lifelong quest to mold her into a proper Haywood, the frivolous waste of life on appearances and the approval of others. She thought about her husband, his misplaced anger, and her own inability to tolerate life when she had everything. It had slowly infiltrated her, this world they were now discussing. And she could recall the moment it began with exacting detail—the glorious summer day when Gayle Haywood first met Troy Beck. It was a day of sports and fine dining at the Haywoods' country club just outside of the city, an annual perk for the firm's executives. Gayle dragged herself there every year, mostly to frustrate her mother by rejecting her latest list of bachelors. That Troy Beck had never made that list, that he was consistently seen as the black sheep in the family firm—the one who was tolerated because he knew how to perform on Wall Street, but whose pedigree was less than par—had been the first thing to draw her in.

Looking back, it was so clear that she had misread him. They had shared many laughs about her stuffy family, teased each other about being the clan outcasts, the nonconformists. Their wedding had been on Martha's Vineyard, a beautiful, exclusive island, but an island nonetheless. Getting there was a hassle, finding accommodations for the lengthy list of invitees an immense headache. The family pleaded for the club or the Plaza. There were close to five hundred people they needed to include, and it was insulting to expect so many of New York's aristocracy to travel so far. Every roadblock they placed in her mother's path had been a savory slice of payback for the years she had controlled Gayle's life. Standing on the pier at Edgartown's Lighthouse Beach, a mere fraction of her parents' friends in attendance, Gayle had been certain she had found her soul mate in Troy Beck.

The glare of headlights shone through the gates. Gayle checked her watch, a panicked look gripping her face. It was after ten.

"Troy is home," she said flatly, as if somehow Paul would know what that meant, as if the meager minutes of intimacy they had shared had given him a new window into her marriage.

But that was not the case. Catching a hint of despair in her eyes, Paul looked at her curiously, trying to make sense of the things about her that were still unknown. For a brief moment, he saw something akin to pleading in words that were otherwise benign. *Troy is home.*

A wall of resignation slowly washed over Gayle before she looked away.

"Thank you for tonight," she said, standing to go.

Paul jumped from the bench and took her hand before she was out of reach. "Gayle?" he asked, still trying to understand what had happened—why her husband's presence had so transformed her.

But she broke away, moving quickly toward the house. When she got to the doorway, she looked back briefly.

"Good night," she said. Then she disappeared.

THIRTEEN

DENIAL

"So there's nothing wrong?"

With Baby Will squirming in her lap and Jessica hiding under the loose flap of her hospital gown, Love tried to concentrate on the X-ray film.

Dr. Stallard shook her head as she waited to get Love's full attention. "That's not exactly what I said. The X-ray doesn't show anything wrong with your spine, but . . ."

Love gave her a puzzled look as she interrupted. "Right. Nothing's wrong."

Dr. Stallard looked around Love to Jessica, who was now tearing pages from a magazine.

"Jessie!" Love reached down with her free arm and took hold of her daughter. "Come and sit up here with us." Her face was gripped with pain as she helped her daughter climb onto the examining table.

"Love, this is not my area of expertise," Dr. Stallard said as she reached out to help. Her voice was soft and equal parts empathy and frustration.

Having delivered Love's three babies, she knew her patient well. If she was here with the two little ones in tow, something was definitely wrong.

"How long did you say you've had the pain?"

"About a month."

"And there's no pattern to when it comes or how intense it is?"

Love shook her head and shrugged at the same time.

"This is just not a gynecological issue," the doctor said, leaning back against a counter. "Look, I was happy to order the X-ray. And it is good that there's nothing structural. But pain is pain, and I can tell that it's pretty intense."

Love nodded, though the relief remained on her face. There was no disc out of place. No giant tumor growing on her spine. That was all she needed to know.

"I'll be fine. I probably just pulled a muscle."

Dr. Stallard was still concerned. "Is there a reason you didn't let Bill check you out?"

There it was, the question of the hour. Love had rehearsed her answer in the car coming over, but now after hearing the words spoken out loud by another human being, the truth weighed heavily upon her. She felt the blood rush to her face. *Why haven't I told my husband?* She knew. Of course, she knew. Keeping Bill in the dark about her pain, about the letter, about the past—all of it felt imperative.

"He worries a lot," Love said as she hopped off the table. Placing Baby Will on the floor with a rattle, she reached for her clothes, hoping to end the conversation.

Dr. Stallard got the hint and began to fold up Love's chart. "You really should see an orthopedist. There's a good one here in the hospital. Can I write his name down for you?"

"Sure," Love answered cheerfully, though she had no intention of calling anyone else about this. She had come here out of responsibility to her children, to make sure she wasn't dying. With that settled, she was certain she could push through it.

"Here." Dr. Stallard handed her a piece of paper, and Love folded it up and slid it into her purse.

"So you'll call?"

"Sure," Love said again.

Dr. Stallard searched her face but found nothing she could decipher. "Take care, Love."

Love said good-bye, then waited for the doctor to leave before letting the air out of her lungs. It was a risk, coming to Cliffton Hospital. Bill knew all the doctors here, and most of them knew Love. She'd dragged the kids out of the house, kept them entertained in the waiting room for half an hour, then again in the exam room while the X-ray was developed. Nothing about this visit had been easy.

She felt the surge of agony crawl through her shoulder blade and up her neck. It made her want to scream, and not just out of sheer pain. She had an alien living inside her and she wanted it gone. She had enough on her plate as it was. But the more she struggled against it, the worse it seemed to become. And at the moment, Love was certain it was incredibly pissed off at her latest attempt to find it. *OK—I get the message!* Love thought to herself. She had begun these internal dialogues with the alien last week, though the alien didn't seem to be listening.

"Can we go now?" Jessica was restless, and Baby Will needed his nap.

"Yes! Let's go."

Gritting her teeth, Love finished zipping her jeans, then gathered her children and headed home.

FOURTEEN

FARRELL V. FARRELL

"CAN I GET YOU anything? Water, coffee?"

Marie looked at Carson Farrell from the other side of the small conference table. It was their third meeting, but each time he seemed different to her, almost a complete stranger. Dressed in the suburban uniform—khaki slacks and golf shirt—her client carried almost no expression, not on his face, in his body language, or anywhere else that was visible to the outside world. There was not a trace of anger or sadness or fear, emotions that Marie had become adept at recognizing even in their most subtle configurations. Yet that was not possible. His youngest child was dead. His marriage was ending. His wife wanted to keep him from the other children. Somewhere inside the man, the flames had to be burning. Still, there were no signs of smoke. As she watched him shake his head, his eyes averted, shoulders at ease, Marie had the distinct impression that she was watching a chameleon.

"Then let's get started. We have a lot of ground to cover."

With the air conditioner buzzing in the background, and the young

Randy Matthews sitting quietly to her right, Marie covered the logistics first. As with any custody dispute, the process would be long, weaving its way through depositions, evaluations by court shrinks, hearings to cover the temporary arrangements. The financial affidavits would be picked apart, every expense, every variable source of income. The negotiations would seem endless, and for the most part, pointless as well.

"It's going to be a long fight. And, unfortunately, it's going to get personal. Are you ready for that?" Marie asked.

Carson Farrell looked up from the table where his eyes had been fixed. Barely into his forties, he seemed far older to her. And it was more than the receding hairline, the dull, sunken eyes, or even the mature definition around his cheekbones. He had a weathered look about him, which Marie decided was sadly appropriate under the circumstances.

Looking at her now with the same inhuman, ghostly absence of feeling, Farrell muttered a quiet *yes*. Marie took a deep breath to calm her nerves. It wasn't exactly the watershed she'd been hoping for. But it was more than her client's evasiveness that had her so frustrated at the moment. She was self-conscious, which wasn't at all like her—to think about how she looked, or rehearse the clever lines that on every day before this one simply emerged with ease. On any other day she would be working on an internal autopilot, jumping from question to question almost without conscious thought. She was that good, that skilled at her job. And before yesterday morning, she had worked alone in her lawyer's lair, lost in her cases, talking herself through a thousand mundane tasks all at the same time without a soul to hear. But now there was someone listening, watching, taking in her every move. She'd felt it from the moment he walked through the door, the young intern who said so little and did as he was told, all the while defying the submissiveness such behavior implied. And though she continued to fight the urge, it had proved impossible not to wonder what he made of her. Even now, she could not help but watch herself through his eyes.

"The first order of business is to prepare you for the deposition next week," Marie said, trying to focus on the task before her. "This round is most likely going to be on the financial discovery and the issues germane to custody."

Marie paused to let the message seep in. There was no way to get around it, yet this was new territory for her. Never before had she been faced with asking a client how his child had died.

"Tell me about the kids. Names, ages, personalities. Whatever comes to mind."

Carson Farrell cleared his throat, and for the slightest second Marie discerned a tensing in his jaw line.

"Sam is nine," he began. Then, with an incongruous detachment, he continued to describe the surviving children with the kind of intricacy that usually went unnoticed by fathers. Sam was like his mother, soft-spoken and fragile. Kara was seven, stubborn and bossy, and she had trouble making friends. The youngest was Michael. He was four now, and doing typical four-year-old things, with an emphasis on anything that involved transportation—cars, trucks, trains, and the like. From the broadest stroke to the finest pinpoint, Carson Farrell laid out a picture of each child that brought them to life. Marie could see each one clearly. She could picture them in their rooms, wearing their favorite clothes. Nothing about them had escaped their father, which was precisely why Marie knew the indifference in his demeanor was a lie.

"So there haven't been any problems, no adjustment issues after the move? You lived outside Boston—is that right?"

Farrell nodded, and again there was a slight twinge in his jaw.

"They've done great. No problems."

"Is that what their teachers will say?"

"I don't know what they *will* say. Only what they should say."

"But there have been no reports home, no discussions of any kind about adjustment issues?"

"Not that I can recall."

Marie sat back in her chair, relieved that she was no longer as aware of the second pair of eyes upon her. The dance had begun, and she felt a sense of power that she was leading the steps.

"Carson, it seems evident to me that your memory is quite comprehensive. So if you say there have been no meetings to discuss issues about the children, then I will be confident that is the case, and I will proceed accordingly."

"There have been no meetings. The kids have done just fine."

Marie nodded and smiled as though she were letting the issue go.

"How about psychiatrists? Counselors? Have the children ever been in therapy?"

Had there been any doubt before, Marie's question put it to rest. The kids, the move, it all paled next to the matter of the dead baby sister. One of them was going to have to bring it up, and Marie was relieved when Farrell took the cue.

"Look. It was a rough time up there. We all saw counselors. But the kids are fine now."

"Good. I'm glad to hear that. I can't imagine what it must have been like for you," Marie said. Having opened the door with concern for the children, it was time to turn the light on her client.

Farrell cleared his throat again, this time twice, and with his eyes closed. Still, he held on tight to his composure as tension spread out across the room.

"It was not easy. Probably the reason our marriage came apart. We thought the move would help, but it all just followed us here."

Marie nodded again, looking at her client with compassion. But she was not about to be satisfied with the small tidbit he'd just thrown her.

"Why did the marriage fall apart?"

The man shrugged.

"If I asked your wife why your marriage fell apart, what would she say?"

"There really hasn't been much communication since the accident."

With a steady tone, Marie glided into the next question. "Tell me about that, if you're able. About the accident." Her voice was soft, but firm.

Farrell didn't miss a beat. Lifting his palms from the table, he shrugged slightly. And this time, there was not the slightest crack in his armor.

"Not much to tell. She fell down the stairs when I wasn't watching."

The words came out with a chilling remoteness that Marie could feel in her bones. Before her eyes, she could see the image of a tiny body, twisted and still at the bottom of a staircase, a frantic father rushing to the scene after hearing the fall, the distinctive thud of dead weight against a hard surface. Then the look of panic, despair, anguish, as he rushes to the phone to call for help, knowing all the while that it is too late, that the child who was crawling through the house moments before was now dead.

Still, when she blinked and looked again, she saw that same father, vacant, distant—as if the event had been completely erased from his soul, remaining as a mere set of facts to be recited as need be. Had she not been a mother herself, she might have accepted those facts and moved on. Had she not become an expert at detecting the signs of emotional shutdown that the guilty employ in the name of self-preservation, she would not have been as worried as she now found herself to be. Farrell was looking straight at her now, waiting for the next question as though they were talking about the size of his shoes. And everything about his demeanor—the calmness in his face, his hands neatly folded in front of him on the table—told her that this moment had been carefully rehearsed.

"I'm very sorry for your loss," she said. Then she went on to talk about the questions that would be asked at the deposition, the answers that should be given. And when they were done, she escorted Carson Farrell to the door.

"So what did you think?"

Standing at her desk, the same navy suit from the day before now slightly wrinkled, Randy Matthews took a moment before answering.

"That you covered everything. That it's complicated."

Smiling now, she watched him as he waited for her response, his feet firmly on the ground and that same understated confidence lurking behind the façade. She thought of telling him that he was dead wrong, that they hadn't even scratched the surface with Mr. Farrell. But that would become more than apparent in the coming days.

"This is not what client interviews usually look like."

Randy nodded. "I imagine not."

"I usually start with the marriage. Though it's not in our best interests as lawyers, we have an obligation to make sure the client really wants a divorce, and that the marriage can't be saved."

"How can you tell the difference?"

Marie smiled inside. He always knew the next question to ask.

"Marriage isn't easy. Especially with small children. And, I think, especially in the suburbs." Marie started to pace as she gave her spiel. "Kids make you tired, they make free time scarce, pit the two parents against each other. It stops being about taking care of your spouse. I try to tell my clients that it's something every couple goes through."

"And the part about the suburbs?"

"What?" Marie asked, now lost in a train of thought.

"You said it's harder in the suburbs."

Again, he was right. And, again, he was holding on to her every word.

"I think couples become alienated. Men work in the outside world. Women tend to the children and the homes. There's very little that husbands and wives share. They don't understand each other's lives and it goes downhill from there."

"Huh." Randy seemed perplexed.

And Marie had to know why. "What?"

"I guess I always saw divorce as a result of love that died."

"Well, yeah. I mean all those factors play into the love dying, or hiding at least."

"So you try to figure out which one it is. Hiding or dead."

"That's one way to put it."

Randy was standing next to his desk now, his back propped against the wall, arms crossed. He was getting more comfortable in their surroundings, and this was confounding Marie's ongoing investigation into his psyche.

"So which is it with the Farrells?"

Marie shrugged her shoulders. "That's what we need to find out. And if we can't, we need to at least help him gain access to the kids."

"OK," he said, smiling with satisfaction. He was enjoying this as much as she was, the search for answers inside the private lives of strangers.

"OK. Now see if you can get me the police report on the death of Simone Farrell."

FIFTEEN

FALLING

THE PICKUP LINE AT the Hunting Ridge lower school was particularly long, and Baby Will was growing restless in his seat. Love tapped her fingers on the steering wheel to keep herself from screaming. It was more than Will's crying and Jessica's whining pleas for Love to make him stop, or the anger at herself for not getting to the school earlier to be first in line. The night had been long, one more sleepless odyssey that had left her exhausted, and the pain in her neck was now running down the right side of her back.

It was her own damned fault, she knew. No mother in this town would fail so miserably to sleep-train their children. She had the knowledge, but lacked the will, and at four thirty she'd found herself asleep in the rocker with Baby Will wiggling in her arms. Then came the pleas from next door.

"Mommy . . ."

Henry had called out. At five he was still not a steady sleeper, and already showing signs of the lopsided intelligence she'd handed down. He was unusually sensitive, and far too perceptive for a boy his age—waking with disjointed thoughts that occupied his little head along with the big ears and floppy brown hair.

"Is it time to wake up?" he'd asked, and she'd scrunched herself up beside him to help him back to sleep.

With the sickness of exhaustion in her gut, she'd managed to muscle through her day. Getting them all dressed, packing up the bags—Henry's backpack, the diaper bag, Jessica's swimsuit and towel for her class. She'd loaded them in the car as Baby Will screamed. Driving, screaming, all day. Now the last pickup, then home again. Her head was pounding, and although she could fight the urge, she knew already that she would make the coffee. There was no chance of getting through the nighttime routine without it, even though it was probably getting into the breast milk and stunting Will's development. Another rule broken. And yet she had sworn to herself again and again that there would be no mistakes. Not this time. Not with her children.

Sitting in the car now, with the baby crying and her pain growing, she could feel the desperation push to the surface.

"Mommy!" Jessica was pleading. "Make him stop!"

"I'm sorry, sweets. I can't right now. He has to stay in his seat."

In a matter of seconds, Jessica began to cry, and Love didn't blame her. Were she not a mature woman, had she not been socialized over the course of thirty-eight years to ignore every unpleasant human impulse, she would be screaming herself—perhaps even slamming her foot on the accelerator and ramming the car ahead in a fit of insanity.

In the end, it was too much to bear. Riding a wave of rebellion, Love waited for the Lexus in front of her to move forward, then maneuvered her minivan out of the line—*the* line that was dictated by school policy and strictly enforced. Only if a parent had good reason could they park in the lot and walk to pick up their child. There simply wasn't enough room for all the cars, not to mention the mayhem that would result from the mix of cars and pedestrians in the lot. Love understood the reasons. And like everything else in Hunting Ridge, universal conformity was the very thing that kept the community so pleasant.

Still, the children were crying.

With her eyes fixed on the road, Love ignored the stares from the other mothers as she drove past car upon car, making her way to the front of the school. She pulled into the adjoining parking lot, and weaved through the lanes. There were spots open, but only in the back three rows.

"No way," Love said out loud. She stepped on the gas, drove to the front row, and pulled into a handicapped spot. It was the worst kind of transgression—clearly illegal, unambiguously defiant. But Love didn't care.

"Come on, Jessie," she said, pulling her daughter from her seat. Jessica wiped her eyes, a look of surprise coming across her red face. *What is Mommy doing?* Next came Baby Will. Reaching his mother's hip, he too stopped crying and assessed the situation. With wide, curious eyes, he looked to his mother for an explanation. She was always there to make sense of things. *Stairs, toilet, hair dryer*. But today she was silent, in some other world where he couldn't reach her.

They started to walk, but Jessica refused to move.

"Carry me," she said.

Love stopped and looked down at her pink-clad child, little blond ringlets flying every which way and tears still wet on her cheek. How could she refuse? She was carrying Will. She always carried Will, as Jessica was quick to remind her. From the moment he entered this world he'd been attached to Love like a fifth appendage. And when she tried to remove him, he reacted as anyone would to a person severing their own limb—with utter dismay. In his mind, they were one. It was that simple, and it had been but a matter of time before Jessica wanted a piece of the action. On this afternoon, giving in to her daughter's pleas—and her own guilt—would prove to be the crucial error. But Love didn't have it in her to reason with a three-year-old.

"Here," she said, bending down to scoop up her little girl. With thirty pounds on her right hip, and sixteen on the left, Love crossed the grass median, then squeezed between two of the SUVs and Mercedes wagons waiting in the line. Stares of disbelief, disapproval, and—most of all—envy, burned a hole in her back as she approached the children lined up by the school's entrance.

"I need Henry, please," Love said to the teacher handling the dismissal.

Like much of the school's staff, the woman was young, just out of college, with an air of self-importance that verged on disrespect. Dressed in a skimpy skirt, matching blouse, and shoes whose shape defied all rules of geometry, she looked Love up and down through eyes that were now squinted. And although she pursed her lips tightly and started to speak, she ultimately held her tongue. It was too unseemly to berate a woman carrying two children in her arms, especially one so disheveled.

As the girl turned to fetch Henry, Love could feel herself, her life, in the expression left behind. Wrinkled pants—no time to iron. Hair long and unruly, nails unshapely, skin dry. There was a time when things like this had mattered. The house had been let go as well. The screens on the porch were ripped, the front step loose, jam and syrup crusted on the refrigerator shelves. It wasn't just the little things either—the whole place screamed of chaos. Toys were sprawled out in every room—cars and trucks and hot-wheel contraptions, play kitchens, and big, unsightly plastic dollhouses, and of course, Legos (Henry's obsession) in various stages of construction. When did it become like her to be this way? Or was it? There just never seemed to be time for herself or the house. She was in a state of perpetual motion, and her father's letter had sent her into warp speed—on the run from what she knew was coming.

Love smiled when she saw Henry, though every muscle in her back was starting to tighten.

"Hey, big guy! How was school?"

Henry looked surprised. This was not how things were supposed to be, and even at five, he could sense that his mother had done something wrong.

"Mommy, you're supposed to wait in the line."

"I know. But sometimes things happen and we have to do things a little differently. It makes life interesting!"

Henry wasn't buying it. He knew his mother too well not to see through the sugar coating. With a look of embarrassment on his face, he followed her through the line of cars, acutely aware of the mean looks from the strangers that were now upon him. Deflated, he hung his head and walked close to the rest of his family, hoping he would blend in and escape unnoticed.

As he approached the median, there was a scream, a cry of pain that was both peculiar and haunting. It was not the sound Baby Will made when his mother put him down, or his sister when she didn't get her way. This was the cry of a grown-up, and Henry thought it was the worst thing he'd ever heard. Looking up, he saw something equally disturbing. On the small patch of grass, tangled in a heap of arms, legs, and heads, were his mother, sister, and baby brother.

"Mommy!" Henry yelled, his feet glued to the earth.

Looking back, Love would remember the feeling distinctly. Her back had simply let go. When she took the step up to cross the median, that was how it felt—a complete collapse of her body and with it her hold on the children.

She tried to sit up, locate each child, make sure they were all right. But nothing in her was working. A moment later, she heard the crying—first Will, then Jessica, and for the first time in her life as a mother, she was crying herself with relief at the high-pitched wails.

"I'm OK, Henry," she said, trying to reassure him. There was no doubt in her mind that her oldest and most sensitive child would also be the most unsettled. "I just fell—I'm really OK. Can you come and get the baby for me?"

Henry stood still, fear and confusion mixed together on his face as the tears began to fall.

"You can do it. Can you see him here?"

Love couldn't move her head, but she could hear the baby just beyond her. "Can you see him?"

Henry nodded, but didn't move. In a matter of seconds, a circle of women had formed around them. Jessica was suddenly before her in the arms of a familiar stranger, then Baby Will with another. Voices of concern mingled in a soft hush, and Love knew she should answer, tell them what she needed. But the pain was too intense. Her head became light, full of air, and her vision began to blur.

Then it all went black.

SIXTEEN

THE RESCUE

"LOVEY, CAN YOU HEAR me?"

When she came to several minutes later, the flurry of confusion had given way to a somber, alarming concern. Still laid out flat on the moist grass, Love listened for her children's cries, but heard only muffled chatter and a soft familiar voice close to her ear.

"Lovey?"

It was Gayle, kneeling down next to her. Dressed in one of her expensive pants suits, her hair perfectly styled into place and smelling of fine cosmetics, Love's friend had swooped in and taken charge. She'd been stuck at the back end of the car line when Love fell, but like a row of dominoes, the women had left their vehicles for a firsthand viewing of the event, and Gayle had done the same. Walking up the hill from the road to the school parking lot, she'd seen Henry standing alone, then heard the distinctive cry of the baby. She'd quickened her pace and reached the circle of women standing around. In a tone that was at the same time polite and commanding, Gayle had broken through the ranks and issued the orders.

"Anne, take Henry to Love's car. Joanna—bring Jessica, then come back for the baby. One of you stay with them."

Gayle knew these women. She knew their names and faces, the names and faces of their children, where they lived. She was a fixture in the community, present at every fundraiser from the YMCA to the library to the school book fair. And despite her gentle disposition, she had a strength within her that showed its face at times like this one—when someone other than herself was in need of help.

The women had listened. One after another, the tasks were carried out until there was nothing left to do but wait for the paramedics to arrive.

"The kids . . . ?" Love asked, but Gayle put her hand to Love's lips.

"They're in the car. Everyone's OK. Not a scrape. You need to lie still now."

Feeling her friend's soft hand clasped around her own, Love returned her head to the ground and tried to relax. The pain had become indescribable. Running from the base of her skull, down her right side all the way to the back of her knee, the piercing ache was more than she could bear.

"I hear them!" one of the women said. Then the siren grew louder.

Gayle squeezed Love's hand before letting go. "I'll be right back. Don't move."

Standing over her now, waiting for the paramedics, Gayle was completely unfazed. Nothing mattered to her—not the curious stares of her peers, or the muddy stains on the knees of her silk pants that would never come clean. The concern for her friend was selfless, needing no praise or recognition, and this was precisely what held most people an arm's length away. Despite the way she lived, Gayle's heart was as pure as they came. No one wanted to look in that mirror.

From the ground where she lay, Love watched two young men in blue uniforms rush to her side with a gurney. Her head was placed in a brace, and a board slid under her. Within a matter of minutes, she was hoisted on the gurney and rolled to the ambulance, her friend at her side every step of the way.

"I'll sort out all the kids and meet you at Bill's," Gayle said as they approached the white van.

Love squeezed her hand harder. *No,* she thought, *not to Bill.* But she couldn't bring herself to say the words.

Gayle waited for the men to load the gurney, then pulled them aside. "Take her to Dr. Bill Harrison in town. He's her husband."

The larger of the two, who appeared to be in charge, shook his head. "We're under contract to go to Cliffton Hospital."

"Well, this time we're going to the offices of Dr. William Harrison. You can send me the bill."

The man stopped and looked her in the eye. Her face was soft, her appearance refined. Still, he could tell she wasn't going to waver.

"She'll have to sign a release."

"Fine. I'll be right behind you."

SEVENTEEN

THE DOCTOR

BILL HELD HIS COMPOSURE, though his stomach was in a knot, his heart racing. With an uncharacteristic intensity, he barreled down the long hallway from Exam Room 1, past the reception area, then the laboratory, on his way to the back entrance.

"How is she?" he asked the nurse who had joined him, having taken the call from the ambulance just moments before.

"I don't know."

When they reached the back door, Bill opened it, letting in the warm air. It was just mid-May, and already the temperature was approaching eighty degrees. That did not bode well for a pleasant summer, and this was what he found himself thinking as he waited for the ambulance carrying his wife. But the coping mechanism that on most occasions served him well—thinking of the mundane—was failing him, and his head quickly filled with images of his wife on a gurney. It was how they had started, Love the patient, the situation critical. And it had been a long time since that night, since he'd seen his wife in a fragile state. In time, he had come to see her as the formidable creature she truly was, strong-minded and beautiful. She had endured three natural births, and she'd been a rock through all of them—so much so that he had found himself unnervingly useless. Thinking of her in a vulnerable state felt like a cruel whitewash over the past decade.

"What did they say happened?"

The nurse answered, looking straight ahead. "Just that she fell in the school parking lot."

As the sirens grew louder, his thoughts ran away. Back pain. A fall. It could mean anything. A fall at the school. Where were his children? The fear was profound, but as the ambulance pulled up to the door, Bill drew a deep breath and turned to what he did best.

"Prep for a film. Call Cliffton, set up an MRI."

The nurse rushed off, relieved to have been given a task. Bill walked quickly, but calmly, next to his wife as they wheeled her into the building.

"The klutz gene again, huh?" he said to her, hoping for a smile. With her long legs and tall stature, Love had a tendency for tripping over herself.

"Let's go right to X-ray," he said next, turning to the paramedic pushing the gurney, never letting go of his wife's hand. His presence was understated, yet commanding, and without hesitation his instructions were followed. That was how it was with Dr. Harrison, how it had been on that night so many years before, and Love felt a rush of yearning as she looked up at her husband. It had been simple then, when there was nothing standing in the way of her admiration for him, his awestruck infatuation with her.

"The kids are OK. Gayle has them," Love said, though the pain from speaking those few words sent her head spinning.

Bill squeezed her hand. "I had no doubt. Let's worry about you now."

Love pretended to believe him as they lifted her from the gurney onto the X-ray table.

"It'll just be a minute to set up." The technician disappeared into the small room behind the glass partition where the controls for the equipment were housed.

Holding his wife's hand, Bill turned to the paramedics. "We're set here."

When the others were gone and the room was theirs, Bill looked at his wife.

"What happened?" His voice was soft, though strained.

"I was just so tired. I couldn't hold them," Love answered, reining in the tears.

Bill sighed and looked away. The panic was now unyielding and he found himself at a loss to contain it.

"How, Love? How did you get so tired?"

Losing the battle with her emotions, his wife began to cry. But she didn't answer.

There was so much more he wanted to say, things that had been building since the baby was born. He knew the work it took to care for their children, being home every night, every weekend. He thought it had been getting easier. And yet the house was a disaster, the car even worse. The look of frenzy never left his wife's face. And now this. There was no doubt he was failing her, or maybe it was their life that was failing her. He just had no idea why.

"I'm sorry," he said. "I'm sorry, Love. Let's just get this done."

Bill draped the iron apron down her right side then left the room for a moment. He returned to help roll her onto her stomach, drape the apron once more. The X-rays were taken quickly. As he wheeled his wife down the hall to an exam room, he watched a calm detachment wash over her.

"It's probably just a muscle spasm," he told her, now firmly entrenched in the role of doctor. "There was no acute injury, which is good. I don't think there's damage to your spine, but we'll know for sure in a minute. Could be a tear. That's the worst-case scenario. Let's hope it's just sore tissue."

Love nodded, her focus on a small water stain that had spread across the white partitioned ceiling. She knew all of this from Dr. Stallard, and the guilt from not telling Bill added unbearably to her misery.

Bill squeezed her hand one more time. "I'll see if the films are ready."

Love let out a breath when he was gone from the room. Closing her eyes to shut out the bright track lighting, she tried not to believe any of this. The pain was profound—worse than it had ever been—and there was the matter of her children, especially Baby Will, who would not know what to make of the world from a place that was not his mother. And more than anything, she knew it had been more than her back that had collapsed on that patch of grass.

There was a soft knock on the door before Bill came in, the X-rays in his hand, and Love felt a sense of alarm at the misplaced formality. When did her husband ever knock before walking in on her? As he hung the films on a white-lighted panel, Love could sense the frustration concealed beneath the doctor façade.

He flipped on the light behind the panel, then exhaled deeply.

"The spine looks fine."

Love nodded as she found herself crying yet again.

Bill turned to look at her. "It's probably just the muscle," he said, confused by her reaction.

Yes, Love thought. *It's just the muscle. Just sore tissue. Just three children and a small house and a life that is quickly unraveling.*

There was another knock at the door. Bill reached behind him and turned the handle.

"They wanted to see you." It was Gayle, holding Baby Will, with Jessica, Henry, and Oliver lined up behind her.

"Hey, bud," Bill said, reaching for the baby, then the other two. "Hey, guys. It's OK. Come on in."

Now in his father's lap, looking into the face of his mother, Baby Will wiggled to reach her. When he could not break free, he started to wail.

"I still want to do an MRI at Cliffton," Bill said, now standing with the squirmy baby in his arms. "I'll be back in a minute."

"We'll be just fine," Gayle said.

Bill disappeared with the baby, leaving Jessica and Henry standing on either side of their mother. "See, she's OK," Gayle said to the children, whose heads just peeked over the table.

"Mommy?" Henry's voice was shaky. Then he started to cry.

"I'm fine, Henry. Really. I just have a tired muscle in my back."

Henry nodded through his tears, though the prognosis did little to erase the image of his mother on the ground—or the fear that had taken root inside him.

"Henry," Gayle said, her voice steady. "I need your help. Can you do something for me?"

Henry nodded.

From the yellow counter, cluttered with cotton balls, tongue depressors, and other innocuous medical supplies, Gayle grabbed a stethoscope and attached it to Henry's ears.

"Very gently, put this on Mommy's chest and listen to her heart. Can you hear it?"

Henry nodded, his tears beginning to subside.

"Good. Now keep listening."

Next, she pulled a hairbrush from her purse and put Jessica to work untangling Love's pony tail. It was so like her to know just what to do.

Love looked up at her friend, but said nothing as Gayle studied her face. Within seconds, Gayle's cheerful smile morphed into a look of deep concern. With nothing but friendship between them, an urgent need was unmasked, and Gayle could see clearly now the extent of Love's pain.

"I'll be right back." Gayle excused herself and stepped outside. She followed the sounds of Baby Will, who had gone back to babbling, until she found Bill standing beside one of the nurses in the office.

"Can I talk to you?" she said, pulling him into the hallway.

Bill filled her in on Love's injury. Impossible to tell the full extent, though the MRI would help. Bed rest, pain medication, maybe some physical therapy would be required, but there was little else to do but wait for it to heal. *Probably*. Gayle listened until he was through. Then she asked the one question the doctor had failed to answer.

"That's a good plan for the injury. Now, how are we going to take care of your wife?"

EIGHTEEN

ANIMALS

"NOT YET," JANIE KIRK whispered, in between the sighs. She wasn't ready for the sprint to the finish line.

The man was breathing hard, his movements quick, awkward. Somewhere between removing her clothing and fondling her breasts, he had stopped kissing her and closed his eyes. Then there'd been more fondling, the self-gratifying kind she had at home, followed by a token effort farther down. Janie did her best to send the signals, placing his hands where they needed to be, keeping him from climbing on top of her, with one word playing in her head. *Take, take, take.*

In all fairness, the first night had been fast, explosive. It was not unreasonable for him to bring on a repeat performance. Still, this was *not* the first time in the dead of night, the full moon and sheer thrill bearing down on them. It was the middle of the day, a naughty encounter in an unlikely place—the small solarium in the back of her house. The sun was sifting through the tinted glass, warming their skin. A soft blanket weaved between their limbs, entangled in their embrace. There needed to be kissing, lots of wet kissing. Then touching—soft, lingering, mouth-watering touches leaving her with a delicious ache for more. She wanted to be savored, devoured, every inch of her treasured for the beautiful creature that she had worked so hard to become. That her lover wanted nothing more than a quick release was as familiar as it was bewildering.

"I'm dying here," he said.

They always said that. At nineteen, her boyfriend had said it. *You're so hot, you have to help me out.* Like being attractive, turning him on, somehow obligated her to hand over her body. At twenty-one, her summer fling had said it. *You were so sexy on that dance floor,* his hand on top of her head trying to elicit some oral gratification. Then, of course, there was the one who wouldn't take no for an answer.

"Your body is *incredible,*" he said. It was a valid attempt, luring her with flattery. But after twenty years with the same man, Janie had no interest in being someone's sexual fantasy. After twenty years, she wanted someone to be hers.

"Just wait," Janie said, trying to lure him, educate him.

Maybe it was springtime. Primal impulses. She'd seen it at work on the farm animals at the Hunting Ridge Nature Center. Her kids had loved the place when they were younger—the tiny barn houses, chickens roaming wild. On most days, it was good, clean fun—all the crap aside. But not in the springtime. She'd learned that the hard way. From April through the end of May, it was simply not a place for children, for anyone as far as Janie was concerned. The females were in heat—pigs, goats, cows, horses. Even the damned butterflies. In pen after pen, squeals resounded as the females ran in terror, chased by their horny male counterparts. They would always get caught, pinned from behind by the bigger, stronger male creature. Then would come the yelping, a few thrusts, and the dismount. With their noses to the wind, the males would start sniffing out their next conquest, while the females, Janie could only imagine, thanked their creator that it was over.

It had only taken one visit for Janie to swear off the place when the ground began to thaw. She would not expose her kids to what were, essentially, acts of animal violence—no matter how necessary it all was to the circle of life. Maybe they didn't notice it, or understand what they were seeing. Maybe it was she who didn't want to see it, didn't want to be reminded that the evolution of mankind from its animal origins had, essentially, failed. That the only things separating us from those pigs in the mud were expensive tailored suits.

It was no use. His whining had killed her mood. With her eyes glued to the ceiling, Janie let him finish. Like a schoolboy at the sound of the bell, he climbed on top of her. Three thrusts and a dismount. He tried to nuzzle into her neck, she could feel his smile against her cheek, and she let him stay there. Briefly. Until she could no longer stand the sensation of the life being sucked right out of her by his pleasure.

"You have to go," she said.

As he collected his clothes, Janie sat with her knees to her chest, the blanket wrapped around her. How different he appeared to her now, in the light of day, the evidence laid out clearly before her. There was no escaping the disappointment that was rushing through her. For years, she had dreaded sex, and she'd seen it in other wives. It wasn't often—the skin of deception that grew over the course of their stints as housewives could be thick. But now and again she would catch a glimpse. A woman at the nail salon having her feet done—a look of sad remembrance on her face at the feel of the warm pulsating water, the firm hands massaging her calves. Or the face of a mother nuzzling her infant, holding on to the intensity of that baby love, that primal emotion that will not be suppressed. Janie was not fooled by the smiles, the polite conversations. She couldn't remember the last time she'd witnessed a passionate kiss in the town of Hunting Ridge.

Still, it hadn't always been that way with Daniel. She would not have written off her sex life that easily. No, in the beginning it had been hot, the kind of hot reserved for teenagers, those freewheeling hormonal hostages. And later in their marriage there had been—not fiery—but intimate, sensual moments. Soft caresses, less conservative positions. He had held out longer to please her. That it faded over time was, she presumed, the natural progression in a relationship—each party giving more than they wanted to lure the other in. It had been that way with other men. Accepting that sex would become more mundane, less interesting as the tension died, was the cost of doing business, the deal that she'd made on her wedding day. What she hadn't bargained on was feeling like an anonymous warm body every time her husband needed a fix.

The man in front of her was another story.

When he finished dressing, he leaned in to kiss her.

"Just go now," she said.

He looked back at her, surprised.

"What's wrong?"

Things to say popped into her head as a matter of course. *Nothing, I just think we should end this before it goes too far . . . I really like you, but we can't take the risk . . . blah, blah, blah.* She opened her mouth, then stopped herself. Looking at him without a trace of kindness, she said instead, "I have this at home."

Pulling away, he looked back at her carefully, studying her face. Then he smiled and folded his arms.

"OK. I see what you're saying."

They were silent for a moment, though their eyes were engaged, and the feel of him searching for her thoughts recaptured her interest.

"Next time, we're going to a room. And not in Hunting Ridge. There's a motel off the Thruway in Cliffton."

Janie smiled, curiously. "Why Cliffton?"

He did not hesitate before answering. "Because I can't fuck you properly in Hunting Ridge."

Janie felt a breath rush in, then a blushing around her cheeks. She looked away from him, but could not hold back the smile. With one sentence, one beautifully defiant, irreverent statement, he had begun to redeem himself. And this time she knew exactly what she wanted to say.

"When?"

NINETEEN

PROFESSIONAL RESPONSIBILITY

"SORRY I'M LATE." MARIE charged through the door, making excuses as she rushed past the conference room and into the office. It was nearly eleven o'clock, and after watching Love's children for the better part of three hours, she was almost frantic to get to work. "It's OK. How's your friend doing?" Randy Matthews stood at attention behind his desk, where a casebook lay open. With his jacket draped behind his chair, his sleeves rolled up, tie loosened, he was beginning to fit in with the office décor.

Marie stopped moving and let the question sink in before responding.

"It's not good, actually. She's in a lot of pain and no one knows why." She shook her head, then continued to her desk. "And will you please stop doing that?"

"What?"

"Standing up every time I walk through the door. In case you haven't noticed, I'm not Emily Post."

The reference to the manners guru was lost on Randy, but he took his orders and returned to his seat. "Sorry. Old habit."

"What? Military school?"

Randy laughed and hung his head slightly with amusement. "No. My father was a stickler when it came to formality. Especially with women and elders."

"Did you really have to ruin my day the moment I walked in here?"

"No . . . I didn't mean you." Fumbling to explain, the young intern was suddenly flustered. "I mean, yes you as a woman, but no, not you as an elder."

He was now fully embarrassed, and Marie smiled as she pulled off her own jacket and dropped it on a pile of folders stacked on the floor beside her. Then she kicked off her shoes and pulled a leg under her as she sat down to face him. She could get used to Randy Matthews, having him beside her, listening and watching as though everything she did and said was divinely inspired. It wasn't as if she *ever* got that at home. Her girls loved her, she knew, but the *I hate you*s could easily outnumber the signs of affection they doled out each day. After all, they were girls. Emotional manipulation was their birthright. That left her husband, who had—to her utter bewilderment—left out his cereal boxes again that morning in what one could only presume to be an act of childish defiance.

"Nice try, but too late. Did you say you would be needing a recommendation at the end of the summer?"

Marie's wry smile disarmed him, and Randy Matthews was again laughing. And when he turned his eyes from her face, she found herself studying the creases that spread across his cheeks when he smiled.

"This came on the fax," Randy said, handing her several sheets of paper. "I think it's the Farrell police report."

"What's it say?" Marie asked, consciously avoiding the touch of his hand as she took the documents.

"I didn't know if I should read it, or wait. So I waited."

Marie sorted the pages, placing them in order. As she began to read, she heard the squeak of chair wheels.

"Can I look on?" Randy was close now, having moved his chair to her desk. And though she nodded silently, casually, she became unsettled by the smell of his cologne, the soft ruffling of his starched shirt as he rested his elbows on the desk.

The report was surprisingly brief.

June 12

Victim Simone Farrell, a 10-month-old infant, died from injuries sustained while falling down front staircase in the Farrell home. Father Carson Farrell was at home with the victim at the time of incident, left child unattended in upstairs hallway to make a call. Baby gate was installed at top of stairs, but was not secured at the time of the incident. Cause of death: spinal shock.

There was more paperwork, the ME's report, the names of the officers who responded, the call made to 911.

"Farrell called for help at ten twenty-one."

"Hold on." Randy dug through a separate pile of documents, pulling out a page from a phone bill. "I flagged the bill from that month . . . ," he said, running his eyes down the page. "Farrell called the office at nine forty-five. The next call was to 911 at ten twenty-one."

Marie nodded silently as she continued to read.

"It's like he said, then? An accident?" Randy asked, turning from the report to face Marie.

"Looks that way." When she got to the last page, she leaned forward, clutching the paper with both hands. "Hold on . . ."

"What is it?"

Marie read the last page of the fax.

April 7

Domestic disturbance. 1462 Shelton Avenue. Neighbor reported yelling at residence of Carson and Vickie Farrell. Officer dispatched. No signs of injury at the scene. Officer issued a warning. No complaint lodged.

Marie placed the report down on her desk, then leaned back in her chair.

"Well, I guess things weren't quite as placid as our client implied. Apparently, our Mr. Farrell has quite a temper."

Randy stared at the report and nodded softly. "So what now?" he asked. "Bring Farrell back in?"

Marie sighed deeply and shrugged. The truth was, in her six years as a divorce lawyer, this was the first instance of domestic violence she'd come across. It just didn't happen in Hunting Ridge—or, at least, didn't make it to the surface.

"This is where it gets tricky. We don't know very much about the incident. If we find out more, and Farrell takes the stand, our hands are tied as to what we can allow him to say."

"Suborning perjury."

"Exactly. We have a lot more latitude if we don't know."

"But what if there's more here. What if he . . ."

Marie held up her hand. "One step at a time. If it's relevant to the custody issue, Mrs. Farrell's lawyer will raise it at the deposition. Then we'll see what he says. I'm not worried about Carson handling the question. You saw him. He's as cool as they come. And I'd rather not let on that we've looked into his daughter's accident." Marie stood abruptly as her last statement played out in her head.

"What's wrong?"

"Nothing," she started to say. Then she said to Randy what she would have said to the office walls such a short time ago. "I usually don't go behind a client's back. I can't even say for sure why I did this time."

Randy shrugged with a definitive nonchalance, the innocence all but gone now from his demeanor. "I do."

"Really? Want to fill me in?"

"There are three children involved and you thought Farrell was being evasive. You have an obligation as an officer of the court to report a client who might pose a danger to others, so you checked it out. And, as it so happens, you were dead right."

Marie sighed as she looked at Randy, leaning back with his legs crossed, shoulders held firmly in place—more of a man than she had seen in him before. And for the first time since their initial meeting, he looked back at her not with youthful awe, but with an alarming degree of certainty in her judgment. It was that certainty that the mirror over the bathroom sink had been missing, the very thing she had missed feeling about herself for far too long.

"Don't tell me—you had Professional Responsibility last semester, right?"

Randy smiled sheepishly and nodded. "And?"

"*And*, it's a lot more complicated in practice. I have my reputation, my firm to think about. I'm not even sure I know what that police report actually means, if anything."

"So should we forget about it?"

Marie walked to the window and looked out at the parking lot below. *Yes, Marie. Leave it the hell alone*. But it was not an option. Not for her.

"God help me for saying this, and I'll deny it to anyone outside of this room. But I'm a mother first, and if Farrell is hiding something that could hurt his children, I want to know."

"I think that's right."

"What?"

"Being a mother first. A *parent* first. Especially when they're young. Who else is going to look out for them?"

Marie gave Randy an odd look. "Interesting perspective for a single guy."

"I'm not saying I know what it's like to be a parent. But I *was* a child. And I've seen how you talk about your girls."

"Is it that bad? Do I go on and on like the rest of them?"

Randy laughed. "Who's *them*?"

"You know—people who talk about their children as if anyone else cares."

"I like hearing about your family."

"You like hearing about nail-polish dilemmas, wardrobe disasters, fights over TV and cereal boxes?"

"Yes. And don't forget the tiff with Suzanne's teacher over her math homework, Olivia's irreverent potty talk that has the other moms up in arms—my personal favorite, by the way—and, of course, *golf*!"

Marie hung her head, pretending to be embarrassed—and trying hard not to think about the way his attention to her children was making her feel.

Did Anthony even know about Olivia's potty talk? Had she bothered to tell him?

"The evidence is in. I *am* one of them. Now, what about Farrell?"

Following her lead, Randy's voice took on a more serious tone. "Tell me what I can do."

For starters, you can stop looking at me that way. Then again, did she really want him to stop? It came as a relief that, at the very least, she knew what she wanted to do with her client.

"Let's get into it."

TWENTY

YVONNE

THE FLIGHT FROM L.A. was long. With delays on both ends, the six-hour event had turned into a ten-hour jaunt, and that was before consideration was taken for the travel to and from the airports. Nevertheless, it had to be done.

Yvonne Welsh waited for the driver to come around for her door. Even if her day had passed, she still felt worthy of the respect and not above demanding it. It was true that few civilians recognized her from the daytime television work she'd put out in the sixties and early seventies. And, at sixty-something years of age, she wasn't stopping traffic the way she once had. Still, she was *Yvonne Welsh*—the longest-running daytime drama actress of her time. And though the money was close to gone, the residuals she'd lived on for years steadily dwindling, she kept up appearances as well as any other Hollywood has-been. The ranch house she lived in was small, but it was in the Hills. Her clothes were department store, but she wore them like Prada. With dyed red hair shapely piled atop her head, carefully penciled eyebrows, and the softest skin, Yvonne Welsh would always be a star.

She studied the house from the back seat while the driver pulled the bags from the trunk. *Has nothing changed?* she thought to herself. It had been nearly a year since her last visit to the home of her only child, and her disapproval at the state of things—even from the outside—was diluted only by her own guilt, both new and old. Love was deserving of more than this, bound to a small-town doctor with a mountain of debt, stuffed into this little cottage like those poor Mexicans she'd seen on the evening news back in L.A. She should have had more. Love Welsh had been born with a *gift*.

Standing at the curb outside her daughter's house, a long silk shawl wrapped around her shoulders in a dramatic sway, Yvonne paid the driver and prepared herself for what lay ahead. It didn't matter at the moment what Love could have had. Her child was sick again. Some kind of back injury—a different ailment altogether—though to the mother in Yvonne, this was not reassuring in the least. None of them had dealt with what had happened to Love, and she couldn't suppress the feeling that this was some kind of payback.

With Baby Will riding on his hip, Bill Harrison met her at the door. He had waited three days before admitting the seriousness of Love's condition, praying it would be unnecessary to call for reinforcements. Yvonne had taken the next available flight, and now it was clear that her presence would be a bitter pill for both of them to swallow. Despite her general disdain for the medical community at large, she and Bill had gotten on from the first introduction. For some brief moment in time, she'd found him charming. That she pretended to still feel this way made it all the more awkward between them—Bill finding it humiliating, and Yvonne being too damned tired to pull it off. She would be helpful now, tending to the kids, tending to Love. But in between the colorful Hollywood tales and embellished memories to pass the idle time, there would be plenty of hard feelings for the man who had failed to provide her daughter with the life that should have been hers.

"Yvonne!" Bill said, extending his free arm to offer half a hug.

"Bill. Nice to see you." The mother-in-law pushed past him, taking the baby on her way.

Through the high-pitched cooing, Bill grabbed the suitcases and carried them into the small foyer. Soon, a wave of feet pounded the stairs, announcing the arrival of Jessica and Henry. With their hair wet, pajamas in various states of adornment, the older children surrounded their grandmother and demanded their presents.

"What? No 'Hello Grandmother, how was your trip'? Where are your manners?" Yvonne teased as she handed the baby back to Bill. After a slight delay—just enough to elicit the wide-eyed anticipation—she reached into her carry bag and pulled out two treasures wrapped in the finest paper and ribbon.

Henry ripped into his first, then beamed at the sight of the latest Bionicle Lego. Jessica struggled a bit, but it was worth it. The Pet Pal stuffed kitten in a miniature carrying case, pink, of course, sent her jumping up and down in a giddy frenzy.

"Now upstairs. Bathroom, teeth, pick out books. I'll send your grandmother up as soon as she gets settled," Bill said, relieved that he knew the bedtime routine cold.

When the children disappeared, their excited voices trailing behind them, Yvonne's smile faded. Then she looked at her son-in-law with the most serious of expressions. "Now, *where* is my daughter?"

"She's in bed. You can go up."

"And *how* is my daughter?" Her dramatic tone forced Bill to stifle a smile.

"We did the MRI. There's no tear in the muscle, which was puzzling. She just has pain—pain we can't explain at the moment."

Yvonne looked at him with scrutinizing incomprehension. "I don't understand."

"We're running some blood tests," Bill answered, feeling defensive. "We're going to rule out Lyme disease first."

"Lyme disease!" Now Yvonne was alarmed.

"It's highly unlikely. We just need to rule things out before accepting that it's a muscle strain."

Yvonne nodded and did her best to be gracious. "So you have no idea yet?"

Bill shook his head.

Then Yvonne shook hers. "My money's on a muscle strain. She always did too much, my baby girl."

"Let's hope."

Yvonne walked past him and started up the stairs, where the hushed giggles of children not doing what they were told filled the hallway. Yvonne smiled, but then fought to hold back her disapproval of the state of things—the stains on the stair runner, a cobweb in the ceiling corner, laundry piling up right there in the hall for everyone to see. Standing before her daughter's former study/bedroom—another disgraceful commentary on her life—Yvonne inhaled deeply to swallow all the things she wanted to say.

Then she opened the door and said them anyway.

"Nice to see you, too, Mother." Lying flat on the small bed, pillows propping up her knees and elbows, Love felt a warm current run through her. Had her mother not burst in pointing out her failings to avoid her own fear, it would have been all wrong.

Yvonne shrugged, then struggled to walk to the side of the bed. "Good God, I can hardly get through here!"

"I know, Mother."

"Can I sit? I won't hurt you?"

Love patted the mattress in the spot she'd cleared for visitors—just below the pillow supporting her left arm, just above her hip. The shift in the mattress from another body could be tolerated there.

Sitting now next to her daughter, Yvonne looked at her with conviction. "Your mother's in the house now. You don't have to worry about a thing."

Love studied the regal woman before her, taking in her smell—the sweet perfumes and lotions, the hairspray that was keeping all those extensions so perfectly in place. Her makeup was just right, adding color in a subtle, natural way to skin that had been carefully protected over the years. The delicate pearl earrings, silk scarf, lady's Rolex on her graceful wrist. Those long, elegant fingers and manicured nails. She was as she had always been—a slight and wispy lady, in the truest sense of the word. Still, looking now into her pale blue eyes, so steady and sure, Love could see the steel foundation she had always leaned on. Yvonne Welsh had done the inconceivable—she had survived Hollywood with her integrity, and most of her pride, in tact. It was that woman who defied the fragility of her appearance that Love always saw when she looked at her mother, as she now did. And in an instant, she was a little girl again.

"Come now," Yvonne said, wiping a stream of tears from her daughter's eyes, "your face is getting all puffy and the children will want to say good night."

Love nodded and took a breath, but the tears kept coming. It had been almost a year since she'd seen Yvonne, since she'd felt the comfort of her mother's presence. It was long overdue.

"What is all this about?" Yvonne said, taking her hand. Then she sighed deeply and watched as her baby girl let go. She pulled a linen handkerchief from her bag, and gently patted dry her daughter's cheeks. But that was all she could do, she had come to realize over the years—sit and watch as her only child ran herself into the ground, desperate to keep one step ahead of her past. And now that SOB was dredging it all up. *Damn that man,* she thought. *Damn Alexander Rice.* He was brilliant to be sure, but he was also a born narcissist and philanderer. She had known from the moment they met that he had not been placed on this earth to be a good husband and father. She should have also known he would be nothing but trouble.

It was that way with the great ones, she reminded herself. Able to buy themselves a ticket out of the moral scrutiny of an otherwise unforgiving public. How many years did she suffer him, living on the narrow walk between perfection and ruin, exhilaration and despair? Rice was a habit she'd been too weak to kick, even though she'd faced every morning with the sickness of uncertainty. *Would this be the last day?* she used to wonder. *Is this the day he'll go back to his wife?*

She held her daughter tighter, wishing she could change things, choose a man who would stick around to be a father. But, ironically, it was fatherhood—their greatest moment, the creation of their child—that had driven him away. Their love child (hence the name Yvonne had insisted upon) had cast a black shadow over him, adultery being one thing, and what was essentially bigamy being quite another. His indulgence had resulted in the making of two families, and public opinion had finally turned against him. The year Love was born, he published his tenth book—an inquiry into the corruption of intellectual thought by religious faith. His life became a testament to his own theories as the public discourse focused on his infidelity, leaving his book sales to languish. It soon became clear to everyone in his inner circle that he would have to choose, and Yvonne never doubted which way he would go.

Of course, that had not been the end of it. Rice's older children had fallen into the trappings of mundane existence—marriage, corporate jobs, kids of their own. None of this had been of interest to him. When Love's gift was discovered, he'd come back to claim his prize. He took over her childhood, investing both his money and his wisdom in her education—not to mention his reputation. That all of his efforts would crumble under the weight of his own arrogance was, in hindsight, almost predictable.

Now he was back again, and Love was running even faster. As if that were possible. Three children in five years, no help to care for them, scrubbing toilets and dishes, washing soiled clothing over and over without a thought for herself—trying to accumulate enough virtue to erase events that could not be undone. And yet it was she who had not been able to see what was right in front of her—the know-it-all Yvonne Welsh, who'd been so invested in Love's future that she'd failed to notice the train wreck approaching.

She thought about the letter she'd received from Rice and wondered if somewhere in this house she wouldn't find a piece of that same gray stationery with the chicken-scratch scribblings that neither of them had seen for years. More than this, she wondered if Rice's re-entry wasn't behind everything that was going wrong in her daughter's life.

Yvonne forced a smile and stroked Love's hair. *This stops now,* she thought, making a list of the things she *could* do—hire a housekeeper, watch the kids, whip Bill into shape. She would send him to the grocery store, get him to fix the front porch step that felt loose, put up a ladder and reach that damned cobweb. Despite her image, she wasn't above scrubbing the stains out of the carpet. And, of course, they would do those tests. Thinking of these things—practical things that could be accomplished—settled her nerves as she watched her little girl begin to calm.

When Love's face was dry, Yvonne carefully folded the handkerchief and returned it to her bag. Then she reached out, softly touching Love's face with the back of her hand. In a whisper, but with a firm tone, she said it one last time.

"Your mother's here."

TWENTY-ONE

BROKEN GLASS

GAYLE BECK WALKED THROUGH the quiet house, across the marble-tiled kitchen, up the back stairs to her bedroom. The door was open a crack, the lights left on, but dimmed just right—just enough to allow her eyes to adjust from the dark hallway. Everything was perfect, as it always was. Her staff was well trained. Careful.

One at a time, she pulled off her heels and placed them on the cedar shelf next to the other dress shoes, lined up an inch from either end. She reached back, unzipping her dress, letting it fall to the plush carpet before stepping out. She draped the dress over an antique rack reserved for dry cleaning. With steady, even movements, she finished undressing, slipped on a robe and walked to the bathroom.

None of this was easy with bleeding hands.

She turned on the light but did not look in the mirror. Instead, she pulled open the vanity drawer and removed every brown prescription bottle she could find. Without expression, she lined them up in a row on the white marble counter and read the labels. As her fingers moved over each one, the charges inside her began to settle.

The master bath in the Beck house spanned the length of the bedroom, twenty feet long from window to window. With thick white carpeting, a sunken whirlpool tub encased in black and white marble, his-and-hers water closets and antique vanities, it was meant to be a private sanctuary. Every detail had been carefully planned. The steam shower had an oversized seat. Soft chairs with plush throws sat before a small fireplace. She had given much thought to the design of this room, selecting the fixtures, their placement on the walls. And she had imagined romantic moments, tranquil respites from everyday life. From the children they were planning.

Now the sound of the breaking glass just beyond her shoulder was all she could recall as she stood within the embrace of the gentle surroundings. What had it been about this time? Misplaced car keys? The wrong brand of scotch? Did it really matter? From their first year of marriage, his anger had shown itself, then crept through their lives until it had filled every place that was vulnerable. Her money. His job at the family's firm. Their love-making, which deteriorated steadily, sharply, until there was no love to be found in the act.

There was a time when she tortured herself to find an explanation, identify the mistake she must have made along the way. But the truth had come slowly, in flashes so little she could easily set them aside in her mind as aberrations of an otherwise good marriage. Now, she could see the path that had brought them to this darker place. Troy had come from a modest home just over the Hudson River. A Jersey boy. He'd gone to a local college, worked his way up to a spot on a desk at Haywood, Locke & Ward. And his ability to bring in the cash had brought him job security, and the feeling that he was invincible.

All of that disappeared when he married Gayle. The ambivalent respect he had achieved on the trading floor was compromised by the shadow of nepotism, and he became self-conscious, angry. The pride he had taken in making his own way was gone, a consequence he had not considered. He began to grab hold of anything he could find to satisfy his drowning ego.

The humor they had shared was replaced with angry barbs at her family members. Still, he thrust himself in their midst every chance he could, flaunting his power as the husband of their youngest daughter. He used the Haywood name to get dinner reservations at exclusive restaurants, spent their money wildly on clothes, cars, and she could only guess what else. And when all that failed, he'd turned to Gayle.

Still, she stayed by his side, defended him to her family. She was a steady wife—supporting his flailing career when the market turned on him, enduring eight in-vitro attempts to give him a biological child when they could have easily adopted. Nothing had been enough.

Her hands were still bleeding as she removed two Percocets from one of the bottles. It was an old prescription in Troy's name—painkillers for one of his sports injuries. She could feel the small shards of glass digging deeper into her flesh as she poured water into a porcelain cup, then swallowed the pills. Dr. Ted would not approve. Mixing pills, looking for any way to stop feeling. It was beneath her. But wasn't it beneath her to stay in this marriage? To watch her son evaporate before her eyes? To let Troy do the things he had done? *What will you do, Gayle?* Dr. Ted had reminded her. *You're forty-one. Divorce will mean a life lived alone. People will pity you.* Her mother had agreed. *You chose this man, now you have to live with it. He'll fight you to the death for everything—the money, the house, Oliver. How will you, of all people, handle that?*

His steps were silent as he approached the bathroom door, and he was upon her without warning.

"I'm sorry," he said, standing in the doorway like a contrite child who'd lost his temper.

Gayle was too startled to speak. She had a keen instinct for such moments, and she was now observing everything about her husband—the color of his face, the sincerity of his voice, muscle tension, hand position. She concluded quickly that it was over. But in other ways, just beginning.

Troy approached her, taking her hands, which had quietly set down the pill bottles.

"Look!" he said, as if surprised. "I told you not to clean up. We have people for that."

He let go of her to find tweezers and ointment, his spirits lifted by the presence of a need he could now tend to.

"Here," he said, taking her hands again. With careful movements, he pulled small pieces of glass from her wounds, smiling at her as he might at a child who'd not listened and come home with a scraped knee.

"Silly girl," he said, and Gayle watched him silently, her eyes never leaving his face—cautiously waiting for the signs of change. It never really left, his rage, and where it had gone now—how deeply it had receded—could not be known for certain.

"There," he said, placing the tweezers on the marble counter. Then he applied the ointment. When the Band-Aids were in place, he cupped her face in his hands and kissed her forehead. It was then that she saw it—the need that had not been placated by tending to her cuts. He sighed then moved his body closer to hers, until she could feel his erection against her thigh. His hands slipped from her face, then down her shoulders to her breasts.

It was a reflex, this paralysis that kept her from moving, from screaming—some kind of preprogrammed response that seemed to take her over in moments like this one. Moments of fear.

Troy reached under her robe and grabbed her thighs, pulling her against his groin. She heard the release of his belt buckle, then the sound of the buckle as it hit the floor. He turned her around, leaned her against the sink. Then he was inside her, moaning in her ear. *I'm so sorry,* he said, pushing himself in deeper as though he might somehow erase his transgressions.

It was over quickly. Troy threw off his clothes and stepped into the shower. The smile on his face was pleasant, as though they'd just made love. And Gayle wondered if this was true—if this was what it was. Other women spoke of those things. Didn't they? Complaining about quickies before kickoff time, surprise fondling at the bathroom sink. Maybe that's all this was—the things women laughed about over glasses of wine. For Gayle, there was a familiarity about the rage, childhood perceptions that bred the quiet acceptance of what was now her adult life. Maybe there was broken glass in every home. Perhaps that explained the silence about such things. It was very likely her own internal defect that provoked the swells that were now moving through her.

It didn't take long for the pills to kick in. She felt a lightness in her head as she gathered her robe from the floor and wrapped it around her. It was over now. She had to get changed, get herself downstairs to check the floor for any glass. Oliver would want to say good night.

TWENTY-TWO

GOLF

MARIE HATED FEW THINGS the way she hated golf. It was a deep and complex relationship—Marie and her hatred of golf—that had grown in lockstep with her husband's infatuation with the game. Like a mutant cancer that seemed to afflict suburbanites in disproportionate numbers, golf had gotten under Anthony Passeti's skin the moment he'd smelled the grass in Hunting Ridge. No longer satisfied with a Saturday morning spent puttering through the mail or lingering over the sports section of *The Times,* Anthony had to be at the range, pounding those stupid, dimpled white balls into the air with a stick. And what began as little more than an hour or two each weekend had quickly evolved into six-hour rounds at the public course in Cliffton.

Six hours, followed by lunch and beers for a cumulative total of eight hours—eight precious hours he could have spent with his girls, or his wife. Eight hours every Saturday from April until October, weather permitting, that could have been put to use helping out around the house, grocery shopping, even reading a novel. Anything else. Then there was the endless talk about the round, the false sense of accomplishment if he shot below 90, or the all-consuming frustration when the golf gods failed to smile upon him. It was such a frivolous game, not merely because it demanded so much time, but because of the way it taunted and provoked its followers—giving them just enough satisfaction to keep them coming back, all the while remaining impossible to master. With its elusive allure, it was the worst kind of tease, and it had wrapped itself around her husband's brain, turning his brilliance into outright idiocy.

Marie had planned on fighting the small battles against suburban atrophy with her girls. The uniformity of wealth, the complete separation of the sexes into outdated gender roles, and—the worst offender—the absence of cultural diversity were not subtle forces, and thereby easily subverted through parental education. *Yes, Suzanne, Mommy likes to work.* Or, *We go to the church in Cliffton because we're Catholic.* And Marie's favorite, *You can't have that because it costs money, and money is something that has to be earned.* For all her complaining about Hunting Ridge, she still preferred these conversations to the endless warnings about the dangers of the city. And then there was the grass, though the black spots were starting to get to her. But what she had not planned on, what now had her head in a vice, was the cunning, insidious, disease that had infected her grown-up husband.

Fortunately for Marie, she was a formidable opponent. Unmoved by the physical beauty of the course, unwilling to measure herself by the sureness of any given shot, Marie had decided to fight the foe from within. The girls were older now, spending more time with their friends on the weekends. There was work, but there would always be work. Now was the time to take it on, to save her husband from pursuing a trivial existence. His mind was a treasure, sharp and critical. He could digest the world's news at warp speed, provide engaging discourse on any number of topics—politics, the economy, theories of the universe. He had been her only competition in law school for summa cum laude. He had been the only man who had ever been able to go to the mat with her on matters of the mind. Even now, half bald with a small pot around his waist, he still could hold her attention with his analysis of a case.

Yet, here he was. The newest member of the Hunting Ridge Country Club—an honor that would cost more than they could afford to spend—standing in a queue at the first tee. Watching her husband clench an invisible club, then drawing back for an air swing, Marie knew she was doing the right thing. She had to infiltrate the enemy camp. Painful as it was, there was no doubt in her mind. It was time to play golf.

It had taken him by surprise, as was the plan. Every weekend he would schedule a game. Every weekend, Marie would bitch about it, laying on the guilt at the time he was spending away from the family.

"Why don't you play with me? You'd really enjoy it," he would say, knowing she would rather shovel manure. Golf was a male conspiracy, Marie was certain. Eighteen long holes, shots that could not be rushed, slow play caused by overcrowded courses. It was nothing more than an elaborate excuse for men to be away from home half the day, then return exhausted, in need of some couch time, time spent doing—what else?—*watching* golf. All of that was about to change.

"Do you need some pointers?" Anthony asked after taking his shot.

"I'll just take a swing."

One after the other, Marie took swings, scattering balls into woods and water. It didn't matter. Her complete ineptitude, her utter disregard of the most basic swing principles was working magic on her husband, infecting his own game, compounding his frustration. After three holes, a ranger rode out in a cart and asked them to keep pace. But Marie would not be rushed. Two holes after that, he came out and politely asked them to move to another hole, which they did.

"Marie, you have to play faster. Just pick up your ball after a few shots," Anthony had pleaded.

"How am I supposed to learn if I do that?"

Three holes later, the twosome of men playing behind them had caught up. As she bent down to place her ball on the tee, Marie saw them approaching. In hushed voices, they talked to her husband, gesticulating forward, then back, then placing their hands on their hips. Anthony nodded up and down sheepishly, then said something that Marie surmised was some sort of apology for his wife's poor playing. When the men were done discussing what to do with her—this creature from Venus—Anthony joined his wife on the ladies' tee.

"Pick up your ball. They're playing through." His voice was serious, his expression a mixture of embarrassment and displeasure.

"Why? Aren't there people behind them?"

"Yes. And we'll have to let them through if we can't keep up."

Marie gave him a wry smile. "Oh my God, it's a travesty!"

But Anthony was not finding the humor.

"Come on, honey . . . it's *golf*."

With his face now turned up to the sky, Anthony shook his head. "I just got it."

"Got what?"

"You have no interest in playing. You just want to ruin it for me."

Marie sighed, tacitly admitting that she'd been found out.

"No, not ruin it for you. But maybe help you see that you're wasting your life trying to get this stupid ball in a hole!" Marie held the golf ball up to his face, meeting his stare. "And don't ever apologize for me again. If those men have something to say *about* me, they can say it *to* me."

On it went as they drove the cart back to the clubhouse.

"You are becoming one of *them*! Neglecting the girls, neglecting the house, neglecting our marriage! And what's with those locker rooms? The men's is a goddamned palace and we hardly have a place to pee."

After a very short while, Anthony stopped refuting each point with a counterpoint—an exercise that he once enjoyed, but now found tiresome. There was simply no point in arguing. His wife was right. He *had* been spending more time away from his family, his responsibilities. The burdens were placed on Marie, who spent every waking hour working or tending to their kids. She had always been that way—able to carry the weight of the world on her shoulders and not even flinch. He couldn't match what she did. He didn't want to. He was thirty-nine years old. He'd learned about all he was going to learn as a lawyer. With the thrill of the hunt long gone, it was now just a matter of churning out the cases. The commuting, the boredom of his work, the insatiable needs of the house and kids. Was it really so hard to believe that he wanted to play a little?

"What, you don't have anything to say?" It was so unlike him.

They drove to the car, and Anthony loaded Marie's clubs in the trunk, leaving his bag in the cart.

"What are you doing?" she asked him, though it was readily apparent as he handed her the keys and climbed back into the cart.

"Don't you get it? This is the only thing in my life that I enjoy."

Marie looked him in the eye, the implications of his words growing inside her, burning.

"The *only* thing you enjoy?"

Anthony sighed, his whole body melting into the white leather seat. As he spoke, he seemed deflated, yet strangely relieved.

"I don't have to think out here—not about clients, or bills, or the girls' every spat with their friends, the house falling part, or the fact that I fail you every day by leaving cereal boxes on the counter or wet towels on the floor." He stopped for a moment, and looked away.

"I just don't want to think anymore."

TWENTY-THREE

THE DIAGNOSIS

As she always did, Yvonne Welsh made herself at home in the Passetis' kitchen. With her daughter's house filled to the brim with little humans, toys, food, and general clutter, she had accepted the invitation years ago to stay next door when she came into town. Though it was no larger in square footage, Marie kept a tight ship in her house and was, from what Yvonne could see, an exceptionally organized individual. From bathroom to bedroom to den, only essentials filled the space. One couch, one matching chair in the TV room, a modest table and china cabinet in the dining area, toys carefully shelved in each of the girls' bedrooms—there was room to breathe here. And what was lacking in the sparse, minimalist décor was more than made up for by the family photographs that were displayed throughout, telling the story of their lives to all who entered.

Standing at the counter, waiting for the coffee to finish brewing, Yvonne listened to the young woman vent.

"And then he just drove off," she continued, throwing her hands in the air to emphasize her dismay at the morning's events. "Can you believe it? I'm in shock—shock!"

Yvonne sighed and shook her head. Though she had known for some time that it was the truest of truisms, the thought came to her yet again. *Youth is wasted on the young.*

Pouring the coffee that was now ready, Yvonne handed a cup to Marie and waited for her to settle down.

"You girls," she said, a note of pity in her voice. "What is it with you girls and this idea of equality between the sexes? You make things so complicated."

Marie bit her tongue as they moved the conversation to the kitchen table.

"Things are different today, Yvonne. Women are more than domestic servants. *Thank God.*"

Yvonne smiled. "Are they? Isn't that what you've been complaining about for the past twenty minutes?"

She had a point, Marie supposed. Since returning from that godforsaken country club, Marie had done nothing but go on about the inequities in the house—how Anthony conveniently turned a blind eye to chores waiting to be done, or gave sub-par performances any time he was left to watch the girls—a transparent ploy to avoid the assignment in the future. Then there was the way he'd ask for a beer and expect its quick delivery anytime he dusted off the weed whacker. Not to mention that devil sport of his.

"It's not right. If I can do his job, why can't he do mine?"

"Because he's a *man,*" Yvonne said emphatically.

Marie thought about that, and wondered how many times she'd heard it before. *My husband just can't deal with the children. It's not in him. My husband is just no good at the shopping. He always comes home with bags full of junk food.* Wasn't it convenient that these claims of incompetence were limited to household duties? Doing laundry was not rocket science. And no one knew how to settle a baby—until they'd had to figure it out or lose their mind.

"Oh, Marie . . . It's so much easier if you just accept that men are different from women." It was self-evident to Yvonne, who'd enjoyed more than her rightful share of the creatures and, by a fair accounting, believed to know them well.

Marie shook her head, biting down on what was left of her thumbnail.

"You'll never change that. And besides, wouldn't that be awfully boring?"

For a moment Marie pictured the version of Anthony her demands implied. Coming home from work, hanging up his keys on the right hook. Helping with dinner, engaging in the conversation as they ate. Clearing dishes, wiping the table. His small but growing gut hanging out of his pants as he got down on all fours with a wet sponge to clear the food from the floor. Then sorting whites from colors, pre-spotting stains on Olivia's sun dresses. The image was almost absurd, and it made her wonder. Is that what would bring it back—the desire to climb into bed at night and wrap her arms around him when he was still awake? The feeling had disappeared so slowly, with such subtlety over the years, it was impossible to impart a cause with any degree of certainty.

"Enough about *golf,*" Marie said, shaking off the confusion. "How is Love? Any progress with a diagnosis?"

Yvonne held her palms to the sky with no attempt to hide her irritation at Bill and the medical community as a whole. She had given it a week, watching her daughter struggle in pain, watching the kids worry—Henry in particular. Baby Will wasn't taking his bottle, and Love made herself worse every time she nursed him. She had deferred to Bill because he was the husband, the doctor, and because in her older age she had accepted that traditional medicine wasn't completely irrational. Still, in her heart of hearts she believed in a more holistic, spiritual approach to healing, and her conviction that they were on the wrong path was growing by the minute.

"They drew some blood and tested for Lyme disease. Now they want to rule out lupus, of all things. There's no rhyme or reason to any of it, if you ask me. Not that anyone would—God forbid."

Marie patted Yvonne on the shoulder and got up from the table, coffee in hand. "Come on, let's look it up."

They went to the small study off the living room where Marie kept her laptop. Looking things up on the Internet was Marie's cure for everything perplexing, though it rarely made her feel any better. Too much information could be a very bad thing. After seven years of investigating the various ailments of her daughters, she was now convinced that the word *tumor* could be found on every Web site ever created.

"What should we call it?"

Yvonne shrugged, taking a seat on the small sofa behind Marie's desk. "Muscle pain?"

Marie repeated the words as she typed. "How about *muscle pain symptom disease.*"

She scrolled the first page of search results then chose one at random. "There—sixty-two diseases with muscle pain symptoms."

"Sixty-two?!" Yvonne was beginning to feel overwhelmed.

Marie scrolled down to the "T" section to amuse herself. Sure enough, *tumor* was disease number 47.

"Let's start from the top. Acute bacterial prostatitis, African sleeping sickness, anthrax . . ."

"Stop!" Yvonne couldn't listen to sixty-two ways her daughter might be ill. "Just read the ones that might be possible. I doubt she has African sleeping sickness."

"OK." Marie read the list to herself. "Here's one—chronic fatigue syndrome."

"Can they test for it?"

Marie clicked on the link, then shook her head. "Not really. They just rule out everything else."

"Great—what others?"

Going back to the list, Marie continued to read. Then she stopped suddenly and sighed.

"What?" Yvonne asked, visibly alarmed.

Marie paused, then read the illness. "Depression."

"Depression? Is my daughter depressed?"

Marie swiveled her chair to face Yvonne. She could see on the woman's face that they both knew the answer.

"What's been going on?" Yvonne asked, fishing for information.

Marie sensed something in her tone—a lack of genuine ignorance.

Playing hide and seek was her job, after all. But after years of living in a town of make-believe, Yvonne was equally skilled at playing it close to the vest.

"I thought you might know. It's been going on for a few weeks."

"And you didn't ask her what was wrong?"

"Of course. She said she was tired. Will gives her a hard time."

"Huh."

The two women were quiet for a moment, calculating. Then Yvonne got up, left the room, and returned moments later with a folded piece of paper.

"Here," she said, handing it to Marie.

Marie unfolded the paper, which was worn from handling. "A letter?"

Yvonne nodded. "From Love's father."

Marie gave the woman a look of surprise, then read it to herself.

"Christ!" she said.

"I know."

The letter, curt and brief, was an announcement—a warning, really—from Alexander Rice that a new work was about to be released. It was an autobiography, a self-proclaimed "coming clean" about his life. And in his narcissistic effort to be understood—maybe even embraced—by the world at large, Yvonne knew he hadn't given one moment's pause to consider the impact it would have on his daughter. What he would write, and how much he would betray, was the only question that remained in her mind—and possibly in Love's as well.

"No wonder she's a mess. They haven't spoken for years, and now his face will be everywhere."

That's just for starters, Yvonne thought. No one in this little Hunting Ridge life knew the truth about Love's past, the night that stole her destiny out from under her. No one had to know. But locking it away had only produced a fierce appetite for everything destructive in Love. Drugs, alcohol, men. The desire to be dead. Yvonne wondered how much Love allowed herself to remember now—or if she had found a safe place to keep it all, some kind of internal steel vault.

"She hasn't said anything about it?"

Marie shook her head. "No—and there's been nothing about it in the papers."

Yvonne sighed, and for the first time since Marie had known her, she looked utterly defeated. "Do you think he sent her a letter, too?"

Marie handed Rice's letter back to Yvonne. "I have no idea. She hasn't mentioned it if he did."

"No, she wouldn't. She wouldn't tell a living soul." Yvonne looked at the folded paper in her hand. "He sent her one. That *has* to be what's wrong with her."

"It's just a book. Maybe it won't even do well."

Marie had no idea how little that would matter.

Yvonne pounded her fist into her leg, then got up to pace. "I could kill that man."

She'd come to town thinking her daughter had a physical injury, one that would heal. She would help with the children, then be on her way. Now, she was sure of only one thing.

"We need a copy," she announced.

"I thought it wasn't coming out until July?"

"No," Yvonne said. "We need it *now*—before it comes out. There must be some galleys floating around."

Marie's eyes lit up. She wasn't convinced that Love's illness was some psychosomatic side effect of depression. Love was tough, and practical. If anything, the anxiety over her father's book had probably driven her to overextend herself. Love was telling everyone it was just a pulled muscle, and Marie wanted to believe her. But if getting a copy of her father's book would put her mind at ease, maybe even give her the rest she so desperately needed, then Marie was determined to help.

She picked up the phone.

"I know exactly who to call."

TWENTY-FOUR

ROOM 221

IN ROOM 221, JANIE Kirk felt the hands dig deeper into her flesh, pulling her hips down, then up again. She opened her eyes and took in the room, the cheap, tasteless décor, the bright light of midday. It was a Rosewood Inn, a generic hotel in downtown Cliffton—something between sleazy roadside and luxurious Four Seasons—and it fit the mood to a tee. They were in a hurry. She had to pick up the kids, he had to get back to the office. There was no time to talk, no time for a sultry dance undressing each other. They were here for one reason. To fuck. Straddled over him, watching him smile with hedonistic delight at her abandon, she said the word over and over—first in her head, then fully out loud. *Fuck . . . fuck . . . fuck . . . FUCK!!!!*

They had waited three days, three tedious days, before finding the time to meet. Their last encounter and the promise of the next one had left a residue—an unsettled nervousness in her gut that seemed to be consuming her from the inside. It was familiar. She'd felt it the first time she'd wanted a man—the "butterflies" that moved inside her every time she was near him.

Then again when she fell in crazy, insane love at first sight at the age of nineteen. It had kept her from eating, sleeping—made her want to escape from her own body. In one month, she'd lost fifteen pounds and taken up smoking. At night, she would drink it away, partying with her girlfriends, scouring the campus bars in search of him.

It was here again, that lust heroin that thrust its victim into a state of intolerable withdrawal. Everywhere she went, she saw men. And they saw her. The last one sent her over the edge—the young guy at the gas station in Cliffton where she'd gone to buy cigarettes. Standing there, searching for the brand she had given up nearly twenty years before, she found herself watching him—the strong muscles bulging from beneath his shirt, his fit stomach and scruffy, masculine face. Beyond her control, her thoughts raced to a vision that made her close her eyes for fear that he would see it, that it might come to be—his powerful hands, stained with oil right down to the fingernails, digging into her back as she lay beneath him, right there on the counter where he was placing the cigarettes and punching numbers into the register. She imagined her clean, manicured fingers unbuckling his jeans, then reaching inside.

Every man not her husband seemed to provoke the untenable longing that had grown roots within her. She'd driven fast, as if somehow she might outrun it, smoking, singing at the top of her lungs.

What had she awakened? For days now, she'd felt alone at her core, isolated from the friends she couldn't possibly tell. Her entire world had become some faraway place, though she was still drifting within it in like a phantom. Wanting to feel something again—something for another person—had driven her to act, only now she felt too much to dwell in this benign existence of small talk and shopping and gourmet salads. She missed the mild pleasure of those things. She missed the small moments of joy with her children that were now overshadowed by desire. And so, she had secured the room, turned up the heat, and turned down the bed.

Then came the knock at the door. Without a word, he'd entered and thrown a gym bag on the floor.

"Are you ready to play?" he'd said, looking first at her, then to the bag.

A shock had run through her, the boring housewife who spent most of her life in a station wagon, and the rest in the kitchen.

"Bring it on." She'd said it like an actress in a low budget porn film, and the dirty tone of her own words nearly brought on the climax. He'd waited to touch her, instead removing his suit pants and boxer shorts. Following his lead, she'd done the same, tossing her black stretch pants on top of his shoes.

"Get on the bed." The last words were spoken. Still partially clothed in her spandex shirt and gym socks, Janie had watched him remove the toys from the bag—the same toys that were now sprawled out around her as she lay there, totally spent from the activities that had just taken place.

"Fuck," she said once more, reaching for a cigarette on the side table.

Staring at the ceiling as she lit up, he folded his arms behind his head. "I'll bet you don't get *that* at home."

No, she thought. *Not even close*. Their skin had hardly touched. The kissing was deep and purposeful, and entirely lacking in meaning. He hadn't placed as much as a finger on her breasts—his focus being elsewhere, his hands too busy operating the heavy machinery. There was nothing like this in Daniel's playbook, and she imagined it was exactly this sort of an aberration that was needed after two decades of fucking the same way.

She took a long drag off the cigarette, then watched with childish glee as the smoke billowed past the NO SMOKING sign over the bed. "I could never do this with Daniel."

He looked at her now, his face genuinely intrigued. "Daniel's a stiff, isn't he? I always knew that about him."

But Janie shook her head. "Not really. He reads porn—and not the ones with the articles."

"Janie, *all men* read porn."

Laughing at her as though she were a naïve child, he pulled the cigarette from between her fingers and stole a drag. "Look, I hope this won't offend you, but the truth of the matter is, men like tits, pussies, and fucking. End of story."

Janie gave a sarcastic laugh.

"Lovely."

"Are you offended?"

"No."

"I just thought, you know, since we don't have to do the whole married couple dance, I could say what I want."

"It's OK."

Janie was smoking, and thinking, and her silence had him unnerved.

"I could be wrong. Maybe it's not *all* men. Maybe Daniel is more like that man we all pretend to be when we look for a wife."

"If you have to pretend, then why do you even bother with marriage?"

"Huh," was his answer. But he was only stumped for a moment. "I guess . . . children. Family. The same reasons women look for husbands."

"I think most women look for love, even when they're looking to get married."

"Shit," he said as he shrugged. "Sorry."

Now Janie was laughing hard and out loud. She liked that he wasn't bullshitting her. It was refreshing. And the simplicity of his answers had brought a wave of clarity.

"Now I've done it, haven't I? I've made you too mad to fuck me again," he said, rolling closer to her. She felt him reach over her, then heard a soft electronic buzzing.

She dropped the cigarette in a glass of water. She felt his mouth on the nape of her neck and moaned softly. They had only a few minutes more to put life on hold, and she would savor each second. There was nothing inside her now but her own desire, and it was not the same desire that had drawn her to Daniel so many years ago. The initial attraction, then the slow peeling back of layers until they were completely exposed and vulnerable to one another. Each night in Daniel's bed had been a step closer to the very thing that was now missing in their marriage—a relationship. There was no chance of that here.

She let herself slip again into the physical pleasure, the place that made this man irrelevant in every other way, but at the same time completely essential. Somehow, in the absence of expectation, and in the face of total authenticity, she was free to explore. Now, *she* was the one taking. How odd it was, she thought, that she could never do these things with Daniel. And it was not because there was something deeper between them than sex. It was because there was supposed to be, and because there once had been.

TWENTY-FIVE

THE DEPOSITION

THE DEPOSITION OF CARSON Farrell had been scheduled for noon, but after the usual delays—introductions, chitchat, a lost stenographer who could not grasp the concept that a law office sat above a diner—they were not ready to begin until after one. Sitting between her client and Randy Matthews, Marie folded her arms on the table and sighed with impatience.

"OK. Are we ready?"

The stenographer positioned her hands over the manual recording device, then nodded. "All set."

"Great," Marie said, then turned to the lawyer representing Vickie Farrell. Tim Connely was a smug son-of-a-bitch, and Marie would know, having sat across from him more times than she cared to remember. He was patronizing, condescending, and usually full of shit. He had tried to bluff her on so many cases that she had come to see his crooked little smile as nothing more than a strange birth defect. Still, he was not completely stupid, and this case was far from ordinary.

"Counselor—take it away."

Her tone was casual, relaxed, though inside, the nerves were on edge. Marie had conducted and defended close to a hundred depositions, and in most cases, there was no need for worry. There was always ground to cover, things to get on the record, landmines to dodge when a client opened his mouth. Ferreting out a smoking gun was the highly unlikely exception to what was typically a dull exercise in fact-finding. The deposition was the last phase of discovery, preceded by document production and interrogatories—long lists of questions that each party had to answer for the other. By the time the deposition rolled around, there was little left to know. The facts were on the table—who had the affair, who felt unloved, who didn't get enough sex, who was never home, etc., etc. Though she always hoped for more, the most Marie expected from interviewing the opponent were deeper explanations of the things she'd already learned.

That the Farrell case involved a dead child—that her client was hiding things that went on in the family even before that death—made this case entirely different. Each time Tim Connely drew a breath, Marie held her own as she waited for the next question to leave his mouth. It started out with the mundane—a history of the roles played in the family by the Farrell parents.

"How much of the child rearing did you participate in?"

With his eyes focused on his hands folded neatly on the table in front of him, Carson Farrell answered with a customary lack of emotion. "I was gone early—before they were up. But I was home by six thirty most nights. And I was home most weekends."

Connely, with his weak, strangely pale green slits of eyes, leaned forward, a self-aggrandizing look on his face. "You say you were home, but isn't it true, Mr. Farrell, that the care of the children was left almost entirely to your wife?"

Rolling her eyes, Marie lifted her hand before Farrell could respond. "I think he's already answered the question. He was there most evenings and weekends. We've also provided you with a year's worth of his work calendar showing the days he was out of town on business."

"We're not at trial, Marie."

Marie rolled her eyes again, and gave her colleague a look of disdain.

She really couldn't object to the question. It was just that the question annoyed her. No one was disputing that Mrs. Farrell was the primary caregiver. Still, the time when fathers were denied joint custody for that reason had ended years before.

Nodding to Farrell, Marie let him answer. "I was there whenever I could be, which was quite a bit. When I was home, I spent time with my kids. I have no hobbies. No sports. I worked out now and then, if the desk was quiet. I can't control how you choose to characterize my involvement."

Marie smiled and nudged Randy under the table. Farrell had been prepped well. The answer was excellent. But Randy's attention was elsewhere, his eyes glued to the well-dressed, and eerily quiet woman across the table. Marie had hardly noticed Vickie Farrell. She had said nothing upon arriving with Connely. Still, it was more than the lack of conversation that made her near invisible. From the vacant expression on her face to the dullness of her skin, she appeared lifeless, a human doll. And though nothing was out of place, her sandy hair perfectly combed, makeup applied in the right places, everything about her seemed wrong.

The questions went on and on, their content quickly switching to the Farrell financial situation. *What is the current value of the 401(k)? What is the stock portfolio worth? What have you included in your estimate of travel and recreational expenses?*

Farrell checked his notes, which were set out before him on a legal pad. The questions had been anticipated, their answers scrutinized to match what would be found in the documents and interrogatories. They were nearing the end, as far as Marie could detect, and she was about to be relieved when Connely's squalid face adopted a somber expression.

"Now, Mr. Farrell, I realize this is a painful area. But I'd like to shift our focus to your daughter's accident."

There was no doubt it would come up, and to his credit, Connely had been smart to raise it at the end. Farrell would be tired, his anxiety piqued by the waiting, and it would give a solid punch line for anyone reading the transcript of the day's testimony. Still, it was not this inquiry that concerned Marie. Farrell could handle it—she'd seen him handle it. Her concern was what might come next—the domestic disturbance preceding the accident that had left their child dead.

Farrell cleared his throat. "May we go off the record for a moment?"

The stenographer lifted her hands, trying not to seem interested.

"Carson?" Marie said, looking at her client with surprise. Taking her lead, Farrell followed her into the office and waited for her to close the door.

"What's this about?"

"I don't want my wife in the room for this. There's no point," Farrell said.

Marie shrugged and shook her head. "She has a right to be there, to direct her lawyer to relevant follow-up questioning."

"I won't answer if she stays."

"Can you tell me why?"

Farrell looked at his lawyer with dismay. "Isn't it obvious? She shouldn't have to hear one more time what I did to our child."

Marie studied his stone-cold face as she considered what he was asking. *Who the hell are you, Carson Farrell?*

"I can ask. That's all I can do. It's up to Connely."

Marie cracked the door to the conference room and poked her head inside.

"Tim, may I see you a minute?"

With a loud huff, Connely pushed back his chair and walked around the table to the office door. He did his best to look annoyed, but Marie knew he was enjoying the drama.

"What is this?" he asked, feigning incredulity.

"My client is worried that his wife will be upset by this line of questioning. He would like her to leave the room."

"Huh! I'll bet he would. He killed their child, of course she'll be upset. But it's the heart and soul of her case."

Marie took a moment for his indignation to settle, and to swallow her urge to slap Connely clear across the face. "You can still ask the questions. We all know what happened that day. It's laid out in the interrogatories. You can always step inside and consult with her if you need clarification," she said, in the same tone she used with her girls. "Let's try to maintain some integrity here."

Connely put his hand to his chin, pretending to mull it over. But Marie knew she had him. As much as he wanted to see his client break down, make emotional outbursts that would be captured on the transcript, it couldn't be done without making himself appear an insensitive ass. After a moment, he agreed, and the two lawyers returned to the deposition. Connely kneeled at Mrs. Farrell's side and whispered something to her. Then, without hesitation—or any change of expression—his client got up from the chair, straightened her skirt, and allowed Connely to lead her into Marie's office.

"Randy, do you mind?" Marie directed her intern to babysit Mrs. Farrell. When both were gone, the door firmly closed, Connely went after Carson.

"The accident occurred on June twelfth?"

"Yes."

"That was a weekday. What were you doing at home?"

"I was working from home that day."

"Then why were you alone with the baby?"

"The others had school. They missed the bus, so my wife went to drop them off and left me with Simone."

"And you brought her upstairs with you?"

"Yes."

"And you did not secure the baby gate?"

"No."

"What were you doing when the baby fell?"

"I was on a call to the office, checking in. I put her down on the office floor, and she crawled away."

"Was the office floor a safe place for her?"

"I thought so at the time."

"You thought so. Were there electrical outlets in the room?"

"Yes."

"A desk with office supplies in the drawers—stapler, paper clips—things like that."

"Yes, but she had a bottle. I thought she would sit and drink her milk."

Connely looked at Farrell with disgust. "So she was in danger even before she crawled out of that room?"

"Nothing happened to her in the office."

"But it could have. Let's move on. How long was the call?"

"I'm not sure. A few minutes. It happened fast."

"You heard her fall?"

"Yes."

"And then what did you do?"

"I ran to the stairs. I saw her lying there and ran to her. I felt for a pulse. Then I went to the kitchen to call for help."

"But she was already dead?"

"Yes."

Connely paused for dramatic effect. "Mr. Farrell, your surviving children are still quite young. Do you really believe they are safe in your care?"

Throughout the interrogation, Farrell's composure was steadfast. Marie had expected nothing else. Still, as he answered this last question, there was little doubt he was holding something at bay.

"They were always safe with me. I made a mistake. One mistake that cost me dearly. It won't happen again."

"How can you be sure?"

"Because I have already lost more than I can bear to lose. That's how."

Marie felt herself catch her breath. Even Connely seemed to feel a chill go through him. There was something about Farrell's statement—his bare description of his own despair, spoken so softly, so evenly. As if the despair had swallowed him whole, leaving nothing but a bystander to serve as witness.

The deposition went on—issues of logistics, how much time Farrell wanted with the children, how the transitions would be made. It was not uncommon for fathers to see their children several times a week, and overnights every other weekend. Keeping both parents in the picture was strongly favored by the courts, and Connely would have one hell of a time convincing a judge otherwise. Which was precisely why Marie held her breath now, waiting for Connely to bring up the domestic dispute.

But it never happened. Connely finished his questions and then Marie tidied up with a brief cross-examination.

"We'll see you next week," Marie said when she was finished. Then she escorted Mrs. Farrell and Connely to the door.

As he packed up his notes, Carson Farrell spoke without looking at his lawyer. "What's next?"

"Your wife's deposition."

Farrell did not let her finish. "No," he said, this time looking Marie dead in the eye. "I don't want to depose her."

Marie was beyond confused. "We have to. If you want your kids, we have to be thorough."

"We have the other discovery. What more do we need?"

"There's a lot to ask her. For starters, Connely attacked your ability to be a parent. We can discredit the argument by asking your wife if she ever put a child down in a room with outlets, or forgot to fasten a seat belt. We can show that all parents make mistakes. Then there are the financials . . ." Marie tried to plead her case.

"No. No deposition." Farrell said it as he closed his briefcase. Then he brushed past Marie to the door and left before she could think of a way to stop him.

Alone now, her eyes still fixed to the spot where Farrell had been standing a second before, Marie scrambled to make sense of what had just happened. First, Farrell insisted his wife leave the room. Now, he wanted to keep Marie from deposing her. And Connely hadn't mentioned a word about the police call on April 7, just two months before Simone Farrell's death. Knowing the man the way she did, that could only mean that he didn't know about it. That Mrs. Farrell had not told him. None of this was adding up.

"What's going on?" Randy was beside her now, watching her carefully.

For the first time, Marie had no answer for him, or for herself. "I have no idea," she said. "But I don't like it. I've never had a deposition like that. *Never*."

"It's the baby, isn't it? I mean, that's what ended the marriage. That's why Mrs. Farrell doesn't want him to see the kids."

Marie rolled her head, then reached back to massage her neck. The tension had been thick, and she was now feeling its impact. "Even so, why would Farrell be so afraid to provoke her?"

Randy shrugged and offered an answer. "Guilt?"

"Maybe. Or maybe he's afraid he'll push her too far. Her own guilt from leaving him might be keeping her from exposing his temper. If she gets riled up, she might be willing to go there."

Marie began her ritual pacing. There it was again, the nagging urge to get to the bottom of things when she should just mind her own business and do her job.

"Can you do something for me?"

"Sure."

"See if you can get the names and numbers of the Farrells' neighbors in Wellesley. I may need to get some character references for Carson."

"And find out what happened on April seventh?"

Marie looked at him and smiled. "That, too."

TWENTY-SIX

MEDDLING

YVONNE HEARD THE GARAGE door open. It was nearly three thirty.

"Mommy's home," she said out loud, though mostly for her own ears. Since earlier that afternoon, her daughter had been at the hospital with Bill, running tests. Then they were picking up Henry. It had been a mere two hours or so, barely enough time to get into trouble—especially with the two young ones under foot. Still, somehow, Yvonne had managed.

With lightning speed, Jessica scurried off her grandmother's lap, throwing a book to the floor as she ran to the kitchen to wait. Love had been bedridden for nearly two weeks, and while the novelty had at first been exciting, a calming relief had filled the house that morning when Love walked down the stairs. Now she had gone to pick up Henry, a task that marked the beginning of the nighttime routine. Pick up Henry, play, eat, bathe, brush teeth. Maybe watch television. Then bed. The return to their mundane existence seemed to envelope Jessica's little body with contentment, culminating in a gleeful smile as she stood and waited.

Picking Baby Will up from his spot on the floor, Yvonne felt quite the opposite.

"Come on, Will. Time to face the music."

She had always been respectful of her daughter's space. No diary had ever been read, no dresser drawer pillaged. With the arrogance of a woman naïve enough to believe she knew the world, Yvonne had always trusted her instincts about her daughter, though the signs had been right in front of her. And her blindness had nearly cost Love her life.

She would not repeat those mistakes now, even if it meant overstepping, butting in without being asked. Everything she'd seen since entering this house had convinced her that Love's survival depended on it.

With the baby on her hip, sucking his beloved thumb with fervor, she followed Jessica to the kitchen. A moment later, the door to the garage swung open and Henry bounded in, his overstuffed backpack hovering over him like a giant tortoise shell.

"Henry!" Jessica said, and she leaped at him for a warm, sisterly hug that was most clearly contrived to earn her points with the adult audience.

Henry pushed her aside. "Get off," he said, then continued his march to the playroom. Jessica scowled at her brother for a brief moment, then lit up again at the sight of her mother.

"Mommy!"

When Love passed through the door, Bill was holding her by the arm. Everything about her, from the twisted expression on her face that was trying to form a smile, to the careful movements that were inching her forward—all of it screamed pain. Yvonne shook her head. She had known it this morning when stating her objections to the day's plan. It had been too soon to venture out of bed.

Love did her best to hug Jessica. "Hi, sweets. How was your time with Grandma?"

"Good. 'Bye." Satisfied for the moment, Jessica followed Henry into the playroom where they could watch for the bus. Olivia and Suzanne would be home soon, and they were spending the afternoon while their mom was working.

Bracing herself on the edge of the counter, Love shuffled across the kitchen floor to answer the baby's call. With outstretched arms and a loud wail, Will would not be silenced until he was in his mother's embrace.

"Here I am, baby." Love leaned against the counter as she held her son, the pain ripping through her right side with every move.

Yvonne reached out, taking back the squirming child. "That's enough, now. Get back to bed."

Bill reached out and took his son. "I've got him. You help her upstairs." He was more than happy to be out of Yvonne's way and the disapproval that emanated from her presence. *Yes,* it had been difficult for Love. But the tests were necessary if they were ever going to figure out why the pain was holding on as long as it was.

He kissed his wife on the cheek, stroked her hair gently. Then he left her alone with her mother.

Yvonne took Love's arm and helped her pull away from the counter where she'd been leaning.

"I shouldn't have gone out," Love said.

"I know."

"I know you know. That's why I said it first."

One step at a time, they made their way upstairs. Yvonne helped Love change into a T-shirt and sweats, turned on the heating pad, and eased her back into the bed. In a matter of seconds, Love felt the muscles give in to the soft mattress, the soothing heat. Then came the sense of defeat that had been growing with the pain for the past hour.

Yvonne sat on the edge of the mattress and took her daughter's hand.

"He's not saying anything, but I know . . ."

"What? What do you know?"

"Bill is worried. What if there is something really wrong . . . ?"

"No! Don't think like that."

But Love couldn't help it. She'd spent the day being prodded and tested and there were still no answers.

"I can't take this much longer," Love said as she started to cry.

Yvonne squeezed her hand. She knew what this was about. Some of it was worry—how could it not be? But the rest was something else. No matter how difficult Love's juggling act had become, it had kept her moving fast enough to outrun herself. Now that her world had screeched to a slow crawl, it was all at her doorstep. Yvonne held the word in her head. *Depression*. Bill could run tests, prescribe antibiotics and painkillers. None of that was helping. Now, it was Yvonne's turn.

She took a deep breath. "Don't be angry,"

"Why would I be angry?" Love asked dismissively. What could her mother have possibly done wrong in the scope of a few hours?

Yvonne cleared her throat and looked away. Then, after a long sigh, she turned her eyes back to her daughter. From the pocket of her silk housecoat she pulled the letter from Alexander Rice. The one addressed to his daughter.

Love could barely breathe, let alone speak. She took the letter, fingering the open flap of the envelope.

"Yes. I've read it," Yvonne confessed.

Dear Love. The words had jumped off the page, striking at her heart with devastating precision. The words, the shape of the sentences. And she would never forget the handwriting of her former lover. It was as distinctive as a photograph, a captured image of the past. She'd read it quickly, terrified by her own inventions of what it might say. What it might do. How could this man still yield so much power over them?

"How did you even know to look for this?" Love demanded.

Yvonne said nothing as she pulled her own letter from her pocket and held it in the air for Love to see. It was the same stationery with the chicken-scratch writing.

"Unbelievable." Love's tone was all sarcasm. She squeezed her hand into a fist, crumbling up her father's letter. She'd read it enough times and knew its contents by heart.

Dear Love,

What can one say at a time like this? It's been many years, too many years. I hope I'm not being presumptuous in assuming that you are aware of my autobiography. It is my intention for this to reach you before its release. I have learned many things on this road of self-exploration. There are many things I wish to say to you. I have enclosed my numbers and I hope you will call so we can arrange a meeting.

Your father,
Alexander Rice

"How did you find this?"

"It wasn't easy. I've been searching for days," Yvonne confessed.

Love looked at her mother with unrestrained contempt. "Find anything else while you were at it?"

But her mother ignored her. This wasn't about the invasion of privacy.

"I think you should call him."

"*Do* you? He's a complete ass, Mother. After nearly twenty-six years, all he can manage is seven sentences? And every one is about him. What can *I* say? *I've* learned so many things. Not once does he mention my marriage, my three kids—his grandchildren!"

Yvonne sighed, though she'd been expecting the resistance. She wanted to give her daughter what she wanted—a comrade in arms against the man who had wronged them both. But that wasn't what Love needed.

"I know. He *is* an ass. A self-consumed ass. No one knows that better than I. But you need to call him."

"Did it occur to you, after you pillaged through my house and read my mail, that this might be part of his plan? Reconciling with his estranged daughter, the child freak show turned fuck-up that he had to cut loose? Wouldn't that make just the perfect ending for his story when he goes on Oprah?"

Love covered her face with her hands. The humiliation was unbearable now, even with her mother, who had never left her side—not through any of it.

"Please leave me alone," she said.

Yvonne complied, getting up from the bed and walking toward the door. Then she turned to look at her daughter one more time. Love's eyes were red, her face so tortured. Yvonne wanted to go to her, take her in her arms and tell her to forget the whole thing. Forget Alexander Rice, just keep on any way she could. But that was the problem. There was no other way for Love, and Yvonne now believed that the pain was clear evidence.

"There's no shame in what happened to you," she said as she reached the door.

Looking up at her mother with disbelief, Love stopped crying.

"There's nothing but shame."

TWENTY-SEVEN

THE SLOW BURN

GAYLE COULD SENSE THE slow burn as she entered the room. Invisible to the eye, it was nothing more than a charge in the air, something an animal might sense, like the distant smell of a predator, or the distinctive crackle of brush underfoot. It was a sixth sense for her, hardwired from her childhood, and she could no sooner turn it off than stop breathing.

Oliver was standing near his father in the playroom, and the sight of her child so close to the fire sent a wave of panic through Gayle. Were she a different person, she might casually waft in, making some excuse to pull her son away—some reason that could not be disputed. A doctor's appointment. A swim lesson. Somewhere, someone might be waiting for them, and this could be enough to diffuse the situation. She would take his hand, smile at her husband. *See you later, darling,* she might say. And he would be contained long enough to make an exit.

But she was not that person. Nor was she someone who would stand and fight. For as long as she had memory, she'd been quite the opposite—the little girl standing perfectly still, as though the slightest movement would set the fire fully ablaze, consuming everything around it—as though her silence, her stillness, might reach out and freeze the rage.

Oliver was scared. She could see it in his eyes.

"He's not doing soccer anymore? Is that true?" Troy asked when he noticed his wife in the room.

But Gayle couldn't speak. Her mouth was dry, her will long since taken from her.

"Answer me, goddamnit! Is he taking soccer or not!"

Finally, she managed a word. "No."

"No," Troy repeated, his face flushed with anger. "So our little prince is not going to learn any sports, is that right? I come home from work to take him to practice and the little shit tells me he doesn't go anymore." Troy paused, his focus now on his son. "*I don't go anymore, Daddy,*" he said in a mocking tone.

Gayle looked at Oliver, trying to draw his attention away from the daggers that were being cast. But his face was frozen, his body as still as hers, and she could see in that instant the legacy she was passing down.

"We've been practicing here. In the yard. He'll be ready in the fall for a team." Pushing through the fear, she made excuses. But they were not enough.

Troy bent down on one knee to face his son. With a sharp thrust, he gave the boy a push that made him step back. "You know what happens to you if you're a momma's boy?"

Oliver regained his footing. He shook his head and fought not to cry.

Troy pushed him again. "You get pushed around." He pushed him again, and again Oliver stumbled back.

Gayle could see it before her now, how fear burns itself into the growing mind of a child. How it is then held there, disconnected from its original source, searching for a new home again and again throughout the child's life. How it becomes part of the being, indistinguishable from any other part, and is understood as the truth. As reality. And all of life becomes viewed through its dark prism.

That was what Gayle saw on her son's face—the brand of betrayal, of fear—and it was too much to bear. She ran from the doorway to where they stood. She grabbed Oliver and lifted him in her arms. "It's OK. Daddy's just teasing," she said, knowing the lie could do little to undermine the bare facts before them.

The feel of his mother around him broke the last wall of resistance, and Oliver started to cry. "It's OK," Gayle said again, now walking out of the room with her son.

She called for Celia, and handed him to her, telling them to go upstairs. She knew this was far from over. Her rescue had cast a light on Troy's behavior and he had reined himself in. In some hidden place, he loved his son. None of this was intentional. Still, the guilt of making the boy cry was like gasoline.

Gayle was in the kitchen when he reappeared. He was shaking his head, standing closer to her than ever before, and the change rendered Gayle unnerved.

"You see? He's a little sissy. One goddamn sport. Fucking soccer! And now that's gone? Are you kidding me?" His voice grew louder as he became more certain in his position. Being convinced of his righteousness was the first sign that an escalation was imminent.

"You undo everything, don't you? You think the Haywood money will keep your son from turning into a little sissy? You're damn wrong!"

Gayle was silent again. With Oliver safe, she would let him yell, watch him storm around the room, threatening, but never achieving, a direct strike against her. He might punch a wall, throw something in her direction, and she braced herself for the sound of things breaking.

But he stopped yelling. Instead, he looked at her with something close to hatred. Then he reached out and grabbed her by the arms.

There was a loud bang, the sound of the back door closing hard. Troy let go of his wife and stepped away just before Paul entered the room.

"Good evening," he said, greeting them cautiously, then walking to the hook behind the pantry door where he kept his apron. He was out of breath and his shirt was misbuttoned, though tucked in—and Gayle knew this was the evidence of a hurried rescue.

"Dinner at the usual time?" he asked, looking at Gayle. But it was Troy who glared back, and Paul turned to face him, making his position clear. He was not leaving this room.

They stood there, suspended by an odd tension that held them in place, until Troy broke the silence. "Yes. Fine," he said in a demeaning tone. Then he turned to leave.

For another moment, Paul went about his work, pulling things from the refrigerator, setting pots on the stove. His pace was quick, his hands shaky. Then, suddenly, he stopped.

"Oliver?" he asked.

"He's up with Celia."

Paul nodded. "Good," he said, visibly relieved, and Gayle wondered what he must be thinking. She had not protected her son. The thought was humiliating.

He spoke again, looking at Gayle with great concern. "And you?"

Gayle started to smile nervously. "I'm fine," she said.

"Are you sure?" His face was solemn, his eyes entirely absent of judgment, and she felt ashamed at having brought attention upon herself. There was much greater suffering in the world than her own. And though he seemed sincere offering his empathy, she felt unworthy to receive it.

"Thank you," was all she could say before leaving.

TWENTY-EIGHT

THE GIFT

WAITING ANXIOUSLY ON LOVE'S front porch, Marie watched the Mercedes SUV turn the corner. Slowly, cautiously, it made its way down the street.

"Christ—will you hurry up!" she muttered out loud.

Even in a moment like this one—a moment that screamed out for urgency—Gayle was going the speed limit.

"Sorry I'm late," Gayle said after parking the car. She had Oliver at her side, and he was unusually sullen.

"Hey, bud. How's it going?" Marie patted the boy gently on the back.

Oliver shrugged. "OK."

"The kids are in the living room," Marie announced, opening the door for him.

Gayle bent down and looked at her son. "Go on in, Oliver. I bet Henry is waiting for you."

He didn't smile, and there was no sign of the usual excitement at seeing his friends. Gayle had been waiting for him to come out of hiding, but he was still nowhere to be found.

"How is she?" Gayle asked, trading one worry for another.

Marie gave her a shaky hand signal. "Still in pain. Everyone's going crazy trying to figure out what it is."

"It's not Lyme disease, though."

"Nope. Came back negative. They did another MRI, and took more blood. Honestly, they don't know what to think. Bill is considering a virus now. Apparently, there are all these diseases that can get into our bodies and cause all kinds of hell."

"So he's worried sick?"

"Pretty much. Worried with a healthy dose of fear. But that's Bill. I'm still hoping for the pulled muscle theory Love's peddling to everyone."

Gayle shook her head and let out a deep sigh. "Well—I have it. Should we go in?"

They went first to the living room to check on the Yvonne Welsh day care center. Though it seemed at first blush to be an inherent contradiction, the refined Hollywood star was seated gracefully on the floor, her face now caked with makeup at the hands of three little girls.

"Not too much, now, ladies. Remember—it should look *natural*," Yvonne said, eliciting wide-eyed excitement from her audience. A red velvet cosmetics case lay open beside her, real life treasures overflowing onto the floor as the girls dove in with gleeful abandon. There was an air about her that even she could not stifle—even when playing the grandmother—and the girls were awestruck. They never would have found such joy making up their mothers.

Yvonne smiled at the women. "Do you have it?"

Gayle nodded.

"Wonderful!" Yvonne had been a pot of nerves waiting for Gayle to arrive. "Go on—I've got the children."

Marie and Gayle turned for the stairs. The second floor was dark. The bedroom doors were closed to keep the air conditioning from escaping, leaving nothing but the sunshine from below to illuminate the small corridor. It was just after three. The day was clear, bright. As they approached

Love's room, Marie and Gayle could sense that such a day was not welcome in this part of the house.

"Love, we're coming in," Marie said as she turned the handle.

Lying amidst the carefully positioned pillows, Love lay slightly propped up—an improvement from the past few days. Curled in a ball at her side, his face pressed against her bare arm, Baby Will slept with his thumb in his mouth.

"Shhhh," Love whispered. "He's finally settled." Her eyes were on the sleeping baby as she spoke, and Marie could see they were filled with the tears of a mother's guilt.

Not wanting to say the things that were begging to come out, Marie stood in the doorway.

"Hi, Lovey. How are you today?" Gayle said softly as she approached her friend.

"Better. He's taking a bottle. But he won't sleep unless he's next to me."

Gayle nodded. There was no point arguing with her. That the baby *would* sleep in his bed if left to cry for a few minutes was not what Love was willing to hear right now. It was human nature for a baby to take whatever he could from his mother, even if it left her destroyed, and it was equally innate for a mother to give until she had nothing left. Unless, of course, you were a Haywood. Then, you delegated such motherly tasks to the hired nurse, then the nanny. Watching her friend cradle Baby Will as he slept, Gayle wondered if her mother had ever held her that way. And she couldn't help but believe—whatever the coming years brought to this house—that Will was one lucky baby.

"I brought you something," Gayle said, a small brown bag draped over her delicate wrist.

Love gave her a curious look. It wasn't unusual for Gayle to bring a gift. In fact, she rarely arrived anyplace without some kind of offering. But the presence of Marie, the arrangements that had apparently been made to present this gift, had her worried.

Gayle looked at Marie, who nodded. Then she pulled a large, paperback book from the bag and handed it to Love.

"What is this?" Love asked, though she knew before looking at the cover.

"I know someone who knows an exec at Barnes & Noble. It's an advance copy."

Love felt the pain grip her back as the tension spread through her body. Holding the book in her hands, she let her eyes fall upon the cover. She was not ready for this. How did they even know? Her friends, her mother downstairs—all of it added up to one big conspiracy.

Gayle sat on the bed next to her and placed a hand on Love's arm. "We've been friends for six years, since that damned Easter Bunny thing. I knew we would be friends the moment I saw your eyes rolling—both of you," Gayle said, glancing at Marie, who smiled back. "And yet, in all those years, you've never once spoken of your father, except in some sarcastic, nonchalant way. I have no idea what this means for you—this new book. But we wanted you to have it before the rest of the world."

Love was silent as she looked at the gift in her hands. She had wondered what it might feel like, holding her father's words again, being this close to reading them.

"I don't want it," Love said, tossing the book on the bed. "I'm sorry, I know you meant well." Then the tears came.

"Oh, Lovey," Gayle said, stroking her face.

"Let me see that damned thing." Bounding in from the doorway, Marie grabbed the book and opened up to a random page. "Hmmmm . . . I didn't know the great Alexander Rice had penile enlargement! Let me see what else is in here."

She flipped some pages, then pretended to read again. "He likes to wear women's underwear? Shit—no wonder you don't want to read it," Marie continued with a dramatic sarcasm. Then she pressed the book to her chest and looked pleadingly at Gayle. "Can I keep it? There's some good stuff in here!"

Through the tears, Love felt a smile break free. Still, she wouldn't take the book.

"Come on, Lovey. Just poke through it," Gayle said, feeling a rush of anger. Love was a mess—physically, emotionally. How could a father do this to his own child? She wanted to tear the book to shreds, buy every copy they made and burn them all. More than that, she wanted Love to read it, to be OK with whatever it held. To be well again.

She felt the blood pounding against her temples, blood that had been racing through her all night and into today. She had learned to live with Troy, his fits of rage against her and the acts of contrition that followed. But last night he had crossed a line, and the invisible scars she could sense within her son evoked something more powerful than her walls of tolerance.

And for the first time in a long time, she let some of it out.

"Damn it, Love!" she said, drawing looks of shock from her friends. "What good are all my fucking connections if I can't help you!"

Silence filled the room as the women took in the change. Over the years, they had fallen into their roles—outspoken misfit, fragile caretaker, frantic supermom. With one sentence, Gayle had reshuffled the deck.

Marie was the first to acknowledge it. "Excuse me, Miss Manners—what *would* the Haywoods say about such language?" she asked from across the small room. Then she started to laugh. Gayle followed, and finally Love, until the laughter filled the room. Baby Will opened his eyes, then nuzzled deeper into his mother. He pulled his thumb into his mouth, sucking hard and drifting off again.

"Stop—it hurts!" Love said between breaths, but the release was powerful.

Marie joined her friends at Love's bedside. She placed the book on the nightstand, then leaned down to give Love a kiss.

Downstairs, Yvonne listened to her daughter's laughter. It had been some time since she'd heard it, years perhaps, and it lifted her up to that place reserved for motherly joy. That she had not been the one to break through and incite it mattered not one bit.

"How's that, Grandma?" Jessica asked, holding up a mirror for her grandmother.

Yvonne looked at her bright red cheeks, her frosted blue eyelids. Lipstick covered her lips, and a good inch around them. Her eyebrows were black and full, clashing terribly with her lighter hair. Still, she examined herself with serious scrutiny, shifting her head to catch all the angles as she might before shooting a scene. With the girls looking on with bated anticipation, her daughter's laughter still filtering through from above, Yvonne smiled.

"It's just perfect!"

TWENTY-NINE

SECRETS

THERE WAS A KNOCK on the bedroom door. Yvonne entered before anyone answered. Janie Kirk was trailing behind her.

"What are we discussing today, ladies?" she asked, playing dumb as Janie took a seat in the corner.

"Hi, Janie," Gayle said, greeting her friend with a cautious look.

Marie jumped in to aid in Yvonne's cover. "Golf and cereal boxes."

Yvonne shook her head at Marie and gave her a wink. "Not again. *Really,* Marie. You must get over it!"

Yvonne held her hand in the air, then walked out of the room, closing the door behind her.

"Your mother thinks I should let Anthony remain in a state of Neanderthalic idiocy," Marie noted for the record.

With her baby still nuzzled into her, Love nodded. "Don't get me started. It's the generation."

There was a brief moment of silence to acknowledge the truth of the statement.

"So," Janie said, after getting settled with her folder and a pen. "Besides golf and cereal, what did I miss?"

Love looked at Marie, and Marie knew. She wasn't ready to tell another soul about her father's book.

"Let's see . . . I've got this case with the dead baby, and this damned cute intern looking over my shoulder all the time . . ."

"Poor baby." Love smiled, giving Marie a thankful look.

"I think it sounds sweet—a young man infatuated with his brilliant boss. We could all use some of that," Gayle said, eliciting looks of confusion.

"What?"

"What do you mean, *what*? Marie is flirting with her employee." Love smiled again, and Marie flipped her the finger.

"I am not flirting. End of discussion. Now, what's happening with this fundraiser? Have we done enough to save the world yet, or are there more flowers to arrange?"

From across the room, Marie caught the look that passed between Gayle and Janie. As protective as she was of Love, she sensed something similar now between the other pair of friends.

"Something happening, ladies?" she asked, trying to keep it light.

Janie shook her off. "Nothing." It was almost convincing.

Then Marie remembered. "The vote! Gayle—why didn't you say anything? The meeting was last night, wasn't it?"

Gayle didn't answer.

"Gayle?" Love asked. "What happened?"

The silence in the room provided the answer.

Janie sighed, looked at Gayle one last time, then finally spoke. "They voted for the facility upgrade."

"Throw pillows? You have to be joking! Who voted against you?" Marie was now irate.

Gayle shrugged, her eyes averted. "I didn't go."

Marie was perplexed. "Isn't that what all of this is for? Giving up your house, your time, not to mention all the years of generous donations?"

"I'm sure something came up. She did the best she could," Janie tried, though she was, as usual, at a loss to contain Marie.

"I'll call them," Marie said, reaching for her phone.

Love tried to stop her from her place on the bed. "Marie . . ."

"What?"

"Please, Marie. Just let it be." Gayle sounded desperate.

Holding the phone in her hand, Marie gave it a squeeze as she looked with frustration at her friends. "Fine," she relented. "But I don't understand any of this. They need your money. They need your connections. You have incredible power here. *And* . . . you're right about the direction for the clinic."

Love frowned at Marie.

"What? Am I wrong?" Marie needed answers—to a lot of things at the moment. She would settle for the ones that were right in front her.

Gayle shook her head, then looked down, her thoughts quickly reducing to an image of her mother, the sound of breaking glass, and the pills in her vanity drawer. It was almost five, two more hours and she could stop feeling this way. *Yes,* she had missed the meeting. *Yes,* they had used the opportunity to vote against her wishes for the clinic. She had planned to go, to fight for the program. But after the altercation with Troy, the meeting was more confrontation than she was able to face. How could she possibly explain any of that without revealing everything?

Pulling herself together, swallowing down the anger to the deep well she had built for all things unpleasant, Gayle began to shut down.

Janie stepped in to defend her. "They're a tough crowd. I wouldn't want to face them either."

"Gayle?" Love said. But the chilling vagueness she saw in Gayle's eyes was something she knew too well, and it had her worried.

Marie carried on, reciting her knowledge about boards, and people who used them to feel important. Who cared what they thought of Gayle? The point was to help the clinic. The rest was just noise, tedious, annoying noise that had to be stopped.

Listening, nodding, Love tried to pull Gayle into the plotting to save the situation. But Gayle was nowhere to be found. She waited for a pause in Marie's diatribe, then politely excused herself.

"I have to get home. Oliver needs dinner."

"Gayle . . ." Marie tried to stop her, but Gayle walked through the door without as much as a parting glance.

"I'll go after her," Janie said, rushing to gather her things. "It'll be fine."

When she was gone, Marie stood still, her eyes now fixed on the empty hallway just outside the room.

"What the hell is going on?"

Love sighed and stole a hug from Baby Will. "There's something wrong with her."

"What?" Marie asked, turning to face Love.

"I don't know. Something's not right in that house."

They both knew Gayle's life was complicated—the family that was richer than God, the estate and staff that needed managing, her son who grew more reclusive each year. And, of course, the arrogant ass who tried to pass as a husband, and a man.

"She never talks about any of it," Marie said, checking her watch. As always, she was running late for dinner, homework, and the rest of her life that was waiting.

Love looked at Marie until she finally had her full attention. "Do any of us? Talk, I mean. About what's really going on."

Marie could not pretend to be surprised. They were the best of friends. They knew everything about each other. Their kids' worst moments, their husbands' choice of underwear. How they drank their coffee. Still, Love was hiding behind the present conflict to avoid the book sitting beside her—the book containing her life. And Marie hadn't brushed the surface of Randy Matthews.

"I know, I know," Marie said, waving her off as she leaned across the bed. She gave Love a kiss on the cheek and squeezed her hand. "Even so—nothing in my life is real until I tell you about it. You know that, right?"

Love smiled at her and nodded, wishing that were true.

THIRTY

THE STEPFORD WIVES

"So I would have the children for dinners during the week, then longer stretches on the weekends?" Craig Hewett was trying to get it all straight in his head.

"Yes. That's usually how it works," Marie answered her client.

"And I would live in an apartment, maybe in Cliffton?"

"We'd have to crunch the numbers. We could require your wife to move as well, to a smaller house. Obviously, maintaining two households is more costly than one."

Hewett took a long moment to reflect, and Marie knew what was coming, if not now, then soon, as those secret thoughts played out over the next several days. *Who will clean, who will shop, who will cook for me? And what will I do when I have the kids? Will the nanny come with them? But where would she stay?* It was cynical to make this assumption, that her client would be worried about such trivial details in the face of such a monumental decision. But it was not unfounded. For most of his adult life, and probably all of his childhood, Craig Hewett had been taken care of by a woman. The mundane yet necessary tasks of sustaining a household, of keeping life running on time, had never been on his to-do list, and this would surely be a factor in his decision. And what was ironic to Marie, what was so maddening, was her conviction that his reliance on his wife as a servant was the very thing that was killing their relationship.

Marie covered the broad strokes of the divorce process, the filing of the petition, the mandatory court hearing, and the different roads it could wind down. If everyone was rational, if they stayed calm and focused on the end result, it could be kept under the radar, settled amicably and wrapped up within the year. If, at the other extreme, one of them wanted to cause trouble, the court would be more than happy to stick its nose in every aspect of their lives. The Hewetts could spend their lives being scrutinized by judges and court shrinks, overworked and obstinate bureaucrats who could not possibly know what was best for them, but would insinuate themselves into every aspect of the separation. They could be at it for years, then find themselves with a similar result—only significantly poorer and emotionally spent. In short, it would behoove Mr. Hewett to be nice.

"I'll be in touch when I've figured out what I want to do," Hewett said, ready to leave.

Marie stopped him. "Look, I want you to go home and think about this. Think about whether or not you can get through the next few years. When the kids are in school, and your wife has more time for herself, she may have more to give you as well."

Sitting back now, Mr. Hewett exhaled for what felt like hours. Then he nodded with resolution. "And what if she doesn't? What if we can't ever be happy again?"

"That's the gamble," Marie said. Then she paused. "Look—we only get one shot at a unified family. You might remarry, have more kids. People make it work. But what you have now—two natural parents together with their children—this is it. You can't recreate this or get it back, and there are always consequences when it breaks apart." The words came out from a place deep within her, the same place that had spoken to her every day and every night since her husband began his vanishing act.

Paul Hewett nodded, and Marie could tell he had considered this and weighed it against his own happiness.

Marie sighed. This was, surely, the beginning of the end for the Hewetts. His mind had started down the path. He now had the knowledge that would occupy his thoughts at every possible moment, and those thoughts would, by necessity, be held in secret as he moved farther away from his wife, and their family. He would, instead, begin to ponder his new life. Sitting at the dinner table—flanked by his children as his wife cooked and served, prodding the littlest one to eat her vegetables, then puttered and cleaned up to avoid sitting in front of a plate of food herself—food that she might actually consume and then regret the next day when she squeezed herself into her size 2 AG jeans—Paul Hewett would be thinking about how bad it would be. Marie could see the wheels turning already.

"Just please—think carefully."

Marie watched him leave, knowing he would be back by the end of the month. Then she turned to Randy, who had been silently observing the consult from across the table.

"Ugghh," she said, sitting back down in a defeated posture.

Randy looked at her slumped down in the chair. "Did I miss something?"

"No. It's just that I know his wife."

"And she'll be crushed?"

"Yes," Marie answered, then lifted her head so she could see her young protégé. "And no. She's the perfect Stepford wife. That's why this will crush her."

Randy laughed at her depiction. "How does one detect a robot wife from the flesh and blood variety?"

"Easy. The human form does the housewife detail but bitches about it to her friends. She goes out in gnarly sweats without a shower, has dust under her bed, chronic exhaustion, and secretly longs to be Angelina Jolie." Marie smiled with endearment as she thought about Love, herself, and the small handful of friends she had collected over the years.

"Hell, *I* long to be Angelina Jolie," Randy said, now thoroughly amused.

"Yeah, right."

"OK. Maybe not. But Mrs. Hewett?"

Marie scowled. She had nothing against the woman—except the fact that she was one of the coveted. "Where to start? She has a perfect body, which she parades through town in tight black pilates pants. She lunches with friends but orders nothing but green tea, doesn't drink or smoke, is always nicely dressed, and keeps an immaculate home. Her children are brilliant, uninterested in television, and eat broccoli. She adores her husband, never says no, and never—ever—speaks poorly of him. But the worst part about her is that she pretends all of this is easy, and completely fulfilling. She pretends that it doesn't faze her to never sleep, or eat, or have an intellectual conversation."

"Sounds like the Housewife Olympics."

Marie nodded and smiled. "Exactly! Her purpose in life is to make other women feel like shit for not being her."

"Until her husband bails," Randy noted, his eyebrows raised.

"Ahhh—you have no idea! Divorce means immediate disqualification. Like bikers on steroids."

Randy sat back and folded his arms, his face lit up by the energy force field Marie's diatribe had generated. "You've given this a lot of thought."

"Well, it *is* my life, after all."

"So what is a double H like yourself doing in a place like this?" Randy asked, referring to her two Harvard degrees. "There must be something good out here. Something that made you come."

Marie rubbed the side of her face, as if trying to remember. She knew the answer—the one she told herself these days. But the real reason? She was almost too embarrassed to say it out loud.

"The grass."

"Grass?"

"Haven't you noticed it? The lush, vibrantly green grass? I had this idea that it would bring us serenity. Back to nature and all of that. I wanted my kids to walk outside in their bare feet and feel the ground."

"That seems like a good reason."

"Only they don't do that. My girls prefer to flaunt their designer sandals at the mall. Don't know where I went wrong, but now, I swear to you—I think if I don't keep one step ahead of this place, it might actually catch up with me."

"And the robot Marie Passeti will kill you and take over your life," Randy teased her, an ominous expression taking shape around his eyes.

Marie smiled then dropped her head to the table, her dark hair spreading out around her face. "Sometimes I wish she would just hurry up and do it."

Randy was smiling when he reached out his hand. Marie felt her heart jump into her throat as he shifted her misplaced hair with one finger, careful not to touch her cheek with the others.

"I don't think there's much chance of that."

He laughed when he said it, and Marie smiled in spite of herself as she lifted her head from the table. He was looking at her now, laughing and smiling in a way that made her believe she was actually making sense. There was a time when this would not have reached so deeply inside her, when she carried within her enough clarity to support her own convictions.

Anthony had—once upon a time—looked at her that way. He used to laugh with her about the ladies with their tight butts and lunches without food. When had he stopped? It was too far back to even remember.

Shit. Love's words popped into Marie's head. *You're flirting with your help.* More words followed. *Unprofessional. Unseemly. Pathetic.*

"So where are we on Farrell?" The shift was abrupt, but necessary. There was simply no time to find a clever segue. Still, it only served to underscore the direction in which her feelings were going, and an awkward tension swept through the room.

Randy pulled back into his chair, then scrambled through a stack of notepads. He pulled one out and began to sum up his findings on the Farrell document production, his eyes consciously avoiding Marie. "We have three years of checks from the joint account."

"Anything pop out?" Marie asked, pulling up a chair next to his.

"Hard to say. Lots of doctors."

"Not unusual with kids, believe me."

Randy checked his notes. "Most are ten, fifteen dollars. Insurance copays. But they did pay one doctor anywhere from six hundred to two thousand a month."

Her eyes lit up now, Marie felt the familiar surge of excitement at the puzzle taking shape. "For how many months?"

"Looks like they start two years ago. There's a sharp increase just after Simone's death. Then they stop after the move."

Looking up from his notes, Randy met Marie's eyes, and they both nodded. Without a word, Randy got up from the table and walked back into the office to his desk. Marie was right behind him.

They logged onto the Internet, then entered the name Dr. Keller as it had appeared in the Farrells' check register. Narrowing the field to the Boston area, they found psychiatrist Rachel Keller in Newton, Mass.

"A shrink," Marie said out loud, as they read the doctor's resume. "They're usually not covered."

"The Farrells were paying out-of-pocket." Randy chimed in.

"They were paying a lot. And it started *before* the accident."

Watching the screen intently, Marie thought about what this meant. Farrell had lied about things being fine before the accident. But they already knew that from the police report. His wife's lawyer had handed over the check registers without the slightest protest. That in itself was not surprising. It always helped the case for alimony to prove expenses, to back them up with hard data. But it also meant that Connely had nothing to fear from disclosing the payments to Dr. Keller—or that he didn't know any better.

"Marriage counseling?" Randy asked, pulling Marie back from her thoughts.

"Could be," she said, nodding. "Could be Carson. I doubt it's the wife. Connely never would have given us those records."

"What about the kids?"

Marie shrugged, stepping back from Randy's desk. It could be any one of them.

"So what now? Can we contact the shrink?"

Marie shook her head. "No. Not without a release from Carson."

"Why don't we just ask him?"

That was the question of the hour. Asking Carson was the obvious thing to do, the course most lawyers would take under the circumstances.

But this case, and Carson Farrell, had bothered Marie from the moment he walked through her door.

Randy was watching her now, the way he always did when she was lost in her thoughts. He waited for her expression to change from contemplation to resolve. When she finally spoke, he seemed pleased with himself that he had anticipated her response.

"Let's keep it under the radar. Where are you with the neighbors?"

"I have general profiles going four doors out in both directions, both sides of the street."

"Any with kids of similar ages?"

"Just one."

Marie shrugged. "Then that's who will know."

THIRTY-ONE

ABOVE THE GARAGE

THE STAIRS LEADING TO the garage apartment were in the back, the last piece of the stone mansion before the start of six wooded acres. And although it was easily forgotten, the woods made up the bulk of her property, spanning twice the size of the lush green lawn abutting the main section of the house, the part she inhabited. That was her domain—the grass, the gardens that flanked it on three sides. It was the landscape she looked at from her bedroom balcony, the peaceful backdrop to her flagstone patio where she liked to read. Standing here at the foot of the staircase, she was about to enter another world altogether—a world that had been calling out to her for days. Ever since that night on the patio, that day in her kitchen. Finally, she was going to answer it.

As she made her way to the top, she could hear his footsteps on the hardwood floor. The smell of incense and the sound of soft music drifted from the small opening in the back window. She stopped for a moment, thinking her presence here an intrusion into this man's private life. But each step brought new information, the music becoming clearer, a view into his kitchen opening up, revealing dozens of sketches hanging from the wall. She continued up the stairs, then knocked on the door.

"It's me. Mrs. Beck . . . Gayle," she said, when the music stopped. She heard rushed footsteps across the room, then the turning of a lock.

"Mrs. Beck." He was startled, and unusually self-conscious. Quickly, he began to tuck his shirt, a casual button-down, into draping, drawstring pants. His feet were bare, the shirt partially unbuttoned, revealing parts of him she had never seen—innocuous parts—the tops of his feet, the bones around his neck. Still, had his face not quickly conformed to the serious employee persona he wore in the other parts of the house, she might not have recognized him at all.

"Did you need me early today?"

On most days, Paul took time for himself between the lunch and dinner hours. Working from sun-up to two, then again from five until nine each night, there weren't many hours left for him to claim.

Embarrassed, Gayle shook her head. "No. I'm sorry to disturb you. This can wait." She turned to leave, but he reached out, touching her lightly on the arm.

"Come in," he said.

Gayle took a few steps forward into the narrow kitchen. Closing the door behind them, Paul led her into the small living area. She knew it well, having designed the room herself and overseen its construction. With vaulted ceilings, skylights, and an abundance of windows, it was a comfortable apartment. Still, today it felt like a place she had never been. Standing in the center of the room, she slowly took in the personal effects that had transformed the space so completely.

The furnishings were minimal. A small sofa, a side chair and reading table. Books were piled on the floor, many books, some of them very old. A small CD player sat in the corner, though the music had stopped. And all around her, scattered randomly about, were easels, at least ten of them, each with a sketch drawn in black pencil. They were in various stages of completion, a few being too abstract to identify the subject. But most depicted people, many in scenes that were familiar—the pond at the foot of the town park, the local coffee shop.

"I had no idea you were an artist," she said, walking slowly through the makeshift gallery.

"I wouldn't say that, exactly. It's a hobby. Can I get you something to drink?"

She wasn't thirsty, but it seemed a good idea—following ritual formalities. "Water is fine. Thank you."

Paul disappeared into the kitchen, his voice trailing behind him, then through the small opening separating the two rooms. "When I traveled," he began to explain, "I didn't have a camera, but there were so many things I wanted to capture. Take with me."

As he talked, Gayle picked up a thin portfolio of drawings that lay on the floor. She opened it, and began to turn the pages. The pictures were of people, like the others. But the setting was here, her home. She turned back to the first one, looking more carefully at the images before her. The drawing was of a small child sitting in a field. The stone fountain in the distance was unmistakable. The child seemed a stranger, until she studied his face. The jawline, the shape of his eyes. It was Oliver. Most of the pictures she had of her child depicted a smiling, happy boy. Those were the shots that made it from the pack to the photo albums. But this drawing was also Oliver, the way he looked when he was sad, contemplative, as he was so much of the time lately. Tracing the boy's face with her fingers, there was no doubt that this man had perfectly captured her son.

She turned the pages, recognizing now the subjects in the drawings. Francisco, the groundskeeper, laboring in the hot sun over her garden. Their maid ironing in front of the television, her attention on the latter. She heard the faucet in the kitchen, Paul's voice still telling of the places he had been when he was a young man, a wanderer. She turned the pages faster, until she found the one she was looking for. There was no landscape, no setting. Just a face. Her face.

"Water," Paul said, coming through the doorway. "With a slice of lemon." Gayle was sitting on the chair now, the small portfolio closed and returned to the spot on the floor where she had found it.

"Thank you," Gayle said, allowing her eyes to meet his.

There was a brief silence, a slight but distinct hesitation before Paul sat on the sofa across from his employer, and Gayle sensed the same discomfort that had recently come between them.

"So, what can I do for you?"

"I wanted to explain about the other day . . . when you came in and . . . ," she started to say. But Paul interrupted her.

"You don't have to explain."

"Yes. I do. I want to. It's been on my mind." Gayle paused, looking at the ceiling, trying to find the words that would say everything, and nothing.

"Really, you don't have to." Paul saved her once again.

Gayle nodded, wondering now if the closeness she'd felt between them that night had been entirely of her own making, and tolerated by him as nothing more than an obligatory indulgence.

"I won't keep you then," she said, suddenly self-conscious. She got up from the chair and turned toward the kitchen door, and the safety of the world that waited just outside. Paul stood as well, shadowing her movements closely—more closely than he did within the walls of the main house. She could feel him now, not as the steady fixture that comforted her throughout the day, but instead as a live, unpredictable entity. And it made her stop.

"Can I ask you something?" she said, turning to face him.

He was surprised, but he didn't back away. "Of course," he said.

"How have you lived alone for so long?"

"I'm not alone."

"I mean, without attachment. How do you live without a permanent attachment? A wife, children?"

"Ah," he answered, now aware of the real question. "I was married, once."

It was Gayle's turn to be surprised. She had never thought to ask, and he had never mentioned it. How selfish she had been all these years—going on and on about herself, and never inquiring about his life, as though he existed solely in relation to her.

She studied the sadness in his eyes, and he allowed it to be seen.

"Not much in life is permanent, is it?" he said.

"Can I ask what it was like? Your marriage?"

Paul shrugged, seemingly unsure how to answer. "Immature, I think. We were young. I didn't know what I wanted then."

"Were you happy, though?"

"Yeah. I guess I was for a while. But I found marriage difficult. I was changing, she was changing. We started wanting different things."

Gayle moved toward the door, not sure of what to say next. "I should go," she said, and this time it was Paul who stopped her.

"Wait," he said, reaching out for her arm. "What did you come here to tell me?"

Gayle looked away. "Nothing."

But he did not back down. He took her right hand in his and exposed the small cuts on her palm that were almost healed.

Standing in the doorway to the kitchen, Gayle stepped back until she felt the hard wood against her shoulders. She leaned into it, wishing it would give way and swallow her—taking her from this place and back to the house she could see through the window.

"How much do you know?" she asked. In his face it became clear that her question had given her away, or at least confirmed the evidence he surely had gathered over the past few weeks—if not from years of living in such close proximity to the catastrophe of her life.

"What do you want me to say?" he asked, his demeanor uneasy.

"Please." Her voice was quiet and pleading as she pressed him. He *had* to understand.

Paul looked away for a moment, calculating the decision. When he looked up again, his expression was definitive. She had opened this door and he was charging through it.

"OK," he said in a gentle tone. Then he continued, speaking slowly and with compassion.

"I know about broken glass. I know about pills and head shrinks with bad advice. I know about two women possessing one body, and a scared little boy. I know about fear. And I know that I'm not the only one who lives alone in this house."

There. He'd done it—listed her crimes. Gayle was flustered. The blood flooded her cheeks. She watched his hand as it moved slowly from his side to her face, the back of his fingers gently pressing against her skin.

"I'm so sorry," he whispered.

She moved away, walking into the kitchen to break the connection. "It's hard for him. At the office, living here. There's no measure of a man beyond his income—how well he provides for his family," she said, surprised at her need to explain her husband. "I make that impossible for him."

Paul remained in the doorway. "Is that what they've been telling you?" His voice was calmer, but there was an urgency that lingered just below the surface.

Standing at the sink, Gayle turned to face him. "I think if I were a stronger woman . . ."

"Don't do that."

"You don't understand."

Gayle shook her head vehemently. But Paul wasn't letting go. "You grew up with it, didn't you? It's familiar. That's why you can't see it."

The presence of the truth overwhelmed her, and she felt herself gasp for breath. Never had she spoken of the rage in her childhood, carrying it about like a cancer beneath her skin. Avoiding it, ignoring it, trying in vain to belittle it with indifference. It had been a substantial undertaking, not just in her present situation, but throughout her life. And she could hear now the sound of her mother's voice, the red heat that would seep from the woman's body in those moments when she lost control, burning into Gayle the scars that no one had ever seen before.

She felt the tears come, and she didn't hold them back. She couldn't have. Instead, she looked at Paul and told him. "My mother," she said, watching him carefully as though the weight of her words might somehow destroy him. But he was still standing there, his face steady.

Gayle took another breath, wiping the tears from her cheeks. She smiled out of sheer reflex, and was, in the end, not able to say any more.

Moving closer to her, Paul reached for her hand and pulled it to his chest. "You didn't deserve this," he said.

He wrapped his arms around her then, and she let her body fall into his, accepting his embrace. Strong hands stroked her hair, caressed her back, and she let him hold her longer than she should have, until the sound of Celia's car in the driveway jolted her from the moment.

"I have to go," she said, abruptly pulling away.

Paul followed her as she rushed to the back door. "Gayle!" he called after her. She was halfway down the stairs before he could get the words out.

She stopped then turned to face him, still wiping the tears from her face. "I'm fine. Really. I'll be fine."

Leaving Paul on the landing, she hurried down the stairs, around the side of the garage to the driveway. Celia was pulling up with the groceries. She stopped and rolled down her window.

"Aren't you getting Oliver from his swim class?" she asked, her voice scolding. It was almost five.

Gayle rushed past the car to gather her keys from the house. As she ran into the mud room, past the jackets and shoes and their other belongings, she felt a strong disconnection. Her body was moving, grabbing the keys, hurrying back outside to her car. But part of her was not there. Part of her was still upstairs, over the garage. On the other side of the world.

Standing in the driveway with a bag of groceries, Celia watched her. But Gayle avoided her discerning eyes.

"I'm going now," she said. Then she pulled away.

THIRTY-TWO

NEW AGE SHRINK

"WHAT ARE WE DOING here?" Love asked, though it wasn't really a question. She knew where she was, and why she was sitting in the hallway outside the office of Dr. Keri Luster.

Yvonne did not look up from the literature she'd been poring over since they arrived. She was at home in this place, on this little planet from the universe of alternative medicine. The smell of herbal candles, the little sand garden with the rocks and doll-sized rake on the table, and of course the barrage of pamphlets explaining why Western medicine was one giant conspiracy to sell pharmaceuticals. All of it spoke to the L.A. earth mother in Yvonne.

"It says here that one of the founders of sensory work suffered from debilitating back spasms. She discovered the methods while trying to find a cure."

"Great." As usual, Love wasn't buying any of it. She was, after all, married to a medical doctor. Scientific studies, clinical tests, and pills were the way to go. Maybe, if pressed, she could get her head around traditional psychotherapy—talk about your problems, understand your issues. This was in another realm. Connecting her back pain to something going on in her head was as asinine to her as it was insulting.

"It's all about the mind-body connection. It makes perfect sense." Yvonne was bubbling with optimism.

"It's completely out there, Mother. Even for you."

"And using leeches to cure disease—that was rational?"

"That was like a hundred years ago."

"And a hundred years from *now* sensory-motor therapy could be the standard for treating illness."

Love sighed. "Thankfully, I'll be dead by then."

"Love!" Yvonne was exasperated by her daughter's cynicism, and Love could almost hear her thoughts. This was going to be it—the answer they'd all been searching for since the fall. Yes—the evil medical community, with all its sophistication and wisdom, had failed to come up with a damned thing. And she wasn't wrong on this point. Lupus, Lyme, cancer, and a whole host of other diseases had all been ruled out. Disc trauma, muscle tear—also eliminated. They were down to Love's muscle-strain theory, though Bill insisted this was wholly inadequate to account for the intensity and duration of the problem. He had his own theory—some mystery virus that had settled in her tissue and was making plans to attack her entire being. No one could agree, and this was playing right into Yvonne's hands. *That's right,* she now reasoned. *When in doubt, the doctors make something up.*

Back and forth they had gone, testing, hoping, researching and arguing. It had become unbearable. So Love had come up with her own plan. She humored her husband by going for tests. Now she had to find a way to appease her mother.

Love looked at the woman—*really* looked at her. The wide eyes, the knowing smile. It was all coming back to her—the wacky world of Yvonne Welsh. She had tried it all through the years. Menstrual cramps? Acupuncture. Headaches? Meditation, aromatherapy, shiatsu massage. Got a cold? A cleansing fast followed by vitamin supplements that make you shit all day for several days. Yvonne was always immersed in some time-consuming (and usually expensive) regimen, and Love had come to hide her ailments just to avoid the treatments her mother would subject her to. Was it any wonder Dr. Bill Harrison had been so appealing? God bless Motrin.

But this was making the woman happy. Perhaps it would even buy a few days of peace.

Yvonne spoke as she read. "Dr. Luster has a booming practice in Hunting Ridge. Doesn't that say *something*?"

"Sure, Mom."

"We were lucky there was a cancellation—she's booked for months!"

The door opened and out came a mother with her daughter. The girl was around six, maybe seven, and Love wondered what could possibly be so wrong with someone so little. No matter—it was their turn. Yvonne patted Love on the knee.

"Time to go."

She helped Love to her feet, then braced her as they made their way into the office. Dr. Luster was waiting.

"You must be Love Welsh!" she said, extending her hand. She was a small woman, maybe five feet, with a round figure and china white skin. Her gray hair was pulled up in a clip, exposing dainty diamond stud earrings. Her clothing was casual but oddly preppy—mid-calf khaki skirt, button-down oxford, leather loafers. She seemed lost in the 1980s, and all of this fed directly into Love's theory that the woman, and her practice, must be out to lunch.

Even so, Love greeted the woman politely and followed her to the treatment area. It was a pleasant room, brightly painted and cluttered with toys in one corner and a soft examination table in the center.

"Why don't you lie down while I go over a few things. I can sense that you're in pain."

Love smiled. *What was your first clue?* she thought to herself, though Yvonne somehow heard it and pinched her lightly on the arm.

"OK," Dr. Luster began. "So I assume you had a chance to read some of the literature outside?"

"Yes," Yvonne answered for them.

"So you know that what I do is a blended approach. I have studied many methods—Hakomi, Rubenfeld, among others. I like to focus on integrating past traumas into present feelings so they can be released from the body."

She leaned over the head of the table and laid her palms on Love's forehead. "You see, trauma that is not assimilated or acknowledged is held in our bodies, resulting in energy blocks that can cause tension, imbalance, and quite often pain. I use the body as the point of entry to treat this—to release the emotional pain so the energy can flow freely as it was meant to."

Love's eyes were closed, but she rolled them anyway. Standing beside her, Yvonne was intrigued. This was everything she had always believed about the human body—the intricate connection between the physical and emotional. The body and mind. And now it was actually a field of practice.

"So what do you need to do?" she asked.

Dr. Luster smiled warmly, reassuringly. "I'm just going to do some body work on Love. I will ask questions and talk to her, and while I do this I will place my hands on different parts of her body to see how they react. If we can find where the trauma is being held, we can help to release it as an *emotional* feeling—freeing the body of physical pain."

Yvonne nodded.

"Does that sound OK to you?"

Love shrugged. "Sure."

Her answer was quick and riddled with indifference. Dr. Luster took a long, cleansing breath.

"Have you worked on your body before—massage, acupuncture, anything like that?"

Love looked at her mother. "You could say that."

But Yvonne refused to be embarrassed. "I am a strong believer in the mind-body connection."

"That's good. Then why don't we begin?" Dr. Luster directed Yvonne to a small wooden chair in the corner of the room. Then she asked Love to roll over onto her stomach.

"Are you ready?"

"Sure," Love said. *As ready as I'll ever be*. She was telling herself to relax and get through the session—how bad could it be? It wasn't shock therapy. Still, something inside her was growing uneasy.

Dr. Luster asked Love to raise her right arm into the air and try to resist her attempt to push it back down to the table. "I will apply some pressure—see if you can hold firm."

Then, with her eyes closed as though she were summoning ghosts from Love's past, Dr. Luster began whispering things to Love, each time pushing against her arm. *I am a child . . . I am safe . . . I am not safe . . . I am scared.* Love's arm broke its hold and was pushed to the table.

"You see," Dr. Luster explained, "when your muscles can't hold, that tells me there is a break in the energy forces within your body. The energy gets blocked by the negative reactions your body is holding when these thoughts are introduced."

She continued with the left arm. *I am seven . . . I am nine . . . I am eleven . . . I am thirteen.* Again, her arm released.

They continued this way for close to twenty minutes, Dr. Luster mumbling things as she tried to push Love's arms and then her legs back to table. She touched Love's stomach, then reached underneath where the pain was, letting Love's weight fall against her hands, whispering statements that were at the same time generic and intensely personal. Things about her father, her mother, her children, lovers, friends, self-esteem, guilt, shame, and regret. Each time she broke the hold, Dr. Luster let out a little sigh—an *aha!* that was growing more and more annoying to Love. Wasn't there a more precise way to measure the body's energy blocks? Some sort of electromagnetic detector with special probes that could be attached to the skin? Wouldn't that be more scientific than pushing her arms and legs to the table?

My body . . . my person . . . my space . . . I am fifteen . . . I am twenty-one. Yep—Love was an easy patient. Every year since her birth had been difficult. Her warped intelligence had made her a problem child, thinking things before she could physically speak. She was chronically bored and frustrated until she was "diagnosed," and then she was bombarded with knowledge that she pressured herself to grasp. Pick a year, any year, and Love could think of something that had been terribly dysfunctional. She wasn't in denial about it. She thought about it all the damned time. If her body was still holding on, what could she possibly do about that?

Still, she felt unnerved as Dr. Luster continued—her voice soft and even, inviting the emotions to come to the surface. It was the last statement that caused a tear to roll down Love's face.

I am at peace with myself.

"We're almost done," Dr. Luster said. She walked around to the head of the table again and pressed her palms to Love's face. She brushed the tears away without saying a word about them, then placed her finger tips on Love's temples.

"I'm going to say some reaffirmations, then we can talk, OK?"

Love nodded as she fought like hell to pull back the tide.

I can be at peace with myself and my past. I can feel the pain from what happened to me and let it go. I can be well again.

The doctor paused for an interminable moment. Then she drew a long breath and returned to her normal voice.

"There. All done. Why don't you sit up and I'll tell you what I found."

Love climbed off the table and joined her mother in a chair by Dr. Luster's desk. She could feel the flush on her cheeks and prayed it had gone unnoticed. *Almost finished,* she told herself. *Keep your shit together.*

"So," Dr. Luster explained again, "what I was doing was called muscle testing. You see, when I said something that triggered a subconscious emotion, the energy was blocked and you were unable to hold firm. I was able to push your arm or leg down. The body is amazing—it holds the truth about each of us." Her face was lit up with the wonder of it all, and Love was thankful for the comic relief. Casting her most cynical light over Dr. Luster, she could feel herself returning to reality. To the kids, the house, Bill. Even the pain. A return to a life that was far too full to dwell on her displaced emotions.

"Your mother told me that you fell?"

"I was carrying both kids."

"And your muscles couldn't hold strong," the doctor continued in an earnest voice, almost as though she were desperate for Love to understand. To believe. "You have suffered great trauma in your past. I'm sensing something in your early teen years. It has to do with a man, and I'm sensing something physical as well as emotional. Also, I got something when I spoke of your father. I'm not sure if it is a separate trauma—perhaps a developmental trauma rather than a particular incident. In any case, your body is holding on to these things."

She paused then to let it sink in. "I'm guessing they were not assimilated, or properly felt, at the time and now they are living inside you—physically. I think there is more, much more—enough to make you fall—and now the pain has no place to go. But we have done what we can for the first session."

Yvonne sat quietly, though her heart was in her throat. Wasn't that what she'd wanted? To prove that Love's illness was linked to some kind of depression, something that wasn't going to do her in? She thought about the letter, the book that sat untouched next to Love like a noose waiting to be tightened around her neck. She believed in this, maybe too much. Maybe that was why Dr. Luster's treatment felt so dangerous.

Dr. Luster waited for some elaboration on the traumas she had identified to see if she was right. But Love was silent, her mind shut down now as she waited for this to be over.

Yvonne cautiously pushed forward. "So what do we do next?"

"Well, I'd be happy to work with you. We can do more body work to integrate the feelings—to give them a proper home by attaching them to the events. We would do more muscle testing and perhaps talk about whatever events might be the source of the blockage. I can see if I have any cancellations this month—try to fit you in?"

Love looked nervously at her mother.

Yvonne sighed. "Why don't we call you? I don't think Love brought her planner."

Love shook her head. "No—no I didn't. We'll have to call."

Dr. Luster smiled. She'd seen this before. They weren't ready.

"That's just fine. I wish you luck with your pain." Her voice was kind and warm. She shook their hands and saw them to the door.

When they were down the hall, Yvonne stopped walking.

"I think you should come back. *Alone* next time."

Love was quick to respond. "No." She had agreed to one session, and that would have to be enough for her mother.

"But what if she's right? She knew all those things—things about your childhood . . ."

"That's what these people do, Mother! Every thirteen-year-old girl has trauma about men. It's puberty! They tell you things that are just specific enough for you to tie it to your own life, but it's really stuff that happens to everyone. *Oh, I'm sensing something when you were an infant—birth, maybe.* It's a trick."

"And what if it's not? What if all of this is about that night . . . ?"

"It's a goddamn muscle pull! Leave it alone."

Love kept walking, leaving her mother behind in the hallway. Even as she put distance between them, she could feel the pull of her mother's guilt. Yvonne had done everything imaginable to fix Love when her life got turned on its head. Everything but stand up to Alexander Rice.

From down the hallway, Love heard her mother call after her.

"I will not leave it alone. Not this time." And Love knew exactly what she meant.

THIRTY-THREE

REJUVENATION

AFTER A NIGHT OF fitful sleep, Love willed herself out of bed, got dressed, and walked slowly down the stairs. She was getting better at this. She'd been to the hospital twice for tests that had proved futile. She'd stood up and walked around the room so Bill could examine her posture, and she'd gone to see Dr. Luster for her mother. Now Love was getting out of bed for herself.

Marie was waiting.

"Where's your mom?"

Love leaned against the kitchen counter, fighting the pain. "She took the kids to the park."

Marie nodded as she held out her hand. "So this is a jailbreak?"

"Something like that."

"Great. I'm gonna catch all kinds of hell."

Marie helped Love out through the garage and into her car. The weight was substantial against her as they moved, a clear indication of the pain

Love was in, and Marie began to wonder if she shouldn't have refused the pleas to take Love to the meeting.

When they were on the road, Love caught her breath. "I really needed this," she said.

And she did. All night she had thought about Dr. Luster, the things she'd said and the demons she'd provoked. Now she was in need of distraction, and the busy work of the benefit planning was just the thing.

Marie did the driving, taking it slow, avoiding the bumps of potholes left over from the winter months, giving the curves a wide berth. When they got to the gates of the Haywood-Beck estate, Love turned to Marie.

"Have you spoken to her since the other day?"

Marie shook her head. She'd left Gayle alone, and Gayle had done the same.

"I see. Well—this should be fun."

Marie brushed it off. "It'll be fine. Gayle's a master of avoidance and I've been working on my self-control. Anyway, you're going to be the talk of the day. Out and about like there's nothing wrong with you. They're going to want a rundown, you know."

"I have nothing to tell. It's just a pull. I was carrying both kids, for God's sake."

Marie sighed as she waited for the gates to open. *Denial.* That's what this was. No one was really believing the pulled-muscle theory anymore—not even Marie. And how could they when Love's esteemed husband now looked like a little boy who'd lost his way in a crowd? Not to mention Yvonne's melodrama. Still, she let it go as they drove up the driveway and slowly made their way into the house.

"You made it!"

Seated at the table were Gayle and Janie Kirk.

"I have to lie down." Wasting no time because the pain was gathering speed, Love dropped herself to the oriental carpet and let out a sigh. The remaining three women gathered over her to observe.

"You OK down there?" Janie asked.

Gayle rushed to the doorway that led to the living room. "I'll get a pillow."

Still standing over Love, Marie tried to minimize the growing concern in the room. Love wanted distraction and she was going to have it.

"You look like one of those dead animal skins people throw on the floor and use as rugs."

Love managed a smile. "Just keep the NRA away and I should be fine."

Gayle was back with a pillow, which she carefully slid under Love's head. "There," she said, as if the pillow had just saved the world from certain disaster.

"Thanks. Now everyone sit down. *Please!* I get enough of this at home. I have a pulled muscle. End of story."

Marie grabbed some linen samples from the table and handed them to Love.

"OK. OK. Don't get all bitchy on us," she said, returning to the table. Gayle sat, too, but said nothing to honor her friend's request.

"This one," Love said, reaching out with one of the swatches in her hand.

Marie took it from her. "See—isn't this easy? Now look at napkins."

A collective sigh followed. No one had mentioned the events of their last meeting, and the tension between Marie and Gayle was felt by all.

Janie stepped in with characteristic ease. Small talk was a suburban necessity and she had it down cold. "Does anyone have a good ob-gyn?"

Trying to make nice, Marie was the first to answer. "The Hunting Ridge group is good."

Janie looked first at Marie, clearly surprised, then covered her mouth with one of her manicured hands.

"What?" Marie was now agitated.

Love spoke from her spot on the floor, her voice reaching Marie from under the table. "You might as well tell her."

"Tell me what?!"

Janie shrugged. "They're closing down. Dr. Olson is moving to a Manhattan group, and the male doctors are turning the practice into some kind of laser clinic. They sent a letter. Didn't you get it?"

"I guess I missed it. What are you talking about? Plastic surgery? How the hell can a gynecologist switch fields to plastic surgery?" Marie said, bending down so she could catch a glimpse of Love's face, which was now straining to hold back a smile.

"It's not exactly plastic surgery," Love managed to get out before the smile took over.

"Then what?"

Gayle decided to jump in. There was no use prolonging a full disclosure. "It's called Laser Vaginal Rejuvenation. It was all in the letter."

"Vaginal rejuvenation? What the hell?!" Marie was now standing, and Love was laughing out loud in spite of the pain.

"You know—when things are not quite the same down there after pushing out the babies. They can pretty up the scars, permanently remove hair. And, of course, tighten it up," Janie explained as she held two napkin samples out for inspection. "They have a Web site and everything. It's the latest trend in cosmetic enhancement."

And you would know, Marie thought, directing her anger at Mrs. Suburbia as she tried to comprehend the fact that there was more demand in this town for tight vaginas than prenatal care. "You see?! It's the goddamned patriarchy! Am I the only one upset by this? We're supposed to bear all these children, then undergo surgery so our husbands can have a better time fucking us?"

The women were quiet for a moment. Gayle and Love knew there was no point trying to calm her down—she'd already broken last year's resolution not to say *fuck*.

"If it's any consolation, the literature stresses that the procedures are meant to increase the *woman's* sexual pleasure. They specifically caution against undergoing surgery at a man's urging," Gayle added, knowing full well that none of this would placate Marie.

"You see! They're already covering their asses because they *know* this is about male pleasure. Just like Viagra and Levitra—always pitched as ways to better serve women, when every woman knows it's about men. How can a doctor trained to deliver babies betray women like this? And you notice that the only woman in the practice wanted no part of it!"

A collective sigh followed—what could be done?

"It's like they want to erase our lives." Marie was in deep thought now.

Everything could be erased—all evidence of having had children, having lived with a man so long there was nothing left to discover. Sure—shrink your vagina and it will all be new again. It was so ridiculous, glaring yet covert, manipulative. Like the seemingly innocuous pods from *Invasion of the Body Snatchers*. How many women, she wondered, would now be pulling out their compact mirrors, crouching over to inspect their imperfect vaginas? How many husbands would now wonder if a minor laser procedure could be the answer to their mundane sex lives? And there wasn't a damned thing Marie could do about it.

She glanced at Janie from across the table, and it was—at last—apparent to her why the woman got under her skin. No one would believe she was the forty-two-year-old mother of four.

"Down with the patriarchy! Let's revolt," Love said with sharp sarcasm.

Feeling Marie's thoughts upon her, Janie threw her hands up. "What patriarchy? This whole thing was probably concocted by one man with a little dick."

Everyone laughed, including Marie, who couldn't resist something crudely funny—even if it came from Janie Kirk.

Love forced herself to settle down as the pain began to crest. "Can we finish here? I don't think I can stay like this for long."

Returning to their tasks, they made the decisions, completed the order forms, and faxed them to the various vendors. The last item on the agenda was the plan for the yard. Removing it from the floor next to Love, Gayle felt a quiet unsettling in her stomach. These were the plans that had brought her to the garden with Paul that night, the night that had changed things between them.

"OK. Let's get started," Marie said, looking over Gayle's shoulder. But the drawing appeared to be finished.

"Actually, Paul and I worked on it."

Love strained her neck to look at Gayle. "Paul? Paul from the kitchen?"

"Yeah." She said it casually, though nothing had been casual about Paul since that night on her patio, since her visit to his apartment.

Marie said a quiet *oh,* raising her eyebrows, but otherwise holding back. "So, we are done. And I have to get the prisoner back."

Marie gathered her things, then helped Love up from the floor.

"Well, I guess I'll see you ladies at the dinner. We can handle the rest over the phone and e-mails, right?" Janie seemed eager to leave.

Gayle walked them out, waving after the last car as it made its way down the driveway. When she turned back toward the house, she saw a shadow in the room above the garage. On any other day, she would have thought little of it. She would have walked back into the house, cleaned up the glasses from the dining room, straightened the papers one more time before picking Oliver up from school. Today, she just stood, watching.

THIRTY-FOUR

TOO MUCH TALKING

"Do you still fuck your wife?" Janie asked while he was still inside her. She could have waited to ask. She could have not asked at all. But their meetings had become as much about irreverence as sex.

He propped himself up with his elbows so he could see her face. But he stayed on top of her, inside her when he gave his answer. "Sure."

"You say that like it was a foregone conclusion."

"Don't you still fuck Daniel?"

"I avoid it when I can."

He brushed a stray hair from her cheek. "Why? Are you in love with me?"

Janie laughed out loud. "Good God, no. But I can be myself here."

He pulled out of her and rolled over to the nightstand for a cigarette. "And you can't be yourself with Daniel?"

"No."

"Why?"

Janie waited for him to light up, then reached out for a drag as he sat beside her. "I don't know. I guess when you've been in love with someone—you know, when you've made love, felt them hold your face and look at you with desire and passion and adoration—real love, and then it's 'What's for dinner' followed by a closed-eyed quickie . . ." She paused for a sigh, trying to find the words to explain herself. "I feel betrayed."

He laughed now, but looked at her sweetly. "That's marriage, darling. What the hell did you expect?"

"Fuck off," she said.

"No, really," he said, his face as serious as she'd ever seen it. "See, I knew what I was getting into. All that stuff you feel at the start—it's just body chemicals. It can't last, the chemicals are there to make you want to fuck so the species will carry on. The *marriage*, on the other hand, is there for family structure. Children. It's a bargain."

"So you no longer desire your wife, but you still fuck her?"

"Yeah, I suppose that's right," he answered, then shrugged.

"Why?"

"Because she's my wife, and it's better than beating off."

"Do you think she likes it?"

He shrugged again, his face going for a look of innocence, but failing. "I don't know."

"What do you mean, *I don't know*? Does she moan, sigh, grab your ass to pull you deeper inside her? Does she kiss you when it's over?"

"OK, I see your point."

"Christ! Does she even climax?"

He looked at her and knew he was in trouble. *Did his wife cum when they fucked?* He really had no idea.

"Fuck, Janie! It's marriage! It's me. I'm a complete shit for cheating, but I'd never leave her. This is life, not some pretty little fairy tale."

"Oh, I am becoming more aware of that by the second. But let me ask you one more thing."

"Oh shit, here we go."

"Do you think your wife is glad that you don't leave her? Did you ever wonder what she thinks about when she lies in your bed tolerating your dick?"

He would have been offended if he were capable of it, but instead he smiled and waved his finger playfully in front of her face. "Aha! I know what this is about."

"You do?"

"Yes!" He crushed the cigarette into an empty glass, then crawled across the bed and back on top of Janie.

"You are not my wife, and I am not Daniel. My wife doesn't think about all this stuff. We're married. We fuck. We go on with the business of life."

Janie drew her arms to her chest, then pushed him off of her. "Great. I'm first in the shower."

He reached for her arm, but she slid it out from his grasp and began to gather her clothes from the floor.

"See, all this talking is just not good," he said, flopping back onto the bed. "Now you really are too mad to fuck."

With her arms overflowing with every trace of herself she could find in the room, Janie gave him a sarcastic smile, then retreated to the bathroom, slamming the door shut behind her. Hearing his laughter through the wall, she dropped her clothes and turned on the faucet. As she let the water run down her back, she found herself hoping he would leave, and not just because he was such a prick. He had never hidden that from her. And the truth of the matter was, she wasn't angry. At least not with him. But everything was changing between them. When they first started this thing they were doing, an affair for lack of a better name, he was at her beck and call. Making excuses at the office, he would drive out to meet her whenever she had a free moment. Now there were constraints on his time. Client meetings were suddenly in the way. They were settling into a kind of routine, the kind where his life was more important than hers. Maybe because of his job, or the drive from the city he had to make. Or maybe just because he was the man. Whatever the reason, the result was the same—she was now having to be more creative with her time, and the feeling that he wasn't worth it was beginning to take hold. They had done everything there was to do, exhausted their bag of tricks. The "body chemicals" he liked to blame his actions on were starting to fade. With no friendship between them, no shred of real intimacy, they were running out of road.

She heard him say something, then the sound of the door closing. He'd given up on the shower and rushed off, which was just fine with Janie. Rinsing her hair one last time in water that had become lukewarm, she turned the faucet handle and reached for a towel. It was not enjoyable, this shower in Room 221. The pressure was weak, the hot water fleeting. The plastic curtain stuck to her legs. That it gave her an excuse to retreat from the bed each time had become its only redeeming quality.

With the dry end of the towel, she wiped the steam from the mirror. She checked her face for any running makeup, the eyeliner being the worst offender most days, then picked up her clothes, which lay in a pile by the closed door. Pressing her face into the fabric, she inhaled deeply, checking for the smell of his cologne, or that sickening-sweet odor of stale cigarette smoke. It was getting old—all this worry. The effort to check for evidence of the two bad habits was becoming rote, and consequently vulnerable to slip-ups. Did she remember to hide the cigarettes in the glove compartment? Was the phone bill about to arrive, the only piece of physical evidence that might cause suspicion? These were the thoughts she had to concern herself with, the worries that woke her in the night. The morning would bring fresh resolve to give them up. After dropping the kids at school, she would toss the pack of cigarettes in the garbage bin in the back of the parking lot, screen the incoming calls on her cell. She would busy herself with errands, go to pilates. But the resolve always faded with the passing hours of the day, and before noon she would find herself at the gas-station counter, buying a new pack. She would find herself back in this room, smelling her clothes.

The ringing of her cell phone caught her by surprise. Still naked, she pulled her belongings to her chest as though the caller could see through the connection, finding her undressed in a motel bathroom. With the clothes clenched in one hand, she dug through her bag for the phone and checked the caller ID. It was Daniel's office.

Her heart pounded, almost choking out her breath. He never called her on her free afternoon. The kids were home with the sitter until five. It was her time, and he had always respected that. She reminded herself that it was just a phone call. *She was in a store. There was no noise because she was in the dressing room. Doing some shopping for summer clothing. Bathing suits.* She would find nothing that fit, feign her disappointment when he came home later, asking to see what she'd purchased.

She took a breath, then hit the answer key.

"Hello?" she said, her voice upbeat.

"Janie?" It was Daniel's secretary.

"Hi, Beth. What's going on?" Again, her voice was casual, and this time more natural. It was not unusual for Beth to call to check on dates for client functions.

She was beginning to feel relieved when the news was conveyed. "It's Daniel, Janie. I'm sorry to tell you on the phone, but I thought you'd want to know right away."

Janie pulled her clothes closer and leaned against the door. "What is it?"

"He had some sort of attack. He's at St. Vincent's." Her voice was somber. "They took him in an ambulance a few minutes ago."

With the phone pinned between ear and shoulder, Janie searched for her underwear, her mind focused on the quickest path to the hospital. "Was it his heart? What happened?"

Beth recounted the event. The chest pain, the shortness of breath. The medics taking him quickly. They hadn't said much.

With shaky hands, Janie hastily buttoned her shirt, then slipped on her shoes. She grabbed her things—a hairbrush, mouthwash, sunglasses—and shoved them into her bag. She ran for the door, car keys in hand.

"I'm on my way. Call the hospital. Tell them—I'm on my way."

She threw the phone on the passenger seat, her mind skipping forward to the worst outcome. She started the car and backed out of her space. Racing out of the parking lot to the road, she saw the faces of her children—young children who wouldn't understand. At her core, she was a realist. She knew these things happened, and rarely did they surprise her. The human body was a walking time bomb. Still, despite everything she told herself as she drove, nothing could chase the thought from her mind. Nothing ever would. She let it come forward, and the words left her mouth with resounding certainty.

"I did this."

THIRTY-FIVE

THE EVOLUTION OF MARRIAGE

MARIE WAS ALONE IN the office, and she could no longer resist the urge. She logged onto Yahoo! and typed in the words *laser vaginal rejuvenation.* The Hunting Ridge doctors had the top listing, apparently being the first practice in the nation to actually specialize in the tightening of vaginas.

With a tense jaw, Marie read through the flowery prose meant to sell the procedures to women who, until now, had most likely never given the appearance of their vaginas much thought. There was designer laser vaginoplasty to aesthetically enhance the vulvar structures through creative treatments. Or laser reduction labioplasty, in case your inner lips projected out beyond the outer. Of course, if you just wanted the look of a youthful vagina, then laser perineoplasty would be the way to go. You could even have your hymen reconstructed and actually become a virgin again. *Yippee!* There were package deals for all the treatments, and if you wanted head-to-toe rejuvenating, you might consider combining your vaginal procedures with a breast implant, liposuction, and facelift.

"Unfuckingbelievable. Now I have to get a designer vagina to live in

Hunting Ridge." Marie was in mid-sentence when she heard Randy come through the door.

"What?" he said, setting the bag with their takeout on his desk.

Marie started to close down the page. "Nothing."

She was too late.

"Is that a Georgia O'Keefe?"

Marie looked at the abstract flower in the right-hand corner of the Laser Vaginal Rejuvenation Web site and shook her head. "No. It's just a flower. Got it?! A flower."

Randy smiled, his eyebrows raised, as he watched the page disappear from Marie's screen. "Sorry. I just thought I saw the word . . . you know."

"What? Vagina? You did see it. But it wasn't Georgia O'Keefe." Marie was now standing and beginning to pace. "Georgia O'Keefe would be appalled by that Web site."

"So, what was it?"

He was teasing her now, baiting her to divulge the source of her more than apparent irritation.

"No. I will not corrupt you further. Did you get plates?"

Randy shook his head. "Sorry."

"I'll get something." Marie walked the few steps to the bathroom. When she returned with the roll of paper towels, Randy was standing over her computer.

"You sneak! Get away from there!"

Marie shoved him back to his desk, then closed her screen again. When she looked at him, he was holding back a smile.

"OK, fine. It seems the local obstetricians have opened a clinic to rejuvenate vaginas—and that is all I plan on saying."

Randy laughed. "Are you serious? Is that what it sounds like?"

"Yes. It's exactly what it sounds like. I told you—this town should be renamed Stepford."

"That is unbelievable. Is that something—I don't know—that women do?"

"Apparently," Marie said, shaking her head as she sat down. "I'm sorry, Randy."

Without a hint of the embarrassment that, by any accounting, should have been present, Randy pulled the containers from the bag and handed one to Marie.

"What for?"

"What for?! Christ, Randy, the things you've seen. I feel like I'm stealing your youth. After this summer, you're either going to be the most popular man at Yale Law, or—I don't know—joining the priesthood."

Randy laughed again, harder this time. "I'll let you know how that turns out."

"I'm serious. How will you ever get married after seeing this parade of crap?"

"I don't believe in marriage." He said it matter-of-factly in mid-bite, as though it didn't call into question the bedrock of nearly every society across the globe.

"You don't believe in marriage?" She tried to look at him in brief increments as she ate, maybe catch some expression on his face that might temper the impact of his statement. But there was nothing. He was dead serious.

"No. Have you ever studied it? Marriage?"

Marie sighed. From the tone of his voice, she knew—he was off again, in that overanalytical head of his. Aside from exercising one's intellect, what was the point of studying something that had been around forever—that was embraced as sacrosanct in every modern culture, from the West to the East, to the most primitive Third World societies. Marie was more concerned with figuring out how to make the damned thing work.

"The Evolution of Marriage, I think it was called."

"I bet you were the only guy in the class."

"There were two of us. Me and the professor."

"And what did this professor teach you that made you stop believing in marriage?"

"Just that the concept behind marriage—the lifelong monogamous union of a man and a woman—is contrary to the most basic aspects of human nature. Did you know there are only a handful of animal species that are monogamous? And scientists aren't even sure they truly are."

"But we're different from other animals. The most advanced species."

Randy let out a sarcastic laugh. "Supposedly."

With exacting conviction, he laid out his professor's theory on the origins of marriage. "Look, from everything we know about human existence, marriage in one form or another has been present since the beginning of recorded history. Before that time, we were cave dwellers, functioning like the small communes that can still be found on the fringe of some societies. The men were the hunters, leaving in packs for long stretches of time to find meat. The women were the gatherers, tending to the children and to each other, gathering plant-based foods to eat and to store for the months when the land was barren. Procreation was random, spreading genes throughout the clan, ensuring a wide cross-section of human offspring. It was Darwinism at its best.

"But over time, man began to herd animals, developing skills that enabled the clan to remain in one location indefinitely. This bred the desire to own property, and men began to carve out the land. Then they started to have desires about that land, putting so much work into the harvests and herding. They wanted to leave it to *their* children. That's where marriage came in. In order to leave property to *their* children, it became necessary to know whose offspring were whose. So, after thousands of years procreating at the whim of their desires, men found it necessary to have dominion over a woman, or several women as the case may be. They had to know that the children were by their seed, and no one else's. Henceforth, marriage was born—and now continues on as an artificial construct to facilitate property ownership."

Marie was quiet for a moment. What the hell could she say to *that*? She hadn't done much thinking about the history of mankind, or anything existential for that matter, since having children. There was simply no time, not when she had enough to analyze right outside her door. Still, her brain was far from atrophied.

"OK. Assuming all that is true, it seems to me that marriage also stems from the evolution of human intelligence, every bit as much as our sophisticated economies and understanding of the world. It's the evolution of love."

"Love is love. Marriage is about possession. Think about it. Think about everything you've said about Hunting Ridge housewives." Randy's face was serious, and it scared Marie that she had helped foster such cynicism in a man so young. "The complete division of labor where men work and women serve them, the submission of woman to man as the head of the household. With the exception of monogamy—which is really a myth when you look at the statistics—marriage has done very little to change the basic social structures of our ancestors. Yet people, as individuals, have evolved greatly. Hence—the persistent discontentment of the masses who subject themselves to marriage."

Marie put her fork down and popped open a Diet Coke. She looked at Randy, so casually eating away and spewing forth his theories as though they had no bearing on his life. And she'd actually started to believe she had him figured out.

"So you're saying that marriage is antithetical to evolution."

"Right."

"That people who get married will be forever stuck in the cave-man days."

"Right, only worse. Stuck in the cave with one cave man, one cave woman."

"Then how can you explain the fact that every movie, every love song, every school daydream is based on finding a spouse? Don't you believe in lifelong love?"

Randy was quiet for a moment, but only a brief moment. And in his response, Marie detected a sad resolve. "I don't know about love. But the rest of it is straight, unadulterated socialization. We're told to crave monogamous love from the day we're born. Of course it preoccupies us. Then we move on to money, religion, finding redemption before we die."

"I'm sorry," Marie said when he was finished.

He looked at her with a puzzled expression. "What for?"

Marie smiled. "I can't imagine life without the dream of love. Even when it's hard. Even when my ass of a husband is out playing golf. There's a reason I fight to get back to that place with him."

"I don't get that. You're one of the smartest people I know."

"You're young. Believe me, there are a lot of people smarter than I am."

Randy shrugged.

"Didn't your parents believe in love?"

"I think they did when they got married. But my mother needed her career. She was a professor, and there was a position at Stanford." Randy stopped himself, and Marie could see a piece of him now, clearly, through the small window her question had pried open.

"My mother left when I was four."

Marie drew a breath and, with everything inside her, held back from reaching over and taking his hand. In an instant, with that one statement, the things she had wondered about Randy Matthews dissolved into understanding. His obsession with marriage, his views on life and love. The reason he was pursuing a career in father custody law.

Feeling her pity, Randy looked at her squarely, the nonchalance returning to his face—the window closing. "I'm not who you think I am. Some poor, motherless kid."

"I don't think that."

"Yes, you do. But that's not who I am. I faced those demons a long time ago. I'm at peace with it. I have great respect for my mother. She made the only choice she could. She was miserable being a housewife, and my father refused to alter his career to accommodate hers. It was an impossible situation, manufactured by the institution of marriage. I can't help it that I see things for what they are. It's not something I can turn off so I can fit in with the rest of the world."

Marie smiled, nodding her head in a show of respect for his wishes. He did not want to be pitied, or judged, or stamped with a label, though she was not at all convinced he had escaped his childhood unscarred.

"OK," she said. "Is there anything else you'd like to share this afternoon?"

"No. Not unless you want to talk some more about vaginal rejuvenation." He was smiling now, his lighthearted spirit having taken over the room once again.

Marie crumbled up a paper towel and threw it at him, catching him squarely between his eyes.

They were still laughing when the phone rang.

THIRTY-SIX

THE REAL MRS. KIRK

JANIE DROVE THE CAR, unable to comprehend the thoughts that were in her mind. *Can he smell the smoke? What did I do with the key card?* Now beside her, his seat fully reclined to keep the blood flowing and a hospital band still attached to his wrist, was her husband.

Her fears had been put to rest the moment she arrived. It was a mild anxiety attack, one that was quickly resolved with medication. There was no imminent threat to his health. They had placed him on a monitor, prescribed a mild sedative. Then they'd released him into the care of his wife.

Listening to the doctor's explanation, his instructions for the next few days, and the longer-term plan to stave off compounding stress—never had she felt so disconnected from herself. She was the woman standing *beside* Mrs. Daniel Kirk—the other woman, the cheater, the liar, the ungrateful woman. Not to mention the closet smoker. There were so many secrets it seemed unbelievable that no one saw through the doting wife to the woman walking her husband to the car, helping him inside.

And now she was worried about getting caught.

"Are you OK?" she kept asking him again and again, as if acting the part might somehow transform her.

"Yes! I'm fine. Please, stop worrying," Daniel said. He was more embarrassed than worried, the attack having occurred at the office where explanations would now be required. Once he was certain that he was out of the woods, he had asked the doctor twice: *Are you sure there's nothing else wrong with me?* And his disappointment at the answer had surprised everyone but her.

"We'll think of something to tell them. Your medical records are private. They'll never know," she said, thinking she'd found a way to help.

"I can't let them think I'm weak, Janie. I'll be put out to pasture."

"What about a blood clot? In your leg, maybe. It cut the blood flow, made you dizzy. They can fix blood clots."

Daniel was watching her now, a strange look on his face. "I forgot how good you were at that."

Janie smiled, looking back at him for a second as she wound her way through the back roads of Hunting Ridge. "At what, Dan?"

"Lying."

The word stopped her cold. Still, she held the smile and managed a laugh. He was talking about her teenage years, the stories she'd shared with him about sneaking around her parents. She had been a wild child, and there was a time when he'd found that irresistible. He was referring to those years now, making an off-color joke to add some levity to a day that had terrified them both. That had to be it. That, and the sedatives—maybe.

Still, as good as she had been in covering her tracks, there were some things that could not be manufactured, subtle distinctions between those in love and those faking it that he might have picked up on. The weakness of her arms as she wrapped them around him to return a hug, the shortness of her looks when their eyes met across a romantic restaurant table. Her recoil at his touch in the bedroom. They were signs that were often spotted in retrospect, after a break-up, small details that in hindsight were glaring. It was possible Daniel had made an early detection.

Her throat felt constricted as she turned her eyes back to the road. How odd it was, this sense of utter panic at the negligible possibility of his knowing. Every time she'd been with the other man, from that explosive first encounter, to the things they'd done in that motel room, she had wondered if she wouldn't embrace her freedom if it were thrown her way. Yes, it would be complicated. Yes, the children would suffer. But she would not be human if the thought never came to pass. *What if he knows?* And now the answer stood before her, so clearly that it felt unshakable. She did not want him to know. Not because newfound love had magically washed over her. No—looking at him next to her, she could feel the same dearth of emotion that had driven her to abandon her own conscience. But the answer was there just the same. For whatever reason, she could not let go of her marriage.

THIRTY-SEVEN

THE PAST

"MOMMY, WHAT ARE YOU doing?"

With *Dora the Explorer* just ending, Jessica turned her attention to her mother and the book on her lap. Curious now, she moved closer until she was almost on top of her sleeping baby brother.

"Can I see?"

"There's nothing to see. It's grown-up reading," Love said, pulling the book away from her child. It was just paper and ink, but she felt an instinctual fear that it might somehow be toxic.

"Can I see?" Jessica asked again as she maneuvered around Baby Will and sat on a pillow near her mother's head. Love sighed, then opened to a page. Looking down at the words, Jessica pretended to read as she had seen Henry do, her face squinting with a concentrated stare.

"It's grown-up writing, Jess."

"About real monsters?"

Love tried not to laugh. In a futile attempt to bridge the television gap between Henry and Jessica, Love had made any movies with "real monsters" off-limits for Jessica. Scooby-Doo cartoons were OK, Harry Potter was not. Inadvertently teaching her three-year-old about real monsters was not exactly a proud parenting moment.

"No. No monsters. It's just about life."

"My life?"

"No. Nobody you know. Just a man."

Nobody you know . . . just a man. Just the girl's grandfather, whom she would likely never meet. For the best, Love imagined. Still, there was something terribly wrong about that.

The sound of Bill's voice in the hall downstairs had Jessica scooting off the bed.

"Daddy!" she yelled, and then she was gone, her attention fully diverted.

Love smiled as she watched her daughter bounce out of the room. A little blond jumping bean.

She returned the book to the night stand. She hadn't read it—not one word—and her defiance was comforting. That man was from her past, from another universe. And it was in that universe she had ended up in the hospital, nearly dead from a handful of pills. For years she had placed her father in the bin with everyone else who had written her off. Friends, the few she'd had, admiring researchers who'd followed her progress, investing their time and energy. She'd spun out of control, placed their reputations in jeopardy. Her self-destruction had been almost passionate as she immersed herself in degradation. But none of it could take back that night when she was still a girl, or quiet the shame that ate away at her day after day until, finally, she could take no more. Her mother's pills had been right there, the ones Yvonne had been too righteous to take. Those with front-row seats had orchestrated the spin to keep the story quiet—that after years of a troubled existence, Love Welsh had tried to take her life, but like everything else had failed.

It was in the aftermath of that ugly truth that she'd met Dr. Bill Harrison, the reason she had these three beautiful children. Still, no one ever spoke about it. Not her mother, whose Valium she'd taken—an old prescription that Yvonne had been given when her own mother died. Not Bill, who'd been on his ER rotation. Not even her father, who had been cunning enough to keep it from the media, releasing a statement from New York that very night to the effect that his daughter had been admitted for dehydration and exhaustion following a flu. There'd been no way to prove that she'd suffered an overdose without violating medical confidentiality, so the tabloids had printed the bullshit story, then left it alone. And, as it turned out, the public cared so little about her by then that the story died before the slightest amount of speculation began to gather speed.

Even so, her world had finally crashed that night, leaving her adrift. Still alive but immersed in the sickening feeling of death, she had ruled out another suicide attempt. And yet the same emptiness was there, taking the more subtle form of depression where a powerful anxiety had once been. She'd taken to sidewalk cafés where she could drink coffee and smoke, and most of all, not be home where her mother's guilt stared her down in every room. At twenty-five, her life had felt over.

Six months later, she'd heard his voice over her shoulder. "Don't I know you from somewhere?"

She'd braced herself for the humiliation—turning to face some L.A. star-seeker who would quickly realize she was one of the fallen. As it happened, it was far worse.

"Dr. Harrison," she'd said, lighting a cigarette. "Yeah, you know me. Give it a second and it'll come to you."

Dr. Bill Harrison had been the only thing from her overdose that she'd allowed herself to remember, and she had used the thought of him to comfort herself in the dark moments that came and went. When he was before her again, the fear that he would reflect on her weakness with disdain had been more than she could bear. She'd taken a long drag on her cigarette and masked her feelings with a façade of indifference.

But with disarming kindness, the young doctor had simply smiled.

"Love Welsh." His voice had been full of delight.

"Nothing gets past you, Doctor," she'd said, still feeling irreverent.

"May I?" He'd pulled out a chair then and sat down at her table before she could answer.

"How are you doing?" He was concerned, and his sincerity had pulled her in.

"I'm better," she'd lied. And he'd seen through it.

"Really? You look kind of thin. Have you been eating?"

They talked then, about her, about suicide and depression. Bill spoke from his brief experience on a psych-ward rotation, and as the son of parents who lived their lives in a state of perpetual unhappiness. Without the slightest hint of judgment, he'd pulled from her things she had told only a select few, things she had thought she would never tell another living person. And he'd listened with the patience that was his way.

"I have to go. I have rounds," he'd said at the end, and Love felt like grabbing him and never letting go. Then, with a boyish nervousness, he had continued. "But maybe we can do this again. Can I call you?"

Closing her eyes now, Love thought about how easy it had been. She'd written down her number, and he'd called the next day. And the next, and the day after that. On their third date, she'd laughed for the first time in a very long time, and by the end of that month, she never wanted to look back. When Bill gave her a way out, she took hold without thinking. Moving east to raise a family, leaving L.A. for dense woods and suburban charm had been the surest path to leaving it all behind. And the illusion that she no longer cared still meant something. Happily married, content with the sacred occupation of motherhood—all of it protected her from the scrutinizing glare of her own failings. She'd sent little cards to some of her former teachers, announcing the arrival of each of her three children. And some had sent back gifts and kind notes. *So happy you've found a life for yourself . . . congratulations . . . looks like everything worked out.* If they suspected for a moment that she cared about the life she'd thrown away, they would think her pathetic, and that was not something Love could bear. Especially not from her father.

She looked now at Baby Will curled up beside her, then at the book on her other side. It didn't matter what her father had revealed. The past was back, living inside her. She could feel it now, now that she was stopped dead in her tracks. The daily tasks that had occupied her for years were being done by others—her mother, Bill, and her friends—as she lay in bed, her back in agony. There was nothing for her to do but think. And remember.

THIRTY-EIGHT

GETTING IN DEEP

"I'LL GET IT. YOU go home," Randy said, reaching for the receiver. Marie mouthed a *thank you*, then started for the door.

"Wait!"

When she turned around, he had his hand over the mouthpiece. "It's the Farrells' neighbor," he said in a whisper, his eyebrows raised.

Marie dropped her bag at the door and bounded back to the desk, waving her hand for the phone.

"Can you hold on a second?" Randy asked the woman—the one neighbor who had children in the same age range as the Farrells'. Randy had left a message for her two days before, but had since given up on hearing back. He hit the *hold* key, then looked at Marie.

"What's her name?"

"Andrea Rasman. Three kids—ten, six, and two. The two-year-old is a little girl."

"That's how old Simone Farrell would be."

Randy nodded. "They're a few houses down from the Farrells' old place."

"OK." Marie exhaled deeply as she reached for the phone. She looked at the red blinking *hold* key, but did not touch it. There was no doubt in her mind that something was not right with the Farrell case. The domestic disturbance that no one had mentioned—not even Connely, Carson's fear of Marie asking too many questions of his wife, and his insistence that Marie help him get to the other kids—increased visitation, overnights, vacations. He had not sanctioned an interview with his neighbor. In fact, he had instructed her not to dig into their past beyond what he himself was willing to disclose. She was violating his trust, her fiduciary responsibility to him as a client.

But there were three small children whose baby sister was dead.

She looked at Randy for reassurance, a first-year law student who couldn't possibly know which call to make. She looked to him just the same because he knew what was going through her mind and, at the very least, could share her uncertainty.

"Want me to do it?" he asked, giving her an out. He wasn't a lawyer yet. The worst thing that would happen to him was a scolding from their client.

Marie shook her head, then placed the phone on Speaker and released the Hold.

"Mrs. Rasman?"

"Yes."

"My name is Marie Passeti. I'm a lawyer down in Hunting Ridge, Connecticut. I was hoping you could help me with a case. It involves the Farrell family."

"The Farrells?" The woman sounded curious.

"Yes. Did you know them?"

There was a slight pause before the answer arrived. And when it did, Marie could tell from the woman's tone that a decision had just been made. "We did. They don't live here anymore."

"I hope you don't mind the Speaker. I've got my hands full at the moment," Marie lied. She wanted Randy to hear the call, but wouldn't risk involving him further.

"No. That's fine."

"I'm representing Carson Farrell in the divorce."

Andrea Rasman let out an audible sigh. "Oh," she said. "They didn't make it?"

Marie looked at Randy, who was now taking notes at his desk.

"No. And now Mrs. Farrell wants sole custody. Because of the accident, she's claiming Carson isn't fit to care for the children."

"That's too bad," she said, and Marie found herself surprised at the woman's apparent sincerity.

"It is. I was hoping you could give me your impressions—about both parents. Carson appears to be a good father."

"He was. You know, from what I saw. Mostly I was with Vickie and the kids. They all went to school together. Most afternoons they'd wind up in one yard or the other."

"I know how that goes. I have two of my own. It's great living so close to other families."

"We knew all the kids. They moved here just after their second was born. Then they had the next two. It was so tragic. Simone was the sweetest little girl."

"That's what I hear. Carson is still shaken up about it."

There was no response.

"Is there anything you can tell me about the family—the Farrells' relationship, or any problems with the kids?"

"Oh, no. Those kids were angels. Did great in school."

"Did any of them see a psychiatrist for any reason?"

"Not that I knew of. They were always home after school. No regular appointments or anything like that."

"And the parents?"

"That I wouldn't know," she said, then tried to explain further. "Vickie and I were friends because of the kids. We really didn't talk much. Just phone calls to make sure we knew where everyone was. Whose house they were at. They really kept to themselves. I tried for a while to get them to come over for dinner, but she always made excuses. Finally, I just stopped asking."

Marie felt herself tensing up. This woman had to know something useful after living three doors down for five years.

"What about the incident with the police? A little while before the accident. Did you know about that?"

Again, there was a distinct hesitation. "Who did you say you were representing?"

Randy looked up from his notes, holding his breath.

"Carson Farrell."

Marie waited, trying to interpret the silence on the line. She was close to giving up on Andrea Rasman when the voice came through the box.

"I knew. Everyone knew. We had some new neighbors—an older couple who moved in. It's the house on the right of the Farrells' old place. We were all used to it. No one liked it, but calling the police? That's a little over the top. I suppose they didn't know what was happening, maybe thought someone was in trouble."

"Was it really that frequent?" Marie asked, pretending that none of this was news to her.

"I'm sure Carson played it down. He's like that. Very private."

Marie felt a surge of adrenaline. "How often did they fight?"

Andrea Rasman spoke, and now seemed committed to telling what she knew. "*Very* often. After Simone was born. To their credit, they kept it away from the kids. There was a lot of anger, from what I could tell. I think the fourth child pushed them over the limit. You could hear her at night—especially when the weather turned warmer and the windows were open."

"You said *her*. You mean the baby?"

"Not the baby. *Vickie Farrell.* Honestly, Carson had the patience of a saint."

Marie turned to look at Randy, who was now standing beside her.

"He's a good man," Marie said, trying to cover her confusion.

"Yes, he was. *Is*. I hope he gets to see his kids. That's really all I know. I'm sure you got all of this from Carson."

"It's OK. I'm glad to have an outside source if we wind up in court. You've been very helpful."

"OK."

"Have a good night," Marie said, disconnecting the call.

"Damn." Randy was sitting back down. "What's going on here?"

Marie felt her heart pounding. This was not what she had expected, and her mind was spinning with the possibilities.

"What do we know about Farrell's firm? Is there anyone there we can talk to?"

"Marie . . . ," Randy started to say. It was one thing to snoop around the neighborhood with people the Farrells would never see again. But the firm was far riskier.

"Just tell me what you know."

"It's a small retail operation. They used to have offices in Manhattan, Boston, and Chicago but the market decline left them only in New York. Boston closed when the Farrells moved. It's the reason they moved. Chicago folded last year."

"Farrell got transferred to New York. What about the rest of the place?"

"Not sure. I can look up the company annual reports and do a cross reference of names."

"No. I need his secretary. How can we find her?" Marie asked, already thinking of an answer herself.

"We have to go back through *everything*. Phone records, check registers—maybe he gave her a Christmas bonus. The deposition transcript. I need to find her name without raising any eyebrows. Then I need to find her."

Randy studied Marie's face, thinking he could understand where she was going with all of this. "I'll do it. You go home. The girls are waiting."

Marie got up from her chair, then sat back down. She reached for the phone and hit the speed dial for Anthony's office. "No," she said, waiting for the connection. "They can hang out at Love's until Anthony gets home. For once, he can put my work first. This is too important."

THIRTY-NINE

EMPTY ROOMS

"Have you seen Paul?"

He had stayed in the shadows since that afternoon, the day Gayle could not chase from her thoughts, but today he was literally nowhere.

Celia shook her head, and when she did, Gayle caught something in her expression that was alarming. It was a look of innocence, a quality the young woman did not possess.

He was always back by five. Neatly dressed, clean-shaven, unobtrusively moving through the kitchen to prepare dinner. It was almost six thirty now.

"Did he say anything to you?" she tried once more, though she knew the answer.

"No." Again, the feigned ignorance sent Gayle into a panic.

"Watch Oliver," she said.

Rushing out the back entrance to the driveway, Gayle turned her eyes to the apartment above the garage. No lights were on. She kept moving, around to the back, up the narrow staircase to the door. She knocked hard several times, unconcerned with how this would all seem if he came to answer—the worried look on her face, the hurried breath. She knew he was not coming. Cupping her hands at the window, she peered inside to the kitchen. It was just as she thought it would be. Empty.

She turned the knob. It was unlocked. She walked inside, this time taking it slow, delaying the discovery that was now inevitable. So much was as it had been—the chair, the lamp, the easels. The couch where she had sat with him. But there was no sign of Paul. The easels were empty. The sketches, the portfolios—everything was gone. The only personal effects remaining were the books, stacked neatly in the corner.

Standing dead center in the room, Gayle let out the breath she'd been holding. He was gone, and she'd known it before reaching the top of the stairs.

Hearing a car pull up, Gayle moved to the window. It was Troy, and it was too early for him. She backed away, out of sight, then waited for him to pull the car in and make his way to the house. Paul was gone. Her husband was home. And the thought that had been submerged for days began to rise, inching out the heartache that was beginning to take hold. With cautious movement, she left the room, the apartment, and closed the door behind her. She walked down the steps, then around the formal side of the house, the part that would be empty. Like a criminal, she stayed close to the walls and ducked under the windows until she was at the front door. She pushed it open, slowly, then went inside. She could hear the voices in the other room, Troy trying to roughhouse with his son. Oliver's strained laughter. Quietly, she walked up the front staircase, then down the hallway to her room. She closed the door, went to the bathroom, then closed that door as well, locking it shut.

She opened the vanity drawer and searched for the Xanax. She removed two, then swallowed them with some water. She walked to her chair and sat down, looking at herself in the mirror. She thought of the sketch she had seen so briefly, the ageless, beautiful portrayal Paul had made of her. Looking at that same face now with indifference, it occurred to her that for the first time in her life, she had been able to see that beauty, as though the image Paul created had been transposed onto her flesh. And she had begun to believe that he saw her that way as well. How ridiculous she had been, thinking about Paul like this. As a friend, a confidant. And, if she were truthful, as more than that. Still, she had thought those things and they had made her happy. Even as thoughts and little more, they had filled her with a lightness that she had not fully appreciated until just now—now that they were gone.

She waited until the light buzz rang in her ears. Then a calm started to trickle in. She walked downstairs where Celia was making dinner for her son. At the stove, stirring pasta, the young woman was laughing at some banal comment made by her husband—something said to Oliver that had left him unamused. Sitting at the island on a bar stool, Troy put his arm around his son, jostling him hard.

"That's my kid for you. Can't take a joke."

Gayle said nothing, but lifted Oliver into her arms.

"Paul left today," she said matter-of-factly.

"I know. We'll find someone else," Troy answered. Then he shot a look at Celia, who looked back with questioning eyes.

Through the haze of the medication, and with her vision partially blocked by Oliver who was draped around her like a rag doll, Gayle could still see it. The sequence of events rolled out before her. Her visit to Paul's apartment. Celia watching her as she left, asking why she was late to pick up her son. Paul's interruption that horrible day in the kitchen. Now Paul was gone and Troy was not asking questions—not bitching about the unreliability of the underclass. Instead, he was exchanging guilty looks with the nanny.

She would have found it comical, the two puerile creatures standing before her in her own kitchen, in the room that Paul once occupied. But instead, she imagined what was said to that kind man, the berating, chastising statements that her husband undoubtedly spewed forth along with his order of dismissal. That was why there had been no good-bye, not even a note explaining his departure. Compromising her further was the last thing Paul would do.

"Mommy, I'm tired," Oliver said in her ear. She squeezed him hard, then set him down. Taking his hand, she led him out of the room.

"We're going to read a book. Call when dinner's ready." Her voice was dismissive, and it caught the others by surprise. Still, she imagined they were relieved that she was going, providing them with a chance to get their stories straight.

FORTY

THE POWWOW

THEY MET ON THE Passetis' porch, the two generals in charge of Love's illness. Yvonne, who had called the powwow, settled the four older children in front of a video and rocked Baby Will to sleep in his stroller, leaving Bill with no excuses.

He gave his kids one last check before joining his mother-in-law, who had already made herself comfortable on a wicker chair.

"I only have a minute," he said. "What's this all about?"

Yvonne squinted her eyes at him and shook her head. "Oh, sit down already. The kids are fine."

She waited then for Bill to pull a chair over from the other side of the porch—his every movement exaggerated as though she were making him dig trenches in cement.

"OK. All set?"

Bill nodded, then leaned back in the chair. "I suppose so."

"Good. Now I want to talk to you about Love."

"Really?" Bill said sarcastically.

Yvonne ignored him. "I've heard you out—all your talk about these viruses with no name that can hurt people. I've helped her out the door for the tests. I've filled the prescriptions for the painkillers, the antibiotics, anti-inflammatories, and all the other pills. I've told her to take them even though they knock her out and kill her appetite. All I ask now is that you hear me—start to finish."

With his blood pressure rising, Bill drew a long breath and pretended he owed her this. Hadn't he let her subject Love to that pseudo-shrink? It was days later and there was no sign of improvement.

"OK. I'm listening."

"Are you, really?"

"Yes. I'm really listening."

Yvonne's face relaxed then, relieved to have his attention. Still, she spoke carefully, knowing this could be her last chance.

"Can you also assume for this conversation that there might be some possible connection between Love's emotional state and what has happened to her, even if it's simply to consider that her emotions put her under stress that made her body vulnerable—to the fall, the virus, whatever?"

Bill nodded, again breathing deeply to control his growing impatience.

"Good," Yvonne said, nodding with satisfaction. "Now, has she told you about the—"

"Letter? Yes, I know about the letter. The one you found in her papers. She told me the night you dug it out." His tone was judgmental, and Yvonne let it slide. She probably deserved it, and she didn't care.

"And do you understand what her father's book could mean for her?"

Now his impatience was pulling ahead. "Yvonne, she's my *wife*. Do you remember how we met?"

"Yes. Of course you know about her troubled teen years, the suicide attempt, the estrangement from her father . . ." She paused then, almost afraid to go on. But she did.

"What I need to know," she said, leaning forward to see into his eyes, "is whether she's told you about the night it all began."

Bill looked away, not wanting to witness the agony that was taking shape within the contours of her face. It was always there in traces—even the lines burrowed through her soft skin seemed to reflect the years of pain. Still, she hid it well, through a false smile or haughty know-it-all expression. All of that was gone now, exposing the force that had become her core.

He struggled to answer her. "I think so. The night of her father's party. Is that what you mean?"

Yvonne cupped her face with her hands as she shook off the emotions that were building. She needed to get through this, get through to Bill. This could not turn into a therapy session for *her*.

"Yes. So you *do* know."

Bill nodded. "It was the night her father told her he was ending her studies. That he needed to focus on his own career."

"I see." Yvonne stopped to gather her thoughts, realizing now that he knew very little. How could she possibly make him understand? Still, it wasn't her place to tell him.

"She's never confronted her father about that night. She's never asked him why he abandoned her. And now—for months—she's been living with the fear that he's planning to tell the world about everything she did. No one could endure that much despair without consequence."

Bill pulled on the ends of his eyebrows as he always did in the face of this much discomfort.

"Have you read it?"

Yvonne shook her head. "She won't let me go near it. I promised her."

"What if he didn't betray her?"

"It wouldn't matter much. The point is that he's back in her life, even if only as thoughts and memories." She looked at him with conviction. "Bill, she has never dealt with that night and the years that followed. *Never*. She's managed to hide behind all of this—the house and kids. But it hasn't worked, can't you see that? The letter was just the key that opened the door."

"OK," Bill said, trying to bring the conversation under control. "So what are you proposing?"

"I want her to see him. He's in L.A. for a few weeks trying to hammer out a movie deal for his book. I want her to fly home with me and see him."

Bill stood up, his face growing angry. "Are you crazy? She can barely walk down the stairs and you want her to fly across the country and dive into the center of the storm? How the hell is that going to help her?"

"It just is," Yvonne answered, struggling to remain calm. She had expected his reaction and practiced her own. But she hadn't expected him to be blinded by the fog of misinformation.

"That's it—enough pretending and assuming. I'll give you that she hasn't dealt with her issues from her crazy childhood. But she is sick. You have to understand that. My wife, your daughter—their mother," he said, pointing toward the house, "is *sick*. And if we get distracted by anything else instead of trying to get her well . . . I can't even think what might happen." He turned from her then as he felt the swell inside him. Since the day of the fall, he hadn't allowed himself to come to this place—the place inside him where he held the worst possible fear. And it was more than he could bear. He felt the flush in his face, the tears, then the gentle hand on his shoulder.

"All right," Yvonne said. "It's all right. We're all more scared than we let on. And I don't want to argue with you. I just want you to think about it. Maybe not now, but later when you've had some time."

Bill shook his head. "I will never allow it. Never."

He brushed her hand from his shoulder and marched toward the front door to retrieve his children.

FORTY-ONE

THE KISS

SORTING THROUGH THE FARRELL documents, they'd been over it again and again.

"I just don't get why Carson Farrell is protecting her. *She* was the one losing her temper, and I have little doubt now that she was the one seeing the shrink. Now she wants to take his kids and he's holding back." Marie had been so focused on Farrell's evasiveness she had overlooked the obvious. Now they had more questions than answers.

Randy caught her eye, then smiled. "Don't ask me. You're the one who believes in true love."

Marie had considered love as the answer. For the better part of an hour, she had placed herself in Farrell's shoes, asked herself how far she would go to protect Anthony from embarrassment if he were trying to take the girls from her. Taking into account even the truest of loves, the answer was indisputable. Anyone trying to take her children would face the fight of his life.

"The police report alone should have forced Connely to back down. He should have had Vickie Farrell at the settlement table from day one. And that's not even bringing in the shrink."

Randy nodded, enjoying his role tonight as Marie's audience. He had come to understand her need to reason out loud, and to enjoy the bird's-eye view into her mind. There weren't many situations she couldn't dissect—most things having a cause and effect that could be uncovered. She could trace the lines, follow the motives of the players, even when they were mired in emotional muck. There was only one place she fell short, and that was where they now found themselves—facing the irrational.

"It's the wild card," Randy said when she stopped talking. "Some people, some things just can't be explained."

Marie thought about his mother, wondering if she was the reason he could accept the unacceptable. They might not know what was lurking in Carson Farrell's psyche, but that did not mean it was unknowable. Everything had an explanation.

"We have to find this secretary. She would have handled the medical reimbursements for the shrink. And that would make her curious, listening more closely to Farrell's conversations, tuning in on office gossip. She could know more than anyone."

"Now look who's stereotyping."

Marie laughed, then reached for her phone. "I'd better call the girls."

She stopped laughing when Love's mother answered her phone. "Yvonne? Where's Anthony?"

Yvonne sounded calm—or, rather, *calming*. "Don't worry. Everyone's fine."

"Anthony should have been there by now."

Yvonne was silent, and Marie knew she wasn't going to like whatever it was that was not being said. "What?" she asked.

"It's fine . . . ," Yvonne started to say, and Marie knew it could only mean one thing.

"He's hitting balls, isn't he?"

"He called a little while ago. I told him to go. Bill took his kids home—I think he wants some quiet family time," she said, trying not to reveal her worry at his hasty departure. "That leaves me and the girls, and they're no trouble at all."

"That's not the point," Marie said, exhaling loudly.

"Marie? You still there?"

"I'm here."

"It's no trouble. *Really*. It's such a beautiful night. Let it go."

"All right," she said, though there was no chance of that. "Is Love doing OK?"

Yvonne hesitated. "Yes, fine. We're all fine. You just do what you have to do."

Marie thanked Yvonne again, told her she'd finish up and come home soon. Then she hung up the phone.

It was no mystery what had just unfolded. Still, Randy asked the question.

"Is everything all right?"

Marie shook her head. Her face was flushed. "No."

There was so much more she wanted to say out loud, thoughts that were burning a hole inside her. Every night, she made sure she was home for the girls. Every night, she made dinner or fetched the takeout, even when the work was piled up. She could easily stay at the office the way Anthony did so many nights, indulging the desire to stay on top of things—to feel professional, for once. Instead, she took it all on herself, borrowing time anywhere she could, paying the price somewhere down the line. And for this one night, she had asked her husband to be home for her so she could figure out this damned case—the case that had been dogging her since it began.

"Do you want to go home?" Randy asked, not at all sure how to help her.

"No."

Marie pulled a rubber band from a group of check registers. "When did the shrink visits start?"

Her words were clear, but her voice was shaky. Something inside of her was coming undone.

"Just after Simone was born."

She started to check the front of each register for the dates, but they fell to the ground.

"Damn it!" Marie said, reaching to the floor to pick them up.

Randy leaned down to help her. "Here," he said placing them one at a time back on her desk.

He was close now, too close. Marie pushed her chair away, then walked to the back of the office. She tried to focus her thoughts on the case, on the woman they were trying to locate and the things she might tell them. But other thoughts occupied her mind—the frustration from the day, the anger at her husband that had been snowballing for weeks. She was beyond fighting it.

Randy left his desk and approached Marie. Standing before her, he emptied his expression of all expectation, searching her eyes for some indication of what he should do. Helplessness cast a bright light on his youth, his inexperience. Still, the resolve to reach her remained.

Feeling the tears on her face, Marie brushed them off. *Fuck*, she thought. She never cried. She started to speak, but for the life of her could not think of what to say. As complicated as she liked to think herself, Randy Matthews had figured her out in a matter of days—her mind, her guilt, the conscience that was now failing her. He had watched her fall apart, seen her miscalculate. Still, he held onto an admiration that was no longer an awkward presence between them. Instead, it had grown into a deep caring that he now wore on his face.

"I . . ." She started to speak, but he stopped her. Moving forward with conviction, he placed his hands on her face and pulled her to him, his lips pressing against her mouth, which was still searching for words. She felt his chest against her as they leaned into the wall. His hands were strong. The kiss was still, holding them like statues against one another. She thought of one word. *Stop*. She heard it screaming from the inside out but chose to ignore it. She told herself there was no danger here. It was just a kiss, the manifestation of adolescent attraction, which could now, maybe, be put to rest.

That was all this was—her arms wrapped around his neck, his hands glued to her face, open palms softly cupped behind her ears. And although everything about him—from the body she could now feel against her, to the fullness of his wavy hair—was drawing her in, she willed herself to move away. Still, as she tried to retreat, she kissed him harder, as if it were somehow possible to draw from the kiss the way he looked at her, the way she felt when she was with him—so extraordinary, so perfectly flawed and human, and yet superhuman. She kissed him as though she could take him with her, outside of this moment.

Then she stopped. Feeling her pull back, Randy looked at her, his hands still unable to let go of her face.

"I have to go." She slipped her arms from around his neck and gently placed her hands on top of his, pulling them from her. Releasing the last thread of their embrace.

"I'm so sorry," Randy said, still feeling the kiss that had just passed between them, the young intern and the married woman. No matter how little he thought of marriage, never had he imagined himself capable of stepping inside one, pulling at fabric that was already beginning to unravel.

But Marie shook her head. "No. Don't be sorry." Pressing her hand against the side of his face, she smiled at him. "We both know this has been building for a while," she said, then walked back to her desk. She reached for the jacket that she'd left draped over her chair. She checked the clock. Not five minutes had passed. As she gathered her things, she could feel the disruption within her. Each action—packing up documents, searching for her keys—felt intolerably cruel.

"Don't do that." Randy was soon beside her, his actions similarly grounded in the mundane, his mood heavy.

"Do what?" she asked without looking at him.

"Don't be so . . . shit, I don't know. So casual."

She stopped now, this time turning to meet his eyes. "I'm not being casual." Then she took his hand. "This is killing me."

He started to move toward her, but she let go of his hand. "No, I have to go. You know I have to go."

She hurried now, stuffing things into her bag, looking for the keys she'd already found and misplaced yet again.

"Are you OK?" she asked him before turning for the door.

"I'll be fine. I'll lock up when I'm done." He was at his desk now, resuming the search as though nothing had happened. Still, he was immersed in a discernible sadness.

Walking away from Randy Matthews, Marie could almost feel the resistance, each step requiring a greater effort than the one before it. How stupid she had been to think that this would be easy, that her age had somehow imbued her with the kind of wisdom that could battle the most basic human need to be adored, to be seen with such clear definition. That she had surprised herself by pulling away so quickly was meaningless. She could see that now, as she got into her car, closing the door. That kiss—a fully clothed, subtle encounter—was more intimate than any moment she'd shared with her husband in a long time. Years, perhaps. And it was clear to her now that there was more than a trifling flirtation between them. This kiss was the physical embodiment of need, the kind of need that rises from the hollowest spaces. How could she not crave it again and again and again?

As she drove toward home, toward the husband she was mad at, the kids who would be mad at her for being so late, and the life she had built that rendered her so uncertain, it occurred to her that she had been wrong. Letting her mind go where it wanted, she could feel his hands pressed against her face, his soft lips, the warmth of his skin. There was no denying it. She could feel the danger of that kiss.

FORTY-TWO

REACHING IN

JANIE MADE POPCORN, TWO microwave bags that she divided evenly into four little bowls. She placed the bowls on a tray, added juice boxes, a beer, and a glass of wine. It was movie night at the Kirk house—a celebration of Daddy's little vacation from work. It was something he could do with his kids, a way of incorporating them into his new life as a couch potato.

All in all, Daniel Kirk was enjoying the convalescence. He spent his days watching sports, his nights watching sports. Janie brought him food and beer. His kids came in now and again to check on him. He'd caught up on the local news, thumbed through a pile of magazines, and e-mailed everyone he knew. The firm had accepted the small blood-clot theory and his request for a few days off to recover. They'd sent a basket of fruit and a get-well card signed by his coworkers and all the secretaries. And to Janie he seemed quite happy, indeed.

She carried the tray into the TV room, where *The Incredibles* was getting underway. They'd seen it a hundred times, and the kids were already showing signs of boredom. Still, it was more TV than they were normally allowed on a school night—and there was popcorn and juice to be had. No one was complaining. Janie took in the scene as she made her way from the kitchen. Four kids huddled around their dad. A family night. A *family*. She felt the knot in her stomach, the same one that had been there for weeks. *Please,* she thought to herself. *Love this man again.* Was it really that hard to do? He was handsome. He made good money. He loved his kids. And he was faithful.

"Popcorn has arrived!" she announced, setting the tray on the coffee table.

"Mine! Mine!" The cries echoed across the room as little hands reached for the bowl that seemed to have more.

"Guys . . . there's plenty of popcorn! Come on, no fighting."

Janie struggled to sort them all out, pulling them back onto the couch so they could hold their bowls and juice as they watched the television. Daniel grabbed his beer, then gave her a wink as she sat down on the other end of the couch.

"You ready to go back next week?" she asked after a short while, looking at her husband over the heads of their children.

Daniel shrugged. "Sure. I feel fine."

Janie nodded. "You don't think it'll be too much?"

"Nah. I just need to work out more, get rid of the stress."

He was completely nonchalant.

"Do you ever . . . ," Janie started to say, then stopped and took a long sip of wine.

Daniel seemed content letting it go as well, drinking his beer and pretending to be interested in the movie.

But Janie felt desperate to reach inside him—to pull something out that she might connect with.

"Do you ever think that this is all too much? The pressure, I mean."

He was feeling defensive now, she could see it in his face, his body language. "No. I don't. It was one time. Too much work, not enough sleep. You know that."

"I mean, do you ever think about doing something else? Something less stressful? You love sports, maybe you could coach or something."

"Oh, right," Daniel said, becoming sarcastic. "And who's going to pay for all your pedicures?"

"I'm trying to have a conversation here. Maybe this was a wake-up call that we need to think about things."

His face was red, the blood was racing, and that was exactly what had landed him in the hospital. Janie read him perfectly. He was in the first flight, the championship class. And now she was suggesting he couldn't handle it, that he wasn't as good as the rest of them. It was a direct affront to his manhood—the only kind of manhood he understood.

"Whatever. You think about things. I'm watching a movie with my kids."

Janie drew a long breath and let it out slowly. Truth be told, she didn't want to leave this life either. She liked the house, the Mercedes, the schools, and—yes—her weekly pedicures. But could they at least have a conversation? Having conversations—real grown-up conversations where two people listen to each other with respect and interest and understanding—had never been what they were about. And she had never thought of it as a deficiency. But as she watched him now from the corner of her eye, she wondered what was on his mind, in his heart. Was it possible not to know after nearly twenty years together?

Daniel finished his beer and reached across the couch to hand her the empty bottle.

"Do you mind?" he asked nicely. His demeanor had done a 180, now that he needed something.

"Sure," Janie said, getting up to fetch another beer. And as she left the room, she wondered if he had any idea what he'd just done.

FORTY-THREE

PACKING

STANDING IN THE CENTER of her tiny makeshift bedroom, Love scanned the corners for items she was forgetting to pack. It had been years since she'd traveled anywhere without her kids in tow, and her mind was simply unaccustomed to the self-indulgent worries that were now upon her. *Bring a swimsuit or not? Pack two pairs of shoes or one? Remember contact lens solution, face moisturizer, a neck pillow for the plane.* The few times they had ventured forth on a family trip, she'd packed late at night, shoving what she could into the remaining spaces of the bags. After the kids' clothing, toys, books, diapers and bottles, there was never enough room, or time, to consider her own needs. And in the end, it mattered little. The word *vacation* when small children were involved meant nothing more than a trip away from home.

This wouldn't be much different, she told herself. It was a two-day sprint to L.A., accompanying her mother home—and meeting with her father.

She'd fought Yvonne for nearly a week, using Bill for cover. Something had happened between the two of them, some plate-shifting quake that now had them worlds apart—Yvonne convinced that Love needed resolution with the past, and Bill adamantly opposed to the idea. The moment he left for work, Yvonne would sneak upstairs to lobby her cause. *Read that damned book already! Call your father.* And when he returned home, her husband would present her with the latest viral research from around the globe. Back and forth she'd gone in her mind. *I'm fine. I'm dying.* And the uncertainty had become unbearable.

Then, two days ago she'd put a stop to it. For reasons she still didn't understand completely, she'd closed herself in the bathroom with the phone, unfolded the piece of paper with his number, and dialed. Her heart raced with each ring, though she knew what she would say. She had written it down and placed the script on the sink counter where she could see it clearly. The talking points were simple. First, the obligatory inquiries into his state of being: *How are you, congratulations on the book—can't wait to read it.* Then there would be her answers to the same questions: *I'm great, I love being a mom, no regrets.* The conversation would die a quick, awkward death, and the subject would turn to his letter. This is where it would get tricky. *Of course*—she would love to see him, catch up. But this wasn't the right time. The baby was little, her back, no one to watch the kids. Maybe he could contact her when he got back to New York. Maybe they could have a quick lunch. There would be no mention of his meeting her children.

Back in the bathroom now, searching the drawers for old cosmetics, jewelry, facial creams—the things she used to use to look beautiful—it was hard to imagine that her life had taken such a sharp turn. The call that had started out exactly as planned had ended in the unexpected.

"It's wonderful to hear your voice," he'd said, his own voice trailing off at the end with the heavy breath of a surge of emotion in an unemotional man.

"Dad?"

"I'm all right." Then, in a serious tone, he'd asked again. "Please, won't you come see me?"

Love had paused long enough to consider the course she was about to take. Looking back on that brief moment when her father was hanging on the line for an answer, it was clear to her that the decision had already been made. The careful balancing act of reason and fear had, somehow, been completed. The resolve to prevent the disruption in her life abandoned. It must have been, because the words had flown from her mouth. *I'll come.*

She heard Bill now, calling from downstairs. "Where's Jessie's big doll?"

He was beyond furious and she couldn't blame him. There had been little notice, mere days, and the decision had been made without him. In spite of him. It happened too quickly for Love to really believe, though she was gaining conviction with each moment that passed. There were so many reasons not to go. First, and most compelling, was the gamble with her back. The pain was still strong, and Bill was convinced that whatever was causing it would only worsen after two long plane rides. Then there was the fundraiser at the end of the week. She was barely going to make it back for the event, let alone help with final details. Bill, the kids—all of them begged her to change her mind. Bill with his disapproving, terrified eyes. Henry and Jessica with their incessant fighting, and Baby Will with the strength of his little hands as he clung to her neck. But after hearing her father's voice, she knew she had to go before these reasons caught up to her. There was no longer any doubt how gravely she needed to take this chance, how decisively her peace of mind depended on taking it. So she was going to L.A.

At the top of the stairs now, Love yelled back. "It's in my car."

She heard Bill walk away, though he didn't answer. He was hassled on top of everything else, but she couldn't help that—not now. He was watching the kids for two days, and it had taken a great deal of work. Shuffling appointments to the other doctors in the practice, rescheduling others for the following week—Bill had made sure she knew just how much of an effort it had been.

After a few minutes of searching, the doll was found and Bill was back in their bedroom. He tossed his shirt in the dry-cleaning pile, then hung up his tie.

"Do you really think seeing your father is going to fix your back?" His words were crafted as a question, but they did nothing more than restate his objections—the same objections she'd heard since his feud with Yvonne began. *Your mother is crazy. L.A. is crazy. Sensory-motor work is nonsense . . . no basis in scientific research . . . it's all just hocus-pocus.* More than that, he was certain the trip would cause more harm.

"I don't know," returning from the bathroom, Love answered him, a hint of sarcasm in her voice.

"I don't see the point." He put on a sweatshirt, hung up his belt.

"Really?" Love said, her tone just one step behind her own anger, which was pushing its way to the surface. This visit was years—decades—overdue.

After pulling on a pair of jeans, Bill stepped out from behind the closet door. "I just don't see it. That world is what nearly killed you." It was a serious blow.

Love moved to her dresser on the other side of the bed to put some distance between them. They rarely spoke of the night they met. It was too humiliating for Love, too terrifying for Bill. Still, he had pulled it from his arsenal on a few, carefully chosen moments—when she was approached about selling her story for a TV bio, when she'd considered taking classes at Columbia to finish her degree. Watching his face now as he spoke of that night, Love could see the picture coming together. Never had he rejoiced in her potential. Even when they'd taken Henry for an evaluation, Bill had described her mind as "abnormal" when giving the family's psychological history. He loved her, she knew. As a mother, yes. As a wife, yes. But he had been a far too eager accomplice in keeping the rest of her hidden.

"I've wondered sometimes . . . ," she said, feeling the rush of adrenaline, "whether you would still love me if I tried to get some of it back."

This was where he ran to her, told her he would never stop loving her. How could she even think it? But Bill stood by the closet, his face unwavering.

"This is about *you* not wanting to face what might be wrong with your body."

"That's not fair."

"Fair or not, it's the truth. This trip can't help you. Do you even know what your father wants with you after all this time?"

"No. I don't."

Bill stood now, moving toward the door. "Do you know what I think? I think this is all an excuse to go back to that world," he said, an injured look coming over his face. "And here I've been believing this would be enough for you."

With her back leaning now against the wall, Love shook her head. She didn't know how to answer him, and the weight of his disappointment—his worry—came tumbling upon her.

As he was turning to leave, he cast one last stone.

"Have you even stopped to think about your children?"

Love lay facedown on the bed, her arms pulled beneath her. The pain was getting sharper, her head was spinning. She felt the tears dampen her quilt. Her body, her entire life, felt intolerable, and going to L.A. could very well break her. Of course she had thought about her children. They were the reason she had to go. For years now, she had been only half present in their lives. Half there being a wife. And though it was agonizing, Love knew they all had felt it. Henry with his compulsive sense of order, desperate to maintain control wherever he could. Baby Will clinging to her hip. Jessica trying to *become* her. It was the reason for the chronic exhaustion, life's daily tasks being done by half a person. And it was the reason she had become so disconnected from her husband. Part of her could not embrace him—the part that she'd left wrapped up with her past so many years ago. Whether he liked it or not, she had to go back, as much for them as for herself.

She drew a breath and tried to relax her muscles. The decision was made—she had to see it through. *Focus*, she thought. The packing was almost done. Yvonne had organized the kids' things for Bill, written out a schedule. She could do this.

And when it was done, she would face her husband with the truth—and the choices she'd made in the aftermath of despair so many years ago.

FORTY-FOUR

DR. TED

Gayle sat on Dr. Ted's couch in his Upper East Side office, wondering how much to say. Paul was gone, though she could still feel the warmth of his arms around her that day in his apartment. When she closed her eyes, she saw the look on his face when he'd rushed into her kitchen to rescue her from her husband. And when she looked in the mirror, she saw his sketch of her, sad but beautiful. She missed him in the mornings as she descended the stairs. There was no smell of coffee, no sound of china cups being placed on a tray. There was no sound at all after Oliver left for school. There was nothing but a profound loneliness, and her own thoughts that had been churning like a whirlpool inside her head.

"So," Dr. Ted began, as he always did. Nestled in his black leather office chair like a snail in its shell, his expression morphed into a mixture of concern and wisdom—what Gayle had come to think of as his shrink face. "How has the week been?"

Week by week—that was how they managed her existence. A little anxious? Up the Xanax. A little depressed? Up the Zoloft. Gayle would talk about Troy's temper, and Dr. Ted would remind her that she was a highly sensitive person. *Did he strike you or Oliver?* Dr. Ted would ask rhetorically. *No.* He never went that far. It was well established on the invisible patient chart he had constructed for her that she had chosen poorly in marrying Troy Beck. But they had also decided that leaving him would be catastrophic. How would she manage? How could she, possibly, when her life had become *about* being married? An entire social structure had been built around the Becks. Weddings, funerals, dinner parties and charity events that never ended—the invitations that read MR. & MRS. TROY BECK. She had no job, no life of her own anymore. And then there was a small child whose entire well-being rested on her shoulders, on her decisions. How could she leave him without a father? This treacherous landscape had been thoroughly explored, and, as a result, was no longer discussed.

But something had changed. Someone had broken through the wall and seen inside her, and now, through that small opening, she could see out as well. And what she saw was an entirely different picture.

"I've had a lot of thoughts about my childhood," Gayle said.

Dr. Ted looked at her with surprise, though he maintained his poise. "I see. Why do you think that is?"

"I'm not sure," she lied. "But I've been thinking that it affected me."

Dr. Ted seemed relieved. "Well, of course! We're all affected by our childhood."

"But I think I was affected *badly*."

"How so?"

Gayle took a long breath, stalling for time. Her mother was also a patient of Dr. Ted's, and they had an unspoken rule about not discussing her in these sessions. Still, it was the Haywood matriarch who had been on her mind, and the image of her rage that Gayle had been able to see clearly for the first time in her adult life.

"There was a lot of yelling in my house," she said, starting out cautiously.

"Yelling?"

"Yes, and anger. I've been remembering lately."

"Why do you think that is?" Dr. Ted asked again.

"I don't know."

"There must be a reason, some catalyst."

Gayle had not told him about those few minutes in Paul's apartment, and she hesitated even now.

"It may have been a conversation I had with someone about growing up."

"Who?"

Again, Gayle hesitated. But then she answered. "Paul, before Troy fired him."

Dr. Ted seemed pleased, though Gayle could not imagine why.

"That explains it," he said, smiling with unusual empathy. He leaned forward in his chair and looked at Gayle with great intensity. "Don't you see?" He began speaking slowly, the way a teacher might do with a child. "Paul wanted to get closer to you. He honed in on something in your life—Troy's temper, which we all know can be upsetting. Then he used that to pry into your past."

Gayle felt a wave of panic rush in. "Why? Why would he do that?"

Dr. Ted shrugged. "Who knows? These transients can have all kinds of reasons. Maybe he needed money."

"Money?" Gayle said, her mind struggling to process this line of questioning. It was true that she had trusted Paul unconditionally from the start. He had that way about him. Still, it had been three years. They paid him well, he lived comfortably.

"How much do you know about him?"

Gayle thought hard to recall the sparse facts she had gathered over the years. He had come from California through an agency. He'd been married once. Liked to travel. Had she really asked nothing more about him?

Her face grew concerned as Dr. Ted persisted. "Something may have changed—an old debt that caught up with him. A person he felt obligated to support may have needed help. Maybe it was time for him to move on and he was looking for a way to cash in on your trust. You said Troy fired him."

"Yes," Gayle answered through the growing haze of disbelief and self-doubt. Could she have been so wrong all this time? Was she so desperate for attention that she had not seen the truth about him? Could anything be real if Paul turned out not to be?

"Why did Troy fire him?"

"I don't know."

"I think you must have some idea."

"Paul walked in when we were fighting."

"Ah, you see? You opened up to him, and he looked for a chance to come between you and your husband. Then you would have to turn to him."

"Are you saying he was trying to break up my marriage?"

"It's possible. It happens all the time, Gayle. A wealthy but vulnerable woman—it's possible."

Gayle traced the steps backwards. He'd insisted on helping her that night with the gala. Then there'd been the wine and conversation. *I'm not the only one who lives alone in this house*. He'd pressed her on her childhood, left those sketches out for her to see. Had he lingered in his kitchen on purpose—giving her the time to go through them, to find the one of her? Gayle felt a gasp of breath enter her chest.

"No," she said.

Dr. Ted sat back, giving her a moment to face it all. "This must be very painful for you."

Gayle felt the tears wash down her face. They were beyond her control like everything else now appeared to be. She felt helpless, like an infant—wholly incapable of navigating the world.

"Tell me what to do. I can't survive this."

Dr. Ted leaned forward and handed her a tissue. "Yes, you can. We're going to make this all right. No harm has been done. Troy took care of Paul. You haven't done anything that can't be fixed. Your marriage, your son. Everything is still in place."

"Yes," Gayle nodded, following his path of reason. Troy, Oliver, the house. She could get a new cook in a few days from the agency.

Dr. Ted pulled his prescription pad from his coat pocket and began writing.

"I'm going to change your medication."

Resignation settled back into place and the tears stopped.

When he was through writing, Dr. Ted handed Gayle the small, square papers.

"This is not going to be hard, I promise. You *will* be all right."

"What do I do now?"

"Follow the prescription. I've written it all down."

FORTY-FIVE

VANILLA LATTÉS

Marie got in early, staking out her ground before he arrived. Occupying her mind with work at least gave the illusion that nothing had changed. At the very least, it had been productive. She'd uncovered the name of Farrell's secretary the year Simone died and was now scouring the Internet, trying to track her down in Florida where she'd retired.

The night had been unbearable. Anthony had chosen to stay late at work, leaving Marie at home to walk the halls, flip the channels. And remember the kiss. She'd been trying like hell to fight it, working her cases, calling Love to bitch about the fundraiser that was creeping up on them, and to counsel her about the decision to see her father. But it was patient, and it knew how to wait for an opening, a crack in the armor. Then it pounced, like a two-ton tiger. The memory of the kiss would stop her in her tracks, consume her mind, and make her want more. She went to bed with it at night and woke up with it in the morning, when she would attack it with the chores and tasks of her ordinary life in the hope that it might retreat.

She heard the door open and close and took a breath. It was just after nine, just after the hour when Randy was expected.

"Good morning," she called into the other room, keeping her eyes on a document as she used to do. Didn't she? How could it be this hard to remember how she acted before the kiss?

No one answered. Now curious, Marie got up and walked to the edge of the conference room. Janie Kirk was standing just inside.

"Janie. I wasn't expecting you," she said, smiling as well as she could.

"I brought you a latté. Vanilla OK?" Janie placed two paper cups from Joe's on the conference table as though their meeting had somehow, at sometime been planned.

Marie's face grew more puzzled by the second. "Sure. Fine," she lied. Janie was in black stretch pants and a spandex halter.

"Pilates?" Marie asked, taking a sip of the latté, burning her tongue. *Goddamned steamed milk!*

"Eight o'clock class—same as every other day."

Marie pulled out a chair. "Sit down," she said. Then, "What's up?"

Janie let out a sigh as she joined Marie at the table. She pulled off the lid to the coffee and blew gently against the white foam.

Mental note—must blow foam before drinking, Marie thought, trying not to stare at the physical perfection that was seated across from her.

"I'm here for professional advice."

Marie took a breath as she found Janie's eyes. They were dry, but serious, and Marie suddenly felt like a complete shit.

"Janie . . . I'm so sorry. I didn't realize you and Daniel were having problems."

Janie smiled self-consciously, then looked into her latté. As her fingers toyed with the rim of the cup, she laid out the situation—how they'd been growing apart for years, how the kids had put a strain on their relationship.

"Does he know? Does he have a lawyer?"

Janie looked up now, and her face was suddenly alarmed. "No! And he can't know that I was here. I just want advice—on how things might end up if he does leave me."

Marie reached across the table and took Janie's hand. It was an insincere gesture, grounded in the guilt of disliking the woman, and as a result was unbearably awkward. Marie quickly pulled away.

"So just to be clear—you don't want to leave him, but you're afraid he might leave you?"

Janie nodded, her focus having returned to the coffee.

"OK. I'd be glad to help you. Of course."

"And this will stay between us?"

"Absolutely. Once you sat down here, I became bound by our relationship as lawyer and client. Besides, we're friends."

Janie smiled with relief. Then she listened as Marie laid out the workings of divorce, should that be necessary. It took just under half an hour and was interrupted in the end by the appearance of Randy Matthews.

"I'm sorry . . . ," he started to say after bounding through the door, breakfast in one hand, briefcase in the other.

"We were just finishing," Marie said, standing now. Janie followed her to the door.

"Good luck."

"Thanks, Marie. I'll see you Friday. Big day," Janie said, smiling warmly.

"Or big disaster."

"No. It'll be great."

Marie watched Janie's blond ponytail swing as she bounded down the stairs. Then she turned to face Randy.

"Wow. Human or robot?"

"The jury's still out, despite appearances." Marie grabbed the latté from the conference table and carried it to the bathroom.

"What did she want?"

Dumping the latté in the sink, Marie was shaking her head. "Professional advice. Preemptive. She thinks her husband is on the way out." Even as she said the words, they seemed impossible to believe. Daniel Kirk wasn't exactly a deep man, and he was one lucky bastard to have such a compliant wife.

Randy was at his desk, settling in for the day. And getting ready for Marie to make one of her hasty exits. "You sound surprised."

Marie emerged from the bathroom and tossed the empty cup on her way to her desk. "Very. I actually thought *she* was having an affair. But I guess he's the one who's unhappy."

"Huh," Randy said, now deep in thought.

"What?"

"I was just thinking . . ."

"What!"

"I was just thinking that maybe this was preemptive—but not in the way you thought. Maybe she was making sure you could never represent her husband."

Marie threw herself into her chair and stared at the floor. It was true—now that she had agreed to consult with Janie, she would be barred from representing Daniel under conflict of interest rules. And the scenario Janie had laid out had been textbook. It had been almost too perfect.

"Are you saying I've been duped?"

Randy shrugged and tried to think of a way to back out of what he'd said. Marie had strong feelings about Janie Kirk, unruly feelings that were only tempered by her belief that she was infinitely smarter than the woman. "Probably not. I don't know why I said it."

Marie was standing now and pacing as she tended to do when life became muddled. "No. You said it because it makes sense. She's having an affair. She thinks Daniel might find out and file for divorce. She knows I would take his case—small kids, decent father."

"Or not," Randy interjected. But Marie was no longer having a two-way conversation.

"Shit!" she said. "I've been outsmarted by Mrs. Suburbia!"

"Well, she is damned attractive—for an older woman."

Marie stopped in her tracks and pointed a finger at him. "Watch it," she said, holding back a smile. Then she turned to look out the window to the parking lot. She could hear Randy watching her, his silence giving him away.

"Is it all right that I came in?" he asked.

Marie sighed, then turned to face him. "We should talk about it," she said, not because she wanted to talk about it, but because she had to say something to break the mood. It was barely half past nine in the morning and the tiger had already returned.

"OK," he answered, standing now, looking at her the way he had that night—the night of the kiss.

Marie found herself pleading. "I'm married. I have children. There are problems, I know. But that's life. That's part of it."

The words were contrived, standard issue. And they did nothing to stop Randy from walking to where she stood. His arms were pinned safely at his side, for the moment, and his face held a submissive resolve, as though he had given in to the need to be with her even at the cost of his own integrity.

"I just want to kiss you again. I've tried to ignore it. I know you need me to. But I can't."

The room fell silent as he reached out for her. The feel of him defied reason. With her mind in a hazy white unreality, she felt her hands gripping his back, her body pressing into his. This could not be happening again. She'd promised herself, not only for her sake but for his. She couldn't replace the mother who'd left over twenty years ago. He couldn't fill the void in her marriage. Still, the knowledge of this, the promise, hadn't changed a damned thing. Here they were, in the middle of the morning, locked together again.

This time she could not break away, and the kiss went on, reaching deeper inside of her—pulling at her with impossible strength. It was a different kiss than the first. No longer still, she could feel his body moving against hers, his hand on her waist, pressing her into him. Somehow the long, restless night had only intensified the attraction. The passion that had been absent before was not just sneaking in, it was there in full force, and for the first time in her life, Marie didn't know what she was or wasn't capable of doing.

It was the sound of the phone that brought them crashing back down. Seizing the moment of reality, Marie pulled away and rushed to her desk.

"Hello," she said. Her voice was infused with an awkward, phony perkiness.

"It's Love. What's wrong with you?"

"Nothing. What's up?"

"I can't reach Gayle, and I need an answer on the table numbers before I leave."

Marie took a deep breath and sat down, her eyes now on Randy—standing there, his eyes still upon her, his face flushed with desire.

"Can you meet me in town?"

They made plans while Marie looked at Randy. For all the things she knew how to do, making herself not want him seemed an impossible task. Still, with everything inside her, with every ounce of love she had for her girls, and for Anthony if she could ever find it again, she knew she had to do just that.

FORTY-SIX

THE CONFESSION

LOVE DROVE HERSELF TO town despite Yvonne's insistence that they would be late for their flight. They met at Joe's for lack of a better spot, where she found Marie waiting for her in the back with the ladies from pilates.

"You look terrible. Is it that case with the baby?" Love asked as she sat down. With everything going on in her life, it was clear to her now that she had neglected her friend.

Marie shook her head, then blurted it out. "I kissed the young intern. *Twice.*"

Love felt a wave of panic at her friend's revelation. Of all the people she knew, or at least knew well, Marie was the last person she imagined would stray from her marriage. And the thought of it, the implied vulnerability for all marriages that it exposed, turned reason on its head. Still, she nodded calmly.

"How did it happen?"

Blow by blow, Marie let it out. The attraction that had been building, the trouble at home. Without stopping, she laid out her case, her careful analysis that explained the glitch in a carefully planned life. Golf, anger, Randy's mother, the way he looked at her. Love listened intently, following her down the various roads with their sharp curves and deep, cavernous potholes. She waited for her friend to finish before speaking a word.

"What are you going to do?" she asked when Marie was finally silent.

"I don't know. I want to stop wanting him. I want to stop being angry with my husband for five minutes so I can love him again. I want my old life back, the one that I bitch about incessantly but wouldn't trade for all the Randy kisses in the world."

"Just walk away, then. Find him another internship, push him off on Nancy, and avoid the office. Whatever it takes."

Marie nodded. "I know—you're right. I just can't see him."

"No, you can't."

"But what if it doesn't work? What if I can't turn it off—if I can't fix things with Anthony?"

Taking her hand across the table, Love caught her eye. "You will." Marie was still not convinced, but Love had to be. Marie was one of the lucky ones, knowing with such certainty who she was. That she had been tested by a handsome, admiring man, that she'd suffered a moment, or two moments, of weakness in the face of domestic discontentment, would in the end be irrelevant.

"What the hell do I do with this feeling?"

Love wondered if she'd ever really had that *feeling*. She'd gone from reckless one-nighters to marriage practically overnight. Still, she'd had a brief moment of adolescent normalcy, and she drew from that now.

"Remember high school? Those crushes that kept you from eating, or sleeping? The ones you were convinced would never leave you in peace?"

"Of course."

"It always went away, right?"

"I know, Love," Marie said, thinking back on days she would rather forget. Then, leaning in to avoid detection, she whispered, "But what if I don't want it to?"

Marie leaned back again and nodded at the dismay on her friend's face. "I know. That's the problem."

Shaking off the possibility, Love found the resolve yet again. "Close your eyes."

"Why?"

"Just do it!"

Marie sighed, then did as requested.

"What do you see?"

"Randy."

"OK. Now erase Randy and imagine instead a new man, a new made-to-order man. Not Anthony, not Randy."

"What do I want this man for?"

"Love. You want this man for lifelong love, silver-anniversary, miss-him-when-he's-gone, love-of-your-life love."

"OK." Marie sighed again, then fought to clear her mind. "He's smart. Smarter in some ways, but less smart in other ways. Overall, equally smart."

"Good," Love said, smiling at Marie's predictability.

"He knows me perfectly—when to hold me, when to leave me the hell alone. He doesn't take advantage in a moment of weakness. I can cry one minute, then kick his ass at twenty questions the next. And none of this fazes him. He shares my political beliefs. He's passionate about things going on in the world. He's confident, but not cocky, and well-respected at work. He's the first person I turn to for advice—unless the advice is about kissing another man, in which case I come to you. Though I suppose there would be no kissing other men if I had this perfect man."

"Just keep going."

"All right . . . he loves deeply, especially our children, and has enough emotional security to cry with me when they're born. He's funny. Witty. And, if I can have everything I want, he's fucking awesome in bed."

"Marie! That's twice in one month."

"Sorry—he's awesome in bed."

"Good."

Marie opened her eyes and looked at Love. "Yeah, great. And the point of this?"

"The point of this is that you have just described your husband. Well . . . I can't speak to the fucking-awesome-in-bed part . . . but the rest of it. It's certainly *not* a twenty-five-year-old law student who hangs on your every word."

Marie let out one last sigh. She thought about Anthony, the *old* Anthony. The pre–Hunting Ridge Anthony, and could see Love's point—on an intellectual level. Still, she could not erase the image of her husband air-swinging in the backyard, mumbling "swing thoughts" to himself. If he could be that man, he could not possibly have ever been the man she thought he was. She could feel the defiance take her over. And for some reason she needed to let it come.

"OK. New subject. Where are you with this trip to L.A.?"

Love threw her hands up in a show of defeat. "I don't know. This all started with the voodoo shrink, and it just snowballed."

"Maybe voodoo shrink was right, then."

"What? That I'm *holding* the issues of my past—dearest Daddy, his book, my childhood—in my body?"

"Could be," Marie said, feigning serious consideration.

"My body is *feeling* my emotional pain?"

"I love it. It's *sooo* Yvonne!"

"I know. So why am I going to L.A.?"

"Well, if all this with your back *is* somehow related to something . . . *emotional*, for the sake of argument, then it could help, I guess, to have some resolution with your dad. Have you read the book yet?"

Love shook her head.

"It's that bad?"

"There's a lot I've never told you. It goes way beyond my father not being around."

Marie gave Love a soft smile, then reached for her hand. "It's OK. Someday we'll have a long chat. When you're ready."

Love smiled back, grateful not to be pressed on the issue. "Anyway, I don't really buy the Dr. Luster stuff. But I don't feel like I have some horrible virus waiting to kill me either. I don't know what's going on with my body, but this thing with my father is here and I can't ignore it."

Marie drew a long breath and leaned back in her chair. "Could you at least wait until he's back in New York? Your back, the benefit . . ."

Love shook her head. "I might chicken out if I wait that long." Love checked her watch. "I should go."

They got up from the table and Marie walked Love to her car. Once inside, Love glanced up to the office window above Joe's.

"Good luck with that," she said.

"Right back at you, my friend." Marie watched her drive away, fighting the remorse that was beginning to surge inside her. It wasn't just for kissing Randy Matthews, but for the anger at Anthony that she knew would not be so easily dismantled. It would hold on, like a leech, sucking whatever traces of love were still running through her. Looking up at her office window, she felt the tears on her face, and could not hold them back—not even to save face with the good wives who were now glancing at her with a seemingly orchestrated intermittence as they paraded down the street. And having no leg to stand on in judging them today, Marie felt utterly lost.

FORTY-SEVEN

THE HAIL MARY

"ARE YOU SURE YOU'RE up for this?" Janie asked her husband, though she wasn't completely sure herself. It had taken the better part of the morning to build up enough resolve.

Daniel was in bed waiting for her. "Absolutely. I can't wait to see what this is all about."

She was working on a theory now, like a scientist conducting a study. She felt nothing for Daniel, the man she'd been with since she was twenty years old. *Nothing*. Not love, not anger. Just indifference—the absence of feeling. She'd tried conversation. Strike number one. Next, she would try to recreate what she'd found with another man. Great meaningless sex.

"OK, then," she said. She emerged from the bathroom in a black teddy.

"Nice . . ." Daniel seemed happy, and Janie tried to ignore the fact that this disgusted her.

She reached into her night-table drawer and pulled out a box wrapped in red paper.

"What's this? A present?"

"Something like that. Open it."

Janie handed the box to her husband as she crawled seductively into the bed beside him. His eyes were lit up with anticipation as he tore off the paper.

"Let's see," he began as he read the label. "The Erection Blaster 2000?"

Janie raised her eyebrows and ran her hand across his chest. "Yup. Guaranteed to please." She nuzzled into his neck, following the instructions she'd memorized for herself. *Think of him, Room 221.*

But Daniel pushed her away. "What is this?" he asked.

Janie was perplexed. Was he actually angry that she'd bought him a sex toy?

"You just put it on and it—you know."

"No, I don't know. Are you trying to say I need a bigger erection?"

Janie let out a sigh of frustration. "No, it has nothing to do with that. It just makes it easier, that's all."

"Easier for who? 'Cause I don't have any problems."

Janie was on the verge of exploding. "It makes it easier to please both of us at the same time. I thought you would appreciate that."

Daniel got out of bed and began pulling on his clothes. It was the middle of the day and he'd felt awkward about this whole thing from the start.

"Well, I don't. If you have a problem with my dick, just tell me."

Janie didn't answer. She sat on the bed and stared at the floor as she listened to him storm about the room. She was trying, wasn't she? Her heart wasn't in it, but he couldn't possibly know that. He hadn't known or cared about what she was thinking for years. This was an act of desperation. A Hail Mary play. And its total failure was turning her anger to sadness.

"Dan," she said softly.

"What?" He stopped to face her from across the room.

"Maybe we should see a counselor." There—she'd said it. The idea had been with her for a long time. Still, it had been easier to hide behind the wall of their busy lives than open a door that might lead to profound and devastating admissions. What would she say to a counselor. *Why are you here?* There had been so many reasons before. *I feel disconnected. We don't talk. I've changed.* All of those could be handled delicately. Now, the truth would likely bring the end.

Daniel shook his head. "I don't believe this. Are you saying you want a divorce?"

"No," Janie said, her eyes meeting his. "I'm saying we need some help."

"Maybe you need help. First you want to leave Hunting Ridge. Now you bring home sex toys. Maybe *you* should see a counselor. I feel fine. I'm happy with our life."

Janie could see he was serious, and that this was his way of being sympathetic, supportive. But it was not enough.

He walked to her and kissed her on the head. "Sorry about the Erection Blaster. We can do it the old way tonight if you want. I'm pretty sure I remember how to give you a good time."

Janie smiled and returned her eyes to the floor. She stayed that way for a long while, even after Daniel had left the room. Was that it? Had she exhausted the ways she knew how to reach him? She hadn't pressed him *that* hard. Surely if she threatened to leave, told him about the affair, he would be called into action. She considered this, and the possible reasons that she was so attached to believing in the futility of any further efforts. Twenty years was a long time to know someone. A very long time. No—she could feel it now, in that place where the truth patiently waits to be found. She *had* reached Daniel Kirk. She had reached deep within him and she had seen all that was there and all that was absent. Her task was not to investigate, question, wonder, or even despair. Her task was, simply, to decide.

FORTY-EIGHT

THE UNEXPECTED CLIENT

ANTHONY PASSETI SAT AT his desk, a voluminous brief carefully laid out in front of him. They had been there together for the better part of an hour, though the brief was getting little of his attention. It was an important document, the one the team had been anticipating for days, setting forth the defendant's response to their motion for summary judgment—a ruling that, if favorable, could mean a certain win at the settlement table. It was Anthony's job to read every word, then tear it to shreds. They had two weeks to respond, which was hardly enough time to do anything in the legal world.

The case was dull, there was no question. No one would argue differently. But Anthony was used to dullness. For fifteen years, he'd been litigating corporate disputes. Most of the time, it came down to a few poorly worded sentences in a contract, murky questions about one party's performance in the agreement. *Did the parties to said contract intend to exclude blah blah blah . . . was blah blah blah meant to be included in the blah blah blah listed in schedule blah blah blah.* Anthony was the king of word spin. He'd carved out a niche turning clear-cut meanings into actionable ambiguities, and the firm's clients paid him well to do it. Still, thinking up new ways to define words as old as the English language didn't exactly rock his world.

That being true, Anthony could not blame his work for the state of perpetual distraction he'd found himself in lately. For weeks his mind had been focused on one thing and one thing only. It was the reason he'd been slow to review documents, or return client phone calls. It was the reason he'd stayed so late, his normal workload now taking twice as long to execute. And it was the reason he'd stolen every possible moment to hit the golf course, indulging his need to escape the object of his thoughts.

It was all about Marie. He'd been noticing the change in their relationship for years, ever since the girls were born, though it pained him to admit it. He loved them, to be sure, the way fathers love their daughters—with a fierce, protective devotion. But in equal measure he missed his wife. Or, rather, he missed the spontaneous, fun-loving soul that used to live inside his wife. Who was this creature who occupied the other half of the bed? Overscheduled, overly concerned with household minutia, unable to let a damned thing go—he hardly recognized her anymore. That sense of perpetual contentment, those moments of real joy that were certain to come now and again—everything that being in love, and being committed to that love, inspired—was gone. Still, he knew there could never be anyone else. His heart was running empty in a hurry, but it was taken nonetheless. And that, to Anthony's mind, seemed a miserable fate.

Luckily, he was not the sort of man to dwell in the wasteland of emotional analysis. That was, thankfully, the domain of the female sex. No—he was a man, and as such, fully in charge of his own mental energy allocation. Looking at the brief that was now threatening to keep him late—too late to sneak over to the club after the commute home—he decided it was time to stop thinking, and start working.

In short order he was fully engaged, his mind nowhere near the danger zone. It took three rings before he heard the phone.

"Anthony Passeti."

"Mr. Passeti, your one o'clock is here." It was his secretary, alerting him to the meeting with a potential new client.

"Take him to Conference Room A. I'll be there in a minute."

Anthony wasted no time, new clients being the key to everything holy in the legal world. New clients, and billable hours, of course. He marked the page of the brief, swung his jacket on, and headed down the hall. There was a time when meeting a new client had been downright exciting—the intrigue of a new battle, the inside scoop on some corporate mishap or scandal. Not to mention the ego boost of having a top-ranking executive hang on his every word. That the thrill had been killed off, case by case, hour by hour, until all that was left was a sense of ho-hum was one of life's many disappointments.

"She's in A," his secretary said, as he walked past her.

She? As he continued down the hall, Anthony felt a pang of interest. He hadn't had a woman client before. Even with all the progress women had made breaking glass ceilings, this remained true. Not one woman client. Women had been on client teams and women had headed the legal team from his firm. But no woman had ever made the decision to hire him. It was an interesting twist.

The door to Conference Room A was closed. Knocking once, then walking inside without hesitation as he always did, Anthony quickly scanned the room for the client. She was seated at the table, removing papers from an open briefcase and setting them neatly before her. Dressed in a jet-black suit and crisp, white blouse, she was professional to a T. And, if pressed to admit it, quite attractive. He walked to the table and took a seat across from her. At this point most clients would get up from the chair, offer a hand and a verbal introduction. Most clients would then pass over a business card with the necessary contact numbers and other information. But this was not most clients.

This was his wife.

"Hello, Anthony," Marie said, looking up at him just long enough to enjoy the surprise on his face. Surprise—and fear.

Settled into his seat now, and trying to keep an air of dignity, Anthony folded his arms defensively. "Well, you have my attention. What's this about?"

"I'm here to negotiate."

She said it with a straight face, giving nothing away. Anthony's mind jumped like a pinball to a wide array of conclusions. *Negotiate what?* Separation terms. Divorce. Child visitation. Or maybe she'd been hired by an opponent. Who knew what she was taking on these days, spending so much time at work?

Her face remained steady, and he knew there was no way around it. He was going to have to ask.

"OK. I'll bite. What are we negotiating?"

"The terms of our partnership," she said matter-of-factly. Then she handed him copies of three separate sheets of paper. "Schedule A is a list of responsibilities concerning the house. Schedule B sets out the girls' summer activities. Camp dates and times, ballet, gymnastics, summer reading requirements."

Anthony looked over the lists, feeling his world sink that much closer to hell at the sight of so much domestic crap. The first sheet, with the house chores, seemed endless. *Grass cutting, weeding, small repairs*. Repairs could mean anything—things that could take hours upon hours. *Grocery shopping, cooking, cleaning, bill paying and budget balancing*. Then there were errands. *Post office, dry cleaner,* and his personal favorite—*miscellaneous*. The second sheet, with the girls' schedules, was a mind-bending maze. *Drop off Suzanne at camp 9 A.M., then Olivia at the YMCA. Pick up Olivia at noon, grab lunch in town, then drop at gymnastics by 1. Pick up Suzanne at 2, back to get Olivia by 2:10.* And that was just on Saturdays.

While all of this was disturbing, it was the last sheet, Schedule C, that had him most worried. On it was one word. *Golf*.

Tossing the papers back on the table, Anthony looked at his wife. "What is all this, Marie? Do we have to go over this again and again?"

"Apparently so."

"You came all the way into the city to bitch to me about chores?"

"Yes."

"And what's next? A trip to marriage counseling to discuss the cereal boxes on the counter?"

"Maybe."

Anthony looked at her with squinted eyes and a cocked head—the expression he saved for the rare moments when he had the upper hand. "All right. If you want to talk about chores and cereal boxes, then maybe we should get down to the heart of the matter."

"Which is?"

"*Which is,* the fact that you made a choice that you now regret. You *chose* to quit your job, move to the suburbs, stay home with the girls. I'm sorry that some of that job involves chores that are beneath you, but that's the job."

Marie got up and started to pace on her side of the table. "It's just *so* damned easy for you, isn't it? Now that you've drunk the Kool-Aid."

"Oh, for Christ's sake."

"Talking about *choices* and *part of the job*. There is no *real* choice when you're the mommy. You either give up your career to change diapers and iron your husband's shirts, or you work and hire someone else to do it. Your children are raised by strangers."

Anthony was honestly confused. "I didn't say the choices were perfect, just that they exist. No one forced you one way or another."

"No? Do you not find it odd that *you* staying home was never even a consideration? I was making more than you were when I left the firm. They were desperate for women attorneys. Hell, I'd have made partner years ago! But—instead—I'm nickel-and-diming it in a hole above a schizophrenic diner that cooks bacon no one eats with their fat-free vanilla lattés!"

Anthony was silent for a moment, trying to get his mind around the conversation. What was she so pissed off about? His domestic failings? Her office? The Hunting Ridge wives again who didn't eat bacon? There were many injustices in the world, plights far worse than that of suburban mommies.

"*You* chose suburbia. *You* wanted to stay home with the girls. *You* did the spreadsheets on the new mortgage, so *you* must have realized that one of us would have to keep working."

Marie sighed. He was right about the choices she'd made and it pissed her off.

"I just can't believe that having a lawn requires such total and utter submission to the patriarchy."

"Christ," was his first response. His wife could make an argument out of a sunny day.

"Listen to yourself, Marie. *Submission to the patriarchy,*" Anthony said, muttering her words under his breath. "We aren't in college anymore. This isn't a theoretical exercise. This is real life. We have children. We have a house. What is it you want to do? Do you want to restart your New York career? Do you want me to quit mine and play Mr. Mom? We have choices. Just none that you can live with, apparently."

Feeling defeated, Marie sat down.

"There's too much shit between us. I'm angry all the time now, not just part of the time, but *all* the time. If we don't do something there'll be nothing but shit, and I can't live that way. I won't."

Anthony looked at his wife one more time, his heart beginning to feel the onslaught of panic. He knew she wasn't happy. That much had become painfully clear. Somewhere along the line he had accepted the possibility that she just didn't love him anymore. It happens. If you can fall in love, you can just as easily fall out of it. And all the signs had been there. He couldn't remember the last time she looked at him as though she knew him, and believed that he knew her—as if they were intimately connected. There was a time when it had been that way. All the nagging to do things around the house, all the bitching about his golf hobby, had just seemed like noise. Never had it occurred to him that these were really the things erasing her love.

He looked at the sheets of paper laid out on the table, seizing the path that would put a stop to this meeting.

"Is this really what you want from me? To sign up for chores?"

Marie nodded up and down, then side to side. *Yes and no*. She really wasn't sure what to do to change the indifference that was starting to overtake the anger.

"It wouldn't hurt. And place some limits on your golf addiction. As you can see, I left Schedule C open. I'm willing to compromise."

Without looking at her, Anthony reached onto the table for the pages. Marie handed him a pen, and he accepted it. Then they went to work, thinking through their schedules, the trial dates approaching on both of their calendars, and other demands on their lives. Line after line, they doled out responsibilities, the fallout from having a home and a family. They made time for Anthony's golf, though it was nowhere near what he had planned on—nowhere close to what he needed to improve his game. And as they worked, hammering out the details of the future, Anthony could sense a hint of relief in his wife. Her husband was finally succumbing to the realities of their world, joining her in her misery. With each line item, he was signing away the small bits of his life that weren't spent inside these walls, trying to keep up with the Hunting Ridge financiers. And though he knew he should feel hopeful, that perhaps this was all that was needed to be done to win back his wife, the larger part of him was bewildered at the high price of keeping a marriage intact—and wondering if it was worth it.

FORTY-NINE

THE REUNION

LOVE SAT OUTSIDE THE Beverly Hills Hotel in her rental car and let the memories flood in. It was a landmark now, but in the days when Alexander Rice would come their way, it was an overpriced and notorious home for the rich and famous. The Pink Palace had been a perfect fit for a man who needed to feed his ego.

That was what Yvonne used to say when he came to town. That was the explanation she would give Love when he came and didn't call. *It's a full-time job, keeping his ego satisfied.* In reality, his trips to the West Coast were infrequent. L.A. was a town of uneducated, flighty celebrities. Not much for him to do if he wasn't cutting a deal with one of them.

Now he was back again, brokering another deal for himself. How ironic that he'd lived so close for most of her adult life, and yet they were meeting here—at the scene of her many crimes. She closed her eyes hard, but the feeling remained, encasing her in humiliation both old and new. Old, for the mistakes of her adolescence. And new, for accepting her father's pity, which was all this could possibly be. She was convinced of this now. Pity.

Duty. Or perhaps raw curiosity sparked by the deep reflection of his life—a reflection that had written her out completely.

With Yvonne looking over her shoulder, she had read the book cover to cover on the plane, her heart racing at every juncture where her name might have been. Where her name *should* have been. He wrote of his marriage, his children by that marriage—the legitimate children. He wrote of his childhood, his early misadventures and the fascinating people he'd met along the way. It was an interesting read, and Love might have been relieved that she was spared from its pages had it not rendered her so completely insignificant. It had not seemed possible, but she felt more humiliated by her exclusion than if he had revealed to the world her sordid tale from start to finish.

Still, there was no turning back now. Turning back would only ignite the suspicion that she was somehow unable to face him.

She pulled up to the valet, got out, and handed him the keys. From the corner of her eye, she saw her father sitting on a stone bench, looking out for her at the entrance. She took her time as the valet handed her a ticket, then she placed it in her purse. Her mind was working hard to process the image of the man she had just captured. His hair had gone mostly white, and she had to remind herself that he was in his mid-seventies now, that she was close to forty. He was dressed in a loose-fitting, white button-down shirt, faded blue jeans, and sandals that befitted his pretentious, bohemian image.

She looked down as the car was driven away. *You can do this,* she told herself. It was a few moments. Anyone could get through a few moments. But when she looked up, her heart nearly stopped.

"Love?" He was at her side, reaching out to embrace her. She felt his arms pull tight around her back, but she could not return the gesture. Everything in that moment—from the mere sight of him to the smell of his cologne—was overwhelming. She hadn't seen her father in twenty-two years, but those years might as well have never happened.

When he let go and stepped back, his cheeks were flushed. He cupped her face in his hands the way he used to do years ago, and took in the sight of his daughter.

"Let me look at you!"

Love smiled at him, then looked away. But he held on until her eyes met his again, and he could reassure her. "You look wonderful," he said, and Love could see that he wanted her to believe in his sincerity. "Come on inside."

They walked through the front door, talking of small things. The plane ride, the weather on the other side of the country. And as they walked, Love tried to settle her nerves as the memories rushed in. He was playing inside her like an old song, the kind that provokes images of the past so vivid they cannot be suppressed—emotional images that demand to be relived as long as the song is playing, and for some time after. It was upon her now in her father's presence—the unhindered ambition, the invincibility of her youth. The time when she was the golden girl.

"Let's go out by the pool," he said.

They walked through the lobby to the terrace where he ordered her a lemonade.

"Ahh . . . good memory," she said. It had been her favorite, and she found it both endearing and presumptuous that he had chosen it for her now. The waiter seemed to know what he was having.

"It's been a long time," he said, hanging his head in a somewhat regretful fashion. "I'm sorry for that."

Love smiled and looked away. His guilt was awkward, her shame unbearable. They had a history that should never have been scripted for a father and daughter.

"It was a lifetime ago," she answered, shifting in her chair, determined not to show her pain.

The waiter returned with a lemonade and a glass of scotch. They were silent as he placed the drinks before them, and Love allowed her eyes to study her father's face as he swirled the ice in his drink. It was then that she saw it—the childhood memories bending through the prism of her adult life, exposing the source of emptiness she'd felt as a child. She knew now what a parent's love should be. Fierce and unconditional. Selfless. Sitting with her father again after all these years, she could see that Alexander Rice had never felt that kind of love for her—even before she'd given him reason.

"You seem happy. Motherhood suits you," Rice said, breaking the silence.

Love forced a smile. "Thank you." That was all she was going to say about her life. "I got ahold of the book. I read it on the plane."

Rice took a long sip of his scotch, then gently placed the glass back into the water rings that had formed on the table. His initial surprise quickly turned to resignation. "So . . . I guess you know why I wanted to see you."

Love shrugged and held her palms to the sky. "I don't, actually."

He smiled then, seemingly pleased that his daughter was being strategic. "There are a lot of reasons I didn't go into your life."

"You mean reasons why you left me out completely. And Yvonne as well."

Rice nodded. "Yes. I left both of you out entirely."

"Let me guess. Your editor made you do it?"

"No—no. Not at all. Nothing like that."

"Then what?"

Rice sighed and looked at his folded hands resting on the table. "I didn't want everything to be rehashed." Then his face grew concerned. "The drugs, the . . . the other things. Right up to the incident in the hospital. What I'm saying is that there might have been a renewed curiosity in those years of your life—renewed interest in a young person who had everything and then just . . ."

"Just threw it away." Love finished his thought, nodding with the acknowledgment of what was in his head—what was in the head of every person who knew her, or knew of her, so many years ago. Nothing was as it seemed, and no one had ever attempted to find the truth. It had been so easy to believe in the deviant character of Love Welsh.

The anger was beginning to choke her. "Nothing *just* happens. People don't *just* fall apart without reason."

Now he was on the defensive. "Of course not, Love. There was a lot of pressure on you—and I was the worst offender. You were a child. I'm not judging you."

"Everyone judged me. Everyone assumed that I just fell in with the wrong crowd, got too full of myself, lacked discipline."

"I only knew what I heard. I pleaded with your mother to get you some help when she moved you here. Maybe I could have done more, but I didn't know what to do. I was three thousand miles away. Part of me thought you would grow out of it." His eyes were concerned now, but she could not let herself believe in his self-deprecation. It was just not in the man. Still, watching his face, the pieces of her past came before her. One by one she could see them, and for the first time since those dark years, she spoke of that night.

"Didn't you notice that it happened in an instant? And even more to the point—that it happened after a *particular* night?"

Rice nodded, then hung his head as though this were the last place he wanted to go with her. Still, he followed. "The night of my fiftieth birthday."

"Yes. The party at your club. Do you remember what happened?"

"Yes. Love, please . . ."

"And that was?"

Rice paused for a moment as though he were incapable of speaking the words. Still, he managed to give her an answer. "That you slept with Pierre Versande. Your teacher. My friend."

"The thirty-five-year-old professor. I was thirteen."

Again, Rice paused. "Yes."

"And you thought what, exactly, about that?" Love's tone was angry now, and with every word she knew that any chance for a warm reconciliation was being cast aside for a confrontation that was long overdue.

"That you went a little crazy. Drank too much. You were old beyond your years, Love, growing up the way you did, and I accept full responsibility for that. I never spoke to Versande again after that night. It was reprehensible. But I never thought that was the reason for everything that followed."

Love nodded as she took it in, relieved that someone had finally spoken of that night to her face. Now her own perceptions could be confirmed. No one had understood that night, or the reasons she went on to degrade herself so badly. Why she devoted so many years to her own destruction, just to quiet the shame—shame that she herself had brought to bear. Her father had made it perfectly clear that no one knew the truth. And how could she blame them? It was only now, immersed in her past, that she was able to see it. Now, without the protection of substances and well-rehearsed denial, she was exposed, naked before the truth.

When the words came, they were soft but clear.

"It was not consensual." The sentence was formal, lacking even a trace of melodrama. Still, they cut deeply.

"What are you saying, Love? That Pierre Versande raped you that night?"

She was distant as she spoke, trapped behind some invisible shield that kept the truth from sneaking back inside her. "He gave me a glass of champagne. I had a few sips, maybe half of the glass because he was sitting next to me and I wanted to be grown up. I started to feel sick. Dizzy. Pierre said he would take me to lie down."

His voice was still in her head. The room, with its art-deco furnishings and modern paintings was now before her. Then the walk to the back room, the eyes that were upon them, people drinking, smoking pot, snorting coke. There was so much laughter, the music was loud. He closed the door behind them, dimmed the light. She crawled onto a leather couch, relieved to lie down, thinking she would sleep off the champagne and never drink again. Her body was so tired, listless. Her mouth unable to form the words, to tell him to stop when his hands fell upon her.

Her father reached across the table, touching her arm as it rested on the table. "That's enough. I understand," he said. Then, after catching her eye, "I am filled with regret. I should have known. I should have known you enough to realize it was all wrong."

Love searched his face for shock, anguish, rage. Anything that would be appropriate under the circumstances. But instead he held only a distant sympathy.

"Everything is so clear to me now. You were a different person after that night."

She thought back to the morning after, going for her lessons at his house. Versande was conspicuously absent, but the house was filled with her father's colleagues and staff. And from them she'd felt the invisible brand upon her. Within days her few friends stopped calling, their mothers forbidding it. Her reputation had been forged at warp speed and it was self-fulfilling. Within a year she was into everything—alcohol, coke, the pill of the day—until she finally jumped off the cliff with her mother's Valium. And for the first time since those years, she could draw a line to the trigger. She was not the wayward girl who was seduced by an older man. She was at her father's club where she should have been safe. And there'd been more than champagne in that glass.

After a moment, when the air cleared, Love got up from the table. "I should go."

"No, I . . . ," Rice started to say, rising from his chair.

"I want to go."

Her father gave her a sad smile, his face replete with understanding. This was too much for her.

"OK," he said.

She started to walk away, but his words stopped her.

"It all turned out in the end. That's what matters."

But that was a lie. The great Alexander Rice didn't believe in the mundane. She could have been one of the great ones—as great as he, perhaps greater. Still, the weight of his disappointment had somehow been lifted. She had failed at many things, destroyed her own potential. But he was a man who didn't know how to love, and that, to her mind, rendered him incapable of passing judgment on anyone.

She turned to face him again, this time unleashing the anger upon words that soared from her heart.

"You have written your books. You have been admired by many. And I know you have been loved."

The strength of her voice rendered him still as she reached into her purse, grabbing a handful of papers that she tossed on the table between them.

"And you have loved no one but yourself."

The tears came then, flooding her face. Her father had no breath as he looked at the papers. They were photos of her children—his grandchildren. His legacy.

When his eyes returned to his daughter, she was drying her face. She gathered the pictures and carefully slid them back in her purse. She looked at her father one last time, but for the first time as a grown woman. A woman with conviction.

"You tell me who's had the extraordinary life."

FIFTY

OTHER DEMONS

HER MIND WAS ON fire as she drove through the Hills, her back in agony as she tore around the twisting corners, slowed by sightseers with their Hollywood Star maps. She reached her mother's house, pulled into the driveway, and rushed inside.

The memories were relentless. Every moment, every detail of that night at the club was coming back now. The striped pink dress, high-heeled sandals with ankle straps. The makeup and hair her mother had done for her, the manicure from the nail salon. She was Alexander Rice's brilliant child and being present at one of his parties was an enviable state of affairs. There were actors, writers, producers, and editors—and, of course, a broad sampling from the intellectual community. The great thinkers of the day who were always in need of a platform to expound their theories and thoughts. *This is your moment,* her mother had told her when she dropped her at the door.

It was the early eighties and times were good. Her father's new book had been well received, bolstered by the buzz of his young daughter's progress. The décor of the dinner club was dated—a seventies modern glass structure, it was white carpets, shiny chrome, and strange, colorful artwork from wall to wall. Love had felt invisible as she walked in. She was still a child at thirteen, and to many in the room, a hindrance. Barry White was blasting from the massive sound system brought in by the D.J. as guests huddled in small groups, mixing drinks and engaging in the eccentric rituals of drug intake. There were giant bongs, hash pipes, mirrored panels for the cocaine. Her father had rented the club out and hired his own staff to allow the indulgence, and none of it was new to Love.

"She's old beyond her years," her father said when she walked through the door. The sight of her, the out-of-place girl trying too hard to seem grown up, had hushed the conversation. Still, it took only a moment for her presence to be forgotten.

He gave her a quick, inebriated shoulder hug and made a few introductions. But he was quickly pulled away by a young woman with thin legs and fake breasts—still somewhat of a novelty back then. They talked in the corner while Love sipped a Diet Coke. She tried not to stare as her father expounded his brilliance to a woman whose sole concern was with the hand she was sliding down his pants. Thinking back, it was the reason she hadn't moved away when Pierre Versande sat too close to her. Though still a child in many ways, she could feel the flirtation of her teacher. Then came the drink, which she held right up in the air as she took those sips. She did it again and again until her father—looking through the big brunette hair—caught her eye. Watching her father watch her, she took a gulp of the champagne as Pierre fixed the strap on her dress, which had fallen off her shoulder. She was expecting an annoyed frown, some look of disapproval that would make her get up and find a TV to watch. But instead her father smiled, oblivious to anyone in the room but himself. And the woman with the hand in his pants. Not exactly the image he gave the public on all those interview shows. Love carried on in a futile protest, until she could no longer hold the glass. She felt Pierre take her arm and help her stand. Her vision was blurred as they walked to one of the back rooms. But even now, so many years later, she could still see her father smiling at her as the door closed behind them.

"Yvonne!" Love yelled as she burst through the door. The house was small, and she could see through the living area to the pool, where her mother was lounging off the flight. With three long strides, she was at the sliding glass doors.

"You're back so soon," her mother said, turning around when she heard Love's pounding steps. It only took one look for Yvonne to know. Still, she asked the question.

"What happened?" Yvonne was standing now and tried to take Love's arm. But her daughter pulled away.

"No one knew. No one ever knew the truth, did they? Not even Dad."

Yvonne sighed hard, then sat back down. She'd known this day would come. Somewhere inside her, she had even hoped for it. Still, she was somehow unprepared.

"We had to make a decision, darling. You were a celebrity. There was no getting around that."

"And you thought it was better for the world to believe I was a child whore than a rape victim?"

"It wasn't like that. There were rumors about you and that son-of-a-bitch Versande. But it never hit the press. *Never,*" she said, almost proud that they had outsmarted the media vultures. "The truth would have made the headlines for months. *Think about it.* There would have been a police inquiry, maybe even a trial," Yvonne continued explaining. "It needed to go away."

Love looked at her with disdain. "For your sake, or mine?"

"For yours, of course, for yours!"

"And it never crossed your mind that it would look bad for you. A mother who allowed her teenage daughter to go to a party of lecherous drug addicts?"

Yvonne was indignant. "No! You were my daughter, Love. You were—you are—everything to me. I was trying to protect you. I thought I could."

Love exhaled deeply, trying to put the anger back in its place. There was so much blame to assign, starting with Pierre Versande, her father, her mother, and ending with herself for staying on that couch, sipping champagne, and letting him touch her that way. He had been her teacher, and she'd trusted him. She pictured her father's face, the look of indifference as she walked away and into a back room that would change her life.

"That's it," she said, putting the pieces into place.

"What?"

"It was Dad. You called him on it, didn't you? You told him what happened, what I said happened when I got home that night, when you had to carry me out of the club to the cab. You threatened to go public, didn't you?"

"Love, what does it matter now?"

"And he told you he would deny everything, say I got drunk and came on to Versande."

Yvonne didn't answer.

"That was why Versande lost his book deal. You had Daddy derail his career in exchange for your silence." Love paced the small patio as she spoke, the words flowing as the thoughts came together. "Then you both pretended it never happened. God forbid the public found out."

"Oh, Love," Yvonne said. "It was more complicated than that."

"What was complicated? The man drugged me. Then he raped me. You could have brought me to the hospital, done a tox screen. At the very least, they could have nailed him on statutory rape charges."

Yvonne looked away, her face becoming even more evasive. For all these years, Love had carried that night alone, utterly and helplessly bewildered that her mother had not been outraged, driven to the most drastic of actions after what had been done to her little girl. But in her face now Love saw no remorse. Instead, she saw a wall of deception.

"What are you not saying?"

Yvonne shook her head.

"Mother!"

Still defiant, and desperate not to say the words, Yvonne took Love's face in her hands. "Oh, Love, isn't it enough already?"

But the question was answered by the anguish in her daughter's eyes. She had been denied the truth for over twenty years, forced to live with an incongruous past. Yvonne had let herself believe that all of this would be cured by a reconciliation with her father—that gaining his acceptance again could obviate the need for knowing what had really happened that night. She could see now how foolish she had been.

"You weren't drugged." Yvonne finally said the words before she could think better of it.

Love stepped back, looking at her mother with dismay. "What are you talking about?"

"It was just the champagne, Love. You didn't have a few sips. You had half a bottle. That was why you felt sick, why you were unable to stop Versande."

"No, that can't be right."

"I did call a doctor to the house that night. And he *did* do tests. There was no mistake."

Love saw the glass in her hand, the bottle on the chrome coffee table. Her father's smile as he looked over the shoulder of that woman, the wink that came as he watched Versande pull her dress strap over her shoulder. Versande poured another glass, and now it was clear. He poured it into *her* glass, not his own. There was no thought given to any of it—only the bone-deep feeling of a father's implicit rejection, the pull of rebellion as she drew the glass to her lips.

Confounded by her own memories, Love asked one more time. "Are you sure?"

Yvonne held her tightly as though she could somehow squeeze the past right out of her. "You were angry. You had a few drinks. It changes nothing—nothing! Paul Versande raped you that night."

Love pulled away and looked at her mother. "Only you couldn't prove it because I was drunk."

Love already knew the answer. All this time she had been unable to stake her claim as a victim, passively accepting the judgments that had been cast upon her. That she *was* a victim in so many ways had not mattered. It was her own role that night that she'd been too afraid to face.

The two women stood by the pool, lost in a moment that was over twenty-five years gone. Finally, after so much time, it all made sense to Love. What she had done, what her mother had done. Then there was the fallout, the years of self-destruction that could have been avoided had someone told her the truth. And her father—the part he played in all of it, the kind of man he was. She would never understand how a father could love nothing in his own child but the things he sees of himself. The truth was finally on the table. The puzzle was completed and could now be looked at in its entirety, and, someday, maybe even put away.

She felt her mother's arms around her. "I'm so sorry, Love. There are so many things I would take back." Hearing the soft voice, Love closed her eyes and let herself stay in that place—the thirteen-year-old girl in the pink dress. "None of it was your fault." The words reached back in time to that little girl as she lay in her bed, confused and ashamed, knowing her life would never be the same.

After a while, she pulled away and looked at her mother. There was no undoing the past, no going back to rewrite history. And there was nothing to be gained in a life immersed in regret.

"It's OK, Mom," she said, but Yvonne was already in tears. "*I'm* OK."

"Oh, shit. Now my makeup's running," Yvonne said, dabbing a finger under her eyes. Love forced a smile as she helped her mother, gently wiping the black mascara from the woman's soft white skin. When they were done, when her mother had fixed up her face, Love smiled again.

"I love you, Mom. But I'm going home."

FIFTY-ONE

BILL, JANIE, AND GEORGE CLOONEY

WITH A CASSEROLE IN her arms for Bill and the kids, Janie knocked on Love's front door. It felt strange to be there while Love was away. And there was so much she didn't know about all of this—what was going on with her friend's back, why they were all so cryptic at the meeting that day. And now this sudden trip to L.A. Other than asking her to take a shift helping out, no one had told her a damned thing. Had she not been so consumed with her own chaos, she would have been insulted.

"Hello? Bill?" she called out. There was no answer.

Slowly she pushed on the door, which was slightly ajar, and peeked inside. At the foot of the stairs was a little blond child, naked and wet.

"Jessie! Get back up here!" Bill was calling after her from the second floor.

Janie walked inside and set the casserole down on the hall table. "You're all wet," she said. "Did you have a bath?"

Jessica nodded.

"Don't you want to dry off and get dressed?" Janie was kneeling beside her now, seeing her eye to eye.

With a defiant look, Jessica shook her head and crossed her arms against a naked belly. Janie held back a smile. She knew what this was about. Mommy was gone. The house seemed to ache for her already, and Daddy was outnumbered.

"Come on. I have treats, but you have to get dressed." She spoke plainly and in an adult voice. Jessica gave it some thought before turning for the stairs.

Janie followed.

"Hello? Mr. Mom?" She called up to the bathroom in a friendly voice. It was far too playful for an exchange with a virtual stranger, a friend's husband, but she was at a loss to come up with something more appropriate. She heard the reply call out from above.

"Who's there?"

Janie climbed the stairs and followed the sound of voices to the bathroom. She squeezed through the door, which was blocked by Bill's body as he kneeled at the side of the tub. Inside, submerged within a swarm of bubbles, were one little boy and one baby who seemed to be propped up by a very wet Baby Boppy.

"It's me—I have dinner?"

Bill was flustered as he looked back over his shoulder. "Oh, right. I totally forgot."

Janie stood awkwardly with her arms folded and nodded her head. "OK. So we're having an early bath?" she said.

Keeping one hand on Baby Will's shoulder to steady him, Bill strained his neck to look at her again. "We had a problem with an art project."

"That explains the purple water."

"Uh-huh."

Grabbing some towels from the floor, Janie wrapped one around Jessica, then held out another. "Here, let me help you."

Bill pulled the baby out and swung him over to Janie. Henry followed, climbing out of the purple water still covered in bubbles. Together the grown-ups dried the older two, then watched with relief as they scurried to their room in search of clothing. As he emptied the tub, Bill felt a wave of embarrassment. Janie Kirk had always struck him as a model mother. With four little kids, she somehow managed to dodge the mayhem that afflicted the rest of them. Even now, at the end of the day, there was not a hair out of place—and here he was, looking entirely incompetent.

"I'll change him, if that's OK."

"Do you have time? Who's with your guys?"

"The sitter is there. It's no trouble, really. I'm here to help."

Janie brought Baby Will to the nursery, dried him, changed him, then met Bill in the hallway.

"I brought hamburger casserole. Want help setting up?" she asked, handing him back his son.

Bill didn't answer as he busied himself with the baby. He didn't know Janie Kirk well and had planned on going it alone while Love was gone. Now her friends had stepped in to deliver meals and help watch the kids. He was not indifferent to the blow his pride was taking from accepting the offer. Still, he had a lot on his mind.

"That would be great."

Janie was pleased. "You get the kids and I'll put the food in the oven and set the table."

"Sounds like a plan."

Within the hour, everyone was fed, the baby was asleep, and the other two were snuggled on their parents' bed watching a movie. Containment had been achieved.

The kitchen was another story.

"How is this even possible?" Bill asked, standing at the threshold of an incredible mess.

"What you need is a dog." Janie grabbed a sponge, bent down, and began to collect the remnants of the dinner from the floor.

Bill started on the dishes. "A dog . . . ?"

"Yep. A dog and a dog trainer to go with it."

Bill nodded, smiling. "I'll add it to the list."

When she'd finished the floor, Janie joined him at the sink to rinse the sponge. It was uncomfortable being this close to another strange man, another woman's husband, and she moved away quickly. Instinctively, and with the guilt of a woman who had broken the most sacred rule.

"Have you heard from her?" she asked, looking for cover wherever she could find it.

"Not yet," Bill answered.

"I'm sure she's fine. She's just meeting her father, right?"

Bill nodded. "It's complicated."

"What about her back?"

"Don't get me started," Bill said. Then the words flew out. "I didn't think she should go."

Janie looked surprised. "How come?"

He turned off the water and dried his hands. Then he looked at Janie Kirk, thankful she was not Gayle or Marie or anyone else who might know what he'd said to his wife before she left. Here was a blank slate on which he could make his case without being judged by his past indiscretions, and he found himself talking.

"Her back—and L.A. She had a terrible time there when she was younger. . . ."

"What happened?" Janie was interested now, and it made Bill want to tell her everything, get a new take on the situation. Was he a selfish ass for wanting Love to leave the past where it lay? Or was he right in thinking this would bring her nothing but misery? God, how he wanted an answer. He was too close to it now. Reason had abandoned him, leaving in its stead a ball of twisted thoughts. Still, it was not his place to reveal his wife's secrets.

"You know—nothing good ever happens in L.A.," he said flippantly.

Janie smiled, though her face held a trace of disappointment that he had retreated, that there was not going to be an honest conversation. She had so many questions. *Is your marriage in trouble? Does this life feel like a steel pipe—strong but hollow? Am I not alone?* There was something in his eyes, the kind of deep worry that threatened the core, and she wanted to understand its source.

Instead, she joined him in the casual banter. "What—are you afraid she's going to have a fling with George Clooney?"

Bill let out a slight laugh. "I might actually feel better if she was."

"That bad, huh?"

"What—you think George Clooney could win her over?"

Janie smiled coyly. "Well, he *is* a two-time Sexiest Man Alive."

"Then I guess I'll have to hope their paths don't cross."

Bill poured detergent into the dishwasher, his mind occupied by a vision of his wife with a man far more dangerous than George Clooney.

Janie smiled as Bill handed back her casserole dish. Then she turned to gather her things, her thoughts now spinning with theories and questions about what was going on in this house. She believed in her gut that there was no perfect union between man and woman, but it was easily forgotten in a town like Hunting Ridge. Sensing a trace of complexity, of less-than-picture-perfect marital bliss, made her crave answers.

Bill walked her to the door. "Thanks for everything," he said.

"No problem." She turned her back to leave. Then she stopped.

"Love will be OK," she said. "She's not that same young girl anymore. None of us are." There was more she wanted to say, advice she could give after all that had happened. But she didn't want to. God help her, she didn't want to make things better here.

Bill managed a smile. "Thanks."

She smiled back and looked at him for a moment longer. Then she walked to her car and drove off.

When she was gone, Bill locked the door and turned off the lights. As he made his way up the stairs, his mind played back to another time—that sidewalk café where he'd fallen in love with his wife. He pictured her defiance and the pain she was so determined to hide. He knew then that he could take her away from all that, and that giving her a new life would be empowering like nothing he'd ever experienced. Janie was right. Love *was* a different person now. She was strong and she had something that her father couldn't touch. Still, what he'd seen in her lately was alarming—a trace of her former self that was as terrifying as it was attractive. She was brilliant, and her beauty could take his breath away. Alexander Rice would be a fool not to pull her back into his world.

His children were asleep in his bed and he didn't move them. Instead, he turned off the television and crawled in between them. He closed his eyes and put his mind to work, pleading for a lucid thought. It didn't matter whether he was right about the trip to L.A. She was there—right now. And no matter what they all thought of the man, Rice could give her many things. He could thrust her back into the spotlight, reinvent the life that might have been. How could he compete with that? But he would not give up that easily. Somehow, he would find a way to give her more.

FIFTY-TWO

THE SECRETARY

MARIE WAS IN HER pajamas when the doorbell rang. She was exhausted and determined to be in bed before eleven. Anthony was MIA again. This time, he hadn't even bothered with a phone call. But it was Thursday—poker night at the club—which left no room for speculation as to where he might be. At the kitchen table was the master list of things to do for the fundraiser. For nearly an hour Marie had compiled the list from a handful of smaller lists, though having it all on one piece of paper did little to ease her mind. By this time tomorrow night the event would either be in full swing or in a state of chaos. And she was beginning to feel it could go either way.

The bell rang again. Leaving her stack of papers, she walked to the door, praying it would be Gayle. She needed the help to be sure, but after another day without as much as a call from her friend, just knowing Gayle was still alive would be a relief. There was no such luck.

"Christ!" Marie said out loud after looking through the peephole. It was Randy.

When she opened the door, the look of astonishment was still on her face.

"I saw the light on," he said, peeking into the house to assess the situation.

"What are you doing here?" Her voice was soft, a guilty whisper. And it occurred to her in that moment that that was precisely how she saw them both. Guilty.

"I tried to call . . ."

"The TiVo was online."

"You should have it programmed to call in the middle of the night."

"Yeah, yeah . . . I can't figure out how to change it. Technology," Marie said, waving her hand over her head.

"Anyway, I needed to see you. . . ."

Marie stepped outside and closed the door behind her. "I can't do this right now. Not *here*."

Randy kept a safe distance, holding his hands in front of himself. "No, you don't understand. It's the Farrell case."

Suddenly self-conscious in her old cotton pj's, pinned-up hair, and a face shiny from night lotion, Marie felt her cheeks blush.

"I'm sorry. Come in."

As they stepped inside, Randy's eyes scanned each room. He was looking for Anthony.

"He's not here. What else is new?"

They walked to the kitchen. Marie offered coffee.

"No thanks. I'll be up all night."

Marie checked her watch. It was after nine, of course he didn't want coffee. Where was her head? Then she remembered. It was on the adorable young man standing in her kitchen. On his dark, wavy hair, which had twice been wrapped in her fingers. On his strong shoulders, his soft lips. On the hands that had held her face, unable to let her go.

"Beer," she said, reaching into the fridge. As awkward as it was to have him in her kitchen, her personal world, she thanked God they were in a place where her children were upstairs sleeping, where her husband might come through the door at any moment.

"So, what was today's word?" Randy was staring at a picture of Olivia taken at the beach last summer.

Marie cleared her throat, then sat down with Randy at the table. "Still *butt crack*."

Randy laughed, turning from the photo. "Wow. That one seems to be sticking."

"Lovely, isn't it? My sweet little angel walks around all day—*butt crack* this, *butt crack* that. Everything's a *butt crack*."

This was one of those moments in their many conversations about her kids that usually made Marie feel warm, connected. But she couldn't afford those feelings anymore.

"I thought you were working Nancy's trial tonight," she said, changing the subject.

"I am. I went back to the office to get some research and there was a message on the machine. It was from the secretary, Mrs. Anderson."

Randy took a long drink of the beer, conscious of his every move, his every look.

"Did you call her back?"

Randy shook his head, then placed the beer on the table. "I thought you would want to do it. That's why I'm here."

Marie looked at him for a long moment, her head now wrapped around the Farrell case.

"OK. Let's call Mrs. Anderson."

Randy followed Marie into the study. They sat down at her desk, and she dialed the number.

The woman answered in a sleepy voice.

"Mrs. Anderson? Leigh Anderson?" Marie asked.

"Yes. Who's this?"

Marie sighed and looked at Randy. *Here we go*.

"My name is Marie Passeti. I'm a lawyer in Connecticut—representing Carson Farrell."

There was a long silence. Marie and Randy locked eyes as they waited for the response.

"Yes?" she said, cautiously, confirming they had found the right Leigh Anderson.

"Mr. Farrell is in a custody dispute with his wife and we're trying to pin down the events of the morning when his daughter passed. It might be important in helping Carson." Her tone was matter-of-fact, though she wasn't at all certain if this was the right tack. How well did Mrs. Anderson know the Farrell children? Or Mrs. Farrell? Was she partial to one of them? Did she, like everyone else, blame Farrell for his daughter's death? Or did she pity him? Marie didn't have the patience tonight to feel her out.

The woman let out a soft moan. "Such a shame," she said in a solemn voice. "Such a tragic shame."

"Yes. Tragic."

"What is it you need from me?" Her intonation reflected a growing skepticism.

"Just a technicality, really. I'm trying to make sure Carson has all his facts straight for his deposition." Marie's face squinted as she lied. "I wanted to confirm the time of the phone call he made to the office that morning. That's all."

It was a good place to start—something benign that the woman could answer in good conscience. Then they would move on to more important matters.

But Mrs. Anderson was silent. "I'm sorry. I don't understand."

"Oh," Marie said. "Well, I have in my notes that Carson called the office that morning around nine forty. But they're from a while back when I first interviewed him. Do I have it wrong?"

Randy sat back, his eyes wide with concern.

"Yes, you must have misunderstood him. Mr. Farrell was in the office that morning. He *received* a call sometime before ten. Then he left in a hurry."

Marie held back a gasp. Randy was motioning for her to keep going, to draw the woman out slowly. Carefully.

"Right, right. I did have it wrong. Carson was in the office—the usual time—then he got the call and rushed home."

"Yes. That's right. I'll never forget that call."

Of course, Marie thought. It was the call that changed a man's life forever. "We all pray not to get one of those."

Leigh Anderson agreed. "Amen to that."

Marie looked at her notes, the list of questions she had for Farrell's secretary. But everything had just been turned on its head.

"And you remember the call coming in between nine thirty and ten?"

"Closer to ten. Is that all you needed?"

Randy nodded at Marie. "Yes. Thank you for your time. I'm sorry to have disturbed you so late."

"Not at all. And please give my best to Mr. Farrell. He's been through hell, that man."

"Good night," Marie said. Then she disconnected the call.

Randy leaned back in his chair and ran his hands across his face. "Shit."

"Farrell wasn't home that morning," Marie said, echoing his thoughts.

"We have the phone records in the police file. Someone from Farrell's house called his office at nine forty-five. Then they called 911 at ten twenty-one." Randy recapped what they knew.

"No—not *they*. We know it was Carson Farrell who called 911 from the house at ten twenty-one. And now we know someone else called *him* at his office *from* his house at nine forty-five."

Marie's eyes were glued to Randy's as her words sank in. *Farrell was in the office*. He was not home that morning as he claimed, at least not *when* he claimed.

"There's only one explanation," Randy said, taking another sip of the beer.

It was not a surprise that Farrell had lied. For some reason, a reason that had just become momentous, he didn't want anyone to know what really went on in that house. From his wife's postpartum depression, to the fighting, to the domestic disturbance call, and now this. Farrell had been doing a complicated tap dance to keep his children without revealing the truth, and Marie had reached her limit. She was his lawyer, but first and foremost, an officer of the court.

"I need to make some calls," she said, reaching for her BlackBerry.

"To Farrell?"

"Farrell, his wife, Tim Connely, and the guardian *ad litem*."

Randy looked at her, puzzled, as she started dialing the first number. She told each one to be at her office in the morning. She said nothing about the nature of the meeting but accepted no excuses. And as she worked, Randy continued to watch her, reading her face, trying to follow her thoughts. Step after step, he recalled the phone records, the conversation with the neighbor. And now the conflict surrounding Farrell's whereabouts.

When the last call was concluded, Randy had finished his beer.

"Ten thirty," she said, her attention still focused on the electronic organizer.

When she was done, she looked up at Randy. A moment passed when nothing was said, and it was then that he was able to see inside her. It was then that he knew exactly how Simone Farrell died.

Marie grabbed the beer from his hand. "Can you work MapQuest?"

Randy looked at her sideways.

"Of course—stupid question. Can you do some research tonight?"

Randy nodded. Then he grew concerned.

"Are you sure you want to do this?" he asked, knowing the answer, but needing to acknowledge the risk she was about to take.

Marie shook her head. She should have given more thought to the consequences of what she was setting in motion, but she was tired of thinking. And she was thankful to have one thing she actually was sure about.

"This is about the children now."

FIFTY-THREE

THE QUIET HAZE

"Mommy."

Oliver Beck stood over his mother, who was curled up at the foot of his bed. This was the third morning in a row he'd awakened to find her there.

"Mommy," he said again, this time giving her a gentle nudge. "The phone is ringing and ringing."

Opening her eyes to the morning light, Gayle reached out to touch her son's face. She knew she shouldn't be there. But waking up to the sweet sound of his little-boy voice was close to what she was able to bear.

"Just give me a minute, Oliver. One more minute."

Gayle closed her eyes again, savoring the last traces of sleep. Soon the calm pulse of her body would begin to rev, the nerves would once again show their frayed edges and send her reeling in a sea of anxiety. It would begin the moment she lifted her head, the moment her body was no longer fooled by the serenity of her dreams, the presence of her child. It would feel the call for movement as she sat up, sending blood to her muscles, then back to her head, where it would pick up the information. The tenuous order she had created so meticulously was gone. The marriage that had become a lie over the years had been confined to a little box and kept on a shelf with the other little boxes—her mother, the social climbers who wanted a piece of her, the women from the clinic. There were so many now. Still, she had learned to live around them, somehow immune. Until Paul reached out to her, reminding her how to feel. And now that had been a lie as well.

Oliver left the room, returning quickly with the phone. Still lying on the floor, Gayle pressed it to her ear, hoping to find a dead line. Instead, she heard Marie.

"Thank God! I was beginning to think you'd skipped town."

Gayle cleared her throat. "No. I'm here."

It was a straight answer, though Marie had teed her up for a clever, sarcastic one-liner. Their relationship had been strained since Marie confronted her about the board, but there had been some signs of normalcy. Gayle had not missed a chance to keep Marie's feet to the fire, though she'd done it with her trademark dry wit. All of that had stopped in the past several days. Now, there was no doubt in Marie's mind that something was very wrong at the Beck house.

"I can't get there until the afternoon. Something's come up at work. Can you run the circus for a while?"

Again, Gayle's voice was flat. "OK."

Gayle hung up the call, then propped herself up. Oliver sat next to her and waited as she rolled her head from side to side, then, finally, opened her eyes.

"I'm hungry," he said.

Gayle managed a smile as her heart began to pound. It was coming now, and there was a long day ahead. She rose to her feet and took her son's hand. Together they walked to the foot of the stairs.

"Go on down, Oliver. I just need to get something from my room."

She waited for her son to reach the bottom step. Then she turned and headed back down the hall to the prescriptions that were waiting.

FIFTY-FOUR

THE SHOWDOWN

THE CALLS WERE STILL coming at ten thirty and Marie was scattered. The caterer, florist, even the band had last-minute problems, none of which were serious. Still, the collective ineptitude was eroding what little patience she had left, and she was now verging on belligerence.

"Just get your asses there by five. Someone will show you where to set up. Come on—this isn't brain surgery!"

She pounded the phone on the receiver, then let out a frustrated sigh. She could feel Randy watching her from his desk, knowing not to say a word until she found her way back to center. That he knew her this well only added to her misery.

"If I make it through this day . . ."

"It'll be OK. Like you said, it isn't brain surgery. They'll figure it out, and you'll be there well before five."

The sound of the office door pulled them back to the present moment.

"That will be Farrell," Marie said, taking a breath. Nothing about the next hour was going to be easy.

Randy waited for his boss, filing in behind her as she walked to the conference room to meet their client. Carson Farrell had taken a seat at the table, his hands folded in the customary fashion. His face was blank, his demeanor nonexpressive. But through it all, his nerves were showing.

"Thank you for coming, Carson," Marie said, taking a seat across from him. Then she was silent.

Randy took a seat next to her. Everyone was in position, yet Marie was still quiet, and Farrell quickly became unsettled.

"So, what are we doing here?" he asked.

"Right now, we're waiting." Marie's voice was decisive and remarkably calm given the state she'd been in just a moment before.

As for Farrell, the sense of alarm was escalating. "I don't understand . . . ," he started to speak, but stopped himself when he heard the door open. One after another, his wife, her lawyer, and the lawyer for their children walked in and sat down at the table. They all seemed surprised at the full house of guests.

"What the hell is this?" As expected, Farrell's fear had turned to anger when he realized that his wife had been summoned.

"Thank you all for coming on such short notice," Marie said, her tone exceedingly formal. "I first want to say that I am acting here as an officer of the court, not as the attorney for Mr. Farrell."

Carson Farrell sat frozen, shocked into silence.

"That's a tricky position, Marie. Even for you." Tim Connely sounded unusually sincere. Still, Marie could sense his excitement. Farrell's lawyer was jumping ship, which was a sign that there might be blood in the water.

"I know I'm on a limb here. I've weighed my responsibilities to Mr. Farrell against my ethical duties regarding the Farrell children, and this is where I've come out. Believe me, I was up half the night with the bar's Code of Ethics, reading between the lines."

Sitting at the far end of the table, intentionally equidistant from the Farrells, the attorney for the children was now concerned. "What do you mean, Marie? Why are you concerned for the children?" Patricia West had been representing children in custody battles for many years. It was required by the court when custody was being contested, and she had seen her share of ugly battles in the name of the children. What was happening in this room was a first.

"In the course of conducting due diligence in this case, I came across some conflicting information regarding the accident," Marie said. Then she paused, giving the room time to turn back the pages.

"The accident involving the youngest child, Simone?" Patricia West asked.

"Yes."

Farrell was suddenly on his feet. "You had no right!"

"Please, Carson, sit down. You can seek your vengeance later." Marie's voice, her words, were commanding. Still, part of her was uneasy—the part that wasn't convinced she was within her rights to do what she was about to do.

"What do you mean, *conflicting information*?" It was Connely's turn to be worried. He looked at his client for clues but, as before, Vickie Farrell wasn't all there.

Now Marie turned to her client. "Carson, you told the police you were watching Simone that morning. That Vickie had taken the others to school, and you were working from home."

"That's right," Farrell said, his position steadfast.

"There was a call placed from your home to your office in downtown Boston a little over thirty minutes before the call was made to 911."

Carson Farrell shrugged defiantly. "I called to check in. That was when I turned my back, when Simone headed for the stairs."

"No," Marie said, trying to hold steady. "You didn't make that call. You were at the office that morning, and you were still there at nine forty-five when the call was made from your home."

The room fell silent. Farrell, Connely, and Patricia West each scanned the present faces for signs of recognition. Marie and Randy Matthews were the only two who were not visibly taken aback.

"I know about the depression, the outbursts. Mrs. Farrell was seeking treatment, maybe even recovering from what, I can only imagine, was a terrifying experience of postpartum illness. But the fact remains that Carson Farrell was not home at the time of the accident."

Farrell jumped in quickly, attempting to recover a situation that was now getting away from him. "I was home. I was at the office early on, *then* I came home. Vickie left when I walked in the door. Simone fell, and I called 911. Check with the police. It's my voice on the tape."

Marie shook her head. "It's not possible, Carson. The drive from your office to your old house is a good half hour, any way you slice it. There's just not enough time for things to have happened that way."

"Marie, what *did* happen?" Patricia said in a tentative voice.

Marie took a long breath. It was painful, even for her, to rehash the death of the Farrell baby. But it had to be done. "Carson went to the office. The older children were at their schools. It was *Mrs.* Farrell who was home with Simone. We know she was ill, struggling with her emotions. She was taking antidepressants. There were many factors, but in the end, she was the one who left the gate open, who wasn't watching Simone when she crawled to the staircase."

"Stop!" Farrell said, but Marie continued.

"After the fall, Vickie Farrell called her husband at the office. I don't think she realized what had happened. Carson left the office abruptly, making it home to find Simone already dead. That's when he called 911."

"That's ridiculous!" Tim Connely had caught up with it now—he could see where this was headed, and it wasn't good for his case. "We have the police report. Farrell gave his statement."

"That's not the end of the story. That's the beginning. We spoke with Farrell's secretary, who was there that day. She remembers him being there right up to the time when he received a phone call, the same time the phone records show a call placed from the Farrell home to the office. The 911 call came in almost exactly half an hour later—just enough time for Carson to get home and find the baby at the foot of the stairs."

Connely looked at his client. The face that had been as empty as stone was now flushed. All eyes turned to Vickie Farrell as the emotion filled up inside her—until, finally, it had consumed every space. She looked at her husband.

"Is it true? Did I kill our baby?" Her face was riddled with confusion, and it became clear to everyone in the room that Carson had worked hard to protect his wife, even from herself. For years, he had allowed her to believe that he was the one who'd let their daughter fall to her death, and the truth had buried itself in the depths of her mind. Still, it was there, and keeping it buried had required a complete shutdown of emotion, until there was no sign of life at all.

Carson Farrell rose from his chair and walked slowly to his wife's side. Her eyes grew wider as time continued to pass without an answer. "Did I?" she asked again, as Farrell knelt beside her.

"No one killed our little girl. It was an accident," he said. "It's OK. It's going to be OK."

With the answer now confirmed by his avoidance, Vickie Farrell's face began to coil with anguish. "No!" she said defiantly, grabbing at his shirt until he pulled her to him and held her tightly, trapping her arms at his chest. Her cries were too painful to witness, yet no one moved—as if the slightest shift in the air would break the woman entirely.

Finally, Patricia West whispered across the table to Marie. "We need to talk," she said.

Motioning to the other lawyers in the room, Marie got up from her chair and led them to her back office. As she passed by her client, she placed a hand on his shoulder. "We'll work this out. I promise."

But Carson Farrell did not look up. He was lost now, in a place two years ago—the place they should have been had he not tried to shield his wife with impudent devotion. The picture was finally in focus, the price he was willing to pay to spare her the hell she was now facing. He told the lie, but then the lie took on a life of its own, growing like a cancer inside Vickie Farrell. All this time, she had believed it—to the point of leaving Carson and fighting to keep his children from him. Her anger was that profound. And now, it would be turned on herself.

Marie left Randy with them in the conference room. As she turned to go, she gave him a sad smile. There was no victory here, no elation that they had finally gotten to the bottom of this disturbing case. And although the truth was finally out, Marie knew the work in the matter of *Farrell v. Farrell* was only beginning.

FIFTY-FIVE

THE FALLOUT

"LOVE?"

Marie had tried for over an hour to reach her on her cell. Finally, she got through.

"Where are you?"

"I'm in the air. I was held up in Chicago." Love's words came in and out with the signal.

"Shit." Marie said it under her breath but it made it through the line.

"What's wrong?"

It was after four and now apparent that Marie would never make it to the party in time. Sorting out the Farrell case had taken the entire day, and they were still waiting on a call from Patricia West.

"I'm running late. It's a long story. I was hoping you could get to Gayle's to make sure everything gets done."

"I'm sorry. I won't land until after six. That won't put me at the house until nearly eight o'clock."

Marie started to tell her something—not to worry, get there when she could—but the line went dead again. Pacing now, with the phone pressed to her chest, Marie felt it coming on.

They'd done the best they could for the Farrells. For the better part of five hours, the three lawyers had laid out a strategy, made phone calls, researched legal precedents, and—somehow—worked as a team to find a solution. Vickie Farrell needed help, now more than ever. Carson had pulled her out of treatment when Simone died, terrified the truth would come out and push his wife over the edge. For over two years her depression had gone untreated, and now she had the death of a child to grieve all over again. As for the children, everyone agreed they should be placed with Carson until their mother recovered. But Connely fought hard to protect his client's rights. Draft after draft was forged, rejected, revised until they found the terms they could all live with. Farrell would have temporary custody. The divorce would be placed on hold. And Vickie Farrell would be admitted to a nearby private facility for treatment.

Still, when their work was done, the plan had to be executed. Connely and Carson Farrell drove Vickie to the hospital. They picked the children up from their schools, drove them home. Carson brought a bag of clothing and personal belongings. They explained that their mother was sick, that their father would be living with them now until she came home. It was a heartrending scene, and Connely had returned to Marie's office completely spent. For all his repulsive qualities, Marie's least favorite opponent had shown extraordinary compassion in the face of a terrible situation. And that left them where they now were, waiting for Patricia West to get a judge's signature so they could close the file and call it a day. Not that it would ever be that simple for the Farrell family.

As for Marie, the repercussions of her actions would not be known for some time. She had done nothing illegal, and in actuality had aided her client's case for custody. There could be no criminal charges, no malpractice suit. Still, Carson Farrell had one avenue left to vent his anger, and he was, in fact, now hellbent on filing a complaint with the state bar association. After two years of holding back the tide, his wife was now in a mental facility, his children were without a mother, and it was all at the hand of his own lawyer. That his children were at least safe now, that his wife might actually get the treatment she needed was beside the point. At the end of the day, Marie had made the decisions for him, and everyone involved with the case knew she would pay a price for that.

All of this was weighing down on her. Alone in the office, Randy studied the face that once again had captured his attention. She looked close to breaking. He started to get up from his desk, but then stopped, folded his arms, and leaned back in the chair.

"What are you thinking about?" he asked her.

"The party." Marie had stopped pacing in front of the window, and was now peering down at the parking lot.

"Just the party?"

"Yes," she said with resolve to ward off further inquiries. It didn't work.

"And not about the Farrells?"

"Well, Randy, I am now."

He got up and walked to the window. Maybe he was unduly biased from knowing her. Maybe he was too inexperienced to know better. Still, he couldn't help believing that what she'd done was right.

"Vickie's illness led to the death of one child. Carson was being reckless. You saw children in danger—we both did—and you acted." He spoke with fervor, hoping to persuade her.

Marie shook her head. "Well, in any case, it's done."

"No, you're not listening." He was beside her now, and he reached out, gently holding her arm. "What you did took courage. The bar will see that."

She laughed sarcastically. "You don't know the bar, Randy. What they'll see is that I didn't do my job as a lawyer. I made choices against my client's will. It's a cardinal sin."

"Hey," he said, squeezing her arm once, then again to get her attention. She took a breath then turned to face him.

"What?"

"Maybe you acted as a mother first. But you're a damned good lawyer."

Marie smiled, pretending to be reassured. Good lawyer, bad lawyer—those were bold lines in the sand, which would ultimately be irrelevant. She would need subtle strategies now, detailed research of the association's decisions. The investigation into Simone's death and Vickie's illness would have to continue until she could prove that the surviving children had been in danger under their mother's care. Every meeting with Carson, every lie he'd told, nuance he'd manipulated, would be brought to bear. And all of this would be done with a singular intent—to force Farrell to back down. Because in the end, the severity of the sanction would be immaterial to her career. She would not be disbarred. She could wait out a suspension, pay off any fines. What she could not do was save her reputation if a hearing went down on the books.

"Thanks," she said to Randy, meeting his eyes. And what she saw there, for the first time since he walked into her office, was the inescapable chasm that time had carved. She could see how much he wanted to help, how deeply he adored her, believed in her. But none of that could help her now. She needed to talk through the evidence, the arguments she would make on her own behalf. And she needed to do this with someone who was wise, experienced, and mature enough to be impartial for a moment. She needed Anthony.

"I can't think about this now. I have a party to throw, and it looks like I'm on my own."

Randy watched her as she walked back to her desk. "Is there anything I can do?"

Marie tried to smile at the gesture. "No, thanks. You're a great almost-lawyer, but I don't see you arranging flowers."

Randy let out a small laugh. "I'm good at getting coffee, though," he said. "I'll be right back—cream and sugar?"

"And make sure it's cream. No skim milk. I'm not in a fat-free mood."

"I can see that."

Randy walked down the stairs to the street. He walked past Joe's to the corner, where a pay phone was nestled on the front of a stone office building. Without a second thought, though he knew it was lurking inside him, he dialed the number.

"Mr. Passeti's line," a woman answered.

"I need to speak with him. Tell him it's about his wife."

When he returned to the office, Marie was packing her briefcase.

"Patricia called. I have to get down to the courthouse to meet with the judge. She wants to speak with all the lawyers before she signs off on anything."

She sounded tired, and now defeated. There was no way she would get to the party in time for the setup.

"Thanks for the coffee. Let's take it on the road. Do you mind driving?"

Randy felt a deep anguish run through him. The rift between what he had to do and what he so desperately wanted to do was too vast to comprehend. As he watched her rush about packing things up, closing the office, he stood still, paralyzed by his own resolve.

When she stopped moving, she stood before him—coffee in one hand, briefcase in the other, and a set of keys clutched between her front teeth.

"Let's go," she mumbled, and Randy couldn't help but laugh.

"Give me those," he said, taking the keys from her mouth.

She started to walk by him to the door but stopped when she felt the distance grow between them. It wasn't like him not to follow close behind her.

"What's wrong?" she asked, facing him now.

"If you don't mind, I thought I'd finish something up for Nancy's trial."

Marie looked at him, confused. Never had he turned down a chance to be with her, and she could see in his face that he wanted that now. But his words were clear when he said them again.

"If you don't mind."

"No, that's fine. I'll see you Monday?"

Randy smiled and nodded. "Monday."

"OK, then. You did a great job today."

The escape was in place and Marie knew she had to take it. The silent space in the room was begging for something to give, something to pull them either together or apart—ending the uncertainty. There was no question that she had to go.

She heard him call her name as she was turning to leave.

"What is it?"

He waited for her eyes to see him, to return from the place they had already shifted to and be again in this room—on him and only him. Then he said, softly, "Good-bye, Marie."

"Yeah. See you Monday," she said.

Then she left without looking back.

FIFTY-SIX

COCKTAIL HOUR

BY SEVEN THIRTY IT was too late to park in the driveway. The valets were meeting everyone at the entrance of the Beck estate, then parking the cars along the road. A hired policeman was directing the traffic from the street, which was now backed up for a quarter of a mile. Sitting in her Volvo, sandwiched between the Mercedes, BMWs, and seven-seater SUVs, Marie felt dwarfed on all fronts. They were moving slowly, inching their way to the entrance, and Marie wanted to scream. She'd left the last trace of her patience at the courthouse, squabbling with the judge over the welfare of the Farrell children.

It was the one angle she hadn't thought through when she'd staged the coup earlier that day. Connely, West—she knew they'd get on board placing the Farrell kids with their father. But not knowing the case as well as they did, not understanding that Farrell's lie about his daughter's death was motivated by devotion to his wife and not something more sinister, the judge had required a great deal of convincing. They'd tracked down Farrell and dragged him in with the kids. All of them had met with the judge in her chambers. And, in the end, it was Patricia West who'd saved the day. As the court appointed guardian, her opinion weighed heavily, and she had sided with Marie.

Finally, Marie was close enough to see the cop. Leaning over to the passenger side, she rolled down the window and yelled out to him.

"I need to get through!"

The cop shrugged as he mouthed a word to her—*sorry*. Checking the lane of oncoming traffic, Marie waited for it to clear then pulled around the line of cars and into the driveway. Past the cop, who was now motioning wildly at her, past the cars waiting for the valet, Marie maneuvered to the side of the garage and parked in the grass. Finally on the inside, she took a breath and pulled down the vanity mirror. Still dressed in a navy pantsuit, she took off the jacket and unbuttoned her pinstriped blouse to just above her bra. She pulled a small brush from her bag and straightened out her hair, then dug deeper for her lipstick. The morning's makeup was all but gone and her face had taken on the gray tone of worry. She applied a thin coat of Firefox Red to her lips, then rubbed a bit between her fingers and brushed it on her cheeks. That was it—the best she could do with what she had at her disposal, and it was barely bordering on presentable. Behind her, she could see the formal cocktail dresses with their plunging necklines and leg slits, the professional coifs and expensive jewelry. For a second she thought of the dress that was hanging in her closet. She had been so close to pulling this thing off, and now she was three hours late and dressed like Annie Hall. Gayle would have to forgive her.

She got out of the car and walked as gracefully as she could to the front entrance. Forced to slow down by the meandering crowd, she let herself take in the scene. The sun was low, almost gone now, and the sky had taken on a glorious orange hue. The grounds were perfect, vibrant green grass cut low, blooming flowers in small beds around the old oak trees and interspersed with the sculpted shrubs lining the house. The stone walkway was adorned with ivy and loose petals. Somehow, everything was just as it should be.

"Good evening, and welcome." A man in a black tuxedo was greeting the guests at the front door, taking the ladies' wraps and directing them around the side of the house to the party in the back.

Marie followed the nicely dressed people, finding a semblance of calmness inside her as she realized there was no disaster underfoot. The caterers had set up the appetizer stations in the right spots and were now passing hot hors d'oeuvres. The tables were presentable, with white and cream linens and gold-trimmed plates. Round glass bowls with colorful peonies sat in the centers, giving the yard a springtime feel. In the back corner, the band was setting up while a harpist played Mozart. And the weather—the one wild card—had turned out to be perfect, not a chill in the air.

Waving to people she knew, making excuses not to stay and chat, Marie worked her way through the crowd to the back entrance. She found Gayle just inside, speaking with the caterer in the kitchen.

"I'm so sorry!" Marie said, scanning her friend's face for some sign of emotion. Anger, fear, nervousness—something. But Gayle was calm, her movements slow and nonchalant. The smile on her face was like none Marie had seen before.

"Hi, Marie. Do you know Brad?"

Marie looked at her with surprise. Of course she knew the head caterer—she'd been dealing with him directly for weeks.

"How's it going, Brad?"

The man was on the move. He filled her in on the food schedule for the night, seemingly relieved to be speaking with someone other than Gayle. They were handling the cooking from the setup in the garage, as requested, and it was causing all kinds of headaches. Still, it was getting done, and Marie felt a powerful sense of relief that there was no one disrupting the inside of her friend's house. In fact, everything was coming through as planned.

When Brad scurried off again, Marie tried to capture Gayle's attention. "Was it crazy here, getting set up? Did you get my messages? And where the hell is Janie?"

But Gayle was distant, her mind on prescription autopilot. "It's all fine. Isn't this wonderful?"

No matter how well things had turned out, Gayle Beck would never consider a gathering like this one—at her home—*wonderful*. Never.

"Have you heard from Love?" Marie asked, again trying to get Gayle to tune in.

"She's on her way, isn't she? Her flight was delayed."

"That's what I heard. I just thought she'd be here by now."

"Don't worry. Everyone did such a beautiful job, Marie. And Anthony was a trouper."

Now Marie knew something was wrong. She didn't even think her husband would show. "Anthony?"

Gayle nodded. "He got here at five o'clock. Took all the plans, put everyone to work. Really, he was incredible. Why don't you go outside, get something to eat. *Enjoy* yourself."

Searching for clues to make sense of her friend, and now her husband, Marie noticed that Gayle's champagne glass was empty and this satisfied her for the moment.

"I'll see you out there," Marie said. But she didn't go outside. Instead, she walked through the house to the side entrance and headed for the garage. The cars had been removed to make room for the gas-powered chafing dishes and prepping tables. Men and women in white and black uniforms rushed about, filling trays, cooking, cleaning up the spills on the floor. And at the center of the storm was a middle-aged man in a gray suit who looked more like a lawyer than a chef.

"Anthony?" Marie asked, as she got closer.

Her husband smiled. He wanted to put his hands on her shoulders, rub out the tension that seemed to cover her from head to foot. But he hadn't touched his wife in weeks and decided to follow caution.

"How'd I do?"

"The question is, *what* did you do? How did you know I couldn't get here?"

Anthony looked confused now. "Some kid from the courthouse called and gave me your message."

"From the courthouse?" Marie's heart stopped. "What did he say?"

"That you were stuck on a case and needed me to get here ASAP for the setup."

"How did you know what to do?"

"The plans were here. The people showed up. I gave them their orders. Not exactly rocket science."

Marie smiled. *My thoughts exactly*. It was comforting to be on the same page with her husband again. Still, she was unsettled as she thought about what had transpired. Randy had gone out for coffee—that was when he'd made the call. He had known she needed help and somehow he had believed that Anthony would come through, even when she herself had not.

"I don't know how to thank you," she said. But it was more than that. Looking at the balding, slightly bulging man who had just recently slipped from his position as the center of her world, Marie could feel something again. It wasn't a burst of love, an overflowing of attraction. Instead, it felt like a slow trickle from a faucet that was once again open—a stream of hope that her husband was actually still alive inside the man before her.

Anthony reached out now and took her arm. "You can thank me by accompanying me to the party."

Marie smiled and nodded. "That I can do."

FIFTY-SEVEN

THE UNVEILING

THE COCKTAIL HOUR LINGERED well past nine, but no one seemed to notice. The food and wine were flowing, the band was playing, and most of the crowd was in a state of intoxicated abandon. Marie made her rounds, introducing herself to the ladies from the Cliffton Women's Clinic.

"The party is lovely. We're so fortunate that Gayle offered her home," they all agreed, as though she'd had a choice in the matter—as though they hadn't screwed her in the allocation vote.

"Yes. And now you can buy some really nice couches," Anthony said with his trademark sarcasm.

Marie elbowed him as the ladies eyed each other, wondering if they had just been insulted. They were saved by the entrance of their fellow board member, Janie Kirk. Dressed in a short pink silk dress, high-heeled sandals, and professionally blown hair, she seemed to be doing just fine for someone on the brink of divorce. She was, however, alone.

"Isn't this incredible?!" she said to Marie, pulling her away from the clinic ladies.

"It turned out." Marie smiled as she looked the woman over.

"How's Daniel feeling? Did they reduce the clot?" Anthony asked.

Janie smiled. "He's doing much better. He'll be back in the office Monday."

"Give him our best."

"Thanks, I will. Have you seen Gayle?"

Marie shrugged. "She was in the kitchen earlier."

"Better find her. See if she needs anything." And then she was off.

"Uggh," Marie said.

Anthony smiled. "I don't get why she bothers you so much."

"She's just so . . . perfect. She looks twenty years old."

"Maybe she's just trying to fill in the blanks."

"What blanks?"

Anthony gave her a scornful look. "How could you of all people ask about the blanks in the life of a suburban housewife?"

Marie scowled. Why was he always so dead-on right?

As Janie weaved her way through the crowd, leaving in her wake a sea of awestruck men and jealous women, Marie looked at her husband. "Well she's done a much better job filling in hers than I have mine."

Anthony wrapped his arm around Marie's shoulders. "I'll take yours any day of the week."

"Liar," she retorted in a way that was wonderfully familiar.

They watched Janie enter the house through the back door, then focused their disapproval on the scene that remained. Clinging to party tradition, the initial burst of mingling had given way to the established town cliques. Parents of kids at the west side school clung together, as did those who lived on the east side of town. The private-school contingent found themselves in groups of two or three couples, and those without children sipped their drinks and scanned the crowd for social openings. It was all so expected. So restrained. So Hunting Ridge.

They caught Bill's eye as he entered the yard, also alone. Anthony waved him over.

"Hey, man. Looks like you need a drink," Anthony said. And Bill didn't need convincing. They moved in a line to the bar, then found a spot to dull their nerves and wait for Love.

At nine thirty, the buffet was served. The band went on break to allow for an orderly dinner service, and the small clusters moved in packs to the tables under the tent. Seated at the table closest to the house, Marie, Anthony, and Bill looked at the three empty places.

"We know where Love is, but where the hell are the hosts of this party?" Marie said, mostly to herself. Her last sighting of Gayle had been close to eight o'clock, and Troy Beck had just disappeared through the kitchen.

"Maybe they don't know dinner has been served. Should I look for them?" Bill offered, but Marie shook her head. After two glasses of champagne, she was just beginning to shed the day's events from her mind. Vickie Farrell's breakdown, the legal haggling, and Randy Matthews's mysterious phone call—all of it was now muted by the soft buzz of bubbly alcohol. And, feeling a burst of himself for some reason, Anthony had entertained a small gathering of their "in-town" acquaintances with witty comments on local politics. Watching him in action, feeling his presence for the first time in months, Marie was remembering her husband and slowly losing track of the rest of it. The Becks could stay missing right through to the end for all she cared.

Upstairs, Gayle heard someone coming. Quietly, she returned the bottle of Xanax to the drawer, pushed it shut, then switched off the bathroom light. The door was open, but only a crack and there wasn't time to close it. She heard the voices now. Her husband was in their bedroom, and he wasn't alone.

They were hushed, at first, the voices, and broken by moments of silence. Gayle moved closer to the door, her senses now returning from the rush of adrenaline. She heard the rustling of stiff silk, then a heavy breath. It was unmistakable. He was with another woman in their bedroom and the thought of it was unbelievable. Then the voices returned, mere whispers sifting through the opening. She couldn't make out the words, couldn't place the other voice, the voice of the woman who was now in her bedroom. Gayle closed her eyes as she listened and the picture appeared before her. The sound of the silk rustling in his hands. The dress was being pulled up. Then the creaks in the floorboards that came with the shifting of body weight. They were leaning into each other now, maybe against the wall. His sighs grew louder, his tone was pleading. The woman was having second thoughts, maybe out of guilt. Maybe from the fear of getting caught.

The sounds grew silent, all but the whispering. His hands were still as he pressed his body against hers. He was convincing her to stay. Gayle heard the click of metal as the bedroom door was locked, then the floorboards again. There was shuffling, then the muted depression of the mattress as their bodies fell upon it.

She knew her husband, knew his every move of seduction. He was kissing her neck now, with a hand inside the dress, grabbing for bare skin wherever he could find it. His other hand was on her back, holding her firmly in place, making it hard to cling to any semblance of resolve. He knew just what to do, where to touch a woman when he wasn't getting his way—this she remembered from days long past.

Then came the laughter. It was soft, but like a fingerprint, completely distinctive. The picture was now complete. The woman in her bed, lying under the body of her husband, was Janie Kirk. Sitting on the floor like a little girl, listening to her husband make a fool out of her in her own home, Gayle felt the last remnants of pride inside her die. For years she had tolerated his abuse to hold on to their marriage. And for the past several days she had carried on, pretending she didn't see him turning now to their son.

She rose to her feet and walked back to the small vanity table. She opened the drawer and removed the pills, clutching the bottle in her hand. Then she walked to the door and pulled it open.

FIFTY-EIGHT

PROOF

"LOVE!" MARIE YELLED WHEN she saw her friend turn the corner to the backyard. Dressed in casual slacks and a T-shirt, Love was as out of place as Marie and yet, somehow, she seemed to float across the lawn. There was a new serenity about her, in her slow gait and gentle movements, that caught the attention of the table as she approached.

Thinking his wife was nothing short of heart-stopping, Bill became filled with the caution of uncertainty. He'd missed her calls, twice letting the phone ring when he could have gotten there in time. As much as he wanted to know how her reunion went, the larger part of him needed to cling to ignorance, even for just a little while more.

When she was close, he rose from the table and managed an appropriate smile to mask his concern, embracing his wife with a small kiss. "How are you? Are you in more pain?"

Love gently waved him off as she sat down at the table. "I'm fine, really. It's about the same."

"And the trip?" He knew he had to ask.

"It's a long story. Can we talk later?"

Sensing the tension, Marie gave her friend a wink, then filled the silence with chatter about the crazy day that was, thankfully, winding down. With more than adequate embellishment, Marie walked them through the saga of the Farrell case and Anthony's heroic efforts to save the party. Then the conversation returned to the uncomfortable absence of the hosts.

"Where could they have gone?" Love asked, and everyone knew what the question implied. They weren't exactly the sort of couple to sneak off for a stolen moment of intimacy. That didn't *really* happen in the suburbs, and Gayle, in particular, would sooner die.

"That seems to be the question of the day."

Love checked her watch. It was nearly ten o'clock. "Aren't they supposed to give the speeches soon? She has to be here for that."

Marie nodded and shrugged her shoulders. "Maybe she doesn't want to hear about the plans to redecorate."

"Come on."

Love got up from the table, and Marie followed. This was Gayle's night. The party was a success and—the best part—it was almost over. There was no reason for her not to be here, at least not one that didn't have Love unnerved.

Upstairs, the bedroom door was open. A light drifted into the darkened hallway from someplace inside the room, but it was too dim to be coming from the night table. As they approached the room, Love and Marie looked at each other, then stopped just outside the door.

"Should we go in?" Love asked. Marie didn't answer. Stepping slowly, she walked inside.

"Gayle?" she called out. The light was coming from the bathroom, escaping from underneath the closed door. Then the door opened.

"It's just me." Standing in the doorframe with the light at his back was Troy. His jacket was off, his tie askew. And everything about him looked wrong.

"Excuse us, we were looking for your wife," Love said, turning to leave.

"I spilled a drink. I'll be down as soon as I clean up." The answer was strange, not only because Marie had watched him leave the party without as much as a hair out of place, but because there was not the slightest hint of concern for his missing wife.

They said nothing to him but moved as one toward the bathroom. When they were face to face with the man, he held out his arms to block their path.

"I'll be right down." His voice was firm.

Still, Marie took another step forward, taking him by surprise. "I just want to see for myself."

He laughed nervously until she was past him, inside the beautiful white room where Janie Kirk was fixing her makeup in Gayle's mirror.

"You have to be kidding," Marie said, looking back and forth between the two lovers. Barely dressed in the hot pink silk, there could be no other explanation for Janie Kirk to be in Gayle's bathroom—with Gayle's husband.

Janie was suddenly pale as she closed her cosmetics bag and walked to where Love was standing.

"I'm so sorry," she said, first to Love, then again to Marie. Love studied her face, trying to place the look in the woman's eyes. It didn't take long for her to recognize it. Shame. Regret. Resolve that she would now have to face the scrutiny of others.

"Oh, Janie. What are you doing?" Marie asked, not wanting, or expecting, an answer. And none was forthcoming.

"Where is Gayle?" Love grabbed Janie's arms. She had no use for Troy, or Janie Kirk, except to find her friend.

Janie hung her head. "She left a few minutes ago."

"Did she see you?" Marie asked, searching the woman's face for signs of contrition.

Janie was silent as she looked at Troy. Love and Marie didn't wait for an answer.

"I'll check for her car. You search the house." Marie bounded out of the room for the stairs. Holding back her anger, Love looked one last time at Janie Kirk. As she headed for the hallway, she could hear the woman's voice trailing behind her.

"I'm so sorry."

FIFTY-NINE

DREAMS OF A CHILD

Love rushed through the house, searching for Gayle. One after the other, she turned on the lights in perfectly decorated rooms, each one so carefully planned. Gayle's grandmother's antique secretary in the study, the restored wall sconce that had once hung in her room as a little girl, delicate moldings and brass door handles—in every corner were traces of her friend. Year upon year, the Hunting Ridge Women's League had offered to include the Beck estate in the annual home show, and each time Gayle had refused them, instead writing a large check to the League. It wasn't about appearances to her. This home was her sanctuary, the place where she could display the keepsakes of her memories and live among them as if they were the oldest and dearest of friends. In every room, Love could feel her presence. But they were all empty.

Marie caught up to Love in the foyer.

"Her car is still here. Did you look everywhere?"

Love nodded. "Maybe she took another car."

"She wouldn't leave without Oliver."

Love turned toward the stairs. Oliver's door was closed, the hall outside quiet, and Love had not wanted to wake him. Now she was wondering if he was even in there.

"I didn't look in his room," Love said. Marie fell in behind her as she headed up the stairs. Quietly, Love turned the handle. The room was dark with the greenish glow of a night light in the far corner. A window fan pulled in the cool night air and the soft buzz from the party on the other side of the house. Love walked softly across the carpet to the bed nestled in the corner. She could see the plush comforter piled high between large bed posts, and as she got closer, Oliver's floppy hair appeared from underneath. She looked at Marie, who was still in the doorway, and nodded. Then she turned to leave, retracing her steps across the room.

A burst of air swept through the fan and into the room, blowing the sheer curtain from the window and letting in the dim light of the night sky. It was in that light that Love saw the shadow at the end of the bed.

"Gayle?" Love said in a whisper, her heart racing at the unexpected discovery.

Following Love's gaze, Marie stepped inside the room. "Is she all right?" Marie asked of Love, but it was Gayle who answered.

"I just like to look at him sometimes."

Love took a few more steps toward her friend. "He's a beautiful child."

"He's a sad child," Gayle said, her eyes still engaged by the sleeping boy. "Just like in the picture. I never let myself see it before."

Marie and Love approached slowly until they were close enough to see the outline of Gayle's face. "What picture, sweetie?" Love asked. She looked at Marie, who shrugged, equally bewildered by their friend's comment and by the expressionless face that peered into the darkness.

"There's so much sadness."

Love touched her arm lightly. "We know about Janie. We saw them in your room, and we know you saw them, too."

Gayle shrugged, as if to say, *what can you do?* Then she turned to face the women standing beside her. "Marie was right."

"I'm sorry," Love said, still unsure where Gayle's head was. She was far too calm for a woman who'd just caught her husband with another woman, a friend, in her own bedroom.

Through the window they could hear the band stop and the orchestra of voices die down to one. The speeches were starting.

"We should go," Gayle said. "Just give me a minute."

Love looked at Marie, who nodded. "We'll wait downstairs for you."

When they were gone, Gayle took the bottle of pills from her clenched hand and slipped them far beneath the bed. First, she would go down to accept the gratitude from the rest of the board. She would make a toast to the clinic, to her friends who made the dinner possible, to the guests, and—most importantly—to the women who would be helped by tonight's party. She would mingle and charm, then direct the clean-up when it was all over. And when everyone was gone, she would assure her friends that what she'd seen had not destroyed her. Janie Kirk in the arms of her husband making hollow protests as his hands reached deeper inside her dress. Then the looks on their faces when they saw her standing there—the evolution of shock to panic. Without a word, Gayle had walked past them as they held each other on the bed.

It was over in an instant. Still, it was surprising the things she could now recall. The smell of Janie's perfume, the color of her nail polish as she held her hands over her mouth, the way a person does when something terrible has just transpired before their eyes. The plan was derived spontaneously, and it was thin. Check on Oliver, take a pill, hide. She'd slipped inside his room, then closed the door—closed out her husband's voice as he called after her. Standing at the foot of the bed where her friends had found her, she had braced herself for the onslaught of emotion. Instead, she was drawn in by the roundness of his young face. Chubby cheeks, tiny nose, his lips open slightly and curled up at the corners. In his arms was a tattered baby blanket, the one that they weren't allowed to discuss in the daylight but waited for him each night under the covers. He was at peace somewhere, his dreams sweet tonight. The dreams of a child. And as she watched him through the shadows of the room, the plan appeared inadequate. No provision had been made for the mornings, which would come, one and then another. As she stepped into the hallway, her conviction became clear. Something had to be done about the mornings.

SIXTY

LEARNING TO WALK

WHEN LOVE AND MARIE returned to the party the speeches were already underway. At a small podium with a standing mic was the chairwoman, a young ambitious New York transplant who had muscled her way past Gayle for the top spot on the board. She couldn't match Gayle's deep pockets, but she was savvy and knew Gayle would never leave the clinic, even if she were passed over for chair. With confidence and charm, she spoke of poverty, teen despair, class and racial barriers. She spoke of the clinic's work, the services it provided (skipping the controversial things), and the statistics—number of girls served, low overhead percentages in the budget. It was after all of this that her face showed signs of worry. She was down to the end of her list and Gayle was nowhere to be found.

"Should we make excuses for her?" Marie asked Love as they stood in the back corner of the patio.

"What could we possibly say? That she's stuck in traffic?"

Marie sighed as she searched the crowd for their friend. "I don't know. I just hope she gets down here."

"Maybe it's for the best." Love thought about what must be going on in Gayle's head. Listening to the board's plans for the money she had raised could very well push her over the edge, if she wasn't already there.

"I'm going back up." Marie turned for the back door. "Wait here in case she comes."

Love was watching her walk away when she heard the voice on the speakers. Marie heard it as well and stopped in her tracks.

"Good evening everyone, thanks for coming." It was Gayle. She'd come from the front of the house, circumventing the party and the possibility of running into Troy.

There was loud applause, and Gayle managed a smile. She waited a short moment, then carried on in a strong, firm voice.

"The Cliffton Women's Clinic is very dear to my heart. I have served on its board for seven years, and I have followed it through tremendous growth. With the generous gifts from people like yourselves, we have been able to save many young, at-risk girls from the devastating cycle of pregnancy and poverty. You've heard the statistics from our chairwoman, so I won't go on and on. It's getting late, and there's a lovely dessert bar waiting. Let me just say that I am proud to be a part of this fundraiser. With your help, we have brought in over seventy-four thousand dollars!"

Gayle paused as the crowd applauded again.

"Yes, it's wonderful! And with this money we will be able to launch a new initiative—an exciting new program that reaches girls before they even get to our doors. We are calling it Smart Choices, and it will focus on preventive sexual education. Starting at age twelve, girls will be eligible for a free after-school program that will provide information about nutrition, the body, sexuality, pregnancy and STD prevention. We will offer these classes in our facility, and also through community organizations that wish to participate. By using a standard prototype and by training educators, we hope to establish a standard in sexual education for girls that will be accurate, neutral, and effective. Smart Choices is a natural extension of the services we already provide. Controlling the decision to bear children is the cornerstone of individual self-determination. It touches every aspect of life, in Cliffton and around the globe. I thank you for making Smart Choices possible! Enjoy your evening!"

There was more polite applause from faces that were now glazed over. She'd lost most of them after her first few words, but that was irrelevant. What mattered was that the members of the board heard it all, and that they would now be in a pickle if they failed to hold a new vote on the use of the money Gayle had just raised. If Smart Choices didn't come to fruition, it would be a severe embarrassment. And Gayle knew they would all choose to jump on board.

Marie watched her as she stepped down from the podium. "Holy shit," she said.

"Holy shit is right." Love's eyes were glued to their friend as she walked through the crowd. They were up from their tables now, mingling and getting dessert. Everyone except Janie Kirk.

"Oh, no—look." Marie noticed her first, standing in the shadows beyond the patio. She'd been watching the speech from a distance.

Love turned in time to watch Janie dry her eyes, then leave from the back side of the house.

"Thank God," Love whispered.

"Yeah. But what about the other one?"

They both looked for Troy, but he was—thankfully—absent. Gayle didn't seem to care either way as she approached them.

"Well done," Marie said, giving her a long hug.

Love agreed. "*Very* well done."

Gayle smiled at them, though it was empty.

"It's done. Now we'll see." She was not glowing with satisfaction, or optimism. Nor did she seem the least bit excited that she had just turned the clinic board on its head. Instead, she seemed disgusted that the mutiny had been necessary, that her husband had been unfaithful, and that her friend had betrayed her. Disgusted, and perhaps, determined.

"Come and sit with us—have a cup of coffee." Love motioned to the table where they'd left their husbands. "Take a break until the party winds down."

Gayle hesitated. She still had to face the board members who had gathered together at a far table to share their bewilderment and discuss their options. She had to face her husband who was hiding upstairs. Then, she would have to face herself.

"Come on. Screw all this nonsense."

Marie, as always, had called it as she saw it. And for a fleeting moment Gayle pictured another friend who had once been able to make her see clearly.

"OK. Coffee it is," she said, though her mind was on the gentle man with the gray hair who had left so abruptly. And for the first time in days, she felt a hint of peace.

SIXTY-ONE

HOME

Bill drove the car while his wife stared out the window. Making his way through the winding roads of Hunting Ridge, past the mini-mansions, the perfect lawns, and pristine, white churches, their world had taken on an unreal feeling. Troy Beck, a man they'd known for years, was sleeping with Janie Kirk. Two homes, two picture-perfect families shattered. Still, it wasn't the affair itself that held the sting. That was common enough in the world at large. It was the fact that it had happened *here*. There was so much money, such inordinate sums of money, and that money paid for more than the million-dollar homes, the outlandish trips, and private airplanes. That money had purchased a glass wall that stood around Hunting Ridge, protecting it from the unpleasantries of adultery, abuse, the slightest unhappiness. Men went to their jobs, women tended to the homes and the children—keeping everything just so. And while there was idle chatter about life's problems—husbands wanting more sex, wives wanting more help—it was just that. Idle. The ones who acted on it, who actually crossed the line from acceptable complaining to admissions of extramarital desires packed their things and left. They'd heard about these couples from Marie, and through the local chains of gossip. But in the decade they'd lived in Hunting Ridge, no one they actually knew had strayed, or divorced—until tonight. And the repercussions were alarming.

"I just can't believe this," Love said, her eyes still gazing out the window.

Bill glanced at his wife, then turned back to the road. He wanted to press her about L.A., the meeting with her father, what had been decided. As much as he was concerned for Gayle, he wanted to know what was going to happen to them.

"Was she all right when we left?"

Love shook her head. "I don't know."

Reaching out for her, Bill placed his hand on Love's shoulder. "Maybe she's stronger than we think."

"Maybe."

As they pulled into the garage, Love felt the quiet resolve returning. So much had happened in L.A., the answer to questions finally found, though not at all as she had expected. Or hoped. All these years she had been ashamed. Now she was just bewildered—by her father, her mother, and with herself for not dealing with this years ago. How much time had she wasted, navigating her life through lies and misperceptions? How many decisions had been made in the midst of fear—decisions that had landed her right here, in this garage, about to reenter a life where the fate of four people rested in her hands? Foolishly, she had expected to feel transformed—as though knowing the truth about that night so many years ago could change everything. As she walked toward the door anticipating with joy the sight of her children in their beds, yet wondering how she would make it through the next day, she knew that no such miracle had taken place. She had run from the abuse of Pierre Versande into the safe arms of Bill Harrison, and she'd been running ever since.

"I'll get your bag. You go on up," Bill said, popping the trunk.

Love smiled at him. She went into the kitchen, paid the sitter, then walked her to the door. Taking the steps two at a time, she rushed up the stairs stopping first in the nursery. Baby Will was curled up on his stomach, little legs tucked under, thumb in mouth, butt high in the air. The burst of light from the hallway made him stir and open his eyes, just for a second. He sucked hard on his thumb, then drifted back off. Thinking how he would feel in her arms the next morning, Love pulled the blanket back over him, then gently touched his chubby cheek. She walked out softly, then closed the door, turning next to Henry and Jessica's room. They, too, were lost in their dreams, Henry on his stomach clutching a Lego magazine, Jessica sprawled everywhere—arms, legs, every part of her open to the world. One by one, Love pulled blankets over her children and kissed their foreheads.

As she closed their door she heard Bill call up. "I'll be right there."

"No hurry," Love answered. The truth was, she could use a few moments alone. He would want to know about the trip. He would be expecting answers. Was she reconciled with her father? Did seeing him again make her want something more? Was she going to disrupt their family, ruin their lives? But there were no answers to give. What *did* she know? That there was nothing to prove or disprove anymore. That she no longer wanted to go back in time, rewrite history, and claim the golden destiny she had been raised to covet. No—everything that went wrong in her life had led to something that was very right. Still, she thought about the coming weeks, the long summer days with all three children home from school. More than ever her life would be lived for them, and for Bill. There was nothing left to run from, but she could still feel herself in motion, perhaps running toward something instead.

Love walked the short distance to her bedroom, then opened the door. She turned on the light and stood there. The room was different. The bed was made, which was surprising, but it was more than that. In the corner was Bill's small desk. For years, it had been an eyesore of clutter in a space too small to hide, and she had trained her eyes to ignore it. But today it drew her attention. Cleared of his paperwork, his loose change, myriad pens and pencils and other junk that accumulates in the pockets of men, there was nothing on the desk but a stack of brochures and a small lamp. Thinking through the implications, Love walked the few steps to the desk, and gave it further inspection. There were five brochures, catalogues from

Columbia, NYU, Yale, Barnard, and Sarah Lawrence. All top rate universities within an hour of their home.

"I've been working at not being such an ass," Bill said, standing in the doorway now with her bag.

Turning to face him, Love found herself without words. It was just a desk, and somewhere in this house, she knew she would find a box full of junk that would never get sorted out. Still, it was an act of love, a heroic act in the face of fear, which Love knew to be profound.

"There's still time to enroll in some continuing-ed classes. Next year you could apply for the degree program."

Walking over to her husband, Love cautiously wrapped her arms around his neck. It had been a long time since he'd felt her close to him, and for a moment Bill stood still, his arms at his side holding her suitcase.

"There are some things I need to tell you—things I've kept from you. I just don't know how," Love whispered, and the sound of her voice made him drop the bag.

"When you're ready," he said as he wrapped his arms gently around her back. And he held on, praying that he could do enough to make her want this life—and not just for the kids.

"So, what do you think about your desk?" he asked.

But Love was tired of thinking. Clearing the desk was a gesture, a grand gesture for a terrified man, but a gesture just the same. Whether they could afford a sitter and make the time for her to go back to school was yet to be seen. Love had no illusions that her life would suddenly give way to her need for more. Still, what she had in this moment was hope, and for that, she was grateful.

She rested her head on his shoulder, letting her body fall into his. Letting him hold her.

"I think I'm glad to be home," she said.

SIXTY-TWO

PINK SLIPS

THE LAST TRUCK PULLED away just after one o'clock. Gayle made a final walk through the property to assess the damage. In the yard, stacks of tables and chairs lay on the grass. Bags and boxes of soiled linens were sprawled across the patio, along with crates of dirty dishes and glassware. The tent remained fully intact and would not be removed until the next afternoon. Gayle imagined that the raccoons would be very pleased with the remnants of the party. Still, there was nothing here that would not be gone come Monday.

Closing the last of the outside doors, Gayle switched off the lights, then moved room by room collecting stray glasses and plates from the guests who couldn't help themselves from inspecting the inside of her house. The game room appeared to have attracted the most party strays, undoubtedly resulting from some sports event on the TV that the men couldn't bear to miss. Thinking about the strangers who had roamed from the party, Gayle summed it up in her head. *Men watching sports, my good friend screwing my husband.* That was it, in a nutshell.

Walking the glasses back to the kitchen, Gayle added them to a tray, then left the tray by the door. Moving methodically through the downstairs, she closed down each room, turning off lights, shutting windows. When she was done, she moved with even steps up the staircase to her bedroom where Troy was waiting.

Still in his suit, her husband sat on their bed. With his legs stretched out in front of him, arms crossed, and a defiant look on his face, Gayle could not help but stare in wonderment.

"You should know, Janie means nothing to me. It was just a stupid moment."

Standing at the end of the bed, Gayle thought about his words carefully. There had been no apology, no remorse. And she wondered if any woman would be comforted by his admission. Was it really any better that he didn't care about the woman?

"Why are you looking at me like that?" he asked.

His tone had changed. It was slight, but discernible, and she was, as she always was, paralyzed by the rage that was beginning to seep from his skin. Still, something had shifted within her. The agony of her life had surpassed the fear.

Her voice was unsteady, her mouth bone-dry. But she got the words out. "Please go down to the kitchen. I'll be there in a few minutes. We can talk then."

She watched his face, watched the blood flow into his cheeks. Then it changed again, taking on the appearance of a schoolboy who'd been sent to the principal's office, and he slid off the bed and walked past her toward the door. That he had given her this much power over him was clearly unsettling the man as he struggled to find a way out. He'd been caught with his hand in the cookie jar—now there would have to be some consequences. Gayle could almost hear his thoughts as he calculated how much he'd have to put up with before his punishment ended. Before he could turn the tables on her.

When he reached the kitchen, Troy Beck was not alone.

"What are you doing up?" Troy asked Celia, who was sitting on a bar stool in her pajamas.

"Ask your wife," she said with disdain. Gayle had pulled her out of bed and summoned her to the kitchen as well.

They sat in silence, Troy not knowing how much Celia knew about the Janie Kirk situation, and Celia too tired to form a sentence. Finally, Gayle appeared. Changed from her dress into more casual attire, she was also carrying a large suitcase.

"Where are you going?" Troy asked, thinking through the scenarios. *Was she going to her mother's house? For how long? Was she leaving?* A wave of panic shot through him. Everything he valued in his life was tied to this woman—his house, his job, the company car, his social status as a Haywood spouse. And, of course, his son.

"I've decided to make some staff changes. Celia, this is nothing personal, but I want to spend more time with Oliver. Now that he's in school, I really don't need you anymore. I'll give you two weeks' pay, but I'd like you to leave the house tomorrow."

Celia looked at Troy with pleading eyes. This was a damned good job. But Troy knew a scapegoat when he saw one.

"Celia, I'm sorry. It's Gayle's decision," he said, suddenly relieved.

But then she turned to him. "I've packed some of your things. I want you gone tonight."

Troy felt a buzz in his head. The adrenaline was on full speed now as he looked at his wife, walking on shaky legs to the door where she laid down the suitcase.

It was a strange feeling to have his power so disrupted, but Troy was a survivor and his mind worked quickly, making deductions. This was nothing more than a ploy to gain some sympathy, contrition on his part. This was not the moment for taking the upper hand, and Gayle was grateful he saw it that way.

"Honey, I'm sorry. I'm so sorry. I can see that I really hurt you."

His words were hollow, the sentiment almost insulting. Gayle had been a lot of things she wasn't proud of—weak, submissive, a willing victim. But she wasn't stupid.

"That's just it, Troy. I'm not hurt. That's when I made the decision. When I saw you with Janie and didn't care longer than five minutes."

Standing beside her at the door, Troy took hold of her arms and found her eyes.

"Gayle, honey. Come on. Let's talk this thing through."

His grip was tight and it belied the softness of his voice, the pleading of his words. He was close to breaking now, she could feel it. She turned her head toward the kitchen and, finding Celia gone, felt the air leave her body. They were at the door. And although this was only the beginning of what would be a long road to remove him from her life, she was finally on it. It was this thought—this desperation to keep the momentum—that gave her the strength to carry on.

Her eyes were unwavering as they stood inches apart in the doorway, and Troy could see what had to be done.

She felt the hold on her arms loosen.

"All right. I'll go, for now. But I'm coming back tomorrow to talk about all of this. You get a good night's sleep."

Gayle let him believe what he needed to believe to get him out the door. She handed him his keys, held the door for him while he picked up his suitcase and made his way down the walk to the driveway. Twice, he turned around, each time saying the same thing. "We'll talk tomorrow." But there would be no more talking, and no more tomorrows. Not for him. When his car pulled away, Gayle closed and locked the door, then walked straight past Celia, who had returned after hearing the car drive out.

"Leave an address on the counter. I'll send your check and forward your mail." Gayle didn't stop as she spoke, instead letting her words trail behind her.

Upstairs she checked on Oliver. She hovered over him as he slept to kiss his cheek and pull up his blanket. Moving slowly, she knelt down to the floor and grabbed the bottle of pills from under his bed. Then she closed the door and headed for her room.

It was over now—the party, her marriage, and all of the structures she'd built around her life. Without Celia, her days would have to be reconstructed—around her son, the only one who ever mattered. None of this would be easy. Troy was fighting for his own life now, and he would come at her with everything he had. First, with his seductive apologies and pledges to be a good boy. But she didn't want a boy. Not as her husband. And, like an irreverent child, he would then return with anger. She would change the locks, bolster the security system. It would be a long time before she would sleep through the night.

He would turn next to the relatives—her mother being first on the list. No Haywood had ever been divorced. Unhappy, yes. Unfaithful, yes. But not divorced. It was too messy to sort out, too expensive to divide the wealth. They would remind her of where she lived. Hunting Ridge was a married community. People moved in units of two. She would be the token outcast at the charity functions. Where would they seat her? Other couples would have to take sides, choose which one of them to befriend. Husbands would be cautious, disapproving of their wives being with her—just in case divorce turned out to be contagious. There were so many problems.

But none of that worried Gayle tonight. After years of being a pawn, of fearing the unknown should she stray too far from the party line, she was oddly relieved. As she had kneeled in the bathroom listening to her husband grope another woman, something had switched off inside her. Her mother, Dr. Ted, her New York friends, and country club acquaintances—she felt indifferent to the judgments they would invariably levy against her. Her thoughts were already a step ahead to the last battlefield Troy would take them to. Lawyers, lawsuits, accountants—the fight over Oliver and the money would be ugly. But in the end Troy would trade his son for a price, agree to weekend visits in exchange for a settlement. And Gayle would pay it.

The room was quiet. Troy was gone, and with him the anxiety that filled every room he occupied. With the door open, Gayle changed into sweats. She put away her clothes, then went to work packing up his. Boxes and suitcases were filled with every one of his belongings. Through the night, she worked to clear him out of her house and her life.

When she was done packing, the back hall was filled with luggage. It would not end here, she knew. There would be haggling over every wineglass, every television and car and painting. There would be moments of doubt, she told herself, as she made her way upstairs to her room. The intensity of tonight would give way to exhaustion, to fear. She walked into the bathroom where she'd left her pills on the counter. She thought about what her life might feel like without them. It had been years since she'd known, and it would take time to wean herself. But she would find someone to help her, she would use her name and her money to choose the best person for the job, and she would make it happen.

She washed her face, then dried off in the mirror, studying the lines that time had drawn. There had been so many years of unhappiness, of untruthfulness. Tonight was the first step back. Tonight, she had found a way out. And though she didn't know where that life was headed, one thing was certain. The little boy in the sketch would fade away. It would take time, and she would be patient. She was determined. Her son would not live in the shadow of fear.

SIXTY-THREE

THE GOOD-BYE

AT FOUR THIRTY THAT morning, Marie shot up from her bed. It had been nagging at her all night, but with her head filled with worry over the party and Gayle, and Janie Kirk sleeping with Troy, it had simply gone underground. Until just now.

Slipping out of their bed, Marie stepped lightly across the wooden floorboards. Out into the hallway, then down the stairs, the thought was now taking shape. She flicked on the lights in the study and logged on to her computer.

It was the way he'd said it. *Good-bye, Marie*. Not the colloquial sort of *good-bye* that people say as a matter of course. He had said that kind to her every day since he entered her office and turned her life on its head. This *good-bye* had been altogether different, and she didn't like what it implied.

When the computer was up, she logged into her e-mail. There were twenty-two new messages, half of them disposable spam, the rest work-related. The last one was from Randy. Marie stared at the address, not willing to believe that she was right. But she was usually right, especially when it came to people, and this person she happened to know very well. It was in his tone, the conflicted look in his eyes. He had been prodding her to know, hoping she would see what he was doing and then stop him. But she had been frantic. The Farrell case, the party. There had been too much preoccupation. Or maybe she hadn't wanted to see.

Her heart pounding, Marie clicked to open the message.

Dear Marie,

I saw true love today, and knew I had to leave. I'll be in touch.

Randy

Marie stared at the words, reading them again and again. *True love.* What did he mean? Carson Farrell's love for his wife, the kind that blinded him to her illness? He came close to losing his children, leaving them with a woman who was ill in a misguided attempt to spare her further agony. Or did he mean Anthony coming through in the final inning? The last possibility took her breath away. Could he really believe that what passed between *them* was love? *True* love? Randy Matthews didn't believe in that kind of love. He'd come damned close to making Marie a love skeptic herself. And now he was saying that he'd seen it? That it was the reason he had to leave?

Marie got up from her desk, but she had nowhere to go. The message was there, and despite the cryptic part about love, there was no need to decipher the ending. He was gone, and the thought of it tore through her. Day after day, even before that first kiss, she had looked forward to seeing his face. They'd worked together like hand in glove, read each other's thoughts before they were spoken. He had infused her with the defiance of her youth, given her back that part of herself who wouldn't be caught dead in Hunting Ridge attending charity functions. In his presence, she was transformed from a made-for-TV working mom into a competent, intriguing woman. He had been the smile on her face, which had been gone for quite some time.

The thoughts played out in her head. She could call him, tell him not to leave. But if he stayed, what would happen? They both knew. The first kiss had led to a second, and with the second, came an untenable desire—the kind of desire that is not containable, running like water through every opening, filling every space until it is spent. Was that really what she wanted—to be unfaithful to Anthony? She thought of how he'd been tonight, the comfort she'd felt having him beside her. They'd talked for a long time after the party, about Gayle, the corrupting influence of Hunting Ridge, the Farrell case and what lay ahead for her career. Still, who would hang on her every word? Who would study her face to decipher her every worry, then move mountains to take them away?

Returning to the desk, Marie ran her finger across the screen, the last trace of Randy Matthews she had left. She moved the cursor, then clicked delete. It was gone. It had to be. She felt unnerved just the same, lost in the haze of a marriage that had slipped off course and the longing to feel Randy's hands on her face one more time.

She shut down the computer and pulled her legs onto the chair, resting her head on her knees. She knew what would happen next. Time would pass, life's distractions would tug at her day after day, keeping her mind occupied. The memories would fade as others were made and stored in front of them, and before long the smell of his skin would be gone, then the feel of his mouth. Step by step she would reinvent herself again, confronting the Farrell situation, rebuilding her career. She would hold Anthony to their agreement, find a way to live with his need to escape on the golf course. And slowly, perhaps, the love would return—the kind of love Marie believed in. And life would be good again. Or at least what it needed to be.

Still, she felt the tears falling on her skin. She had been flying, soaring above her own existence in a whirlwind of anger and excitement and thoughts of change. None of it was real. She lived here on the ground, in a house, with a husband and two children. She had a mortgage to pay, a job to save. She wiped the last tears from her cheeks and got up from the chair. At the kitchen sink, she let the cold water run through her hands, then pressed them onto her burning skin. Against the darkness of night, she could see her reflection staring back at her in the window. In all her years, with all her wisdom, she never would have seen this coming. Was it a well-kept secret, this ability to go back in time, to revisit the passion of the young? Did everyone carry with them this knowledge? She had many friends, good friends who bared their souls to her, and still, no one had ever confessed to knowing. Maybe Janie Kirk knew. Maybe Troy Beck had shown her. All through this town, the wives walked the streets as if they held the key to life's perfection. Perfect kids, perfect houses, perfect marriages. No. They couldn't know, or maybe they just didn't remember how it felt to be so alive. Marie was beginning to envy that kind of ignorance.

As she turned out the kitchen light and headed for the stairs, she felt herself returning to calm. Already her thoughts were running away from her to her sleeping girls and the plans for the day that was almost upon her. She stopped to look in on Olivia, then Suzanne, and it was their sleeping, peaceful faces that she saw before her as she crawled quietly under her own covers. Olivia with her Powerpuff Girls pajamas, unruly hair, and cherry-red cheeks. Suzanne coiled up like a little doll, her pink nail polish now worn and chipped around the edges. As she closed her eyes, she heard Randy's words in her head and she smiled to herself. *Yes*, she thought. That's what he had seen in her. The mother, above all else. That was why he had left. It was the one thing they both believed in. That was the *true love*.

Marie opened her eyes and sat up to look at her husband. Anthony was snoring, his stomach bulging beneath the blankets. Reaching across the bed she pressed her hand against his chest.

"Wake up," she whispered. But he didn't move.

"Tony—wake up," she said, louder this time.

His eyes shot open, startling her. "What's wrong?" he demanded, his face flushed with alarm.

Marie didn't waste any time. "We're leaving this place."

Anthony sat up and rubbed the sleep from his eyes with the palms of his hands. "What are you talking about?"

"We have to leave this place. I can see that now."

He studied her face. She was serious. Reaching across to the night table for his glasses, he let out a sigh of resignation. There was going to be a conversation.

"All right. Let's go downstairs and make some coffee."

SIXTY-FOUR

THE RETREAT

THE ROOM WAS STIFLING. It was cool outside and the heat had turned on. Janie thought of opening a window, but couldn't muster the will to remove herself from her bed. Through the sheer curtains, the moonlight sifted in and this was as unwelcome as the heat. She lay on top of the covers next to her sleeping husband, her mind and body exhausted. Spent. She closed her eyes and saw Gayle and the look on her face as she made sense of her husband with another woman. With *her*. She opened her eyes and saw Daniel, unaware, but now vulnerable to the same sting of betrayal she had inflicted upon Gayle. The kind of sting that doesn't go away. Ever.

She would not see Troy Beck again. She didn't want to, and in any case, it would hardly be possible now. She could see down that road. He would come to her unencumbered, and the lack of deviance would kill the excitement for him. An awkward, unspoken expectation would crawl into bed with them, and there wouldn't be a damned thing they could do to get rid of it. There could be, at most, a few more encounters before they finally put it out of its misery. Even if she woke up tomorrow and somehow felt the need after everything that had happened, Troy Beck would no longer satisfy it.

She wiped a bead of sweat from her forehead and thought about what lay ahead. Wanting Troy Beck again did not concern her. Nor did wanting any man. This had not been about sex, she could see that now. Not about the bad sex with Daniel. Not about the great sex with Troy. She was missing a connection with another human being, and she hadn't found that with either man.

She could feel the shift inside her—as if someone had pulled a switch. She was retreating back to that underground place where she walked half-dead among the living, speaking with words that were well-rehearsed and known to be acceptable. Attending parties and luncheons and school fairs. Smiling, smiling. Caring for her children. Servicing her husband. Smiling some more. She would impose upon herself a penance. She would be a more perfect, doting wife. She would devote herself to her home and she would not want more.

She thought about the four children down the hall. There was comfort there. She loved them, and they loved her back. It was uncomplicated—caring for them, pouring her love into them, would be her escape. She would remind herself that staying with Daniel, keeping the family together, was a gift for her children. And this thought, too, brought some comfort.

Still, as she lay in bed next to her husband, she felt pieces of herself falling from her being. Withering in the harsh light of her perfect life.

SIXTY-FIVE

THE MORNING AFTER

GAYLE SAT ALONE AT the kitchen counter savoring a cup of black coffee. It was barely past six and the sky was light. Morning had finally, mercifully, arrived.

The adrenaline had been relentless, chasing away any possibility of sleep as she lay in her bed through the remainder of the night. Now her head was pounding, her nerves frayed. A strange mixture of emotions—fear, excitement, anger, sadness—churned inside her, pushing and pulling her toward thoughts she had never had in her life. They were the thoughts of independence, and they were terrifying. She had kicked her husband out of her house. Now she would have to plan the follow-through. He would come back, she was certain, sometime today. There would be a confrontation and she would have to face it head-on. She'd thought of running. She could take Oliver, pack some things, and drive off. She could leave a note on the door and hope Troy would concede the battle. But that kind of fantasy required a depth of denial that she could no longer afford to embrace.

Yesterday, she had been a married woman, a Haywood. She had suffered from depression, and anxiety, and delusion. She'd been medicated, sometimes sedated. And she'd lived in a secret world that, in the end, had become unsustainable. So much had happened to that woman of yesterday that it might as well have been a lifetime that had passed rather than one night.

The sound of the doorbell sent a fierce panic through her. Could he really be back this early? She rushed to a place out of sight from the window. She would pretend to be asleep. She would not answer. A voice called from outside the door and she recognized it instantly. It was Janie Kirk.

"I told Daniel I forgot my purse," Janie said when Gayle finally appeared.

Gayle stood in the doorway. "I'm sure he believed you."

Janie hung her head, accepting the retort. "Can I come in?"

Stepping out of the way, Gayle let her pass, and they walked in an awkward silence to the kitchen.

"Coffee?" Gayle asked, though she had no idea why. She should hate this woman. They should not be sitting and chatting over coffee as though they were still friends—as though she hadn't heard Janie Kirk laughing as her husband ran his hands across her bare skin.

"No, thank you." Janie was as surprised as Gayle. Still, she took a seat next to her at the island counter. Then she pulled a letter from her purse.

"I'm resigning from the board. I'll send copies to everyone."

Janie paused as Gayle scanned the short explanation. *Personal reasons . . . my husband's illness . . . etc.*

Gayle looked up when she was through. "You don't have to do this."

"Yes, I do. You've worked hard for the clinic. You don't need to see my face all the time," Janie said, interrupting her.

Nodding with understanding, Gayle accepted the gesture. "You could have mailed it," she said.

"I know. That's not the only reason I came." She drew a long breath and held back the shame from what she had done. "I don't think it's even appropriate to try to apologize. But I thought I could explain. I suppose that's what I would want if I were in your position."

Gayle thought about this. *An explanation*. Would that make any difference now? Her husband's affair was a cupful of water in the ocean of their troubles. Still, she did have questions.

"OK," Gayle said. Then she listened as Janie confessed the details of the affair, the reasons she'd done it, and the many times she'd tried to make it stop. Speaking of the bone-deep discontentment, confusion, and now remorse, Janie pleaded—not for forgiveness, but for discretion.

"I'm not sure what happened with Daniel. Maybe I'm beginning to understand it. I don't know . . ."

"Do you still love him?" Gayle asked, though she knew life was more complicated than that.

Janie thought of what she should say. But there wasn't much point of hiding now. "No, I don't. But I have four children."

Gayle nodded with understanding.

"I'm going to try. This is not going to happen again. I know what I've done. And I know it wasn't the answer." She looked away, holding back the tears of her desperation. "Not even close."

She vowed then to seek happiness in the little things—reading to her kids, seeing her friends. But she couldn't do it without Gayle's promise to bury what she had seen. And though Gayle was not entirely sure of her sincerity, she knew she could never be the reason the Kirk children lost their father.

"It's not my place to ruin your family. And just so you know, you weren't the only thing that ruined mine."

Janie looked at her with a strange expression, wondering what she was not seeing. Had Troy strayed before? It wouldn't have surprised her.

"I should go," Janie said, getting up to leave.

But Gayle stopped her. She had one more question.

"What kind of man is he with you?"

Janie blushed with embarrassment. Had she not known Gayle the way she did, she might have found this an attempt to humiliate her. But she did know Gayle, and she owed her an honest answer.

"He was selfish, I suppose. He was a little childish, and not particularly remorseful. He had a cynical view of marriage—of life."

Janie was expecting Gayle to be hurt, insulted perhaps to hear these things about her husband. But she didn't seem to care about any of that.

"But was he . . ." Gayle couldn't find the words to finish the sentence.

Janie studied her face and for the first time in four years saw the signs of pain that Gayle hid so carefully. She was beginning to understand what this was about.

"He was fine," she said as gently as she could. And Gayle nodded as though hearing this description of her husband—how he was with another woman—explained everything.

They walked to the door then, and as Janie left she spoke the most obvious words.

"I'm so sorry," she said.

And though Gayle believed in that moment that she knew the extent of their meaning, it wouldn't hit her until hours later, when she reflected on the odd mix of sympathy and regret that hung on those words, that Janie Kirk was sorry for more than what she had done.

SIXTY-SIX

GOOD FRIENDS AND BAD COFFEE

GAYLE THOUGHT ABOUT THEIR conversation as she returned to her coffee, fighting to absorb all that had happened through the exhaustion—and the fear of everything she still had to face. She savored the silence, hoping for a few more moments before having to explain to Oliver the profound changes she was injecting into his little life. But it didn't last.

The sound of a second car pulling up the drive sent her jumping again. She rushed to the bay window that faced the back of the house.

"Thank God," she whispered to herself, her hand pressed against her chest. It was Marie. Then she felt the tears come. She heard the knock against the back door, but she didn't move. The dam had broken and everything was now pouring out, gushing uncontrollably from her body. There was a soft click from the lock coming open, then the sound of the door.

"Gayle?" It was Marie, and Love was right behind her.

They walked slowly through the house, not sure of what they would find. And what they did find was, oddly, the most surprising.

Love rushed to her friend, who was kneeling on the stone tiles, her hands covering her face as she sobbed into them.

"What's happened? Let me see your face!" Love said, afraid of what might have taken place throughout the night. She knelt beside Gayle and wrapped her arms around her.

Marie approached slowly, pulling Gayle's hands from her face. "Let us see you," she said.

Gayle looked up at Marie. "I'm not hurt," she said, reassuring them.

Marie and Love inspected their friend. Her face was red and utterly exhausted, but that was all.

"Come on." Love took Gayle's arm and helped her to her feet. "Come sit down."

"I'll make some coffee," Marie said.

Love and Gayle sat down at the island counter while Marie walked to the coffee machine. It was a professional espresso maker with gold knobs and handles and more spouts than Marie could count.

"What the hell is this?"

Gayle let out a small laugh as she dried her face with a tissue. "Don't worry about it. I already made the coffee."

Marie turned and gave her a look of severe disapproval. "Your coffee sucks. Haven't you hired a new cook yet?"

Sensing a lightness coming into the room, Love chimed in. "I know. The service around here has really gotten bad."

Gayle sighed as she felt the despair release its hold. "Well, get used to it. There's no cook. And last night I fired my nanny *and* my husband. It's going to be self-service in this house for a long time to come."

Love and Marie both nodded, taking in the information.

"Huh," Marie said after a long silence. "You may have to leave this town, Gayle Haywood. *No* cook. *No* nanny. *No* husband. And you haven't even had your vagina rejuvenated."

Gayle tried again for a smile. "I know. *And,*" she started to say, then paused to fight for her composure as the tears returned. "I don't think I'll even make it through one day."

Love rubbed her back and let her cry. Marie found the coffee. And when she was ready, Gayle told them how things had played out—Troy leaving, Celia huffing off, and Janie coming to say her peace.

"I know he'll be back today," was the last thing she was able to get out.

Marie leaned across the counter and looked in Gayle's eyes. "Well, then. It's a good thing you happen to have the best divorce attorney in the state sitting in your kitchen. I *think* I still have a license to practice."

"And I'll drive Oliver to my house. He can play with Henry all day," Love added.

Gayle nodded. "OK," she said, though the thought of having her friends help her was unsettling. She had never let anyone this deep into her life.

Sensing her discomfort, Love reached out and took her hand. "We're staying. Both of us, all day, until he comes. We'll call for new locks, have the gate code changed. We'll tell the post office to forward his mail. What else can we do?"

Gayle took a long breath and nodded. *Yes,* she thought. *Together we'll make the changes.* She dried her face one last time. It was a strange feeling, giving herself over to the hands of others. Strange and unbelievably powerful. It seemed almost possible to let it all go, to freefall from the tightrope she'd been walking and trust that someone would catch her at the end. She closed her eyes and reached for her friends, holding their arms—and letting her friends hold her back.

SIXTY-SEVEN

THE CONVERSATION

THE PASSETIS HAD TALKED for hours that night—the night of the fundraiser—and the conversation had been long overdue. Marie was certain that leaving town was the first step to solving their problems. Anthony was certain that all of the problems were Marie's. They resolved nothing and drank too much coffee, leaving them both angry and wired as they waited for the sun to rise. When it did, Anthony played golf and Marie went to Gayle's, exhausted and pissed off.

It wasn't until late summer that they spoke again of leaving.

"Some broker called. From Brooklyn—know anything about that?"

Anthony was smoldering as he stood before his wife in their study. He had been foolish enough to believe that she would respect his wishes—that this notion of moving back to New York had been removed from the table.

Marie sighed. "Oops."

"Oops? That's all you can say?"

"I was just looking—to see what our options are."

She was not nearly as contrite as Anthony needed her to be.

"I thought we were done talking about this."

"And we haven't talked about this, have we?" Marie said smartly.

"Cute. Very cute."

Marie tugged on his arm so he would at least sit down with her. Reluctantly, he pulled a chair under him and sat. But his anger was not settling. She was going behind his back, making a unilateral decision that would impact all of them. Olivia and Suzanne liked it here in Hunting Ridge. They liked their friends, their school. And they were not alone. Anthony loved his nights, especially now that summer had arrived. He loved weekends on the golf course. He had a regular game on Saturday mornings and his handicap had dropped eight points. He liked the yard, black spots and all. He liked that he didn't have to think about a damned thing once he got off the train, except, perhaps, whether he'd left out his cereal boxes. And he liked to drive his BMW though the back, winding roads lined by nothing but green trees and beautiful houses. He had told her all of this, but now it seemed that none of it mattered.

"Is this about the Farrell case?" he asked, thinking—no, hoping—that the uncertainty that hung over her career was the reason she still wanted to go. The Farrell family was actually getting back on its feet. Vickie was out of the treatment center. Her medication had been adjusted to battle the depression and she was back at home. Carson had returned to work after a short leave, and they had a full-time nanny to make sure the children were safe while they assessed Vickie's ongoing condition. Still, all of this had come at a significant cost to the family, and Marie waited anxiously for Carson Farrell to catch his breath and go after her license.

But Anthony was wrong. This was not about her.

"It's not Farrell."

"What then—you just don't like it here? Is it just too nice for you?"

Marie gave him a harsh look. "No, it's not that I just don't like it here. It's that I don't like *us* here."

She paused for a moment to let the statement sink in. Then she continued. "Look, the girls talk of nothing but material things. Houses and plasma TVs and designer clothes. They worry that our house is too small, that we don't have a pool and don't vacation in St. Barts. I love them beyond reason, Tony, but I don't like who they're becoming."

Anthony sighed. What did he know about any of that? The girls seemed fine to him.

"And me? Do you not like me anymore?"

It was time, Marie imagined, to either come clean or shut up. It wasn't in her to do the latter.

"Actually, no. I don't like either of us."

"Well, I'm so sorry." He was hurt and doing a poor job of hiding it.

"You can't even see what's happening to you! You hate your job, but you can't leave it because it's the cornerstone of our very existence. And because you hate your job—because going to work every day is utter misery for you—you spend what little free time you have numbing your brain with beer and golf and TV. You've gained twenty pounds since we moved here."

Marie stopped only to take a breath. But she was not done. She'd spent months thinking about this, and she knew she was right.

"Look at your life now. You've lost interest in nearly everything you once felt passionately about." She pulled her chair closer to his and grabbed his hands. He *had* to see this, what was happening to him, to all of them.

"You used to care about the world. Politics. The environment. When was the last time you voted? Don't you see? You've lost touch with who you are—in your heart."

Anthony listened patiently. He could see she was serious and that somewhere inside her she must still care about him. Marie didn't waste her time obsessing about things that didn't matter to her. Even so, he had a different take on the situation.

"I hear what you're saying, Marie. And you are right that I don't like the job anymore—that it's a chore to get through the day. But I do it because it's worth it to me. Because the girls are safe. Because I enjoy playing golf and relaxing. I didn't do those things before because I couldn't. We didn't have golf in the city, and we were so infiltrated by social woes that it was impossible not to think about them day in and day out. We worked hard to get here. Why can't we enjoy it a little?"

But Marie persisted. They were addictive, these suburban luxuries, and breaking him of the habit would not be done overnight.

"Will you just come and look? I'm not talking about midtown. It's *Brooklyn.* Townhouses, tree-lined streets. And the Center for Human Rights is there. You'd never even have to get on a subway!"

"Why are you talking about CHR?" Mentioning the Center was a body shot. Anthony had worked there for a year right out of law school and had never been more interested in the law, or being a lawyer.

"Why not? If I started a full-time practice, we could afford for you to work there again. There's a great parochial school in the neighborhood . . ."

"Marie, you're talking night and day. Parochial school for the girls. Both of us working. And we still wouldn't be able to afford a decent vacation."

He was right. It was night and day, the lives that people could live just fifty miles apart. That's what had her so excited.

"I know it would be different. But it's not as though we'd be moving to China. And it wouldn't have to be forever. It could be a little sabbatical for all of us. We could rent out this house, rent one in Brooklyn."

Anthony sat back and rubbed his face with both hands. "Oh, Marie . . ." It was devilish the way she could plant a seed.

"Just come and look."

This was not at all how he'd imagined the conversation would go. He was going to be mad, Marie would be madder. They would fight. And he would leave to hit balls at the club. He almost didn't believe the words as they left his mouth.

"I'll look," he said, and Marie kissed him hard on the mouth.

SIXTY-EIGHT

LOVE

IF THERE WAS ONE thing the East Coast had over the West, it was the fall foliage. Vibrant oranges, yellows, and reds. That near-fluorescent green. When the sun's light shone through the dying leaves from above, there was not a more impressive show of nature to be found. But the ostentatious display was inseparably tied to the cooling temperatures, a precursor to the long, barren winter months, and Love could sense it coming on—wool sweaters, the smell of burning wood, pumpkins, Halloween, and Christmas trees. Life's memories were slowly being roused from their place of rest.

As she made the drive from the city, Love sighed at the thought of the work that lay ahead. The falling leaves, beautiful as they were, would need to be raked. The pumpkins gathered and carved, costumes chosen and ordered well in advance—before they could sell out and leave her kids disappointed and herself feeling guilty. The Thanksgiving feast would then be upon her. The shopping, cooking, and entertaining of Bill's distant relatives would leave her exhausted on too many fronts. And just in time for the weeks of mad shopping sprees, wrapping, decorating, then hiding it all until the morning when the spoils of Santa's miraculous journey around the world could be ravaged. These were the moments she would capture on film and video, the rituals that glued the family together and provoked bursts of joy in her children. But they were also moments littered with potential landmines. The Halloween costumes, an inadvertent misstep with Bill's relatives, a last-minute addition to a Christmas list that could not be procured in time. There was so much room for failure that Love had come to wish it away before the first frost.

No, she said out loud, repeating the mantra she'd been practicing for months. It was part of the new plan, the one where she admitted to herself that being the stay-at-home mommy all day, everyday, was just not in her. It was the plan where she tried not to hate herself for this indiscretion, or for those of the past. It was the plan where she said *no* to all thoughts that had dragged her down before.

Dr. Luster would be proud of her, getting in touch with her subconscious feelings, chanting positive thoughts. In the end she had not gone back for more treatments, choosing instead the therapy of truth. She had told them all about her past, in bits and pieces, over coffee, over the phone. Whenever and wherever she could. She talked and talked until she had nothing left to say. And, slowly, her pain had resolved over the summer months. No one ever knew for sure what had caused it. Of course, Bill remained satisfied with his theory that it was a virus, which had, thankfully, left her. Yvonne, on the other hand, had become a firm believer in Dr. Luster's methods. Back and forth they went. Was it not obvious that the virus had run its course? Was it not apparent that confronting her father and learning the truth about her past had set her on the road to recovery? Love thanked the powers that be every day for the three thousand miles that kept the two of them apart, her husband and her mother. It was bad enough Yvonne had placed them on the *Sensory-Motor Self Monthly* mailing list.

Other than her return to health, there had been no life-altering watershed after the crazy events of spring. Love had waited nearly a week after the fundraiser to tell Bill what had really happened in L.A., instead remaining preoccupied with Gayle and the Janie situation, tending to her friend, avoiding her husband. And in the end, the disclosure of information that she had been certain would blow a gaping hole through Bill's steady demeanor had instead produced barely a fizzle.

"So, you were drunk," he'd said, making sure he was understanding her. Then he shrugged in a *what's the big deal* kind of way.

"I was lucid. I remember that now."

"You were still the victim of a much older man. He should have gone to jail. Your father should have killed him. I would kill anyone who did that to Jessica," he'd said, causing both of them to shudder at the thought.

"The point is that I made a choice, a decision aimed at hurting my father. Only it backfired dead center into my life. Then I went running for cover."

Finally getting to the part of the story that had repercussions for his life, Bill had nodded slowly. "You ran right to me."

"Yes."

They talked then about where that left them, now that Love was no longer in need of escaping. Now that she no longer needed to be someone else, anyone but the disgraced Love Welsh. They talked about what remained when they peeled away the layers of their pasts that had drawn them to each other. And they were still talking, learning to see one another in the full light of day. Hoping to build their love on steadier ground.

In the back seat, Baby Will began to doze. Glancing at his shuttering eyes through the rearview mirror, Love muted the lullaby CD, then returned her focus to the highway. He had adjusted well to the new schedule, taking his naps in the car, accepting the company of new faces at a day-care center near Columbia University. Three days a week she loaded him up and took him with her to New York. She was enrolled in Freshman Biology and Comparative Literature. They were two of the twenty-four courses she would need to complete her degree. At this rate, she would be fifty when it was finally done, and that thought could stop her dead in her tracks.

The decision had been difficult, as was any change that caused this much upheaval. That it wasn't worth the effort was a fear that filled her head nearly every morning that she dragged herself to the city. The routine was hectic—getting everyone fed and dressed and packed up for the day, loading them in the car, dropping Henry at his school, then Jessica at hers.

She wouldn't get on the highway until well after nine, just in time to hit the end of rush hour. If the baby slept, which on most days he did, the drive would be tolerable. On the odd day he stayed awake, it took sheer will power to keep going. She'd drop him at the day care, then rush off to a lecture hall to sit among faces that made her feel like a dinosaur. Still, for all the hassles, all the complaining by Henry and Jessica about being picked up from school by Gayle, and the chaos it had thrown into her marriage, Love knew it was worth it. For the first time in many years she was present in her life, living each moment. She could feel it now, as she drove in silence among the falling leaves, the sense of peace that was edging out the noise.

SIXTY-NINE

MARIE

"JESUS CHRIST!" MARIE SAID under her breath as she looked at the speck of blood.

It was the third time in under ten minutes she'd nicked her hand on the tape dispenser—a device that appeared simple and therefore had her all the more infuriated. The living room was finished. Items carefully packed, sealed, and labeled, ready for the movers who were coming first thing in the morning. But the kitchen was another story.

She checked her watch.

"Christ!" she said again. It was after three. She reached for the phone, dialing with one hand while she turned on the radio.

"Love?" she yelled into the receiver.

"What? I can't talk, I'm in the car."

"Will you get a bloody hands-free phone already! What's wrong with you?"

Love answered, checking in her mirrors for police cars. "It's on my list. Now what's up?"

"It's three!"

"Oh—OK. I'll turn it on."

Marie hung up, then went back to her boxes and the program that was coming on public radio. It was a taped interview with Gayle Haywood, founder of the innovative Smart Choices program that was now being prototyped in New York.

Yes, we have had wonderful feedback from the girls and their parents. Gayle's words floated through the room and Marie was near giddy with pride. *No, it has not been controversial. It's a privately funded program, so there's no state involvement. And, frankly, parents are grateful that their girls are being empowered with accurate, unbiased information.*

She went on for ten minutes, answering questions, getting the message out. And although she sounded nervous to Marie, the rest of the world would hear nothing but an intelligent, passionate woman.

"Christ!" Now it was half past three and she hadn't even finished the glasses.

Weighing the factors carefully, she tossed the tape dispenser on the counter and headed for her car.

It was the last play date they would have. There had been talk of getting together every few months, promises on her part to drive up from Brooklyn and the good intentions of her friends to bring the kids to the city. None of them believed any of it. They were forcing it now. The kids were outgrowing friendships imposed by their mothers, and, as the holiday frenzy ate up every ounce of spare time, Marie knew she would not see Love and Gayle for some time.

They had met every week over the summer months, unraveling the events of late spring. They had talked Gayle through the Janie Kirk incident, with Marie doling out legal advice and Love helping Gayle battle the self-doubt that was always sneaking up on her. In turn, Gayle had listened as only she could while Love worked through the decision to start at Columbia.

For her part, Marie had practically begged them to understand her decision to move back to the city. Not the city, exactly, but Brooklyn, where they could afford a small townhouse. Three bedrooms, two baths, a run-down kitchen and dreary living room, one small patch of grass and weeds out back—it was a far cry from the cute-as-a-button colonial they were leaving behind. Still, it was a house, and Marie was betting everything it would become a home where they could all be happy.

It was clear to Marie now, having spent most of the summer thinking about their life, trying to see herself through objective eyes. She had been slowly disappearing into nothing more than the anti-wife, a modern-day Katharine Ross running from her robot clone. How many hours had she devoted to picking apart the Stepford wives, judging them for being happy with a life that she had also chosen? That she couldn't find her own happiness in that world didn't make them less human. It simply meant that it was time for her to leave.

In spite of this conviction, nothing about the decision had been easy. The house wouldn't be ready for three more weeks, and that meant a midsemester transfer for the girls to their school. And Marie was needed for a trial at her new firm in six days. There would be little help with the logistics now that Anthony had started back at the Center for Human Rights. The commute was ungodly at the moment, leaving little time to help with the packing—let alone golf. That he wasn't completely convinced yet made it all the more difficult. He was doing this for her, she knew full well. They were renting for now, viewing it all as a one-year experiment. And that was how they'd sold it to the girls, whose protests weren't nearly as catastrophic as she had planned for. Suzanne cried to her friends on the phone but then spoke of New York with pride. *I was born there,* she'd say. *And it is the greatest city in the world.* Olivia was too young to understand. She cried because they were leaving the house but had already begun her plans for setting up the new bedroom.

Still, there were many moments when Marie felt the waves of doubt roll in, with nothing other than her family's happiness on her shoulders. But it was done now—it was time to hope for a new beginning.

As for Randy Matthews, absence had done its job, forcing the kisses to recede to a place where she could manage them. And she was more than happy to keep them there.

She'd heard from him in August. As before, it came in the form of an e-mail. And, also as before, it contained few words.

Dear Marie,
How's life in the cave?

She'd laughed out loud in spite of herself, then written a reply. She'd filled him in on the Farrells and their other cases. Her mind had shifted then to Randy autopilot and she started to write about the summer, the girls, the ongoing struggles with the move. But these things were not his concern. Not anymore. Randy had given her a gift, a look at her life from the outside in, and she could now see that life for all that it was and all that it wasn't. And there was no room in it for him.

Deleting line after line, she'd left only the case updates, then added one final note.

Good luck out there.
Marie

There had been no further communication on either side. Randy would go on with his final years at Yale. He would pass the bar and become a brilliant attorney. And, despite the internal protests he would stage, Marie had no doubt that he would not escape love. It was possible that he could dodge marriage, maybe even a lifetime partner, if such a thing even existed. But no matter how deeply he analyzed the world around him, keeping himself at arm's length, he was not immune. She had seen it firsthand. One day, she was certain, he would be a father. Love would find him and he would let it in, embrace it, and let it run away with him.

SEVENTY

GAYLE

"I HEARD A CAR!" Henry yelled from the playroom. He ran to the back door and watched as his mother's van pulled into the driveway. Jessica was right behind, standing on her tiptoes to reach the glass panels of the door.

Gayle came up behind them, watching as Love retrieved Baby Will from his car seat and made her way up the walk.

"Hello, Lovey," she said, giving her friend a hug. But she was quickly outnumbered by two children, now jumping up and down at their mother's feet.

Love bent down and took them in her arms. "Hi, guys! How was school?" It was over in a second. The *we missed you, where have you been all day?* guilt show had been duly performed, and the performers had returned to the project set up in the other room.

"Great interview—as always!" Love said.

Gayle brushed it off. She never would learn to take a compliment. "Was it OK? I couldn't hear it over all this."

"What exactly is going on in here?" Love asked, following her children to the back of Gayle's house. In the center of the wood floor was an enormous sheet of white paper. On each of the four corners of the paper, were little puddles of paint. Blue, red, purple, orange, yellow, green. There were paintbrushes of every size and shape, sponges, crayons, glue pens, and glitter. Olivia and Suzanne were making footprints—stepping in the squishy goo, then walking across the paper. Jessica was busy doing the same with her hands, and Oliver was using three brushes at once to make a rainbow. In the far corner, usurping all the crayons and employing great determination to stay within the lines he had created, Henry was making a picture of a Bionicle Lego.

None of this would have surprised Love had it not been Gayle's house.

"Paint," Gayle said.

Love was still standing in the doorway. "Wow. This is an incredible mess in the name of artistic development."

It was more than a mess. Paint had dripped onto the wood floor, glitter had scattered across the room, landing on fine upholstered sofas and the felt top of the pool table. And it would only get worse when they tried to wash all those little feet and hands.

With the wry smile that had returned to her face in the past few months, Gayle answered her friend. "I know—but it's not what you think. When all of you are gone, I'll be in here with the scrub brushes, vacuum cleaner, glitter-dust detector. By the end of the night the room will be cleaner than it's ever been. Then I'll have a *really big* glass of wine."

Love laughed. In truth, Gayle probably would do those things, or come damned close. Certainly, no one believed she had transformed that drastically. But it was also true that she was aware now—more aware than ever—of the forces that had been driving her into a state of total containment. With incredible grace, she had exorcised Troy from her life and helped Oliver navigate the path of a broken family. She had pared down her commitments, serving as the clinic's spokeswoman for the Smart Choices program, but nothing else—spending the time with Oliver instead. And she had found a new psychiatrist to help her get off the drugs. Now she was pushing herself, going to therapy, facing her childhood and her marriage. She was beginning to figure out what was real and to trust her instincts again. And she was testing her own limits in these small ways—messy paint and children on the loose.

Walking over to her friend, Love squeezed her shoulder and gave her a smile. All of this suited her. It showed on her face.

"And the packing?" Love said, turning to Marie, who was sitting on the couch.

With a cup of coffee in her left hand, Marie held up the right one, which was now adorned with three tiny Princess Band-Aids.

"Boxes?"

"Tape dispenser."

"Ah. I can help tonight—after the kids are down."

"Great! I'll supply the wine."

Gayle frowned at both of them. "Wine? How come you only see me over coffee and kids?"

Marie raised her mug at Gayle. "You come, too. Oliver can sleep over."

Love gave Marie a sad smile. The clock was ticking on these gatherings, and Love could already feel the huge void that Marie's departure would leave.

It was just after six before they had the children clean enough to transport home. One after the other, they marched them to the back hall, put on jackets, sorted backpacks and lunchboxes, and loaded them into cars. Marie and Love thanked Gayle for picking up their kids. They gave each other hugs, which were longer today, and then they were gone.

Turning to Oliver, Gayle bent down to see into his eyes. "Did you have fun?" she asked, and he nodded. "Go on inside. I'll get the mail."

The days were growing shorter, and the sky was almost dark. Without the sun's warmth, Gayle felt a chill as a gust of wind passed through, blowing up the leaves. She pulled her sweater tightly around her and turned her face away until it was gone, until the leaves had returned to the ground. Making her way down the long driveway, she started to think about the paint on the floor, wondering how best to remove it without dulling the finish. Then she stopped herself before the thoughts turned to actions, before she found herself rushing inside to restore the perfect order she had been fighting to disrupt. She would not clean up. She would go in, have dinner with her son, play a game or watch a movie. She would feel the small joy of those things and keep at bay everything else. As she waited for the electric gate to swing open, she drew a long breath. This was how it had been, one thing at a time.

The mailbox was full, as it always was this time of year, with catalogues and other junk making up the bulk of it. The wind picked up again, blowing the leaves around her feet. She carefully pulled the mail out and held it close to her chest. She closed her eyes until she felt the gust settle, then walked to the foot of the driveway. As she waited for the gate to open again, she pulled the mail from her chest and began to flip through it. From between two oversized catalogues a small postcard slipped out and fell to the ground. When the wind picked it up, she thought of letting it go. Her arms were full, the gate was now open, and her eyes were starting to water from the cold. Postcards in the fall were invariably solicitations for some sort of home repair operation—painters, landscapers, and the like. Still, there she was, chasing after it into the road. At least she was smiling at herself—her confounding inability to let a damned thing go. As she caught up with the card in a pile of leaves, she made a promise to let the next one go.

It was later that evening, after Oliver was asleep and she was alone in the kitchen, that she finally found the card again mixed in with the other mail. It was a white card with a sketch of a mountain scene, and she took a small moment to guess the name of the service company that would appear on the other side. *Alpine Lawn Care. Everest Remodeling. Colorado Cleaning Company*. She flipped it over, hoping to be amused, but instead found herself without a breath. The handwriting was unmistakable.

It was postmarked in Oregon, and that was the last place she'd heard he'd gone. Through the agency that had sent Paul to them years before, she had pieced together his journey after leaving her home. He'd been abroad for a while. Chile, Brazil. Then to Mexico and up the California coast. She had asked that he not be told of her inquiries, nor had she explained the reasons for his departure. She had not expected to hear from him again.

His note was brief.

Dear Gayle,

What can I say to you after all this time? I have held on to the conviction that leaving was the right thing, but I fear I was wrong. I have prayed that you and Oliver would be all right. I planned a journey, something that was overdue. But the change in the weather has me longing to return. Are the leaves as beautiful this year as last? I hope to reach you by the end of the month. Of course, I will call first. Give my love to Oliver.

Paul

So little was written, and yet so much was said. He knew Troy was gone. He never would have written had he not known. And he addressed her as *Gayle*, making her think now how foolish she had been not to insist upon this from the very start. Clinging to formalities had left her house so sterile, so lacking in humanity. But he was not her employee anymore. There would be no more *Mrs. Beck*. He had never been the cook, or the butler. He was a man, an honest, compassionate man who had done nothing less than hold their house together—listening to her daily dilemmas, teaching Oliver to dribble a soccer ball. Countless little things, everyday nothing things that together constituted life. It was not until he was gone that she realized what he had been. The string that holds the beads together.

These past months, she had come to know this—to see who this man really was. And yet, at the same time she had become all of those things for herself, and her son. Together they had filled the void and created a new home, and it was a good home—somehow complete even in the absence of a man. Marie would be proud of her now, thinking as she was about the failings of marriage, hers in particular. She had done a lot of thinking about the state of affairs between men and women and the attempts they made to share one life, one home. Was there ever really harmony without one person's submission? And even then, was misery not inevitable?

Still, as she searched for the date of his writing, she felt the pull within her, the unabated excitement as she imagined answering his call before the month's end—hearing his voice, then seeing his face, this time with nothing standing between them. She was a damned schoolgirl again, a wise schoolgirl, but still so easily carried away by the daydreams that were sneaking into her thoughts. After everything she had seen, everything she'd been through, and the mountain of evidence that was undeniable, irrefutable—there she was, just the same. Standing on the edge of a deep pool of possibilities.

Knowing she would dive in.